Fallen
Into the Pit

Fallen
Into the Pit

Ellis Peters

WHEELER
PUBLISHING, INC.

★ AN AMERICAN COMPANY ★

Copyright © 1951 by Edith Pargeter.

Published in Large Print by arrangement with Warner Books, Inc. in the United States and Canada.

Wheeler Large Print Book Series.

Set in 16 pt. Plantin.

Library of Congress Cataloging-in-Publication Data

Peters, Ellis, 1913–
    Fallen into the pit / Ellis Peters.
      p. cm.
    ISBN 1-56895-116-7 : $23.95
    1. Large type books. 2. Felse, George (Fictitious character)—
Fiction. 3. Police—England—Fiction. 4. England—Fiction.
I. Title.
[PR6031.A49F35   1994b]
    823'.912—dc20

                                 94-19116
                                     CIP

To JIM,
and the survival
of
his memory and ideas
through his friends

CONTENTS

I

The Time—

1

The war ended, and the young men came home, and tried indignantly to fit themselves into old clothes and old habits which proved, on examination, to be both a little threadbare, and on trial to be both cripplingly small for bodies and minds mysteriously grown in absence. Things changed overnight changed again next day. Nobody knew where he stood. Even the language was different. At the Shock of Hay you could hear good-nights flying at closing-time in two or three tongues besides English. Blank-eyed, blond youths with shut faces worked side by side with the hard old men in the beet fields, and the sons of the old men, coming home laboriously with the distorted selves they had salved from the blond youths' embraces all over the world, wondered where they had been, and to what country they had returned. But they had known for some time, the most acute of them, that if England meant the country they had left, and Comerford the village, this would be neither Comerford nor England. Fortunately the names meant much more than their own phases, and the lie of the land, obscured behind many changes, remained constant even at this pass.

Those who came back first had the easiest time. Those who had still to linger a year or more of their time away in the tedium of suddenly

3

purposeless armies, or adjust themselves to the fluid situations of other people's crumbling countries, limped home with more bitter difficulty, to find the fields full of displaced persons, and the shops of a new lingua franca evolved for their benefit, the encrustations of pits suddenly congealed into the nationalized mining industry, whole hills and valleys torn out by the roots under the gigantic caresses of surface mining machinery, and in the upper air of the mind every boundary shifted and every alignment altered. It was all a bewildered young man could do to find his way around this almost unrecognizable land. The old did not try; they sat in the middle of it in contemplation, waiting for the eyes to adjust their vision, and the legs to acquire the mastery of this new kind of drunkenness. Only the young had so short a time before them that they could not afford to wait.

They tried, however, to cram themselves back into the old round holes, and mutilated their unaccountably squared personalities in the process. Time eased the fit for some; for some, who had sent their minds home ahead of their bodies, the adjustment was neither long nor unwelcome, though it could not be without pain; to some the whole of Comerford seemed now only a green round hole, not big enough to hold them. They despised it both for what had changed in it and for what had remained the same, because they had lived too long enclosed in the changes and monotonies of their own natures, and could no longer distinguish great from small.

If day-to-day life could halt at such a time, and

give all the lost people time to get their bearings, things would be easier; but it went on steadily, or rather unsteadily, all the time, full of all the old snags and spiteful with new ones. Colliers' sons went back to the pits, and found themselves working side by side with Ukrainians, Poles, Czechs, Lithuanians, Letts, whose wartime alliance was just falling apart into a hundred minor incompatibilities; and soon came even the few screened Germans out of their captivity to fester among their ex-enemies without being able to reunite them. Nice-looking, stolid young men, hard workers, a good type; but they did not always remember to keep the old "Heil Hitler!" off their tongues; and the leftward-inclined youngster with Welsh blood in his veins and a brother dead in some Stalag or other was liable to notice these things. Maybe he picked a fight, maybe some older and cooler minds broke it up, maybe he just got his room at the hostel rifled and his books shredded, or maybe some evening in the dark, pepper found its way into his eyes. No one knew how. No connection with the war, of course; the war was over.

Meantime the topsoil of two small fields and an undulation of rough pasture and furze was scoured off and piled aside in new mountain ridges, and the grabs lifted out the stony innards of Comerford earth to lay bare the hundred and eighty thousand or so tons of shallow coal which the experts said was to be found underneath. As if the earth cried, instant outcry broke out over the issue, one faction crying havoc for the two fields, a smaller and less vociferous group welcoming the leveling of the furze mounds, and tidying of the ground long ago mauled by shallow dog-hole mining. But the small army of weathered men swarming over the site, performing prodigious surgical operations with uncouth red-and-yellow instruments, took no notice of either party in the controversy. They assembled about them every conceivable variety of weatherproof and wearproof ex-Army clothing, making their largeness larger still under leather jerkins and duffle coats, and so armored, they busied themselves in making hills and valleys change places, the straight crooked and the plain places rough. But when they moved on they left a level dark plain, and though inimical voices clamored prophetically of soil made barren for a lifetime, and drainage difficulties had to be stabbed at twice after an initial failure, in one year grass was growing delicately over the whole great scar. Poor grass beside that which formerly grew on the two small fields, but beautiful, improbable grass over what used to be furze, bramble and naked clay.

And from the returned young men themselves, wise and foolish, willing and unwilling soldiers in their time, proceeded outward through their families and their friends shuddering cycles of unrest, like the tremors before earthquake. They came trailing clouds of tattered and tired glory which they could neither repair nor shake off. The unimaginative were the luckiest, or those whose supposedly adventurous Army career had been spent largely among mud and boredom and potatoes; but some came haunted by the things their own hands had done and their own bodies endured, growths from which no manner of amputation could divide them, ghosts for which Comerford had no room. They had been where even those nearest to them could not follow, and daily they withdrew there again from the compression and safety of lathe and field and farm, until the adjustment to sanity took place painfully at last, and the compression ceased to bound them, and was felt to be wider than the mad waste in the memory. Then they had arrived. But the journey was a long one, and others besides themselves might die on the way.

There was, for instance, Charles Blunden, up at the Harrow. His was a mild case, but even he had fought his way in a tidy, orthodox fashion twice across North Africa and all the way north through Sicily and Italy to his demob in 1946, and had then to become, all in a moment, an upland farmer. Or Jim Tugg, who came home three times decorated, trailing prodigious exploits as a paratrooper before and after Arnhem, and shrank suddenly to the quiet dark shape of a shepherd on Chris Hollins's farm. Who believed in it? When he went by, double his prewar size, light as a cat, close-mouthed and gaunt-eyed as a fate, the ground under his noiseless tread quaked a little, and small boys expected lightnings to come out of the ends of his fingers and dart into the earth.

Or, of course, Chad Wedderburn, whose legends came home before him, the extremest case of all. Captured in Italy, bitterly ill-used by both Italians and Germans after three attempts to escape, at the fourth attempt he had succeeded, if that could be called escape which smuggled him across the Adriatic from one mortal danger to another. For the rest of the war he became a guerrilla at large all over the Balkans, living from minute to minute, tasting all the splendors and miseries of the mountain life among the Yugoslav patriots, sharing their marathon marches, their hunger, their cold, their sickness and wounds, for which there was seldom medical attention and almost never drugs or anesthetics. He knew, because he had had to use daily during that last year, all the ways of killing a man quietly before he can kill you; and because he had been an apt pupil he was still alive. It was as if an explosion had taken place in Comerford the day he was born, to fling fragments of violence half across the world.

When he came back in 1949, after a year of hospital treatments in many places, and another year of study to return to his profession, it was an anticlimax, almost a rebuff. He looked much thinner and darker and harder than prewar, but otherwise scarcely different; he was even quieter than he had ever been before, and of his many scars only one was visible, and that was a disappointment, just a brownish mark running down the left side of his jaw from ear to chin. The village tried to bring him out of his shell by drawing him into British Legion activities, and he astonished and offended them by replying decisively that personally he had been a conscript, and he thought the sooner people forgot whether they had worn a uniform or not, the better, in a war which had involved everybody alike, and in which few people had had any choice about the manner of their service.

But this fair warning meant little to the boys at the grammar school, when he returned there at length as classics master. They had caught a reputed tiger, and a tiger they confidently expected. They conferred together over him with excited warnings, and prepared to jump at the lift of his eyebrow, and adore him for it. But the tiger, though its voice was incisive and its manner by no means timorous, continued to behave like a singularly patient sheepdog. They could not understand it. They began to test the length of that patience by tentative provocation, and found it elastic enough to leave them still unscathed. His way with them was not so unreasonably mild as to let these experiments proceed too far, but he let them go beyond the point where a real tiger might have been expected to pounce. On a natural human reaction to this disappointment they began to fear, prematurely and unjustifiably, that what they had acquired was merely the usual tame, doctored, domestic cat, after all. But the legend, though invisible, like the potential genie in the bottle, still awed them and stayed their courage short of positive danger. With tigers, with cats for that matter, you never know.

2

The Fourth Form, who had tamed more masters than they could remember, discussed the phenomenon in perhaps the most unwise spot they could have found for the conference, only ten yards from the form-room window, in the first ten minutes of break, while the latest manifestation of Chad Wedderburn's mildness was fresh in their minds. They had sweated Latin and English under him for the whole of the summer term, which was just drawing to its buoyant close, and got away with everything except murder. That he managed none the less to get the work out of them, and to keep a reasonable and easy order, without resorting to sarcasm or the cane, had escaped their young notice, for work was something on which their minds took care not to dwell out of the classroom. The fact remained that he was not the man they had thought him.

"If you'd planted a booby trap like that for old Stinky," said the largest thirteen-year-old, leveling a forefinger almost into Dominic Felse's eye, "he'd have skinned you alive."

"It wasn't for old Wedderburn, either," said Dominic darkly, "it was for you. If he didn't come in so beastly *prompt* to his classes he wouldn't walk into things like that. Old Stinky was always ten minutes late. You can't *rely* on these early people." He chewed his knuckles, and frowned at the memory of flying books and inkwell, thanking heaven that by some uncanny chance the lid of the well had jammed shut, and only a few minute drops had oozed out of its hinges to spatter the floor. He cocked a bright hazel eye at the large youth, whose name was Warren, and hence inescapably "Rabbit" Warren. "Anyhow, you try it some time. It felt like being skinned alive to me."

"Sensitive plant!" said Rabbit scornfully, for he had not been on the receiving end of the drastically quiet storm, and had in any case little respect for the power of words, least of all when delivered below a shout.

Dominic let it pass. He felt peaceful, for people like Rabbit seldom interested him enough to rouse him to combat. All beef and bone! He looked small enough when he was turned loose with Virgil, Book X!

"But when you think what he's supposed to have *done*," said Morgan helplessly, "what can you make of it? I mean, stealing about in the mountains knocking off sentries, and slipping a knife in people's ribs, and marching hundreds of miles with next to nothing to eat, and rounding up thousands of Germans—"

"And now he's too soft even to lick a chap for cheek—"

"Never once—not all the term he's been here!"

"Of course, we could be rather small fry, after all that," said Dominic, arrested by the thought.

"Oh, rot, he just hasn't got the guts!"

"Oh, rot, yourself! Of course he has! He *did* all that, didn't he?"

"I tell you what," said Rabbit, in very firm tones, "I don't believe he did!"

The circle closed in a little, tension plucking at them strongly. Dominic unwound his long, slim legs from the boundary railing and hopped down into the argument with a suddenly flushed face.

"Oh, get off! You know jolly well—"

"We don't know jolly well one single thing, we

only know what they all say, and how do they know it's true? They weren't there, were they? I bet you it's all a pack of fairy tales! Well, look at him! Does he look like a bloke that went around knocking off sentries and rounding up Germans? I don't believe a word of it!"

"You can't tell by looking at people what they are, anyhow. That's just idiotic—"

"Oh, is it? And who're you calling an idiot?"

"You, if you think you can just wipe out old Wedderburn's record by saying you don't believe it."

"Well, I don't, see! I don't believe he ever killed all those Jerries they say he did. I think it's a pack of lies! I don't believe he ever saw Markos, I don't believe he ever was knocked about in a prison camp, see? I don't believe he's got it in him to stick a knife in anyone's ribs. I bet you he never killed *anybody*!"

"I bet you he did, then! Who do you think you are, calling him a liar? He's worth any ten of you."

"Oh, yes, you would stick up for him! He let you off lightly, didn't he?"

"That's got nothing to do with it," said Dominic, meditating how little he had ever liked Rabbit's face, and how pleasant it would be to do his best to change it.

"Well, all right, then, I still say it's a big lie about his adventures—all of it! Now! Want to make something of it?"

"It wouldn't settle anything if I did fight you," said Dominic, tempted, "but I'm considering it."

"You don't have to, anyhow, do you? Not

12

you!" And he raised his voice suddenly into the taunting chant from which Dominic had suffered through most of his school years: "Yah, can't touch me! My dad's a p'liceman!"

Dominic had finished considering it, and come to a pleasing decision. His small but solid fist hit Rabbit's left cheek hard on the bone, and distorted the last word into a yell of quite unexpected delightfulness. Rabbit swung back on his heels, and with the recovering swing forward launched himself head-down at his opponent with both arms flailing; but before they could do each other any damage a window flew up in the classroom, and the voice of Chad Wedderburn himself demanded information as to what the devil was going on out there. Everybody ducked, as though to be shortened by a head was to be invisible, and the latecomers on the outside of the circle faded away round the corner with the aplomb of pantomime fairies or stage ghosts; but enough were left to present a comical array of apprehensive faces as supporting chorus to the two red-handed criminals pulled up in mid-career. They all gaped up at the window, made themselves as small as possible, and volunteered not a word.

"Felse and Warren," sad the unwontedly awful voice, crisply underlined by the crook of the selective forefinger, "up here, and at the double! The rest of you, beat it! And if I catch any of you fighting again, take warning, I'll have the hide off both parties. Get me?"

They said, in one concerted sigh, that they had indeed got him.

"Good! Now scram!"

It was popular, not classic, language, and it was certainly understood by the people. They departed thankfully, while with mutual recriminations Dominic and Rabbit scrambled up the stairs and arrived panting before the desk at which Chad sat writing. He looked them over with a severe eye, and then said quietly: "What you fellows argue about is your business strictly. Only what you fight about is mine. Understand me once for all, fighting is something not to be considered short of a life-and-death matter, and something I will not have about me on any less pretext than that. It proves nothing, it settles nothing, it solves nothing, except the problem of who has the most brawn and the least of any other qualities. There could be times when nothing else would serve, but they're not likely to occur in the school yard—and they *always* indicate a failure by *both* sides, wherever they occur."

A rum couple, he thought, comparing them. On such an occasion the face is, of course, worn correctly closed and expressionless, but the eyes become correspondingly alive and responsive; and while the eyes of Warren were respectful and solemn and impervious, the light, bright, gold-flecked eyes of Felse were extremely busy weighing up his judge. A little puzzled about him the child seemed, but getting somewhere, and probably not, to judge by the reserve of those eyes, exactly where he would have liked the young mind to arrive. Be careful, Chad! In this small package is unsuspected dynamite.

"Understand me?"

"Yes, sir!" If he said it, he meant it; but the reserve was still there. He understood, bless him, but he did not altogether agree.

"Well, then, let's put it this way. You two have still got a score not settled. Give me your word you won't try that way again, and we'll say no more about this time. Is it a deal?"

Rabbit said: "Oh, yes, sir!" promptly and easily. The other one looked worried, and a little annoyed, even, as if something had been sprung on him before he was ready, and from an unfair angle. He said, hesitating, standing on one leg the better to think, a method by which he often wrestled the sense out of a more than usually tough line of Virgil: "But, sir, could I—?" He wanted Rabbit to go, so that he could argue properly.

"All right, Warren, remember I've got your word for it. Now get out!"

Dominic still stood considering, even after his enemy was gone in a clatter of grateful haste down the staircase. Chad let him alone, and thoughtfully finished the sentence of his letter which their entry had interrupted, before he looked up again and said with a slight smile: "Well?"

"You see, sir, it isn't that I don't think you're right about fighting being the wrong way to do things, and all that. But, sir, you *did* fight."

"Yes," said Chad, "I did fight." He did not sound displeased; Dominic raised the fierce glance of his eyes from the floor, and looked at him, and he did not look displeased, either. "Not, however, at the drop of a hat. And not because

15

some lunatic threw at me: 'My dad's a policeman!,' either." He smiled; so did Dominic.

"No, sir! But that wasn't why I hit him. I'd just made up my mind I would, and that didn't make any difference."

"All right, that's understood, if you tell me so. But I'm still sure that what you hit him for was something a thousand miles from being worth it. And what I said still goes. All the more because you were certainly the aggressor. Either you give me your word not to go and reopen that fight in a safer place, and not to start any more so lightly, either, or else we'll settle our account here and now."

Dominic followed the turn of his head toward the cupboard, with hurt and incredulous eyes. "But, sir, you can't! I mean—you *don't!*"

"On the contrary," said Chad remorselessly, "on this occasion I can and do."

Dominic's mind calculated values frantically. He said in a small, alert voice: "Sir, if a fellow *made* another fellow fight him, you wouldn't blame the other fellow, would you? Even if he'd promised never to fight, would you?"

"In that case I'd hold the attacker responsible for both of them. He'd have quite a charge-sheet to answer, wouldn't he? Come along, now, no sidetracking. I want an answer."

Dominic thought, and squirmed, and would not give in. He said almost apologetically: "You see, sir, it's like this. Didn't you decide for yourself what was worth fighting about? I mean, wouldn't you insist— Well, it isn't even a thing you can put on to conscription, is it? Because lots

16

of fellows, if they felt like that, refused to fight. I mean, it's just *oneself* who must decide, in the end, isn't it?"

He looked a little harassed, and Chad felt sufficiently appreciative to help him out. "You're doing fine. Don't mind me! What's the conclusion?"

"I think, sir, that I ought to decide for myself, too."

"Ah!" said Chad. "Then if you've gone as far toward maturity as that, you have to take the next step forward, whether you like it or not, and realize that in any society you have to be prepared to pay for that privilege."

"Yes, sir!" sighed Dominic, resigned eyes again straying. "I *have* realized it."

Chad was sorry that he had got himself into this situation, and even sorrier that he had dragged this new kind of schoolroom lawyer into it with him. But there was no way out of it now. To let him off would be to insult him; even to let him down lightly would be to make light of his conclusions. Chad dealt with him faithfully, therefore, and left, in the process, no doubt of his own ability. But the persistent child, even when dismissed after the humane minute or two allowed for recovery, did not go. He lingered, breathing hard, with his burning palms clenched uneasily in his pockets, but his eyes once again speculative upon the future.

"Sir, could I ask you—you go home by the road, usually, don't you? I mean—not over the fields—"

"Sometimes," said Chad, examining him with

respect, "I have been known to walk through the fields." The eyes clouded over ever so slightly, but he saw the cloud, and understood it. "But this afternoon I shall be going home as you supposed—by the road." The cloud dispersed, the eyes gleamed. Chad knew himself transparent as his adversary, and the knowledge dismayed him considerably. If they were all like this one, he thought, I'd have to get out of this business; and that would be the devil, because if they were all like this one it would be well worth staying in it.

"Yes, sir! Thank you, sir!"

"You won't, however," said Chad delicately, "be in very good condition to give of your best. Why not change your mind? No discredit to you if you did, I assure you—quite the reverse."

The child, still tenderly massaging his hands in the deeps of his pockets, said hesitantly: "Sir, I hope you won't think it awful cheek, but—well, it wasn't a question of odds with you always, was it?"

The water was getting too deep for him, he made haste out of it, slipping away out of the room before Chad knew how to reply. It was reassuring to find that he supposed any situation to be beyond him.

On the way home by the fields, that afternoon, Dominic finished what he had begun, and conclusively knocked the stuffing out of Rabbit. He was a little handicapped by the puffiness of his hands, but he managed, and the fact that it hurt him somehow added to the satisfaction he got out of it. He marched home flushed and whistling, one cheek a little bruised and the eye discoloring, his hands now hurting at the back as well as the palm, because he had skinned the knuckles, but his crest well up and his self-esteem buoyantly high. One couldn't, of course, even by a roundabout method, tell the person most concerned how the affair had been concluded, but it was really a pity that he couldn't simply know.

The oblique illogic of proceedings which seemed to him directly logical did not worry Dominic at all. If you fight for somebody who doesn't believe in fighting, and has choked you off for it in advance, that's still your own affair. Especially when you have already paid for the privilege and, like the village blacksmith, owe not any man.

3

Dominic came in to tea scrupulously washed and tidied, because Aunt Nora was there, and six-year-old Cousin John; but in spite of all his precautions he did not escape from the table again before his mother had observed and interpreted more or less correctly the various small changes in his appearance. It might not have happened but for the brat John, for he was taking care to keep his knuckles as far out of sight as possible. John had so far resisted all attempts to teach him to recognize letters, and was not interested in figures for their own sake, but he could count éclairs on a plate and people round a table as fast as anyone, and make them come out right, too. Having observed by this means that the éclairs outnumbered the people by one, and that he himself was the youngest and most indulged person present, he had assumed that the extra one would be his as of right; and it was a serious shock to him when Dominic's acquisitive hand shot out and abstracted it from under his nose. He let out a wail of indignation, and seized the offending hand by the wrist as it flicked back again with the prize, and both mothers, naturally, leaned forward to quell the argument before it could become a scrimmage. Maybe Aunt Nora did miss the significance of the skinned knuckles and tender palm, but Bunty Felse didn't. Her eyes sought her son's, she frowned a little, and then laughed, whereupon he scowled blackly, relinquished the éclair, and hurriedly put his hands out of sight under the table. But she didn't say anything. She wouldn't, until the others had gone, and by then, with luck, Dominic himself could be out of the way for an hour or two. Maybe she'd forget, maybe his father wouldn't notice. Inside an hour he could finish his homework and be off to the kitchen-yard of the Shock of Hay to collect Pussy.

Unhappily in his haste to get rid of his homework he forgot to conceal his hands, and the jut of scored knuckles from a chewed pen was too obvious to escape Sergeant Felse's notice when he sat back from his late tea. George wasn't yet so far from his own schooldays that he couldn't interpret the signs. But George had an inconvenient conscience which moved him occasionally to demand more from his son than he had ever provided for his father. He reached over Dominic's shoulder, took the inky hand and turned it about in his own palm, and held on to it firmly when Dominic attempted to slide it away again. Dominic, sighing, thought and almost said: "Here it comes!"

"Hm!" said George. "Interesting! Who licked you?"

Dominic fidgeted, and frowned, and said: "Old Wedderburn."

"Oh, I thought he didn't go in for violence?"

"This time he did," snapped Dominic. "Look out, the pen's going to drip. Mind my algebra!" He wriggled, and was released; he grumbled just above his breath, like a half-grown pup growling, and mopped the small blot in the margin with unnecessary energy, to divert attention from his injuries. But he heard George chuckle.

"What was it all about? Fighting? Oh, don't trouble to duck, I've already seen your eye."

"Does it show much?" asked Dominic, fingering it rather anxiously.

"Going to be a beauty. Somebody else licked you, evidently, besides old Wedderburn."

"He didn't!" said Dominic indignantly. "You just ought to see him, that's all. I bet he'll have more than just a black eye to show by tomorrow." The gleam came back to his eyes readily, brightening them to the color of home-made marmalade. He pushed his chair back from the table to balance it on its two back legs, and wound his own long, flanneled shanks bewilderingly

21

about the front ones, braced on his taut brown arms, suddenly grinning, suddenly gloating, the little devil, about as subdued as a cock robin in the nesting season. Four feet seven of indiarubber and whalebone, with a shock head of dark chestnut hair growing in all directions, and a freckled nose, and an obstinate mouth; a good deal like his mother, only Bunty's hair was frankly red, and her skin fair and clear of freckles. George's resolution to be properly paternal, and read the appropriate lecture, went by the board, as it usually did. After all, he spent all his days being serious, even portentous, about minor crimes, he couldn't quite keep it up after hours with his own boy; and he was well aware in his own heart, though he never admitted it, that while he was more ready to threaten, it was usually Bunty who performed. She had a way of advancing with perfect calm and patience to the limit of what she would stand, and then, only occasionally and with devastating effect, falling on her startled son like a thunderstorm. And George's conscience, aware of shortcomings, impelled him sometimes to express concern ahead of her, so that he might at least appear to be the seat of authority in the house. She never snubbed him, she only smiled, and said with suspicious sweetness: "Yes, darling, you're perfectly right!"

Tonight, when he followed her into the scullery and took the teacloth out of her hand, she turned and gave him the too demure smile which made him feel about Dominic's age; and with a very

22

natural reaction he resolved to be his full thirty-nine years, and be damned to her.

"Our Dom's been in trouble at school," he said with gravity.

"So was his father before him," said Bunty, "many a time. It didn't make the slightest impression on him, either. Dom's all right, don't you worry." Aunt Nora and John were already down the road and waiting for the bus back to Comerbourne Bridge, and Bunty could laugh at both George and Dominic if she pleased, without hurting either of them. She patted his cheek disconcertingly with her wet hand, and snatched a cup from him just in time to prevent him from dropping it. "You're so like him, it just isn't true."

George took exception to this. "He's the spitting image of you, and you know it. Try and make him go the way he doesn't want, and see how far you get with it. But he *is* a little devil!" He recaptured the paternal frown with some difficulty, for heavier things than Dominic had been on his mind all day, and this was by way of self-indulgence at the end of the common task. Sometimes he thought: "Why did I ever go into this police business, anyway?"

"What was it this time?" asked Bunty serenely.

"He fell foul of Chad Wedderburn over scrapping with some other kid. Seems there are some things that get Chad's goat, after all. They had to hunt for a long time before they found one of 'em—it took Dom to do it!—but he's managed it this time. A queer lad," said George thoughtfully.

"Chad, I mean. Would you suppose that his particular red rag would be fighting?"

"I can conceive it," said Bunty, rinsing the sink. "Hasn't he had about enough of it to last him a lifetime?"

"That isn't really any reason, though, why he should grudge our Dom his bash."

"It's on the right side, anyhow," she said comfortably. "Not that Dom usually goes hunting for that particular kind of trouble, to do the little tyke justice. You didn't ask him anything about it, did you?" A hazel eye very like Dominic's regarded him sidelong for a flash, and appeared satisfied with his indignant stare; off duty she found little difference between her husband and her son. "Sorry, darling! Of course you didn't. Neither did I. He looked so on his dignity, I didn't dare. But he won," she said positively, "it was sticking out all over him."

"I wish some of his elders had learned enough sense to quit scrapping," said George. "Win or lose, it's a mug's game, but there are always more mugs than plenty." He hung up the towel neatly and rolled his shirtsleeves down. "Dealing with kids must be money for jam compared with our job."

"The child," murmured Bunty, "is father to the man. I don't suppose there's much to choose. Had a bad sort of day, then?"

"Not exactly—just ominous." He liked to talk to her about his job, at night, when he could kick it out of his mind for a short time if he wished, and therefore with human perversity ceased to wish it. Closer than his skin was Bunty, the partner of partners, and often she could help him to see a little more daylight through the opaque human creatures who vexed and made interesting his days. "I wouldn't care to say that our D.P.s are any less honest by nature than we are, but their dependent circumstances, or all they've been through, or something, has certainly given some of 'em the idea that they're entitled to be carried for the rest of their days. *And* that all we've got is theirs for the taking. Rum, you know, old girl—I could have swallowed that, but they pinch from *one another*. That I just don't get. Nobody dare leave anything lying around in the camp these days. And how the farm workers do love 'em, to be sure!"

"Cheer up," said Bunty helpfully, "the knives haven't been out for three nights, not even at turning-out time."

"Knock on wood when you say things like that, just to please me. Still, the land's awake, all right, maybe we've got to thank the visitors for that. And I suppose they have had the rough end of it for some years, poor devils—but what we'll stand from somebody who couldn't get on with his own country—or hasn't risked trying it—is nobody's business. Mind you," said George scrupulously, "there are some fine chaps among 'em, too. They're the ones I'm sorry for. There may be some place in the world where they belong, but it certainly isn't among their fellow-exiles here in Comerford."

"A man without any national roots," said Bunty gravely, "is the last person to make a good adopted child in another country."

"That's the hell of it. The last person to make any kind of internationalist, either. But we've got 'em, and we've got to try and digest 'em."

It was almost invariably at this hour in the evening, when slippers, and pipe, and a drowsy evening with the wireless floated comfortably in George's mind's eye, that the office telephone rang. It did so now, and Dominic, already on the doorstep with trunks and towel rolled under his arm, shrieked back unnecessarily to inform them of the call, and ask if he should answer it. Either way he was content; he wanted to go and fetch Pussy out from her tiresome music lesson and go swimming in the pool of the Comer, but it would also be gratifying to listen in to the beginning, at least, of some interesting incident. However, he departed blithely when George came out to the office himself, for trouble would keep, and the golden July evening would not.

"Hell!" said George, reaching for the receiver. "This is what comes of drawing fate's attention to— Hullo, yes! Felse here!" Bunty saw the official tension settle upon his face, and heaved a resigned sigh. When he hung up she had his cap already in her hands, and was holding it out to him with a comical resignation.

"Who mentioned knives?" said George accusingly, ducking his head into it wrathfully, ducking a little lower still to kiss her as he hooked open the door. "From now on, woman, keep off that line of talk, you've got me a real casualty this time."

"Where?" cried Bunty. "Not the camp?"

"The Lodge—young miner at the hostel copped it from a P.O.W."

"He's not badly hurt?" she shrieked after him, leaning forward in the doorway as he flung a leg across his bike and pushed off hard along the empty evening road.

"Be O.K., I think—I hope!" He was gone, and the rest of the story with him. Bunty went back dispiritedly into the kitchen and turned up the radio, but it was not much company. One might almost as well not have a husband; D.P.s, labor rows, neighbors swapping punches over a shared front path or a drying-ground, Road Safety Committee meetings, lectures, drunks, accidents, there was no end to it. And now some poor kid in trouble—maybe two poor kids, since most of the ex-P.O.W. recruits at the miners' hostel were no more. Say good-bye to that cosy evening with George, he won't be back until all hours.

"Maybe I should get me a dog," said Bunty grimly, "or take up fancy-work."

4

The Lodge had cost the Coal Board more than it was worth, and more than they need have paid for it if they had had the courage of their convictions; but it was house-room for thirty men. The warden was a decent, orthodox, middle-aged man who expected his troublous family of Welshmen, local boys, Poles, Germans and

27

Czechs to behave in as orderly a manner as children in a preparatory school, and was out of his depth when they did not. The whole setup was too new for him; he preferred an arrangement tried and hardened by use, where the right procedure for every eventuality was already safely laid down in black and white for a simple man to follow. Improvisation was not in his nature. He opened the studded imitation Tudor door to George, and perceptibly heaved all his responsibilities into those welcome navy-blue arms at sight. His wife would be less than useless; she had political convictions but no human ones. If the boy was really hurt they'd better get him out of there, thought George, before she gave him a chill.

"Doctor here?" he asked, halfway up the stairs with the warden babbling in his ear.

"Just ten minutes ahead of you, Sergeant. He's with the lad now." There is a certain type of man who persists in using the word lad though it does not come naturally to him; the thing has a semi-clerical ring about it, a certain condescension. You get the feeling that a young male creature of one's own class would have been a boy, while this person is subtly different.

"Good! No verdict from him yet?"

"There's scarcely been time, Sergeant. This has been a terrible business, it might so easily have ended in a tragedy. This collier's lad—" A shade more of definition, and one step down; we're getting on, thought George.

"Which? You didn't say who the victim was. Local boy?"

28

"Young Fleetwood. He's been here only a month, and really—"

"I know him," said George. "What about the other party?"

"A young man named Schauffler, Helmut Schauffler. I must say he's never given me any trouble before. A good type, I would have said. And, to be quite fair, I can't say he has been altogether to blame—certainly not the only one to blame—"

"Where is he now?"

"Down in my office. My assistant is there with him."

"You weren't there when the thing happened?—wherever it did happen? Was anyone?"

"It was in the day-room. Three other men were present. They were playing darts. I don't know if you—"

"That's all right," said George, marching across the landing, which betrayed its period by being lit with a large stained-glass window in improbable armorial bearings, notably of a violent blue. "Let's see what the damage is, first. Which room?" But the murmur of voices had drawn him before the warden could reply, and he walked in upon the end of the doctor's ministrations without waiting to be led. There were more people round the bed. The warden's wife, holding with an expression of reserve and distaste an enamel bowl of water stained darkly red. A scared-looking eighteen-year-old backed up against his bed in the far corner; the rest of him trying to be invisible, but his ears sticking out on

29

stalks. And somebody long and lean, or appearing long by reason of his leanness, standing with his back to the door and talking down to the boy on the bed across the doctor's bowed shoulder. A quiet, reasonable voice cheerfully advising the kid not to be an ass, because everything would be taken care of, including letting his mother know. The speaker looked round at the small sound the door made in opening, and showed the unexpected face of Chad Wedderburn, the slanting light magnifying his scar. Tonight he had another mark, too, a small punctured bruise upon the same cheek, of which at the moment he seemed completely unaware.

The doctor was a little, grimly gay, middle-aged man with brilliant eyes, and false teeth which slipped at the most awkward moments, and which he plugged testily back into position with a sudden thumb whenever they tripped him. He looked over his shoulder at George, and with a welcoming grin, as who should say: "Ah, trouble!" pulled him directly into consultation. Trouble was the breath of life to him, not because he enjoyed seeing people tormented, but because his energy was tumultuous, and demanded an exhausting variety of interests to employ it through the day.

"There you are, Sergeant!" he said, as if George had been there from the beginning. "What did I tell you? Only a perfectly clean wound, touched a rib, no damage, not the ghost of a complication of any kind. Thinks he's going to die because he bleeds freely. Thinks I'm going to forbid you to badger him, I dare say. Your mistake, my boy! Put you through it as much as he likes, I've no objection. Eat you if he likes! He'd find you tough enough if he tried it!" He was all this time busily finishing a bandage, and buttoning a stained shirt over it again with fingers which flew as fast as his tongue, but more steadily. The boy on the bed looked a little bewildered at the spate of words, but a little reassured, too, and stirred docilely from side to side as the hands directed him. "Good boy! You're all right, I promise you. Nothing in the world to worry about, so take that scared look off your face, and relax. All you've got to do is exactly as you're told for a few days. Something new for you, eh? Eh?"

Apprehensive but faintly soothed gray eyes flickered from the doctor's face to George's, and back again. Young Fleetwood was seventeen, sturdy but small for his age; on his own here now, George remembered, the family had moved south. Clever, idealistic kid, out to save the country and the world, so he bypassed the chance of teaching, and set out to cure what was wrong with the mines. Probably end up as a mining engineer, and maybe that would reconcile his old man, who had been a collier himself and learned to look upon it as something not good enough for his sons. All the more important because there was only this one son now; the elder was dead in the last push into Germany, in 1945.

"I'm taking him into hospital for a few days," said the doctor briskly. "No great need, but I'd like him under my eye."

"Best thing for him, I'd say. How bad was it?"

31

"Quite a gash—sliced wound, but the rib stopped the knife, or it might have been a bad job. The ambulance will be here for him in about ten minutes, but if you need longer—? Let him down easy, he's had a fright."

"That's all right, he wouldn't know how to start being scared of me," said George cheerfully. "Known me all his life." He sat on the edge of the bed, and smiled at the boy until he got a wan smile in return. "Can we have the room to ourselves until the ambulance comes? Let me know when you're ready for him, doctor."

Jim Fleetwood let the room empty of everyone else, but turned his head unhappily after Chad Wedderburn, and reached a hand to keep him, but drew it back with a slight flush, ashamed of hanging on to comfort. Chad said quietly: "It's all right, Jim, I'll come back."

"Stay, by all means," said George, "if he wants you. That's all right with me. I know the feeling." The door closed after the others, and it was quiet in the room. "That's better! How did you get here? Just visiting?"

"Jim asked for me, and his roommate called me on the phone. I was ahead of the doctor. His family are a long way off, you see; I suppose I seemed about as solid a prop as he could think of offhand." He looked, at that, as if he might be. The broken bruise on his cheek burned darkly; he saw George's eyes linger on it, and said evenly: "Yes, I walked into it, too. This was a present from the same bloke. The row was barely over when I got here, everybody was arguing, down in the day-room, what happened and what didn't happen. Schauffler happens to be a kind I know already. He didn't much like being known. But he'd given up the knife by then, luckily for me. I was turning away from him at the time," he explained gently, but with a certain tension in his voice which hinted at stresses underneath. "I had Jim in my arms. The Schauffler kind chooses its time."

"I wish you'd lit into him then," said Jim, feebly blazing. "I wish you'd killed him."

"You're a fine pal, to want me hanged for a Helmut Schauffler!"

The boy paled at the thought, and lost his voice for fear of saying something of equally awful implications with the next breath.

"There isn't going to be any trouble, is there? I don't want my people to get it wrong." He began to flush and shake a little, and George put a hand on his shoulder to quiet him.

"The only trouble you've got is a few days in hospital, and the job of getting on your feet again. Just tell us all about it, and then quit worrying about anything except getting well. We'll see that your parents don't get it wrong. You can trust us. If I don't make a good job of it, Wedderburn will. Now, how did this business start?"

"It's been going on a week or more, ever since I was coming from the showers one day, and saw him just leaving some more German chaps outside. They saluted each other the Nazi way, and said: 'Heil, Hitler!'—just as if there hadn't been any war, and our Ted and all the other chaps gone west for nothing. I dare say I oughtn't to have cut loose, but what can you expect a chap to do? I couldn't stand it. I suppose I raved a bit—honestly, I can't remember a damned word I said, but I suppose it was all wrong and idiotic. I should have hit him, only Tom Stephens and some more fellows came, and lugged me away. I didn't put any complaint in—I couldn't, because I was ashamed I'd made such a muck of it, and anyhow he hadn't done anything to me, only stand there and grin. But ever since then he's picking on me here—nothing you could get hold of, because there never was anyone else around to see and hear—but he'd slip remarks in my ear as he went by—he got to find out about Ted, somehow, I think he's been prying here in my room. But I can't *prove* any of it. I'm telling you, but it's only my word for it. Only, honestly, I haven't made it up, and I'm not imagining it, either."

"I wish you'd had the sense to come to me days ago," said Chad Wedderburn.

"Well, but I didn't want to make trouble for you, and it was all so slippery. You can see it's no good now. I only made you take the same sort of nastiness I've had."

"What about tonight?" prompted George.

"He was down in the day-room, playing darts with three of the fellows. They didn't often invite him in, but I suppose he was there, and they took him on. I didn't even know. I went down there to borrow a fine screwdriver, because I'd broken the strut of Ted's photo, and I was putting a new one on it. When I went in he was sitting by the table, and he had a clasp-knife, and was trimming the end of a dart that wouldn't fly true. I never

34

took any notice of him. I just put the photo on the table—as far from him as it would go, but it's only a small table—and asked Tom Stephens for his pocket gadget, and he gave it to me, and went on with the game. And I went back to pick up my picture." He stirred painfully on his pillow, and shut his teeth together hard to stop a rising gulp. "It's Ted in his uniform—I went and left it down there—"

"Don't worry, we'll take care of that. Go on!"

"He sat there whittling away with the knife, and he looked at me over it, and then he spat—making believe he was spitting on the blade, and then stooping down to sharpen it on the sole of his shoe—but he knew what he was about, all right! He spat on Ted's photo—spattered it all over the face— He spat on my brother, and grinned at me! A dirty little Nazi like that!"

"So you went for him," said George equably.

"Of course I did! What would you expect me to do? I dropped the screwdriver—anyhow it was a little pocket thing, all closed up, like a lipstick—and went for him, and hit him in the face, and he started to get up and lunge at me, all in one movement. The knife went into me, and I fell on top of him, and then the other three came and pulled us apart, and I was bleeding like a pig—and—and I was scared like a kid, and started to yell for Mr. Wedderburn, and Tom went and got him—and that's all."

Not all, perhaps, that could be told, but all that Jim was capable of telling just then, and it was as full of holes as any sieve. He looked speculatively at Chad's darkening cheek, and asked: "What about your little incident? If you had the kid in your arms at the time, *you* can hardly have started the rough stuff."

Chad smiled sourly. "I didn't even call him rude names. It was all strictly schoolmaster stuff. He was sitting like a damp sack until I turned to go out of the day-room, and then he shot up like a rocket and took a hack at me. I—hadn't been complimentary, of course. His poor English might have led him to find words there which I never used."

"Don't put words in *my* mouth," said George hastily.

"Just the words you'll probably find in his. He has them all, there's been time to find the right ones. But it would hold up an assault charge," he said simply, "if you're hard up. Every little helps!"

George thought it might, but discreetly said nothing. He patted Jim with an absent-minded cheerfulness, as he might have done a Dominic smitten with stomachache, bade him do as he was told, like a good chap, and not worry about anything; and with the exchange of a glance committed him again to the surprising care of Chad Wedderburn, who was inexpertly putting together the small necessities of a stay in hospital from the chest-of-drawers. "See him off, and keep him happy. Come along to the station on your way back, will you? I'll take care of brother Ted, you can be easy, you shall have him back safely."

He went down, not very well satisfied, to collect three vague and confused statements from the dart-players. An incident only three seconds long is not seen clearly by men whose minds are concentrated on a dart-board placed on the other side of the room. Tom Stephens, who was the most anxious to back up his roommate, said he had seen the blow struck, and didn't think it was any accident. He had also seen the insult to Ted's photograph, which still lay on the table with half-dried stains of spittle undoubtedly marking the glass, and his firm impression was that that had been no error of judgment, either, but a deliberate provocation. But the other two were less ready to swear to it. The German had started up to defend himself, and the open knife was already in his hand; what could you expect in the circumstances? Jim had hit him first, and quite possibly on mistaken grounds. They wouldn't like to say he had meant any harm.

As for the warden, he wanted everything smoothed down into a chapter of accidents, the eruption of contrary temperaments intent on thinking the worst of each other. Schauffler had always been a good, quiet fellow, a little sullen and defensive in this place where he felt himself unwanted, but anxious to avoid trouble rather than to court it. The position of an anti-Nazi German soldier allowed into industry here was certainly a difficult one, and it was the warden's opinion that hot-headed young people like Jim Fleetwood did nothing to make it easier. All this he poured into George's ear as they went along the corridor to his office to have a look at this vexed case in the flesh.

The warden's assistant was sitting at a desk

near the top-heavy Victorian fireplace, and opposite him in a straight-backed chair, perfectly still
and inert, sat Helmut Schauffler. He was perhaps
twenty-three or -four, blond as a chorus girl, with
a smooth face weathered to dark ivory, and light-
blue eyes a little moist and swollen, as if he had
been crying, and could cry again at will. But the
rest of his face, smooth across broad, hard bones,
was too motionless to suggest that any sort of grief
was involved in the phenomenon. He should,
thought George, be a pretty impressive specimen
when on his feet, broad-shouldered and narrow-
flanked, with large, easy movements; but just now
he didn't look capable of movement at all, he sat,
as Chad had said, like a damp sack, helpless and
hopeless, with his flaccid hands dangling between
his knees. They didn't look as if they had bones
enough in them to hold a knife, much less steer
it into another man's ribs. When George entered,
the blue eyes lifted to his face apprehensively,
like the eyes of an animal in a trap, but the rest
of his face never moved a muscle.

His voice was deep but vague in pitch, fitting
the sullen indefiniteness of his person; his English
was interestingly broken. He burst easily into a
long and pathetic explanation of the whole incident, the burden of his song being that here he
was an outcast, misinterpreted, misunderstood,
that his most harmless gestures were held to be
threats, and the most innocent lapses of his
tongue, astray among the complexities of the
English language, taken as deliberate affronts.
Once animated by his own woes, his body exhibited some of the tensions which had been missing,

drew itself into the compact and muscular mass it was meant to be, with double the adolescent strength of Jim Fleetwood in it. It appeared, in fact, to enjoy its own animal competence. The hands, flattened along his thighs, no longer looked incapable of killing.

"I never wish to hurt this boy, I never wish to insult his brother, never. That one was a soldier, I too, I respect him. It is by a bad chance it happens like that. But the young brother is so hot, all at once he runs at me, strikes me in the face—I do not even know what it is he thinks I have done! When I am struck so, I jump up to fend him off—who not? The knife I forget, all is so suddenly happening, I am so confused. It is only he, running at me, he runs on the knife in my hand— What am I to say? If I am not German, this does not happen. If I am not German, he does not so quickly think the worst in all I do. What is it, to be here in this country a German?"

George reminded him delicately of the Nazi salute which had not passed unnoticed at the colliery. He admitted it, tears of despair starting in his blue eyes.

"Thus we are taught so long, thus it must be done years of our lives, can we so soon lose it? It comes to my hand, so, my will does not know what I do. Never have I been a Nazi, only one must conform, or for parents, family, all, is very bad life. I am young, I do as I am taught. And now it makes me to seem an enemy here, where I would be only a quiet citizen."

His depression deepened when the unwarrantable blow at Chad Wedderburn was recalled to his memory. Five people had seen that, and to deny it was purposeless; even excuses might carry less weight here, but he could try. He enjoyed trying, George could see that. As the tragedy and doom of his eyes deepened, the exultation and sleekness of his body became more clear and insolent, like the arrogant stretchings of a cat before a fire.

"That was a bad thing, I own it, I regret it. But even that I do not mean. I am confused, angry, I am in trouble and afraid, no one helps me, no one explains or wishes to make things easier. This man, it is well understood he is very angry for the boy Jim. But he rages at me—half he says I do not understand, and so perhaps I think it worse than it is. I lose my head, and strike him because I am in despair. But when I have done it I am sorry, I no longer wish to hurt him. I am very sorry and ashamed."

He wept a subtle tear or two; George was impressed in spite of himself. He went away to phone Weaver, and get a car from Comerbourne. This hostel was no place for Helmut Schauffler now, from any point of view; even the warden would be glad to get rid of him, though one felt that he would be equally glad to get rid of Jim. And in view of the fact that somebody, some-where, was due to have considerable trouble with Helmut in the future, maybe a few days in custody wouldn't do any harm; especially as the tears and broken words were due to flow for the magis-trates' benefit even more readily than they had done for George's, and he doubted if a charge of unlawful wounding or causing bodily harm was going to stand up successfully under their weight.

He didn't forget to collect Ted's photograph, clean it gravely of the traces of Helmut's attentions, and commit it to the care of Tom Stephens until Jim came home. It was the usual conventional photograph of a simple young man in uniform: candid-eyed, vulnerable, not too intelligent, very much Jim's brother; easy meat, the pair of them, for a Helmut Schauffler. George felt depressed, and not altogether because of the immediate upsets of Comerford. Something was going wrong here which had also larger implications; it wasn't in a few months' time that the world was due to hear about it, but in twenty years or so, after a few people had shouted their hearts out about it and been shrugged aside as mental for their pains.

George went home at last, late and slowly, and found Chad Wedderburn talking to Bunty in the kitchen. The cut on his cheek was discoloring badly, and by tomorrow would be a focus of extreme interest for the Fourth. George said, remembering the beginning of his evening as if it drifted back to him from a thousand miles away: "I hope Dom hasn't seen that. If he has, you're liable to be sued for breach of contract, or obtaining money on false pretenses, or something."

When Chad laughed, the stiffening cut quivered and laughed with him. "I'm afraid he has. He was a little late getting home, and we met on the doorstep. His eyes popped out of his head,

41

almost. He's probably hanging over the banisters now, all ears."

"I hope," said Bunty, "he's asleep by this time, or there'll be no getting him up in the morning. What would you like him to be told, if he assumes I've got the whole story out of you?" And though she said "if," it was immediately clear to George that indeed she had. She wore a satisfied look, as if she had not been altogether left out of events.

"I leave it to your husband," said Chad, grinning at George. "Or haven't you got a clue, either?"

"I could tell him the truth, I suppose, but he'd be pretty disgusted with you."

"Oh, I don't know!" said Chad, smiling down a little somberly at the curling smoke of his cigarette. "He'd see the arguments for nonviolence—in the circumstances. Still, I do admit—"

"You'd have liked to pulverize him, wouldn't you?"

"It would have been a pleasure," said Chad, in voice and word still understating.

"Why didn't you? Oh, I know, you were thinking about Jim, you wanted him safe out of the rotten business without any more harm—and all that. Still—why didn't you?"

The hard, lean fingers closed gently together on the end of the cigarette and crushed it out. "I was afraid," said Chad, very simply, "that if I started I should probably kill him."

5

Helmut Schauffler was discharged on the bodily harm charge, though with a warning that it was dismissed only by reason of an element of doubt as to his motives, and the extent to which sheer accidental circumstances had framed him. On the assault charge he was fined £2, which within the allotted time he contrived to pay. The magistrates gave full weight to his passionate plea that everybody was against him, and the worst construction automatically put on everything he did; so anxious were they to be excluded from the everybody thus censured that they leaned over backwards to be generous to him, and expressed the hope that he would yet find his niche in England, and settle down happily among his neighbors. The local colliery administration had already decided by then that they would be courting trouble by taking him back, and in their turn hoped that something else might be found for him, something more retired from the frictions of hostel life. Say some job on a farm. He was able-bodied, and a hard worker by inclination; if he had to deal only with a very small group of individuals who were prepared to take a little trouble with him, the results might still be admirable. The magistrates called this case to the attention of any local farmers who might be in need of a hand, and hoped one of them would feel able to make the experiment.

Gerd Hollins read the local weekly religiously from front page to back every Saturday evening. She put it down and looked at her husband over the carefully folded sheets at last, and was quiet for a long time. Whenever she fixed her eyes on him thus, Chris Hollins felt their plucking as the strings of a harp feel the fingers that wrest music out of them, and had to look up and meet her dark glance before he could have any rest.

They had been married now for ten years; she had been in England for twelve, and her speech was flawlessly English, perfected even with the leisurely country softness of Comerford, where she had learned most of it. But she kept still some little opulent gestures and elaborations of manner which set her apart as clearly as an accent would have done. She had been assimilated without being changed; sometimes it was merely plain that she was not English, sometimes one could safely judge her country to be Germany. Always, though her quietness withdrew it into the background of her personality, the discerning eye could be sure that she was a Jewess. Her father had been a teacher in Dessau; there had been three brothers, and one more sister. Now there was only Gerd. She had escaped in the autumn of 1937, and by interminable ways round Europe arrived in England, where she had found domestic work, and begun to scrape together all the money she could, in readiness for the day when some other member of the family should follow her. But nobody ever came. It was only by the most elaborately capricious of chances that she herself had ever arrived. Long after she had married Christopher Hollins she had gone on hoping and believing that the others would turn up, after the war; and after the war she had traced at least her youngest brother, but to a cardboard box of ashes on a shelf in a room of the crematorium of Osviecim. And that was all.

Gerd was in the middle thirties, and already less handsome than she had been; but Chris was fifty, and found her very beautiful. Even if her figure had rounded and spread far more disastrously, and the understandable gray in her smooth, rather coarse black hair been more obtrusive, he would still have thought her a beauty, for he was still in love with her, and probably always would be. He had lived all his life in the constant round of his little lands, a hill-farm just above the village, mostly sheep-pasture; but she had brought here in her person all the romance and all the tragedy of Europe, and in spirit he understood it better, and burned with it more deeply, than many who had wandered through it in uniform and seen it for themselves, but without an interpreter. Most people found him narrow and dull and virtuously uninteresting, but inside the placid shell she had found house-room for all the havoc of humanity's hopes; and living alone with him was not boring to her.

She folded the paper more firmly, the dry half-column of "Magistrates' Courts" framed between her hands. "Chris, have you seen this?" She gave it to him. He read it silently, and looked at her again, and gravely.

"Perhaps you'll think it a counsel of desperation," she said, "but I want you to take in this man."

"But all these years," he said, astonished, "you've avoided having any contact with Germans. Why should you suddenly want to have one here? I'm dead sure it would be a mistake. Better not to think of them, even, not to remember they exist."

"I know! I've been wrong to avoid the issue. If by trying one could really forget they exist, that might be well. But I have tried—as you say, I've tried for years—and without success. How long can one go on running away from a fact, I wonder? Chris, I haven't done you or myself any good. You can't pretend things haven't happened. I'm tired of trying. If I could make this effort, it would be better for us both."

"It's too big a risk," he said. "We should be fools to go looking for trouble. He'll only remind you all over again, every time you look at him. That's no way to get rid of memories."

"I've tried smothering them," she said, "for years. It's no good that way, Chris. I can't forget things that way. There's only one thing for it, and that's to admit everything and accept everything, and find some way of living that doesn't mean always sitting on top of a chest of grudges, trying to keep the lid from opening. If I could get used to the idea that Germans are much the same as other flesh and blood—if there could be some ordinary boy, stupid perhaps, difficult perhaps, I don't care—only someone who could have something in him worth forgiving—"

"You seem to have picked a difficult case if you want this one," he said bitterly.

"There are no easy ones. Anyhow, what would be the good of an easy one? It would mean nothing. But he's young—and if it succeeded, I should be a lot happier. Chris, I want to try. Let me try!"

"I don't know!" he said. "I'll have to think about it. Give me a little time to consider. I'm involved in this, too."

"Yes," she agreed, "because you, too, would be happier if we could get rid of this past that follows us about."

It is not easy to shake off memory by any method; and gentle and still as she was, and spotlessly innocent of any act which should haunt her afterwards, and unfair though it is that the acts of other persons should haunt us, Hollins had felt her always being followed by the hate and horror which even she could not escape. He did not reflect that her nature was soft, and should have been unretentive. He was not given to thinking except by such processes as lift the shoot to the light. But he could perceive, and he perceived that she made the best of things, and even enjoyed some happiness, always with the footsteps treading on her heels. Ten years had not achieved a cure by leaving well alone; it might be worth even the risk of meddling.

So he thought about it, and sought another opinion because thought was such unfamiliar country to him. He talked it over with Jim Tugg, in the late afternoon when he came back tired from the last of the dipping. Jim listened, and his black brows drew together over the gaunt deeps of his eyes.

"Your wife's a saint," he said, wasting no words, "but she's a fool, too. If you do a daft thing like that, you'll be buying trouble for everybody."

"That's what I'm afraid of," admitted Hollins, "but she's set her mind on it."

"More fool her, to think it could do any good. And more fool you, if you let her have her way. Forgive! You might as well forgive an adder for being an adder, and pick it up in your hand, and expect it not to bite you."

He was no comfort. He said the same things to Gerd, and in much the same words. She heard him attentively, fixing her great, black, young, sad eyes on him trustfully, for he was friend as well as shepherd. When he had done, she said: "You may be right. Yet if it could be only one accidentally decent boy, he would do. If I could *like* one of them, and be able to bear it that I came from the same race, it would be enough. And there must be some who are good—you know it is impossible there should be none at all."

"Some there may be," he said, "but don't look for them here. The best go back, they want to do something for their own country. What do you expect to find here? There's so little in any of them except what someone with more will has planted—they've got no bones of their own to stand up by."

"I cannot go on all my life hating," said Gerd. "I wasn't made for it."

Jim turned his dark, massive face toward her

48

and said: "While there's hateful things going on every day side by side with us, what's wrong with hating?"

"It's painful. It deforms one. Perhaps it even kills."

"Not a chance!" he said with a fiery smile, sultry and sudden like the red of a bonfire breaking through the damp smoldering blanket of sods. "It keeps alive, sometimes. With no other solitary thing to live for, hate can keep you alive."

"It is not a way in which I can maintain life," she said, looking at him plaintively; but she was never angry, never condemned his angers, never said things heatedly without considering first if she truly meant them. And therefore, for one who loved her, it was necessary always to listen to her earnestly, and try to make the adjustments which alone could help you to understand her.

"No," he said, staring at her steadily, "no, I don't suppose you could." She did not know, because she thought so little of herself she did not guess, even when he looked at her like that, that he adored her. Why should she suspect it? She was a few years older than he, and looked older still; she was graying, her figure was growing soft and shapeless and middle-aged, and her face had never been striking, even in first youth. "Try, then!" he said, and abruptly turned away. "Have it your own way! If it doesn't come off—if he's all I think he might be—there's always me around to deal with him. But if he turns out to be the usual kind," said Jim Tugg, "I'll kill him."

She did not think anything of that, not because he was given to saying such things, but because everyone says them sooner or later. Her mind had gone too far with the idea to turn back; if she had retreated from her purpose now it would only have been one more ghost close on her heels, like the spectral bastard of the older memories.

So Helmut came. He came lumpishly, defensively, with closed face and warding-off eyes, as if he feared everyone he met might hit him. They received him without fuss or too much favor, like any other hand, lodging him in the attic room over the house end of the stables, and feeding him at their own table. But getting his head out from between his shoulders was a labor for Hercules during the first few days, and tools were needed to prise out a few whispered words. He worked willingly, even anxiously, and looked years younger than his age because he seemed so lost and timorous; but it was true that the actual lines of his face, in their solidity and stillness, did not quite bear out the unformed, grieved questing of his eyes. He seemed so young that Gerd was moved, and the warmth of it came into her heart gratefully, and she believed she had succeeded.

She was not even very unwise. She called him Helmut, because Jim was always Jim, but used it very seldom because it came stiffly to her tongue. Only if she had to use a name for him, that was the name. And on his part there were few words except: "Yes, Mrs. Hollins!" and "No, Mrs. Hollins!" like a dutiful boy new from school. Jim behaved to him with careful but competent coolness, as to an awkward gate-post freshly painted. And in a few days Helmut began to expand to his full size, instead of going about shrunk defensively into himself; and in a few days more, when he had his true height, only an inch below Jim's, and his great, loose young breadth of shoulder spread for all to see, his gait and all his movements, down to the extending of a hand to accept a plate, acquired a glossy, exultant smoothness, his step an effortless spring, his voice a resonance hitherto unsuspected.

"He comes to himself," said Gerd, and was pleased, as if the triumph had been hers.

He did come to himself, and with a vengeance. He was late in to his dinner one day, having stayed to finish a repair job on one of the distant fences; and by the time he arrived Hollins was away again, and Jim just leaving. She served Helmut alone. He watched her as she came and went, and his light blue eyes had quite stopped being young and pathetic, and were bright, opaque and interested. They traveled all over her, and enjoyed their sapience. Suddenly in the very same tone in which he had just thanked her for his pudding he said in German: "You like it better here than at home, do you? The English are more long-suffering?"

Her step faltered for only the fraction of a second. She put a cup of coffee at his elbow, and said quite calmly and levelly: "Do not speak German to me. I prefer not to use it."

"You want to forget it?" he suggested sympathetically, and flashing up at her a quick, cold grimace which was not quite a smile.

"I prefer not to use it. If you speak in it I shall not answer you."

"In English then," he said, and laughed so

51

briefly that the sound was gone almost as soon as recognized. He stretched himself, leaning back in his chair to have her the more securely in view. "Do you think even the English do not tire at last? There are some who are tired already of harboring you. They make little noise yet, but the time will come when you will hear it, even in this very nice comfortable place."

No protests came to her lips, because there was no use in them. She turned her back and went away from him, carrying dirty dishes into the scullery, as if he did not exist, or only as precisely the same rather lumpish and harmless young man he had been five minutes before. Behind her he said, a little more sharply for her apparent calm, but still with a shy, subtle quietness: "You hear already, but a Jew crawls away only when he must. Even when you kick him out at the door he creeps in by the window again."

She closed the door between them, and began to fill the sink, as if nothing in the world had happened; her heart in her breast was like a white-hot stone, heavy, dragging her body down into a dark place she did not know, but she began to whisk soap powder into the water, to slide the knives into it, and clatter them out again on to the draining-board.

Presently he brought his dishes in to her there, the door opening almost apologetically as on his first day, and his big, fair body coming in side-long. She felt him there, though she did not turn her head, and all she saw was his hands as he put down the plate and cup on the table at her right hand. Then, as he was going, he touched her;

his fingertips, first so softly that the contact was hardly perceptible, then with a sly, savoring firmness, in the soft flesh of her back, drawing lines, drawing a subtle shape there on her body.

"Even in this nice country," he whispered, with a stupid little giggling breath of excitement and pleasure in her ear, "you will wear here, some day, a yellow star."

He was gone, even a little hastily in the end, shutting the door loudly over her motionless silence. She stood there at the sink staring at her raised hands with a slight, concentrating frown, while the lather dried on them in little iridescent bubbles with the smallest of moist, bright sounds. She seemed to be contemplating some domestic complication such as the next week's grocery order. What she was actually seeing was a long, dark earth corridor, and six people walking down it, father, mother, Walter, Hans, Frieda, Josef; and at the end of it a crematorium trolley, into which, one by one, they quietly climbed and vanished.

II

The Place—

1

The farms at Comerford, cheek by jowl with the collieries, lay round the rim of a misshapen bowl which circled a bend of the River Comer. Over all the high ground sheep-pasture jostled with the waste tips and shafts of the mines, and the relics of old forest filled every cranny of the hills still left to them. But the greatest acreage on these levels belonged to new and fantastic forest, which had eaten at the pastures until almost sixty percent was absorbed. The pits had begun to dump here a hundred and fifty years ago from great numbers of sudden, shallow shafts; and having created about itself queer mud-pie shapes of clay, each shaft finally failed and was abandoned, the area being thereupon left for the wind to plant again, and the seasons to reclaim. On the better places a wild, deep, elastic grass grew, then heather, then the unconquerable silver birches which came from nowhere, by fragile-seeming colonies, to seed and flourish upon starvation. The casing of the shafts fell in, their perfunctory wooden surrounds disintegrated or were impounded in bad winters for firewood, and there remained, quite simply, a series of highly dangerous holes in the ground, which were nobody's business. Presently about these death-traps the high woodlands thickened with bramble and heather and bilberries, and made soil enough for other trees to feed there; and a few more enterprising landowners, like Selwyn Blunden of the Harrow, covered the barren places with young plantations, and turned parts of them into preserves, since they would raise no other crop. So from forest Comerford circled round again to forest, but these woods had the bizarre outlines of the high places of Assyria, instead of the suave folded lines of the primeval England.

Slithering inward from the cooler winds, the village coiled itself inside the bowl, three convoluted streets, so involved that one could nowhere see more than fifty yards ahead, and a maze of footpaths kept clear by the obstinacy of the inhabitants, who used them on principle even when they proved to be the longest way home. And downward still from the village went the rich, sheltered fields of the lower farms, greening, greening into the black prolific water-meadows, and the serpentine curves and bright calm pool of the Comer.

The main road, winding up the valley, made the passage of the village perforce, for as yet there was no bypass to spare motorists the convolutions of the Comerford street. The railway was just over the coal-rim and out of sight, with the local station nestling a lane's length from the last wood of the Harrow preserves.

On the rim the opencast unit camped like a giant circus, leisurely stripping up the more naked of the clay hills, under which the coal seams ran obliquely toward the Harrow; and on this sacred land, too, the Coal Board had designs, so that the contractor and his men sat and looked with shining eyes at the fat wooded lands, and the heathery open levels extending from the edge of their present site round to the skyline above the river. Old Blunden had shrugged his shoulders over the hectic changes in the landscape, in the social pattern of England and Comerford, even in the day-to-day business of farming, and had seemed to accept the necessity of adjusting himself to all these things; but he was human, and when the encroaching finger of change tried to creep over his own boundaries he stopped being quite so philosophical about it. The odds were that if the fight went against him he would pay up and look big, for he had always been a sporting old chap; but he would see to it that there was a fight first. His appeal was a massive responsibility, for he was one of the powers in the district still, for all his virtual retirement. The farm might be nominally his son's responsibility now, even his son's property, but their voices in this matter were one voice, and that was the old man's.

Meantime, the large, leather-coated, weather-beaten Gypsies and their monstrous machines went on methodically building new mountains and gouging out new valleys, and the dark topsoil, neatly isolated, began to grow a fresh young grass even in the autumn, in the first decline of the beautiful year. And for the time being this edge of Comerford looked like a stretch of the baked clay deserts of Sinkiang. People who had never turned a hair about the open shafts in the woods were never tired of lamenting this temporary devastation. Even the more thoughtful residents looked forward to the day when the lie of coal would be exhausted, and the site would be folded level and bare again to heal slowly in the soothing flow of seasons. Only the little boys, exulting in strange friendly men and the pleasures of change, collected new grotesque tractors and grabs and loaders as they had formerly collected cigarette packets and stamps, and gravitated to the site on their way home from school as dogs to a bone. Just as the twentieth-century nomads, the new navigators, gravitated inevitably to the pubs of Comerford in the darkening evenings, and boiled among the regulars like an incompatible ingredient in some chemical mixture, with larger bodies, louder voices and different accents, a race of good-humored giants left over from the primitive world.

The Shock of Hay was the largest pub in the village, snug under the shadow of the church tower, with the trim oval green drawn around it like a nicely arranged skirt about a demure woman posing for her portrait. It had a creaking picture-sign so faded that it might have been anything, and a large stable-yard from the heyday of horses, and an erroneous reputation of being a coaching inn, though the truth was that no coach in the history of transport ever ran so crazy a route as to pass through Comerford. The house was warm and red and squat, with ceilings rather low for Georgian, but rooms of the commendable spaciousness which gives a large man license to stretch his legs as he sits, without tangling them in the iron stand of the next table, or tripping up his neighbor in the gangway. The sunshine miners liked it because they could sprawl; but they liked it also, as everybody did, because it possessed the inestimable asset of the person of Io Hart.

Joe Hart owned and ran it. He had been born there, and his father before him, and though he had had a few vicissitudes in his young days, sown a few unexpected crops here and there, been a boxer and a fireman and a lumberjack for brief periods, it had always been taken for granted that when the old man died he should come here and take over the business. And so he had, as to the manner born.

Mrs. Hart had been dead for four years now, but Io, the elder daughter, who was twenty-two, had everything at her finger-ends, could manage the whole diverse flow of customers year in and year out without disarranging a curl of her warm brown hair, and make her father, into the bargain, do whatever she wanted. When she knew what she wanted, which wasn't always. Folks were beginning to say that she didn't know which of two young men she wanted, and that was shaping into quite a serious matter, especially when they would come and do their quarreling in the snug, and over any mortal thing under the sun except Io. Luckily, the only other girl was thirteen, a safe age yet. Her name was Catherine, but it had been shortened to Cat early in her schooldays, and from that had swiveled round into Pussy, by which unexpected and in many ways unsuitable name everyone in Comerford knew her. She was an extremely self-possessed young woman, shaped like a boy rather than a girl, though not so lumpy at the joints; she could outrun most boys of her age, skim stones over the Comer with a flick of the wrist like a whiplash while the shots of her rivals sank despondently in mid-stream, climb like any monkey, throw from the shoulder, keep up her end one-handed in school or out of it, and had generally, as her father proudly said (though not in her hearing), all her buttons on. She would never be the beauty Io was, but in another way she might be pretty disturbing in a few years, with her direct green eyes and her snub nose, and all that light-brown hair now impatiently confined in two long plaits, one over either shoulder. But the only kind of cat she recalled was some rangy tigerish tom, treading sleekly across the gardens in long strides with his soft, disdainful feet; not the kind of cat one would call Pussy. Because of its inappropriateness the name stuck; people are like that.

Io was darker of eyes and hair, though fairer of face. She had a pink-and-white skin which glowed softly, and when she smiled, which was often, the glow seemed to brighten and deepen, warming her whole face. She was one of those fortunate people who are dainty by nature, invariably dainty without any effort on their part, whose clothes always fit, whose hair always curls, and to whom dust never adheres, while mud-splashes in the street deflect themselves from touching even their shoes. Her very gestures had a finished delicacy, and no spot ever spilled overboard from a glass while she carried it. She was plump, frankly plump, with some shape about it, the new feminine turn of fashion might have been designed expressly for her soft, firm figure. Her arms even had dimples in them near the elbows, dairy-maid fashion, and even those village connoisseurs who theoretically were devotees of the attenuated celluloid lovelies of Hollywood found this generosity of Io's person singularly agreeable to behold. In fact, the chief drawback of the Shock of Hay was that sometimes even its ample spaces became uncomfortably full.

The two who were seriously upsetting the peace of the place on Io's account were Charles Blunden and Chad Wedderburn. Not that they ever came into the open about it; they just sat there in their particular corner of the snug, perhaps one or two nights a week for an hour or less, and bristled at each other like fighting terriers. But it was quite obvious what goaded them, by the jealous way they sharpened their words and threw them like darts whenever she came near them. They were always arguing about something, and the something was never Io; it might be politics, it might be books, or music, or even football; but most often it was something abstruse and high-flown, amply provided with long words and formidable terms, so that their neighbors admired the more as they understood the less. They had always been friends, and for that matter had always argued, in a casual way, so that the effect was not of a change, but only of a sudden and devastating acceleration in the inflammable progress of their relationship. But it left people with an uneasy feeling that some day it might get really out of hand, and refuse to stop.

Now wouldn't you think, said Comerford to

itself, that two young men who had been half across the world during the war, and lived through two or three lifetimes of adventure and discomfort and danger, could be trusted to behave with some restraint and calm over the simple matter of a girl they both admired? Yet that was the one thing that set them both off like the fuse to explosives; after all they'd been through! True, there were lulls of common sense between, chiefly when Io, who had a temper of her own if it came to that, had visibly been pushed to consider knocking their heads together. Then the odds were that one or other of them would laugh, though rather discomfortedly, and they would come to their senses and go off together apparently friends, and both out of spirits.

Charles, of course, would have been quite a catch for any girl, with all the Harrow land in his hands; but the other one had still the rags of that glamorous reputation of his, for all his attempts to claw himself naked of them. Most people, when they thought about the issue at all, thought Io would be a fool if she didn't take Charles; and most of the observers who had watched the rivalry, in its comedy setting, most closely, gave it as their opinion that in the end that was what she would do. They claimed to see the signs of preference already; but the only person who really saw them, with cruel clearness, was Chad himself. He saw them all the time, whether they existed or not. And to tell the truth, his temper was not improved by the fact that as often as not he was ashamed of his subjection, and knew himself every kind of fool. Diagnosis, however, is not cure, and a fool he continued, kicking himself for it all the way.

2

An hour before closing time, on this particular evening toward the end of the August holidays, they were arguing about the Blunden appeal, which hung in suspense somewhere in the legal wilds, as yet unheard. It had come up because the sunshine miners were making vast, unpleasing harmonies in the bar, and their presence had reminded Charles how the grabs were steadily scooping their way nearer to his boundary fence.

"They say there's nearly two hundred thousand tons of the stuff under the heath and the top pastures," he said gloomily. "As if that's worth tearing the guts out of those fields for! At the price it costs 'em to get it, too!"

"Only about twenty acres of the ground they want from you is pasture," said Chad unpleasantly and promptly, "and you know it, so don't go around pretending they're proposing to take good agricultural land in this case. *I* can't see why you're kicking."

"They very often have taken good agricultural land, and you know that. Years and years to get it back into shape!"

"I've seen that view questioned by better-informed people than you. It doesn't take half so long to put it back in condition as you people make out. Read some of the books about soil, and see if they don't bear me out."

"I'm a farmer myself, and I know—"

"But farmers disagree about it themselves. And in any case, this time it's just twenty acres of not so brilliant high pasture, and no more. The rest's all waste land, being used for precisely nothing, not even building. Fit for nothing! If it was leveled at least it could be built on." He had begun simply by taking the opposite side because he must, but by this time he was serious, dead serious, on one of his queer hobby-horses, almost all of which consisted in finding the good to be said for anything which was being denounced publicly and loudly, and in some cases with suspicious facility, by the majority of other people. He leaned across the table and spread his lean, nervous hand under Charles's eyes. "Look! I know it looks like hell, I know it makes a positive wilderness while it lasts, I know it's the fashion, almost the rule, to damn it out of hand. I know it *does* put land back from its full usefulness for some time—we needn't argue how long, the experts are busy doing that—and I even know some bad mistakes have been made in judging the priorities in some cases, and good land *has* been taken. But for heaven's sake, do consider this particular case on its own merits, and don't just hand me out the arguments that might be justifiable if you were growing wheat on every acre they want to take up."

"Twenty acres is twenty acres," said Charles obstinately. "And they want the whole of the preserve, as well."

"Oh, don't let's pretend that's of any great value! You and your old man like to play with a little shooting there yourselves, but that's all there is to it. The woods there are pretty enough to look at, but it isn't a case of valuable timber or loss of soil. I bet you that land could be pasture at the most three seasons after it was relaid—I could show you land that was bearing a pretty good grass the second year after—and that's what it's never done in my lifetime or yours."

"I very much doubt it. And anyhow, it's an asset as it is—it's woodland."

"Private woodland, about half of it, with your fence round it, and not so hot at that. Come off it, Charles!"

"As much an asset, at any rate, as two hundred thousand tons of rubbish at an uneconomic price."

"But the plant's here, the labor's here, it's a continuation of the very job they're doing, and if you let them carry on you'll be bringing the price down, and handsomely. That's the point!"

"Never within miles of the cost by the old way," said Charles positively and truthfully; for his grandfather had been in the dog-hole colliery business in the later stages of Comerford's shallow-mining past.

"Are you seriously holding up the old way as a present-day possibility? As an alternative to surface mining?" Chad really looked startled, as if his friend had proposed a return to the stage-coach; so much startled that Charles colored a little, his broad, florid face burning brick-red under the dark, pained stare. But he felt the

67

weight of listening opinion in the snug to be on his side, and answered sturdily:

"Why not? It got the coal out, didn't it? Not that we need, in my opinion, to get such poor stuff as this out at all!"

"But it's there, and the odds are it will be wanted out at some time. And it may as well be while the site here is open—clear the whole lot, and let's have the ground back in service—whether in two years or ten, at least once for all. If you win your appeal, and they re-lay this site and go away, sooner or later that shallow coal left under your ground *is* going to be wanted. Supplies aren't so inexhaustible that we can suppose any deposit of two hundred thousand tons can be ignored forever. Then how do you propose to get it out? Shallow shafts?—like last century?"

"Why not?" said Charles defiantly. "It was effective, wasn't it?"

Words failed Chad for a moment to express the deadly effectiveness of uncontrolled shallow mining in Comerford. He leaned back with a gusty sigh, and reached for his beer. Io, watching them from the doorway as she went out with a tray, thought them unusually placid tonight, but did not suspect that for the moment she was forgotten. Her reactions if she had suspected it, however, would have been simple relief, only very faintly tinged with pique.

"Shallow mining," said Chad, carefully quiet as always when he wanted his own prejudices to stop overweighting his case and erecting Charles's defenses against him, "has done more damage to this district than any other kind of exploitation. Just at the back of the Harrow—off your land—there's a perfect example, that little triangular field where all those experimental shafts were sunk when we were kids. You know it. Could you even put sheep on that field?"

"No," admitted Charles, after a moment of grudged but honest consideration. "I suppose you couldn't. Anyhow, *I* wouldn't care to risk it."

"No, and if you did you'd lose half of them. It's pitted all over. They've had to wire off the path and take it round the two hedges instead of straight across, for fear of losing somebody down one of the holes; and even under the hedge the path's cracking and sliding away. Until that ground's finished subsiding it's done being used for anything. And that may be for good, it's certainly several lifetimes. You can't even hurry the process. If you put heavy machinery on that ground to try to iron it out, you'd simply lose your machines. But it could be stripped and opencast, and at least you'd have some sort of usable land again."

"But that's a very extreme case," objected Charles. "It's hardly fair to judge by one small field that's been ruined. The rest of the shafts round the district are fairly scattered."

"Pretty thickly! Do you know there are at least fifty on your own land?"

They were warming again to enmity, perhaps because Io's blue dress filled the corners of their eyes, and Io's small, rounded and pleasing voice was saying something gay and unintelligible to a group of colliers just within earshot.

"Candidly, I don't believe it," said Charles, jutting his square brown jaw belligerently.

"You mean to say you don't know?"

"I'm as likely to know as you, but no, I don't know the exact figure. And neither do you! But I don't believe there are anything like fifty!"

"All right, let's prove it! One way or the other! Come round with me on Saturday afternoon, and I'll show you shafts you didn't know were there."

"It's likely, isn't it?" said Charles, jeering. "I've been going around with my eyes closed all this time, I suppose?"

"I suppose so, too."

"My God, I never saw such infernal assurance!" spluttered Charles.

"Well, come and see! What have you got to lose?"

"Damn it, man, it's *my land*!"

"All right, then, *you* take *me* all round it, and show me how little damage your precious shallow mining did to it."

They would go, too, wrangling all the way in precisely the same manner, with the same more peaceful intervals, in which they would discuss the problem earnestly and even amicably, but disagreeing still. They were temperamentally incapable of agreeing upon any subject, and the more serious they were, and the less obsessed by their differences, the more sharply defined did those differences become. The inhabitants of the snug listened tolerantly and with interest, grinning over their beer; and the vigorous singing of the sunshine miners in the bar subsided gently into the tinkling of the piano, and reluctantly ceased. It was at this moment of calm that the lower pane of the window suddenly exploded inward with a shattering noise, and slivers of glass shot in through the curtains and rang like ice upon the table.

A single voice, indistinguishably venomous and frightened, began bellowing outside in the lane, and there was a sound of heaving and grunting struggle under the window, but no second voice. The snug rose as one man, emptying glasses on the instant of flight, to pour out by the side door into the lane and see who was scragging whom. They were not greatly surprised, for fights, though comparatively few, were potentially many these days; and the usual speculations came out in staccato phrases as they left their seats, answering one another equably.

"That Union Movement chap again with his ruddy literature, maybe—said he was asking for trouble, coming here!"

"D.P.s, I bet!"

"More likely sunshine miners and colliers arguing the toss."

They tumbled out by the side door to see for themselves, all but Chad Wedderburn, who sat regarding his linked hands on the table with a slight frown of distaste and weariness. Even when Charles got up with somewhat strained casualness and said he might as well see the fun, too, Chad did not move. The sounds of battle had no charm for him. Io came in resignedly from the bar, and found him still sitting there, finishing a cigarette. He looked round at her, and even for her did not smile.

"What, one superior being?" said Io, none too kindly. "Are you made of different clay, or something?" She sounded hard-boiled, and a little ill-tempered; but she looked upset, and more than a little scared. It was all very well pretending, but she didn't like it much, either. She went to the window, and began to brush tinkling splinters of glass out of the curtains and down from the sill; but at every louder shout from outside she started just perceptibly. A dozen people were talking at once, now, and the heaving and crashing had almost ceased; there was just a breathless trampling, a babel of argument and expostulation, and then the virtuous youthful tones of Police-Constable Weaver, pitched high, to assert who was master here.

"Now, then, what's going on? What's going on here?"

He was very young, he liked to say the correct thing, and Chad was tempted to suppose he even practiced the tone in which it should be delivered.

"All over!" said Chad, smiling at Io. "The law's arrived. No need to worry about possible bloodshed anymore."

"I wasn't worrying," said Io smartly, kneeling over the dustpan. "I couldn't care less! Men! They're no better than dead-end kids, got to be either hitting someone else, or watching two other men hit each other. Even a football match is no good unless it ends in a free fight!" She marched away furiously by one door as the dispersing spectators came in by the other in a haze of satisfied excitement, with fat voices and shining, pleased eyes, doing their best to justify her strictures, and settled down contentedly to their drinks again with a topic of conversation which would last them all the rest of the evening.

Charles, tweedy and broad-set, the perfect picture of the young yeoman farmer, came back to his chair rather self-consciously, trying to look as if the spectacle of two men trying to take each other apart had really rather bored him. In fact the mind of Charles moved with a methodical probing caution which ruled out boredom. He said with a shrug and a smile:

"Another case for the old man's bench next week! Disturbing the peace, or assault—if they can sort out who hit whom first—or whatever is the correct charge these days." But he couldn't disguise the excitement which flushed his fine, candid face, ruddy and solid and simple with all the graces Chad's black-visaged person lacked. He leaned over the table as if he had a secret, though a dozen full-voiced conversations about him were tossing the same theme. "It could have been a bad business. Didn't you see them? My God, Jim meant making a job of it this time! I knew there'd been some bad blood up there, and I believe they've already been pulled apart a couple of times, but this looked like being the real thing."

"Jim? Jim who?"

"Tugg. Good Lord, didn't you really look? Lord knows it does seem asking for trouble to take in a German laborer on the same farm—"

German?" said Chad, his lean brows
...ng together. "Schauffler?"

Whatever his name is! The fellow they've got
up there. Big, fair-haired chap nearly Tugg's own
size. I heard Hollins had had a bit of trouble with
them already. Seems it's Jim who usually starts
it—"

"Yes," agreed Chad thoughtfully, remembering another, safer, easier Jim who was just out
of hospital and back at the hostel, with only a
long scar on his ribs to show for it, "yes, it would
be."

"Oh, I don't know!" protested Charles, failing
to understand. "He's usually a reasonable
enough chap, I should have said. There must be
something behind it. Tugg doesn't just fly off the
handle. But a German, of course—it was a fool
trick to have him there, if you ask me."

So everyone would be saying, of course, and
so perhaps it was; but where, thought Chad, as
he finished his drink and quietly took his leave,
where *is* the right place for the Helmut
Schaufflers? What's to be done with them? No
keeping Helmut on the Hollins farm after this,
however big a something there is behind it; and
no other farmer will touch him with a barge-pole,
with the certainty of upsetting all his other labor.
And yet we can't get rid of him. If he does something too blatantly his own fault and no one else's,
we can deport him, he's still German; but he
won't ever be left visibly the *only* guilty party in
any clash; it will always be the other fellow who
begins it.

He was depressed. He went out, and began the

green walk home by the field path, up toward the rim of the bowl; and before long, as he walked slowly, someone overtook him, and he found himself walking side by side with Jim Tugg. Jim was quite untouched, that was easily seen in the early dusk; he was neat and light and long in his walking, quiet of face, content but dark, gratified but not satisfied. He greeted Chad from the outer edges only of a great preoccupation, but in a friendly tone, and accepted a cigarette. He didn't have to act as if nothing had happened, because everyone knew by now that it had. No need even to wonder if it had reached this particular person; it had reached everybody.

"That'll mean a summons for assault, I suppose," said Chad.

"Be well worth it," said Jim serenely, narrowing his far-gazing eyes against the blown smoke of the cigarette.

"What did he say to you?"

"Who? Weaver?"

"Helmut. What was it he said, to make you hit him?"

Jim turned his big, gaunt face and looked at him narrowly. "What makes you think he didn't hit me first?"

"The Helmuts don't—not unless you're small, peaceful, and at a disadvantage—and they have no other immediate way of getting at you."

The dark look lingered on him a long minute, and then was withdrawn, and Jim gazed up the rise of the fields again, and walked intact and immured in his own sufficiency.

"Didn't say nothing to me. I got tired of waiting."

"He knows how to angle for sympathy," warned Chad.

"He can have all of that."

"Well, you know your own business best. But you could find yourself in gaol unless you're more forthcoming in court. If you don't put him in the wrong, he'll take jolly good care he doesn't put himself there."

"Thanks for the goodwill, anyhow!" said Jim, and smiled suddenly, and went on up the rising path with a lengthened stride, to disappear in the twilight.

3

The chairman of the magistrates was Selwyn Blunden, the old man himself, Charles's father. He behaved admirably, eliciting, as on the bench he frequently did, some less obvious aspects of what on the face of it was a simple case. As a result of which astute activities, the bench discharged Jim Tugg on payment of costs, and with a warning against taking the law into his own hands. His previous unspotted record of civic usefulness, especially his war reputation, stood firmly by him; his plea of guilty, which spared everybody the trouble of lengthy evidence, did him no harm. Even Helmut's able display of hunted and frustrated good intentions, his portrait of a misunderstood young stranger in a very strange land, did not appear completely to convince Blunden. He delivered a short but pointed lecture on the responsibilities of an ex-P.O.W. to a country which had made repeated efforts to find a niche for him. It had been a generous gesture on the part of Hollins, said the chairman, to take him in after a previous conviction, and it could not be accepted that the failure of the experiment was due only to Tugg; it would appear that something in the nature of a special effort was now required from Helmut himself, if he was to remain *persona grata* in this country.

Afterwards he admitted to George that he had some qualms about Helmut. Maybe the difficulties of his position had not been sufficiently appreciated. Maybe England still owed him one more chance; but how was it to be arranged, in order to protect both parties? People must be a little tired of taking risks on Helmut.

"To tell the truth," said the old man candidly, "I have a horror of doing the young wretch less than justice. Maybe I'm leaning over backwards to avoid it—I don't know—if he were anything but German it would be easier to discount the feeling. But at any rate, I would like to see him have one more shot before we decide he's quite irreconcilable."

"The difficulty," said George, "is what to do with him. He might have ideas himself, but I very much doubt it. I think he intends to be carried. He'll work—oh, yes, everyone admits that!—but he won't take one crumb of responsibility for himself if he can leave the load on us."

Selwyn Blunden pondered, and stroked his

broad brick-red forehead, from which the crisp gray hair had receded into a thick, ebbing wave. He was very like his son Charles; the authentic yeoman flavor, indefinably not quite county, glossed him over healthily and brightly, like a coat of tan. He was between sixty-five and seventy, but he still looked somewhere in the fifties, walking as straight as his son, carrying himself, thought George, rather like a retired general, if generals ever retired in such good condition. He had a beautiful big white moustache, behind which he was accustomed to retire when deep in thought, caressing it meanwhile with a large and well-shaped hand to enlarge the screened area.

"I could say a few words for him in quite a few directions," he said thoughtfully, uttering no more than the truth, since he probably carried more influence than any other man in the district, "but I want to see him somewhere where he can't do any more mischief—and not on false pretenses, either—must let 'em know what they're biting off, whoever's bold enough to take him on. Wouldn't bother about him, as a matter of fact, only the fellow's so young, after all." He fingered the moustache's gleaming curves, emerging from its shelter reluctantly. "Tell you what, I think the best bet might be the opencast contractors. Tough company there, all right, tough enough to hold him down, I should think. They're still taking on men when they can get 'em, I'm told, and everybody admits the boy does at least work."

"Seems to be his one virtue," said George.

"Well, no harm in trying, at least. I'll have a

word with the contractor's man, give him the facts straight, and we'll see how he feels about it." He frowned for a moment, and George guessed that he was thinking about the delicate matter of the appeal, still pending, still threatening the effectiveness of the unit's operations in Comerford. "Hm! Equivocal position, very!" he said cryptically, but shook the embarrassment away from him with a twitch of his big shoulders and a flash of his old, bold blue eyes. Better-looking than Charles, on the whole; sharper-boned, more acid in him. "I'll have a word with the young fellow, too," he decided. "Might do more good in private. I don't know—never been a P.O.W. myself—I dare say it does seem as if we're all incurably against him." He shook his head doubtfully, sadly but firmly, and marched away. It was curious that the back view of him undid some of the effect of talking to him face to face. His gait, after all, wasn't so young; he bowed his shoulders a little, he leaned forward heavily. One was reminded that he was getting old, that he had had his reverses in his time. From behind it was possible to be sorry for the old man; from in front one wouldn't dare.

When Bunty heard the story, her eyes opened wide, and she laughed, and said: "The cunning old devil!" almost in her son's tone. "What effrontery!" she said, but with admiration rather than indignation. "He pretends it's an embarrassing position for him, to have to approach those people when he's doing his best to keep them off his own ground; but he knows jolly well they'll jump to do as he asks them all the more eagerly, because they'll think, if we oblige the old boy over this he can't very well go on being awkward about the appeal. Maybe that would be their reaction, but it won't be his. No amount of favors done for him could restrain him from being awkward where his own privilege is concerned, and they ought to have sense enough to know it by now. They'll find out later!"

"He says he's abiding by the result, bad or good," said George, "and I believe he means it. The old chap's getting a streak of fatalism in his latter years, and honestly, I don't think he minds as much as he would have done ten years ago. The world's changing, as he's never tired of reminding us."

"He's fondest of reminding other people of that, though," said Bunty, grinning. "He might not be so keen on having it pointed out to him." She added, thoughtfully tossing the probabilities in her mind: "Bet you five bob, evens, Helmut gets taken on!"

George looked scandalized, pulled her hair, and told her she would get him into trouble yet. The truth was, as Bunty maintained, that he was afraid of losing his money. By and large, Blunden was the next thing to God around here.

However, he was absolutely frank with the agent in the little concrete hut office above the gouged-out valleys of the coal-site. The name of Gerd Hollins had not even been mentioned in court, but for all that, the old man had not missed her significance; and the story he told was the full story.

"I'm no racialist myself, thank God! But that

boy's had the principles drummed into him ever since he began school, I suppose, and we can hardly be surprised if he retains 'em still. Telling's not much use to that kind of fellow. Now if you could surround him with Jews doing the same work, doing it better than he does, and well able to knock him down if he reverts to type—well, to my way of thinking it might be more effective. But that poor, well-meaning lady at the farm has had more trouble, I fancy, than she's let anyone else know. Tugg has eyes, and a brain. I may be wrong! I may be quite wrong! But I fancy that's very much what happened. A Jewess is still a Jewess to Helmut, and a Jewess going out of her way to be kind to him was asking to be trampled on."

"That at least couldn't happen here," agreed the agent, watching him respectfully. He was a young, hard, experienced man, but he was not past being flattered; and besides, if the old boy could bring himself to ask favors, even in this fashion, he could be handled, he could be sweetened. Up to this they had had no direct contact, and men can keep up an enmity on paper which won't survive the personal touch. "If he steps out of line here he's liable to get hurt; and being that kind of chap, he'll have gumption enough to size up the odds, and stay in line."

"I can't guarantee it, but I think he will. And the one good thing about him, as everyone agrees, is that he will work. Strong as a horse, willing, handy, even, in that way, entirely trustworthy. It's an odd thing, that, but at any rate it gives one some hope of him. I tell you frankly, he'll need keeping in his place; but duly kept there, he could be a useful man."

He could, if he only managed to place the old fellow under a very small, but strongly binding, obligation. Costs on this site had been, to tell the truth, alarmingly high, and though the extended range was a desirable way of bringing them down, if Blundens were going to put all their weight into the appeal and fight every inch of the way, frankly it wasn't going to be worthwhile pushing the matter. But if this tiny seed of love was going to stay the defending hand, ever so lightly, and let the thing go through in comparative peace, then it was going to be very well worth it. One hypothetically troublesome hand, thought the agent contentedly, was a very small price to pay for that consummation.

"All right!" he said, making his decision. "He can start, if the employment people O.K. it. We'll make the experiment, at any rate. I take it he'll want help with getting somewhere to lodge? There might be a vacancy where some of the men are staying. Anyhow, we can see to all that for him."

He thought: This really ought to be worth a little goodwill. Hope the old boy appreciates it! And it appeared to him by small but gratifying signs—for of course one must not expect too much too soon—that the old boy did.

Helmut came, and it appeared that he did too, for a more anxiously accommodating, earnest, subdued young man had never been seen on the site. He had shrunk a little from his full size again, his face was tight shut and gray with reserve, he applied himself grimly to the safe outlet of work, picked up things very quickly, and heaved his weight into the job as if his life depended on it. Perhaps the old man, briefing him for this third onslaught on reconciliation, had succeeded in impressing on him the fact that, indeed, his life did depend on it.

4

Charles and Chad came down through the silvery woods, between the quivering birches, the intervals of naked whitish clay crunching and powdering softly under their feet after the hot, dry summer. They were still arguing, in much the same terms as they had argued three weeks ago, when this expedition had first been suggested.

"I still don't see that such poor-quality coal is worth getting at all, at a time when there's no shortage of deep-mined stuff. The question of *how* to get it ought not to arise."

"But it would arise some time—or there's a long chance it would."

"Not in my time, or yours," scoffed Charles, as if that clinched it.

"And that's all you damn well think about! My God, you sound like something from the nineteenth century! 'It'll last our time!' Is that all that matters?"

The suggestion that anything else ought to matter certainly jolted Charles, but some sensitivity in him recognized at once, against the whole armory of his training, that he ought to resent the implication of his short-sightedness.

"I dare say I do as much thinking a generation ahead as you do, for that matter—"

"So you never put a plough into the ground, or plant a tree, until you've calculated whether it's going to be you or your grandchildren who's going to get the benefit of it! Leaving clean out of the question anybody else's grandchildren!"

"You're a damned sanctimonious prig!" said Charles, and unexpectedly scored a hit. Chad was sometimes horribly afraid that he was. His dark cheeks flushed. But even if it was true, it couldn't be helped; and what he had said of Charles was certainly no less true.

"Sorry! It's something you've got to decide yourself, I suppose. Do it how you like!" He kicked at the thick blond tussocks of grass, and the trailers of bramble in his path, and moved a little aside from Charles to skirt a place where the rains of many years had made a deep channel, too permanent for even this dry season to obliterate. Aside among the scattered trees and clearings of new saplings, funnel-shaped pits, a dozen yards across and often as deep, punctured the level crest of the mounds. These were so frequent, and so taken for granted, that the infants of Comerford, though reared only a mile from genuine and normal hills, thought it more fitting to have them of waste clay, and pitted with holes.

Charles, strolling moodily with his hands in his pockets, thought: I suppose we do rather tend to talk about uneconomic propositions where we can't look forward to covering costs inside a very few years. Maybe it is a mistake, at that! Only it seems crazy to have to look thirty years ahead for a thing to pay for itself—even if it saves no end from then on. And even the entertainment of the doubt was new to him, and made him feel like looking guiltily over his shoulder.

"Anyhow," he said generously, "you were right about the numbers. I didn't think there were so many shafts—never bothered actually to count 'em."

"And about the mess they made?" asked Chad, with a fleeting grin.

"Oh, well, I knew they didn't exactly improve the place. Being brought up in the middle of it, one forgets about it, rather, but the facts were always there to be seen. It didn't need you to point 'em out."

"Some of the ground could be put back into use, I'm sure of it. Oh, I know it sounds odd to be recommending surface mining as a method of reclaiming land, but it does happen. There was a piece of the old canal-bed running round one side of a field at Harsham, and they had it all up, and put it back level. Farmer's got a field double the size now. If it does nothing else, it certainly can iron out the creases, and you must admit you've got more than your share of the creases up here."

"Oh, in that way there isn't all that much to lose, I suppose. Except that even a rather seedy wood with some sort of growth on it is better than a bare patch. After all, hasn't this generation got its rights, too, as well as the next? They've had their fair share of ugliness, I should have said. Is it so selfish to leave a bit for the future?''

Chad said nothing. They came to the hedge, and the gate in it, and leaned looking down on the undulating slope, and over into the crater where the scored underworld of red-and-yellow machines lay, with its knife-edged deep where the water drained down into a dwindling mud-circled pool. Deep as a quarry in places, with lorry tracks running up the beaten clay mountains, and the larger, crueler marks of tractors patterning the whole surface. A growth of huts lay on the distant rim from them, with the canyon in between made deeper by the blue evening shadows.

"I'm not really so sure," said Charles, gazing into the depths, "that they're as keen on going here as they were. They haven't had much luck lately, and they say the cost per ton is getting rather alarming—I mean alarming even to the people who believe in the method. Naturally the contractor isn't going to carry the can back if he can help it. Did you know they lost a digger over the edge there the other day? Lord knows how! Sort of accident you get sometimes in stone quarries—probably the driver's miscalculation, but there's no knowing. The kid driving was pretty lucky to come out of it alive, but the digger's a dead loss. Crazy expensive business! The boy's in hospital, but they say he'll be all right."

"I heard about it," said Chad. "They've had quite a run of accidents lately. Must have some pretty deadly mechanics, to judge by the number of tractors they've had to send away for major repairs."

"You hear all about 'em, evidently," said Charles.

"What my boys don't know about every piece of machinery down there isn't worth knowing. We have no train-spotters any more, only tractor-spotters. On the whole I think it's a safer amusement."

They moved on, detaching themselves with a countryman's reluctance from the top bar of the gate. The undulating ground, dryly prolific with brambles and bilberry wires, descended with them on its many and complicated levels, here and there cracking and falling away into new funnels about the bricked-over shafts, more often falling clear into holes, only half-boarded up, and already rotting away within.

"The old man had a lot of these filled," said Charles, "in 1941, after he lost a calf down one of 'em at the back of the long field. It wasn't a very good job, because labor was busy on other things, and all they could find time to do was rush round about twice with a tractor, and shove as much clay and stuff down 'em as the machines could move. But they didn't do the lot, and even those they did do are falling in again. Some of 'em have sagged yards in these few years, and I wouldn't care to trust any stock around them now. I hand you that much, if it's any use to you."

"You don't need me," said Chad, surveying the wreckage of land still beautiful. "It speaks for itself. What made your old man suddenly decide to fill the things, just when labor and machinery were nonexistent? Not," he added frankly, "that that isn't typical!"

"Oh, I suppose the calf touched it off, turned it into that particular channel; but the fact is he was trying to work himself to death at that time, any way that offered, to take his mind off his troubles. Don't you remember the business about my stepmother? But I suppose you were walled up somewhere in Europe at the time, it wouldn't reach as far as that—not even my dad's troubles carried that far in 1940. She left him, you know—went off with some fellow he didn't even know existed, and left him a characteristic note saying it had all been a failure and a mistake, and he wasn't to try and find her, because she could never be happy with him. I dare say you heard bits of it afterwards. They still talk about it round the village, when there's no more recent stink to fill their nostrils."

"Oh, yes, I did hear something about it, of course. Not very much. But I remember seeing her around, just prewar—she was rather pretty, wasn't she, and quite young?"

"Not so frightfully, but too young for him. Old man's folly, and all that. *I* wasn't surprised," said Charles, "when it went smash. Tell you the truth, I never could stand her myself. Stupid, fluffy-brained, self-centered woman—I never could see why it cut him up so. But you know, it wasn't so much being deserted, it was the way she did it. It was 1940, and the scare was on, and lots of people, especially comfortably-off old-style lads like my father, were talking about getting the women and children out of the country and clearing the decks for action—expecting invasion any minute, and all that. She had quite a lot of property in jewels, and securities and so on—not terribly rich, but it was a good little nest-egg, all told. She went about quietly realizing the lot, turned everything into cash, explaining in confidence to every dealer that the old boy was sending her to the U.S.A. to be safe and off his mind. Her nerves! She was one of those women who have nerves! Well, you can see it made sense, he was just the chap who might do exactly that. Then she disappeared. Just left him this note, saying she was off with her lover— Well, he's a stiff-necked old devil, and he didn't try to find her, he let her go, since that was what she wanted. But it knocked him, all the same, especially as the rotten story leaked out gradually, as they always do. That was the first he'd heard of this tale she'd put up. Poor, silly old devil, he was the only one who knew nothing whatever about it! People didn't talk about it in front of him once they had the rights of it—but how would you feel, having been made to look that kind of a doting fool?"

"Not so good," admitted Chad. "So he went about working off his losses any way he could! Ramming up these holes in the ground for one thing—well, he might have done worse!"

"Oh, it's an ill wind! And mind you, I believe he does realize by now that she was no great loss, but I'm dead sure he'd never admit it. Funny thing!" said Charles pensively, "everything he touched after that seemed to turn up trumps. He prospered every way except the way he wanted. That's the way things often work out in this world."

"Surely your old man never had much to complain about in the quality of his luck," said Chad, with recollections of a childhood in which Selwyn Blunden had loomed large and fixed as any eighteenth-century squire.

"Oh, I don't know! It hasn't been all one way with him. Just before the war he had a bad patch—not that he ever confided in me, I was still looked upon as a bit of a kid. But I knew he'd had a disastrous spell of trying to run a racing stable. It wasn't his line of country, and he should have had sense enough to leave it alone. He did, luckily, have sense enough to get out of it in time." Charles laughed, but affectionately. "A great responsibility, parents! It was after that woman left him, though, that he first began to seem almost old. When I came home he was glad to turn over the farm to me, I think, and sit back and feel tired."

"Not too tired to continue calling the tune," said Chad provocatively.

"It would be diplomatic to let him think he called it, in any case. Besides, his tune usually suits me very well."

"This appeal, for instance?"

"This appeal, for instance! You haven't made me change my mind, don't think it."

They went on amicably enough down the rutted track through the blond grass, toward the spinney gate and the dust-white ribbon of the lane.

"If you did change your mind," said Chad to himself, "I wonder, I really wonder, which way the tune would be whistled then?"

III

—And the Loved One

1

Gerd Hollins went down to the end of the garden in the late September evening, past the small green door in the high wall, which Jim Tugg had painted afresh that afternoon. The screen of the orchard trees separated her from the house and from her husband's uneasy, questioning eyes, and now there was no living creature within sight or sound of her but the silly, self-important hens, scratching and pecking desultorily in their long runs. They came screeching to meet her when she went in and filled their troughs. She filled her basket with eggs, going from shed to shed, stooping her head under every lintel with the same patient, humble movement, rearing it again as she emerged with the same self-contained and self-dependent pride. But as she was dropping the peg into the last latch, her back turned to the narrow path by which she had come, she stiffened and stood quite still, her fingers frozen in the act, her breath halting for a moment. She heard and knew the step, though he walked on the grass verge to soften it. She had asked Jim to lock the door in the wall when he finished the job, but he must have forgotten. She could scarcely blame him, when the door had never been locked before in his experience.

"You didn't expect me?" said Helmut, in the soft, pleased voice every inflection of which she knew and hated. "You are not glad to see me? It is ungrateful, when I go to so much trouble to pay you these visits. How would you remember your own language, if it were not for me?"

Gerd let the peg fall into place, and picked up the basket. When she turned to face him, she saw him astride the path, where it closed in hedge to hedge, so that she could not pass him unless he chose to let her. Everything about him was now hideously familiar to her: the heavy spread of his shoulders, the forward jut of his head upon the thick young neck, the blond, waving hair, and the coarser, duller fairness of the face, now fallen a little slack with enjoyment. He had scarcely to speak at all, only to appear, and drink and eat the quiet despair and loathing of her looks; he did not need to have any power to touch or harm her, because he was a reminder of all the harm she had already suffered, all the rough hands which had ever been laid on her.

"I like to spend a few minutes with you," he said softly. "It is like home again for you, isn't it? Like home, to see someone look at you again not like these stupid sentimental people— someone who doesn't weep silly tears over you as a refugee, but sees only a greasy, fat, aging Jewess, a creature to spit on—" He spat at her feet, leisurely, and smiled at her with his blue, pleased eyes. "You Jews, you like to have a grievance, it is bad for you when you cannot whine how you are persecuted. I am something you need—why are you not grateful to me?"

"Why do you come here?" she said, in a very calm and level and unreal voice. "You have been beaten already, more than once. Do you want to be killed for this amusement? Is it worth that much?"

She had never spoken to him like that before; in the whole incredible relationship she had spoken as little as she could, in his enforced presence remaining still and withdrawn, shutting him out from her spirit as well as she might. Now she came suddenly out of her closed space to meet him, and he was stimulated by the new note in her voice, and came closer to her, giggling softly to himself with pleasure. He put out his big right hand, and felt at her arm, digging his fingers into it curiously, probingly, as into a beast.

"You Jews, you think to grow soft and fat on this country now as you did on us. You are like slugs, without bones. You will not take much crushing, when the English learn sense."

"You had better go," she said, "if you wish to be safe. You've had your fun; be warned, it can't last forever."

"Safe? Oh, I know already where your men are, both of them. I am quite safe. Presently I will go—when it pleases me—when the smell of Jew is too strong for me."

"Why do you come here?" she said. "What do you hope to gain? You can't harm me. We are in England now, not Germany. I am protected from you here."

"You are not protected," he said triumphantly, "because you will not claim protection. Why don't you tell your fool of a husband how I come to torment you? Because you want a quiet life, and still you hope to find one. You don't want to tell him, or the other one, either, because they will want to kill me if they know, and it will be nothing but trouble for you all, whether they succeed to kill me or fail, only trouble. And then to help them you would have to stand up in court and tell all this for the papers to take down, and they would make a good story with all your sad past in Germany, for people to buy for a penny and read, people who don't know you, don't care more for you than I do. You will die before you do that—you have only one kind of courage. So you hope if you keep very quiet and pretend not to hear, not to see me, this bad time will pass, and no trouble for these men of yours, and even for you only a short trouble. No, you don't go to the law! Not to the law, nor to your husband! It is just a nice secret between you and me, this meeting. I am quite safe from everyone but you. And you are too soft to do anything—too soft even to be angry."

She looked at him without any expression, and said in the same level tone: "It might be a mistake to rely too much on that."

Helmut laughed, but looked over his shoulder all the same, and took his hand from her arm, which had all this time refrained from noticing his touch sufficiently to wish to shake it off. He was, for him, very careful now; he appeared only when he was sure of finding her alone. There was no hurry; if he went softly he had a whole lifetime in which to drive her mad.

"Bah, you would even lie to him, to keep him from knowing. I have the best ally in you. But it is an offensive smell, the smell of Jew, and even for the fun of seeing you hate me I cannot bear it long. So I am going, don't be afraid. It isn't time for you to be afraid yet—not quite time. You have not to go back to the ghetto and the camp—yet!" He laughed again, and touched her cheek with his hard fingertips, and shook and wiped them as if her pale, chill flesh had soiled them. Then he turned carelessly on his heel, and went away from her in a quick, light walk, and slid through the green door in the wall, closing it gently after him.

Gerd stood for a long time staring about her, while the empty twilight deepened perceptibly about her and grew green with the green of the trees. She ought to have become used to it by now, and yet the shock never grew less, was always like the opening of a black pit under her feet. She had almost forgotten, until he came, that it was possible to hate anyone like that. He was all the shadowy horror of her life rolled into one person, and he came and went protected and secure and insolent about her, reminding her softly that he had been the means of destroying her family, and would yet be the means of destroying her; for in spite of the war and the peace and all the good resolutions, it appeared that governments were still on his side, not on hers.

She went on into the house, bracing herself to meet her husband's eyes and tell him nothing. She had brought him sorrow and trouble enough. But Hollins was not in the house. She supposed that he had merely gone out into the yard upon some late job or other, or up the fields on his usual evening round; but she sat with her sewing for a long time, and he did not come in.

She sat and thought of Helmut. And continually out of nowhere the thought of Christopher's old service revolver came to her mind. She looked at it calmly, and did not either embrace or put away the suggestion, but only let it lie there in her mind, like a seed patiently waiting to grow.

Helmut went up through the woods toward the rim of the bowl, his hands deep in his pockets, his feet muttering in the scuffle of pine needles and drifted twigs under the trees, and silent in the deep grass of the open places. He whistled as he went, for he was very pleased with events. He liked his job, he liked being in a private lodging, he liked the money he jingled in his fingers as he walked, he liked the evening, and his errand, and the feeling of well-being which his methodical visits to Gerd gave him. He liked his own cleverness and everyone else's stupidity, which fed it without effort on his part. He liked the large black eyes of the Jewish woman, defying him but believing him when he told her that he was only the vanguard, that racial hate was not far from her heels, even here, and would bring her down at last.

Behind him in the shadow of the trees, out of hearing and screened from sight, someone walked with him, step for step.

2

Pussy and Dominic came down the wilderness of hills on an evening in the second week of the autumn term, crossed a discouraged little field full of nibbling sheep-tracks now thick with white dust, and came to the squat brick hut of Webster's well. It lay in an arm of hedge at the rim of the next woodland, the ground falling away behind it in a staircase of sheep-paths, with only fringes of tired grass between them, to the channel of the brook and the shadows of the trees which overhung it; while on the other side, the homing side, the path wound uphill among clumps of silver birch saplings for a time, and then descended along the rim of the Harrow preserves until it reached the lane, and the road into the village.

The brook passed along the side of the field, gathered in the powerful overflow from the pipe in the back of the well and spread itself wallowing over the whole basin of low ground behind the brick hut, carrying so strong a flow of water that in winter it was a small lake lying there, and even now after the dry summer there were two or three considerable channels threading the churned-up bowl of clay mud, trodden into great, white, deep holes by the drinking cattle. Only the supply of water in the well never seemed to decline, for it enclosed two vigorous springs, and the overflow sprang out from its pipe with force enough to strike your hand away if you held it against it. Dominic and Pussy knew all the interesting things which can be done with a strong jet of water, provided you do not mind getting a little draggled in the process. They had outgrown most of them, but tonight they had lingered longer than usual in the Comer pool, and emerged already far too late to get back to Comerford in time for the Road Safety Committee's lectures to senior school-children, to which an hour and a half of their evening should have been dedicated; they felt, accordingly, guilty and abandoned enough to enjoy playing babyish games with water for a further twenty minutes or so, while the sun went down.

"They'll be halfway through by now," said Pussy cheerfully, wringing out water from the ends of her pigtails, when they were tired of making fountains.

"Not worrying about it, are you? It was an honest mistake, anyhow. I really didn't notice the time."

"You're the one who has to worry," said Pussy heartlessly. "Io might nag a little, but Dad hardly dare pretend to be concerned about road safety, I should think—not until his own driving improves a bit. You're the one who's going to catch it! Penalty of being the police-sergeant's son!"

"Most of the time," said Dominic peacefully, "I can manage him pretty well. But he does get parentish sometimes—I guess he has to, really, in his position. And I suppose it was rather letting him down, to stay away when he's got to give the lecture. But I didn't do it purposely." This fact alone was enough to make him feel as virtuous as if he had not done it at all. He sat teasing burrs out of his wet hair with his fingers, and making faces over the snarls he found in it. "Got a comb, Puss? I seem to have been rolling in a patch of burdocks."

Pussy had reached the stage of carrying a comb constantly upon her person. She fished it out of the top of her stocking, since the pocket of her skirt had somehow contrived to slit itself wide open in a thorn-bush on the way up the slope from the river; and having detached it from the folds of her handkerchief, she flicked it across to him, and went on wringing drops from the ends of her hair.

"What time is it?" asked Pussy then, flinging the plaits over her shoulders as a mettlesome horse tosses its mane and starts at the touch of it. She scrambled up from the grass and went to the well, to cup her hands in it and drink the icy water.

"Nearly half-past eight. They'll be at it for another half-hour yet. Bit of a nerve, when you come to think of it," said Dominic, stiffening into belated indignation as he squinted out from behind his tangled chestnut forelock with horrible grimaces, "to expect us to go to a lecture, *and* do our homework, and then go straight to bed, I suppose, without any fun at all. I didn't forget the time on purpose, but I'm rather glad, all the same. And I don't care if they do check up on us, either, it was worth it."

The inconsiderate female administered

comfort as cold as the water she was drinking: "Your father would be sure to look for you, anyhow. Almost anybody else could be missing without being noticed, but *you* can't expect to." She added, as a casual blow over the heart: "*Our* homework was excused!"

Dominic emerged to gape at her in incredulous envy. "Ours wasn't! And I've only done part of it yet, too. My goodness, you girls get away with everything." He thrust the dark red mass of his hair back from his forehead, gave it a last smooth with his hand, and waved the comb at her disgustedly. "Here, catch!"

The throw was strong and astray, perhaps with the injured weight of his unfinished homework behind it, and Pussy's hands were wet. It sailed through her grabbing fingers, and flew over the top of the well, to vanish soundlessly down the dimpled slope below.

"In the brook, probably," she said, giving him a hard, considering look. "Now you can jolly well go and find it—or buy me another, which you like."

"If you weren't such a muff—" he grumbled, nevertheless climbing docilely to his feet.

"If you could throw straight, you mean!"

Dominic went over the crest, and began to trot down the slope from path to path toward the watery hollow, looking about him on the ground. When Pussy looked over the roof of the well again he was down among the tree shadows, looking before him into the water, and paying no attention to her. She called impatiently: "It can't have gone as far as that!"

Dominic turned his head and looked back with a start. His eyes seemed very big in the shadows, his face suddenly and rather unwillingly serious. "No, it's all right, I've got it. It's only—wait a minute!"

He went nearer to the stormy clay sea, with the two or three murmuring tides still flowing through it in deep channels, green with the reflected green of the overhanging trees. She saw him leaning forward, peering; then, as she began to follow him down the slope, he turned and came back at a stumbling run to meet her, crying as he came, in a peremptory tone which made her hackles rise at once: "Don't come! I'm coming now! I've got it!" As if she cared about the comb, when her thumbs had pricked at the wide light gleam of his eyes, and his face so white that the freckles looked almost vermilion by contrast. But when he reached her he caught her by the wrist, and turned her about quite roughly, and hustled her back up the slope with him, tugging and furious.

"What is it? What on earth do you think you're doing, Dom Felse? Let me go! Do you want a clip in the ear?"

But she was only angry as he was masterful, by reversion from some other emotion not at all understood. She wrenched at her wrist, and at his fingers which held it, and panted: "What did you see down there? Loose my arm! I'm going to look what it was."

"No!" said Dominic, with quite unexpected violence. "You're not to! I'll hit you if you try it!" But before he had dragged her a dozen yards past the well on the homeward path his pallor became suddenly green, his knees quaked, and he leaned helplessly into the long grass and lost all interest in Pussy. She did not wait to hold his forehead, but with a ruthless singleness of mind flew back to bound down the hill like a chamois, and probe the depths where he had seen whatever it was he had seen. Between sympathy and curiosity Pussy plumped for curiosity, though she would not be the first cat it had killed. Dominic, for the moment, was too busy being sick to observe that she had deserted and disobeyed him, and in the circumstances he would not, in any event, have expected anything else. Only in extremity would he have thought of giving orders to Pussy.

By the time he had recovered sufficiently to see and hear again, she was just coming back, at a rather automatic walk, and half her face was a green, scared shining of eyes.

"You would go!" said Dominic with pallid satisfaction.

"Anyhow," said Pussy, equally malevolent and equally shaken, "I wasn't sick!"

"I'm sick easily. It's a ph–physical reaction."

Pussy sat down in the grass beside him, because her own knees were none too steady. She sat hugging her hands together in her lap, while they looked at each other forlornly, but with the dawning of a steadying excitement deep in their eyes. When you have something to do in an emergency, you are not sick, and you forget to be frightened.

"He's dead, isn't he?" said Pussy.

106

"Yes." Saying it made it at once more normal; after all, it is normal, there are funerals every week in almost every village, and you hear your parents talking about this one and that one who has died. Not always old, either, and not always naturally. And then, books and films have made the thing a commonplace, even if parents do frown upon that kind of film and that kind of novel. It only takes a bit of getting used to when you suddenly fall over the thing itself in a corner of your own home woods. "Did you see who it was?"

She shook her head, ashamed to admit that she had not waited to look closely, but on recognition of a man's body in the nearer channel of the brook had turned and run for her life.

"It's that German fellow—Helmut Schauffler." His voice quavered hollowly upon the words, for giving the body a name somehow brought the issues of life and death right to his own doorstep.

"He must have fallen in," said Pussy strenuously, "or fainted, or something."

"No, he—no, I'm sure he didn't. What would he be doing down there, leaning over the water, if he felt faint? And besides—" But his voice faded quite away before the details could come tumbling out.

"What have we got to do?" asked Pussy, for once glad to lean on him for guidance; and she drew a little nearer in the grass, to feel the warmth of his shoulder near her, in the sudden chill which was not altogether the fruit of the falling evening.

She began to shiver, and to be aware that she was wet and cold.

"We've got to get my father here at once. One of us ought to stay here, I think—I'm almost sure—to make sure nothing's disturbed until he comes."

"But there's no one to disturb anything," protested Pussy, thinking of the long run home alone, or, far worse, the long, chilly wait here in this suddenly unpleasing place.

"No, but there might be before he came. Anyhow, I shall stay here. You go and get Dad— please, Puss, don't argue this time, do go! You can run, it's all downhill, nearly, and you'll get warm if you run. Will you?"

And she did not argue, nor complain, nor tell him frankly that he was no boss of hers, nor do any of the things which might have been expected of her, but with exemplary sweetness suddenly smiled at him, and jumped to her feet.

"He'll still be lecturing, but you'll have to interrupt. He won't care, when he knows why. But don't let anybody shush you and make you wait, promise!"

She could give him that assurance with goodwill; and indeed, the curative effect of having something definite and essential to do in the matter had brought back the color to her cheeks and the flash to her green eyes. Even the prospect of insinuating herself with shocking news into the middle of the Road Safety Committee's lecture began to tickle her resilient fancy with suggestions of enviable notoriety. She actually made a spring upon her way, and then looked back and suddenly peeled off her blazer.

"Here, you have this, if you're staying here in the cold. I shall be warm enough, running. You *would* come out without a coat of any sort, wouldn't you?"

"Well, it was quite warm enough then," said Dominic, startled and recoiling.

"Well, it isn't now. Don't be silly, put it on. You look pretty green still." She thrust it into his arms, and ran, and her white blouse and flying plaits signaled back to him from the rising path until she crossed the crest, and disappeared from view without a glance behind.

Dominic sat where she had left him, hugging the blazer and staring after her. He felt hollow, and queasy and limp, and if he did not actually feel cold, he was nevertheless shivering; and besides, he had given himself inevitably the inactive part which left him nothing to do but think; and thought, at this moment, was no very pleasant employment. He had lived no nearer to this sort of thing than Pussy had, but he knew instinctively rather more of its implications. The first, the worst, shock was that it could happen here; not in someone else's village, in some other county, but here, less than a hundred yards from where he sat huddled in the grass like a rather draggled bird. Once that had been assimilated, the rest was not so bad. And most potent of all, he had his share of curiosity, too, and curiosity can cure as well as kill.

Something else was in his heart, too, something presumptuous, perhaps, but none the less authentic and strong and full of anxiety. Dominic felt himself to be a piece of his father, accidentally present here ahead of the rest. Every crisis is also an opportunity. And he wanted George to do everything surely and perfectly; he was very fond of George, though he had never bothered to be aware of it. That was the chief reason why he pulled himself up out of the crushed grass, and went back to the hollow of clay behind the well, dragging Pussy's blazer about his shoulders as he went. And with every step his brand-new, burning zeal to be helpful flamed up a little higher. He needed its warmth badly to take him down the darkening slope, for he felt very empty within, and the air was growing acidly cold, and the silence and loneliness which he had not noticed before hung rather heavily upon his senses now that he had such quiet and yet such unforgettable company.

The light was failing, but it was still sufficient to show him most of what he had seen before. He stepped down to the trodden edges of the water, where the tufts of long grass were powdered with clinging white dust; and climbing out upon the corrugations which the cows had trampled up to bake in the sun, above the small pits of dark, oily, ocherous water, he looked closely and long at the body of Helmut, face downward, composed and straight under the trembling flow of the water.

Pale things at this hour had a lambent light of their own, and the back of the blond head, breaking the surface with a wave of thick fair hair, was the first alien thing he had seen, and fascinated him still. The face he could not see, but the head was just as unmistakable from the back; and the clothes, too, the old Army tunic faded and stripped of its buttons and tabs, the worn gray cord trousers, the soft woolen scarf round his neck, these were familiar enough to identify him. He lay there half-obscured by the cloudy, ocherous quality of the water, which reddened him all over, all but the patch of fair hair. And to Dominic, staring intently with eyes growing bigger and bigger, it seemed, as it had seemed at first, that the arch of skull under the hair was not quite the right shape.

3

Pussy sneaked into the chapel schoolroom by the side door, and found the room full of people, and all dauntingly attentive to George, who was in full flood, and doing rather well. Interrupting him was not, after all, quite the picnic she had foreseen; the respectful hush of concentration, real or simulated, shut her firmly into the obscure area off-stage for several minutes before she recovered breath and confidence and a due sense of her own importance. The vicar, as chairman, was firmly ensconced between her and her quarry, and hedged about with cardboard models and miniature working traffic lights, George looked as inaccessible as any lighthouseman from the mainland. But he also looked large, decisive and safe, and she wanted this most desirable of reinforcements to reach Dominic with all speed. She edged forward among the cardboard buses, and became for the first time visible to the audience as she plucked the vicar by the sleeve. The audience stirred and buzzed, deflecting its keenest attention with suspicious readiness; the vicar frowned, and leaned down to her to say: "Hush, little girl! You can ask your questions later."

Pussy recoiled into a cold self-confidence which had needed some such spur as that. She said very firmly: "I must speak to Sergeant Felse at once—it's urgent!"

"You can't interrupt now," said the vicar with equal but more indulgent firmness. "Wait ten minutes more, and the sergeant will be closing his little talk."

This conversation was conducted in stage whispers, more disturbing by far than firecrackers; and its quality, but not its import, had reached George's ready ear. He looked round at them, and paused in mid-sentence to ask directly if anything was wrong. The vicar opened his lips to assure him confidently that nothing was, but Pussy craned to show herself beyond his stooping shoulder, and said indignantly: "Yes, Sergeant Felse! Please, you're wanted at once, it's very serious. *Please* come!"

And George came. He handed back the meeting to the vicar with the aplomb and assurance of one presenting him with an extra large Easter offering, slithered between the cardboard showpieces, and in a few minutes was down with Pussy in the wings of the tiny stage, and heading for the quiet outside the door, steering her before him with a hand upon her shoulder until they were out of earshot of the audience.

"Now, then! What's the matter? Where've you left Dom?" For it went without saying that Dom was in the affair somewhere. "He isn't in trouble, is he?" But the excitement he saw in Pussy was not quite of the kind he would have looked for had any accident happened to Dominic.

"No, Dom's all right. At least—he was sick; and I nearly was, too, only don't tell him—and besides, he really looked, and I only half-looked—" She threw off these preliminaries, which were supposed to be perfectly clear to Dominic's father, in one hopping breath, and then took a few seconds to orientate herself among events, and become coherent. "He's at the brook, just behind Webster's well. He said when one found something like that one ought to keep an eye on it until the police came, so he stayed, and I came to get you. We found a man in the water there," she said explicitly at last. "He's dead."

"*What?*" said George, jolted far past the limit of his expectations.

"It's that German who had the fight with Jim Tugg—Helmut something-or-other. But he's quite dead," said Pussy, large-eyed. "He doesn't move at all, and he's right under the water."

"Sure of all that?" demanded George. "Not just something that might be a man who might be that particular man?"

"I didn't look *who* it was, but it was a man, all right. And Dom said it was *him*."

"Did you come straight down? Any idea what

113

time it was? Did you hang around up there—before or after finding him?"

"I came straight down, as soon as—as we thought what we ought to do. Only a few minutes before we saw him I asked Dom the time, and he said nearly half-past eight."

"Good girl! Now listen, Puss, you go home, drink something hot, and talk Io and your father silly with all the details, if you want to—get 'em off your mind. Don't bother about anything else tonight, and I'll see you again tomorrow. Got it?"

"Oh, but I'm coming back with you!" she said, dismayed.

"Oh, no, you're not, you're going straight home. Don't be afraid you're missing anything, Dom will be coming home, too, just as soon as I get to him. I'll see you in the morning. O.K.?"

Pussy was at once displeased and relieved, but he was the boss, and as one accidentally drafted into service she was particularly bound to respect his orders. So she said: "O.K.!" though without any great enthusiasm.

"And go to bed in good time, when you've spun your yarn. No wonder you're shivering, running around without a coat." He turned her toward the Shock of Hay, and set a rapid course for the bright red telephone box nestling in a corner of its garden wall.

"I had a blazer," said Pussy, liking the feel of the official hand upon her shoulder, "but I left it with Dom. He hadn't got a coat at all."

"He wouldn't have! Lucky one of you had some sense. He shall bring it over when he comes home. All right, now you cut off home, and forget it."

She wouldn't, of course, it wasn't to be expected; but she went home like a lamb. He thought Io would get the story in full before another half-hour had passed, but with Pussy one could never be quite sure. Io might not be considered sufficiently adult and tough to be entrusted with such grisly secrets.

George called Bunty, and asked her to send Cooke up to Webster's well after him as soon as he came in, which he was due to do in about a quarter of an hour. Then he called Comerbourne, and passed on the warning to the station sergeant there, so that ambulance, surgeon and photographer could be on tap if required; and these preliminaries arranged, he plucked out his bike from the backyard of the chapel school-room, from which the vicar had not yet released his audience, and rode off madly by the uphill lane out of the village toward the woods.

Dominic was down in the hollow still, prowling up and down the tussocks of grass and ridges of clay carefully with his light weight, as if he might obliterate the prints of tell-tale shoes at every step; though in fact every inch of ground above the water was baked hard as sandstone, and armies could have tramped over it without doing more than flatten the more thin and brittle ridges. He had searched right from the edge of the field to a hundred yards or so downstream from the body, as closely as he could by the fading light, and had found absolutely nothing except adamant clay, rough strong grass insensitive to any but the heaviest tread, and the old stipplings made by cows coming to water; and all these were now frozen fast into position, and had been unchanged for weeks. He didn't know quite what he was seeking, but he did know that it wasn't there to be found, and that was something to have discovered. No one ever picnicked here; there wasn't even a toffee-paper, or a sandwich bag. There was only the man in the water, lying along the stream's channel and almost filling it, so that the water made rather louder ripples round him, and a faster flow downstream from him.

Nobody falls into a stream as neatly as that; it fitted him like his clothes. Nobody deliberately lies in a stream in such a cold-blooded, difficult fashion, no matter how fiercely determined he may be upon suicide. Not with the whole of the Comer just over the heath and down the hill! And nobody climbs painfully across twelve yards of crippling lumpy clay in order to faint in one yard of water, either. So there was only one possibility left.

It seemed to him that George took an unconscionable time to get there, and it grew colder and colder, or at any rate Dominic did, perhaps because of the emptiness within rather than the chill without. When he looked at his watch he was staggered to see how short a time he had really been waiting. He knew he mustn't touch the body, even if he had wanted to; but he went and sat on his heels precariously balanced among the clay ridges, to examine it at least more closely. The light was going, it was no use. And now that he looked up, the light was really going, in dead earnest, and to tell the truth he didn't like the effect very much.

George appeared rather suddenly on the iris-colored skyline by the well, and Dominic started at the sight of him with a first impulse of fright; for after all, it wasn't as if Helmut had died a natural death. But the same instant he knew it was only his father coming loping down toward him, and the leap of gratitude which his heart made to meet him frightened him almost as much as the momentary terror had done, because it betrayed the state of his nerves so plainly.

To George, springing down the slope with a reassuring hail, his son's freckled face looked very small and pinched and pale, even by that considerately blind light. He kept his torch trained on the ground, away from the shivering boy who clearly didn't want to be examined too narrowly just now.

"I thought you were never coming," said Dominic querulously. "Did Pussy tell you everything?"

"Only the fact," said George, and balanced forward to pass the light of the torch slowly and closely along the length of Helmut's body, strangely clothed now in the surface gleam of the water, quivering over him like silver, and stirring the intrusive pallor of his hair like weed in its ripples. "Well, that's Helmut, all right! No doubt about it."

"I thought one of us ought to stay here," said Dominic, at his shoulder as he stooped, and clinging rather close to its comfortable known bulk. "So I told Pussy to come and butt into your

117

meeting, and I've kept an eye on things here. That was right, wasn't it?"

"Absolutely right!" said George, still surveying the busy, untroubled flow of water round the blond, distorted head; but he reached for Dominic with his spare hand, and felt a trembling shoulder relax gratefully under his touch.

"Where is she? Didn't she come back with you?"

"She wanted to come back, but I sent her home to bed. And that's where you're going, my lad, just as soon as you can get there."

"I'm all right," said Dominic, promptly stiffening. "I want to stay and help."

"You can help better by not staying. Comerbourne are hanging around for my next call, and you can go down and tell your mother to ring them. I'll give you a note for her."

"But—"

"No buts!" said George placidly. "You can stay until Cooke comes up, and fill in the time by telling me exactly how you dropped on this affair, and what you've been doing while you waited for me."

Dominic told him, fairly lucidly, even to his own inadequacy. George sat on his heels the while, and passed his fingers thoughtfully through the obtrusive clump of fair hair which now held all the remaining light seemingly gathered into its whiteness. Everything was evening itself out from a chaos into a methodical channel of thought, and the steady flow of probability was certainly carrying both their minds in the same direction.

"He couldn't have fallen in," said Dominic. "If you even tried to fall into the bed of the stream just like that, I don't believe you could do it. And if you did, unless you were stunned you'd get up again. There aren't any stones just there to stun him. And—and he's sort of really wedged into position, isn't he? Like a cork into a bottle!"

George turned his head, and gave him a long, considering and rather anxious look, switching the torch off. "I see you've been doing some thinking while you waited. Well, then, go on with it! Get it off your chest."

"There wasn't much to do except think," said Dominic. "I went right back to the hedge there, and all down the stream to the bend, looking for just any kind of mark there might be; but you wouldn't know there'd been anything here but cows for months. The only bits that could hold tracks now are deep inside these clay holes, where the water's still lying, and they're shut in so hard you couldn't get to them. You might as well look for prints in solid concrete. But the light got so dazzly I couldn't see anymore, so I stopped. Only I didn't find even the least little thing. Maybe— on *him*—you know, there might be something, when you get him out. But even then, that flow of water's been running over him for— Do you think he's been there long?"

"Do you?" asked George, neither encouraging nor discouraging him, only watching him steadily and keeping a reassuring hold of him.

"Well, I think it must have happened last night. I mean, this way isn't used very much, but in the daytime there might always be one or two odd people passing. It was broad daylight still when Pussy and I got here tonight. So I think last night, in the dark—wouldn't you?"

"It might have been more than one evening ago, mightn't it?" said George.

"Yes, I suppose so, only then he might have been found earlier. And—they begin to look—different, don't they?"

The more he talked, and the more staggering things he said, the more evenly the blood flowed back into his pinched, large-eyed face, and the more matter-of-fact and normal became his voice. Thinking about it openly, instead of deep inside his own closed mind, did him good. A rather tired sparkle, even, came back into his eye. Helmut dead became, when discussed, a practical problem, and nothing more; certainly not a tragedy.

"Even if a man wanted to drown himself," said Dominic, knotting his brows painfully, "he wouldn't choose here, would he? And even if he did, and lay down here himself, he wouldn't lie like that—look, with his arms down by his sides— When people lie down on their faces they let themselves down by their arms, and lie with them folded under their chests or their foreheads— don't they? I do, if I sleep on my front."

George said nothing, though the grotesque helplessness of the backward-stretched arms, with hands half-open knotting the little currents of water, had not escaped him. He didn't want to snub Dominic, but he didn't want to egg him on, either. Just let what was in his mind flow headlong out of it, and after a long sleep he would have given up his proprietary rights in the death of Helmut, and turned his energies to something more suitable.

"Besides," said Dominic, in a small but steady voice, "he was hit on the head first, wasn't he? I haven't touched him—and of course you can't really see, and there wouldn't be any blood, after the water had kept flowing over him—but his head doesn't look right. I think somebody bashed his head in, and then put him here in the water, to make sure."

He couldn't tell what George was thinking, and his eyes ached with trying to see clearly in a light meant only for seeing earth and sky, comparative shapes of light and darkness. He gave a shivering little yawn, and George tightened his embracing arm in a rallying shake, and laughed gently, but not because there was anything funny to be found in the situation.

"All right, you've used your wits enough for one night. Time you went home. I can hear Cooke coming down the path, I think. Want him to come back with you?"

"No, honestly, I'm all right, I can go by myself. Does Mummy know why I'm so late? And I didn't finish my homework—do you think they might excuse it this once? It wasn't my fault I went and found a dead body—"

"She knows it's all on the level. And if you like, you can tell her all about it. Forget about the homework, we'll see about that. Just go straight to bed. Here, hold the torch a moment, and I'll give you a note for Bunty." He scribbled rapidly the message which would launch upon him all the paraphernalia of a murder investigation. Why not call the thing by what was, after all, its proper name? Even if it seemed to fit rather badly here! A lamp flashed from the crest of the ridge, and the incurably cheerful voice of Police-Constable Cooke hallooed down the slope. "Hullo, come on down!" cried George, folding his note; and putting it into Dominic's hand, he turned him about, and started him up the slope with a gentle push and a slap behind. "All right, now git! Make haste home, and get something warm inside you. And don't forget to return Pussy's blazer as you go through the village. Sure you don't want company? I wouldn't blame you!"

"No, thanks awfully! I'm O.K.!"

He departed sturdily, swapping greetings with Cooke as they met in the middle of the slope, quite in his everyday manner. George watched him over the brow and out of sight, frowning against the chance which had brought him this particular way on this particular evening. If Comerford had to have a murder case, he would much have preferred that Dominic should be well out of it; but there he was, promptly and firmly in it, with his quick eyes, and his acute wits, and his young human curiosity already deeply engaged; and who was to get him out again, and by what means? George feared it was going to prove a job far beyond his capacity.

Cooke came bounding down the last level to the mud-side, and strode out across the dried flats, to gaze at Helmut Schauffler and whistle long and softly over him. Whereupon he said with no diminution of his customary gaiety: "Well, they say the only good one's a dead one! Looks like we've got one good one, anyhow!" And when he had further examined the motionless figure under its quivering cloudy veil of ocher water: "I wouldn't say the thing had a natural look, would you?"

"I would not," said George heavily.

"And I doubt very much if he was the kind to see himself off—whereas he was precisely the kind to persuade somebody else to do the job for him."

George agreed grimly: "It certainly looks as if Helmut got himself misunderstood once too often."

"Once too often for him. What d'you suppose happened? Coshed, or drowned, or what?"

"Both, but it'll need a post-mortem to find out which really killed him."

"This means the whole works, I suppose!" said Cooke, with a slow, delighted smile. He saw parking offenses and minor accidents and stray dogs suddenly exchanged for a murder case, the first in his experience—for that matter, the first in George's, either—and the prospect did not displease him. "Makes a nice change!" he said brightly. "Sounds the wrong thing to say, but if he had to turn up in a brook, it might as well be ours. Not that I expect anything very sensational, of course! He certainly went around asking for it."

George stood looking moodily at Helmut, a trouble-center dead as alive. He saw what Cooke meant. In the books murders are elaborate affairs carefully planned beforehand, and approached by a prepared path, but in real life they are more often sudden, human, impulsive affairs of a simple squabble and a too hearty blow, or a word too many and a spasm of jealousy to which a knife or a stone lends itself too aptly; tragedies which might never have happened at all if the wind had set even half a point to east or west. And the curious result seemed to be that while they were less expert and less interesting than the fictional crimes, they were also more often successful. Since no path led up to them, there were not likely to be any footprints on it.

Consider, for instance, this present setup. Ground baked clear of any identity, no blood, no weapon, no convenient lines to lead back to whoever had met Helmut, perhaps exchanged words with him, and found him, it might be, no nastier than Fleetwood, and Jim Tugg, and Chad Wedderburn, and a dozen more had found him on previous occasions—only by spite or design hit him rather harder. There, but for the grace of God, went half of Comerford! And short of an actual witness, which was very improbable indeed, George couldn't see why anyone should ever find out who had finished the job.

But unnatural death sets in motion the machine, and it has to run. Even if everyone concerned, except perhaps the dead man, wherever he is, would really rather it refused to start at all.

"I tell you what!" said Cooke. "This is one time when the coroner's jury ought to bring in the Ingoldsby verdict on the nagging wife—remember? 'We find: Sarve 'un right!' But I suppose that would be opening the door to pretty well anything!"

"I suppose so. Among other things, to a final verdict of: Sarve 'un right! on us. Tell me," said George, "half a dozen people who would have been quite pleased to knock Helmut on the head!"

Cooke told him seven, blithely, without pausing for breath.

"And all my six would have been different," sighed George. "Yet, believe me, we're expected to show concern, disapproval, and even some degree of surprise." All the same he knew as soon as he had said it that the concern and disapproval were certainly present in his mind, even if the surprise was not. For murder is not merely an affair of one man killed and one man guilty; it affects the whole community of innocent people, sending shattering currents along the suddenly exposed nerves of a village; and the only cure for this nervous disorder is knowledge. Censure, when you come to think of it, habits in quite another part of the forest.

IV

First Thoughts

1

The word murder once uttered in Comerford, everyone began to look at his neighbor, and to wonder; not with condemnation, not with fear, only with concern and disquiet. For the crack in Helmut's head was also a crack in society, through which impulses from the outer darkness might come crowding in; and of disintegration all human creatures are mortally afraid.

When George saw Helmut in the mortuary for the last time, still and indifferent, stonily unaware of the flood he had loosed, he felt even less sympathy for him than on the occasion of their first meeting. Then at least he had been a young, live creature in whom there might yet be discovered, if one dug long enough and deep enough, some grains of usefulness and decency; now he had not even a potential value, he was past the possibility of change. Nasty, devious and unwholesome, he had run true to type right to the end, and dead as alive had turned in the hands of chance, and put his enemy in the wrong; and in his death, as in his life, George suspected that his enemy had been something at least finer and more honest than the victim.

George, in fact, would have been disposed almost to regret that justice must be done, but for the fact that he had realized to whom justice was due in this case; and it was not out of any zeal for Helmut's cause that he fixed his eyes obstinately on the end and went shouldering toward it by the best ways he could find. It was not even simply because it was his job, though his conscience could have driven him along the same ways with only slightly less impetus. It was the thought of every man turning suddenly to look at his neighbor and wonder; for the sake of everyone who hadn't bashed in Helmut's head, for the sake ultimately even of the one who had, George wanted to travel fast and arrive without mishap.

Others were traveling by the same road, and it was by no means certain that they would always be in step. Inspector Logan, for instance, whom Cooke deplored and Weaver resented, and of whose heavy but occasional presence George was glad. He was a decent old stick in an orthodox sort of way, and capable of giving a subordinate his head and a free run over minor matters, but a murder was something with which he couldn't quite trust even George. And at the other end of the scale of significance there was Dominic. He was very quiet, very quiet indeed, but he was still there, saying nothing, trying to make himself as small as possible, but keeping his eyes and ears wide open. He had been warned, he had been reasoned with, he had been urged to forget about the whole affair and attend to his own business; and when that failed to remove him from the scene of operations, he had been threatened, and even, on one occasion, bundled out of the office by the scruff of the neck, though without any ill-will. The trouble about telling Dominic to get out and stay out was that he couldn't do it even if he wanted to; he was in the affair by accident, but climbing out of a bog was easy by comparison with extracting his tenacious mind from this mud of Helmut's making. And George didn't like it, he didn't like it at all. That was one more reason for making haste.

The evidence of the body was slim enough. The doctors testified that his fractured skull had been caused by three determined blows with some blunt instrument, but probably something thin and heavy, like a reversed walking-stick or the head of a well-weighted crop, or even an iron bar, rather than a stone or a thick club. What mattered more exactly and immediately was that the injuries could not have been self-inflicted, and could scarcely have been incurred by accident. They were precise, neat and of murderous intention; and the coroner's jury had no choice but to bring in a verdict of murder against some person or persons unknown. In a sense Helmut had been twice murdered, for though the doctors expressed certainty that he had died from his head injuries, he had done so only just in time to avoid death from drowning. He had breathed after he was put into the water, for a negligible amount of it was in his lungs. And though everyone agreed that he had asked a dozen times over for all he finally got, there was still something terrifying about the ferocity with which he had been answered.

On Thursday evening the children had found him; according to the doctors, he had died on Wednesday evening, at some time between nine and eleven. As for the exact spot where he had been attacked, no one could even be sure of that; George and the inspector and all of them had been over the ground practically inch by inch, and found nothing. What could be expected, after such a dry season, and on such adamant soil? There was no sign of a struggle, and it seemed probable to George that there had been none. The blows which had smashed Helmut's skull had been delivered from behind, and there had been no great or instant flow of blood, according to the medical evidence. Somebody's clothes, somewhere in Comerford, might bear marks, but probably even those would be slight. And no time had been wasted in carrying or dragging the body at least across the trodden level of clay, and possibly down the slope. By his size and weight, Helmut had not been moved very far to reach the water, and even over a short distance considerable strength must have been needed to carry him. Could one rule out the possibility of a woman? George was very wary of drawing conclusions from insufficient premises. There is very little, when it comes to the point of desperation, that a woman cannot do. A body can be rolled down a steep slope if it cannot be carried. Grass will bend under its passing and return, dust will be disturbed and resettle; and when the body has been in the brook under a strong flow of water for twenty-four hours it will tell you nothing about these things.

So that was all they got out of Helmut or the field or the basin of clay. No weapon, no blood, nothing. His pockets had kept their contents relatively unimpaired, but even these had little to say. His papers, surprisingly well and carefully kept in a leather wallet rubbed dark at the edges with much carrying, but nothing there except the essentials, no letters, no photographs; a disintegrating ten of cigarettes and a paper of matches; a small key, a handkerchief, a fountain pen, the same clasp-knife which had marked Jim Fleetwood; another wallet, with a pulpy mass of notes in it; and a miscellaneous handful of small change. Rather a lot of money for an ex-P.O.W. to be carrying around with him; twelve pound notes, old and dirty notes of widely divided numbers, which pulled apart in rotten folds when separated. And finally, a strong electric torch, heavy enough to drag one coat pocket out of line. There was one more interesting thing; the lining of his tunic on the left side was slit across at the breast, making an extra large pocket within it, but the interior yielded nothing but the usual accumulation of dust, sodden now into mud, and some less usual fluff of feathers, over which the experts made faces because there was not enough of it to be very much use to them.

His lodgings, a single furnished room in the same house with a husky from the coal-site, confirmed the interesting supposition that Helmut's life had been run on a pattern of Prussian neatness. He had not many possessions, but every one of them had a place, and was severely in it. His actions and thoughts appeared to have been the only things absolved from this discipline. Perhaps he had learned it in the Army, perhaps even earlier—in the Hitler Youth, which he had at one time decorated with his presence and enlivened with his enthusiasm, to judge by the few photographs he had left behind in one drawer of his table. The key they had found in his breast pocket opened this particular drawer, and all his more personal papers were in it, including a diary which disappointed by recording only the dispatch and receipt of letters, and an account of such daily trivia as his laundry, his wages and expenditure, reminders of things he must buy, and small jobs of mending he must do. Of what went on inside his head nothing was set down, of his prim housewifely domestic existence no detail was omitted.

The most interesting thing was that in the table drawer they found another bundle of notes, rolled in an elastic band. Counted, these produced no less than thirty-seven pounds, in notes old and much-traveled, a jumble of any old numbers, like those which had been found on his body. The daily record of income and expenditure in the diary made no attempt to account for any such sum; here were only the few pounds he earned weekly, and the slender housekeeping he conducted with them. Nor, to judge by his records, could he possibly have saved up so much gradually from his pay.

"It looks," said George, fingering through the creased green edges of the notes, "as if Helmut had got himself a nice little racket on the side. Ever hear of him in any of the regular lines?"

"No," said Cooke thoughtfully, "but now that I come to think of it, the lads on the site seemed to think he was uncommonly flush with money.

None of 'em had anything much to do with him off the job, except maybe the bloke who lodges here with him, and he professes to know nothing."

"So does the landlady. He was just a fellow who paid for his room, as far as she was concerned." The house was one of a row built on the outskirts of the first colliery district just outside the village, a bit of industrial England suddenly sprawled into the fields; and the landlady lived on her pension and what she could get for her two small, cluttered rooms, which was every reason why she should accept a good payer thankfully, and ask no further questions about him. "She's obviously honest. And besides, he'd been here only just over a month; even if she'd been a busybody she hadn't had time to find out very much about him. And anyhow, how much identity have any of these exiles got? Scarcely anything they have about them goes back to any time before captivity, or any place outside this country. We know no more about them than if they'd fallen from Mars. No more about their origins, their minds—or their deaths, either, as far as I can see yet."

"He had plenty of enemies," said Cooke, summing up with extreme but acute simplicity, "and more money than according to all the known facts he should have had. About some people who get themselves murdered we don't even know as much as that—native English, too."

But this point, from which they started, seemed always to be the same point where they also finished.

All of this came out at the inquest, and after that airing of their very little knowledge the atmosphere was not quite so oppressive; but the intervening days were bad, because everybody had the word murder in his mind, but was studiously keeping it off his tongue until authority had spoken it. It is not, after all, a word to be bandied about lightly. Conversation until then was a matter of eyes saying one thing and lips another. Suspicion seemed the wrong term for that emotion with which they eyed one another; it was rather an insatiable curiosity, sympathy and regret. The state of mind which had led to the act, the states of mind to which the act had led, these were the wrong and terrible things; the act itself was nothing. By whatever agency, however, the crack in the known world was there, was growing, was letting in the slow, patient, feeling fingers of chaos.

Take just one household, involved in only the safest and most candid way. Dominic hovered on the edge of his parents' troubled conferences, all eyes and ears, and inadvertently let slip the extent of his knowledge one evening. Pussy was there, or perhaps he would not have been so anxious to cut a figure, and would have had more sense than to interrupt.

"Dad, do you think he could have been making his extra money on the black market? You know some chickens were missed a few weeks ago at the poultry farm down at Redlands."

"Extra money?" said George, frowning on him abruptly out of the deeps of a preoccupation which had blotted out his existence for the last half-hour. "What do you know about his money?"

"Well, but I heard you say to Mummy that—"

"How many times have I got to tell you to mind your own business? Have you been creeping about the house listening to other people's conversations?" George was tired, and irritated at the reminder of his worst personal anxiety, or he would not have sounded so exasperated.

"I didn't listen!" flared Dominic, for whom the verb in this sense involved hiding behind doors or applying his ear to keyholes. Dominic didn't do these things; he just came quietly in and sat, and said nothing, and missed nothing. "I only heard you say it, I wasn't spying on you."

"Well, once for all, forget about the whole business. Keep your nose out of it, and keep from under my feet. This is absolutely nothing to do with you."

So Dominic cheeked George, and George boxed Dominic's ears, a thing which hadn't happened for over three years now. Dominic wouldn't have minded so much if it had not been done in front of Pussy, but as it had, his feelings were badly hurt, and he sulked all the evening, very pointedly in George's direction, and was sweet and gentle and obedient with Bunty to mark the difference. Pussy, not caring one way or the other about the actual clout, was enchanted to discover that it gave her such an unexpected hold on him, and preened herself in his tantrums, experimentally teasing him back into resentment whenever his naturally resilient heart threatened

137

to bound back into good-humor. By the end of the evening George's hands were itching to repeat the treatment upon Dominic, and Bunty's to duplicate it upon Pussy. It was wonderful what Helmut could do in the way of putting cats among pigeons, even when he was dead.

These stresses seemed slight, and were slight; they seemed to pass, and they did pass; but they also recurred. And what might be the atmosphere up at the Hollinses' farm, for instance, if it was like this even here, in this scarcely affected family?

Bunty did a little scolding and persuading in two directions, and received a double stream of indignant confidences, all of which she kept faithfully, without even wanting to reconcile them. She said what she thought, and listened to what you thought, and that was the beautiful thing about her.

"I only wanted to help him," said Dominic. "You'd have thought I was trying to muck things up for him, instead of that. And I *haven't* listened when I wasn't meant to—if he didn't want me to be here when he was talking about it he could have told me to go right away, couldn't he? He could *see* I was here! I can't *not* hear, can I, when I'm in the same room? And I can't help *thinking* about it. Surely it isn't forbidden to *think*!"

"Now, you understand him a great deal better than that, if you'd be perfectly honest with yourself," said Bunty serenely. "He's worried that you should be spending your time thinking about this particular subject, and whether you like it or not, you know quite well it's on your account he's worrying. He'd be a great deal happier if you didn't have to think about it at all—and frankly, so would I."

"I don't have to," said Dominic. "I want to."

"Why? Is it a nice thing to think about?"

He considered this with some surprise, and admitted: "No, not nice, I suppose. But it's there, and how can you *not* think about it? I suppose it might be rather good not to know anything about it; but it's interesting, all the same. And *how* can you not know anything about a thing, when you've *seen* it?"

"It can't be done," she agreed, smiling.

"Well, but he won't see that. You can see it, why can't he?"

"He can," said Bunty. "He does. That's what worries him. He wouldn't be so unreasonable about it if he wasn't fighting a losing battle."

"Well, if I'm not allowed to talk about it," said Dominic, between a prophecy and a threat, "I shall think about it all the more. And anyhow, he shouldn't have hit me."

"And you shouldn't have given him that final piece of lip. And the one wasn't particularly like your father, and the other wasn't particularly like you—was it?"

Dominic, aware that he was being turned from his course, but unable to detect the exact mechanism by which she steered him, gave her a long, wary look, and suddenly colored a little, and again as suddenly grinned. "Oh, Mummy, you are a devil!"

"And you," said Bunty, relieved, "are a dope."

George wasn't quite so easy, because George was seriously worried. Maybe he would eventually get used to the idea that his son had senses and faculties and wits meant to be exercised, sooner or later, beyond the range of his protective supervision; but at the moment he was still contesting the suggestion that the time for such a development had arrived.

"It's sheer inquisitiveness," he said stubbornly, "and unhealthy inquisitiveness, at that. You don't want him to grow into a morbid Yank-type adolescent, do you?—lapping up sensation like ice cream?"

"Not the least fear of that," said Bunty, with equal firmness. "Dom got pulled into this, whether he liked it or not. Do you think you could just forget about it, if you were in his shoes?"

"Maybe not forget about it, but I could keep my fingers out of it when I was told, and he'd better, or else—"

"I doubt very much if you could have done anything of the kind," said Bunty severely. "The same conscience which makes you try to head him off now would have kept you in it up to the neck then. So for goodness' sake, even if you feel you must slap him down, at least don't misrepresent him."

George, as a matter of fact, and as she very well knew, already regretted his momentary loss of temper; but he had not changed his mind.

2

The local inhabitants were left to George because he knew them every one, and they all knew him. Such a degree of familiarity raises as many new difficulties as it eliminates old ones, but at least both sides know where they stand.

He went up to see Hollins on the day after the inquest. Mrs. Hollins met him in the yard, and brought him into the kitchen and sat down with him there with the simplicity of every day, as if she did not even know that a man she had hated was dead; and yet she had had dealings with the police before, and could certainly recognize the occasion. George began the interview wondering about her calm, and ended understanding it. She had been through such extravagances of persecution, suspicion and compression already that nothing in this line was any longer a novelty to her, and therefore there was nothing to get excited about. It was as simple as that. Her linked hands, rather plump and dark upon the edge of the table, had unusual tensions, but it did not seem to him that they had much to do with his visit; her eyes were certainly wide, luminous and haunted, but he thought by older things than the death of Helmut Schauffler. On the whole it seemed to him that she was not steeling herself up toward a crisis, but relaxing from one.

"You'll want to see Chris, I dare say," she said.

"He'll be in pretty soon now, all being well. Let me make the tea a little early for once. You'd like some, wouldn't you?"

He didn't object. The easier the atmosphere remained, the better pleased he would be; and she had a kind of graciousness which he wished to assist and preserve for her sake and his own, instead of putting clumsy official fingers through it. They sat in the hearth of the big, dark farmhouse kitchen, under the warped black beams stuck with iron hooks; there were seats set into the ingle on either side of the fire, and only the firelight, no daylight, lit their faces here. It was a room looking forward to winter before summer was over the hill; and she was a tired, autumnal woman, content with a retired quietness and a private warmth for the rest of her life. She had seen too much and traveled too far already to have any palate left for wilder pleasures. However, they drank tea together, and blinked at the fire, which she kept rather high for so bright an autumn day.

"I came to ask you about Helmut Schauffler," said George. "Your husband, too, of course."

"But it's a month now since he left us. I'm afraid there's nothing we can tell you about him since then." She looked up and met his eyes without a smile, but tranquilly. "You know already all about that affair. It was an experiment that failed, that's all."

"I wouldn't care to say I know all about it," said George. "I always wondered what made you take him on."

"Considerations which ought to have kept him out, I suppose. It was my suggestion." She gave him a long, clear look, as if she wondered how much she could express and he understand. "I am legally an Englishwoman, perhaps, but I am still German. You can't get rid of your blood. I lived for years by ignoring mine, but you can't even do that forever. I hoped to be able to reconcile myself with my race through just one man who should prove to be—at any rate, not altogether vile. It sounds romantic, but it was in reality very practical. I was asking for very little, you see, even an occasional impulse of decency would have done—even the most grudging effort to live at honest peace with me. It would have been like recovering a whole country."

"But it didn't work out," said George. "I see!"

"He was what he was. He was satisfied with what he was. You must know it as well as I do by this time."

"I doubt if anyone knows it as well as you do," said George, watching her squarely. "Better tell me exactly what did happen to the experiment. It wasn't so simple, for instance, was it, as if you had been merely an Englishwoman who took a similar chance on him?—or even any other German woman!"

"No," said Gerd, after a long minute of silence, during which her eyes seemed to him to grow larger, darker and deeper in her still face. "My case was that of a German Jewess, exactly as it would have been in 1933. I think, Sergeant Felse, you have wasted your war!"

"Tell me!" said George. And she told him; from the humble entry of Helmut to the shock of his first expansion, through dozens of similar

143

moments, nightmare moments when she had been left alone with him only by the normal routine of the day, only for seconds at a time, but long enough to look down the dark shaft of his mind into the abyss out of which she had climbed once at terrible cost. "And you think you have changed something, with your war! You think you have drained that pool! It's only frozen over very thinly. Wait for the first, the very first thaw, and the ice will give like tissue-paper, and you will be swimming for your lives again. And so shall we!" she said, with piercing quietness.

"You didn't tell your husband anything about this persecution. Why not?"

She told him that, too. He believed her. She was accustomed to containing her own troubles rather than make them greater by spreading them further, like ink through blotting paper.

"But Jim Tugg found out? Or at any rate, suspected!"

"I never told him anything, either, but he is better acquainted than my husband with people like that boy. He often pestered me with questions, and I tried to put him off. But yes, he knew. Knew, or guessed. There was some trouble between them once or twice, and Jim began to try to stay in between us. It was—sometimes—successful. Not always!"

"And the night when he attacked Schauffler in the village? He told us as little as possible to account for it, but it was a determined attack, and my impression is that he'd followed him that evening with a very definite purpose. He meant driving him off this farm at least, if not off the face of the earth." George watched her eyes, but they met his gaze emptily, looking through him and beyond, with a daunting, dark patience. "What happened to bring that on? Something even worse than usual?"

"Only the last of many scenes like those I've described already. But I was tired, and Jim came at the wrong moment, and I said more than I meant. It was a weakness and I was sorry for it. But it was too late then. He went away to find him, and there was nothing I could do to stop him."

"Did you want to stop him?" asked George simply.

Her look remained fixed, and a little strained. "I would sometimes have been very glad to see Helmut Schauffler dead. Why not admit it? I had every reason to dislike him. But I have never quite reached the point of wanting someone to kill him. There has been more than enough killing. Yes, I would have stopped Jim if I could. But if you know him you certainly know he is not an easy man to stop."

"And so you got rid of Helmut," said George, "without much cost to Jim, as it turned out. But your husband must have had more than an inkling of what was going on, by then? He could hardly miss it, after that, could he?"

"There was no longer any need to make a secret of it, when the boy was gone. I told Chris all he needed to know—there was no need to dwell upon details. It was over."

"Was it?"

She looked at him with the first disquiet she

145

had shown, and raised her head a little warily. "What do you mean?"

"He was still in the village. Didn't he come near you again? It could happen."

"After Jim had beaten him like that? Helmut was brave only when he *knew* the odds were on his side."

"But very painstaking and persistent in seeking situations where they *were* on his side. Remember," he said, "I've seen him in action before, on a boy who was probably much less capable of dealing with him than you were, but in similar circumstances. I know how patient and devious he could be in pursuit of amusement."

"He didn't trouble me again," she said firmly.

"He never came here—when you were on your own, for instance?"

"No, I had no more trouble."

"Then you can't give me any more information about his movements the day he was killed? He was at work as usual during the day, came back to his lodgings at the usual time, about half-past five. In the evening he went out again, the landlady saw him leave the house about a quarter to seven. A boy tinkering with his motor-bike by the side of the road at Markyeat Cross says he saw him pass soon after seven, and climb the stile into the field. Since then no one seems to have seen him until he turned up the following night in the brook. That field-path leads up this way. I just wondered if he'd been here again."

"I haven't seen him since he was in court," she said.

"And Jim? He hasn't run into him, either?"

"Jim hasn't seen him," she said. "Why should he? Jim knows nothing at all about him since they fought, and you know that part already. That's finished with."

"I hope so," said George equably, and watched her for a moment with curious, placid eyes. "But you never know, do you, what's finished with and what isn't? How well do you remember that evening? Can you tell me what you were doing here while Helmut was coming up the field-path?"

"Wednesday!" she said, recollecting. "Yes—I was ironing most of the evening. I fed the hens, as usual, about eight o'clock, and collected the eggs, and then finished the ironing. And then I went on making a dress, and listened to the wireless. That's all!"

"You didn't go out at all that night?"

She smiled, and said: "No."

"Nor your husband, either?"

"Oh, yes, Chris went out halfway through the evening, to see Mr. Blunden at the Harrow. They were planning to transport some stock together to some show in the south. But he can tell you all about that, better than I can."

"What time did he get back?"

"Oh, I suppose about half-past ten—I can't be sure to a quarter of an hour or so. He's a little late, but when he comes he can tell you more exactly, I expect."

And when Chris Hollins came, clumping in a few minutes later from the yard, he did fill in the picture with a few dredged-up details; the time of his call at Blunden's, about nine o'clock, as he remembered, for the wireless was on with the news; the route of his long and leisurely walk home; his arrival somewhat before half-past ten. He had taken his time coming home, certainly; it was a lovely night, and he'd felt like a walk. But as he had chosen the more obscure heath pathways, and the woodland tracks, he had met hardly a soul after leaving the lane by the Harrow, until he had stopped for a moment to talk to Bill Hayley the carrier almost at the foot of his own drive.

He was not, naturally enough, so accomplished at this kind of thing as his wife, and he exhibited all the signs of guilt which the innocent show when questioned by the police. George in his unregenerate 'teens, coming away from the orchard-wall of this very farm with two or three purloined apples in his pocket, had felt himself going this same dark brick-red color even upon passing close to a policeman. Besides, there are so many laws that there exists always the possibility that one or two of them *may* have been unwittingly broken. Hollins's lowered brow, broad and belligerent as the curly forehead of his own bull, did not quicken George's pulse by a single beat. Yet he was deeply interested. Chiefly in the way they looked at each other, the stocky, straight, blustering, uneasy, kind husband and the dark, quiet, relaxed wife. After every answer, his eyes stole away to hers, seemed to circle her, looking for a way into that calm, to bruise their simple blueness against it and withdraw to stare again. And she met them with her dark, self-contained gentleness, closed and inviolable, and did not let him in. However often he scratched at the door, she did not let him in. Like a fireguard, fending him off, she spread the grieving glance of her black eyes all around her to keep his hands out of the fire. But deep within her head those eyes were watching him, too, more inwardly, with less of composure and quiet than she had in keeping her own counsel.

George did not know nor try to guess what was going on between them in this absence of communication; but at least he knew that something was going on, and something in which they both went blindfolded as surely as he did.

"You didn't see anything of Schauffler, then, on the day he was murdered?" said George, choosing his words with deliberation. He added, snapping away the pencil with which he had noted down the scanty details of Hollins's walk home: "Either of you?"

She didn't turn a hair. She had lived with the reality of murder, why should she start at the word? But her husband drew in his head as if the wall had leaned at him.

"No, we didn't. Why should you think we had, any more than anybody else around the village? He'd left here a month before. He hasn't been up here since. Why should he?"

"Why, indeed?" said George, and went away very thoughtfully from between the two fencing glances, to let them close at last.

But for some reason he did not go down the drive. He turned aside when he left the yard, and went along the field-path by the remembered orchard-wall. There was a narrow door in it, almost at the end, he recalled. It had just been painted, bright, deep green paint, maybe a few days old.

3

Jim Tugg was quite another pair of shoes, a pair that didn't pinch at all. He looked at George across the bare scrubbed table in his single downstairs room, as spare and clean and indifferent as a monk's cell, and stubbed down tobacco hard into the bowl of a short clay pipe which ought to have roasted his nose when it was going well, and made a face as dark as thunder in contempt of all subtlety.

"Turn it up!" he said, bitterly grinning. "I know what you're after as well as what you do! I'm one of the possibles—maybe the most possible of the lot. God knows I wouldn't blame you, at that. Too bad for you it just didn't happen that way!"

"You didn't have much use for Germans in the lump, did you?" said George thoughtfully, watching the big teak-colored forefinger pack the pipe too full for most lungs to draw it.

"I'm calculable, but I'm not that calculable. Men don't come to me in the lump, they come singly, with two feet each, and a voice apiece all round. Germans—maybe they rate more rejects than most other kinds, but even they, when they go out go out one at a time. If you mean I hadn't any use at all for Helmut Schauffler, say it, and I'll tell you the answer."

150

George gave him a light, and said: "I'm listening."

"I hated his guts! Who didn't, that ever had anything to do with him at close quarters? I could have killed him and liked it, I dare say. I did bash him, more than once, and I liked that, too, I liked it a lot. I should have liked to bash him again on the twenty-sixth of September, and I wouldn't have minded even if it had turned out one bash too many, either. Nothing more probable ever happened. Only this didn't happen. I never saw him that day, or it likely would have done—but I didn't see him, and it didn't happen."

"What had he done to you?" asked George with deceptive mildness.

"Nothing. He was like a leech creeping round me feet, he loved me the way a leech loves you. Until I hit him the first time. Then he kept out of my way all he could, unless there was half a dozen other fellows close at hand."

"Then what did you have against him so badly?"

"You know already," said Jim, looking up under his black brows from cavernous dark eyes. "You've been to the house, I saw you come round the orchard to my gate. You know what I had against him."

"Only the persecution of Mrs. Hollins?"

"Only?" said Jim, and small, rose-colored flames spurted up inside the dark pupils of his eyes, burning out the angry center of his being into a hollow, sultry fire.

"Don't mistake me! Nothing on your own account?"

151

The flames subsided. He sat leaning forward easily with his elbows on his knees, and his hard, sinewy forearms tapering down strangely into the lean, grave hands which held the pipe between them, ritually still. He thought about it, and thought with him was leisurely on the rare occasions when he let it come of itself, instead of igniting it like explosive gas while it was still half-formed. He narrowed his eyes against the spiral of smoke, and said: "Yes, maybe there was something on my own account, too, growing out of all the rest. Sergeant, we only just finished a war. I don't kid myself I won it single-handed, but I had my hand in it all right, and what's more, I knew what it was in there for. I wanted my war used properly. God damn it, didn't I have a right to expect it? And every time I looked at that deadly, dirty, arrogant, cringing little spew of a Nazi, and knew him for what he was, I knew we'd won and thrown the whole stakes away again, poured it down the drain. Look, Sergeant, I don't know what other fellows feel, but me, I didn't much like Arnhem, I didn't much like any damn part of the whole dirty business. It's no fun to me, in the ordinary way, to get another chap's throat between my hands and squeeze—and the hell of a lot of fun it was picking up the pieces of other chaps I knew who didn't squeeze hard enough. Well, it made some sense while we thought it was *for* something. But if the Schaufflers can come squirming out of their holes only a few years later, and spit on Jewish women, and tell 'em they're marked already for the camps and the furnaces—here in our own country, my

152

God, in the country that's supposed to have licked 'em—will you tell me, Sergeant Felse, what the hell we tore our guts out for?"

George looked somberly between his boot-heels on the bare wooden floor, and said: "Seems to me someone else, though, was due to collect that particular bash on the head—if everybody had his rights."

Jim grinned. It was like looking down the shaft of a pit, such improbable dark depths opened in his eyes.

"Ah!" he said, "if we only knew where to deliver it! But Schauffler was here under my feet, something I *could* get at. I could land off at him with some prospect of connecting. Only I didn't. Don't ask me why. I let him alone so long as he let her alone; and if he didn't, I thrashed him—when I was let, but there were too many of your lads about, half the time. He got a bit more careful after the first mistake, but he only went farther round to work, and kept a bit sharper an eye on me. He couldn't leave her alone, not even to save his life—after all, torturing people was what he lived on."

"But after all," said George, arguing with himself as well as with the shepherd, "he couldn't actually harm or kill her here."

"No, he couldn't kill her, he could only sicken her with living. She had a war, too, and it looked as if all her efforts were gone to hell, same as mine. You ought to try it some time," said Jim acidly, "it's a great feeling."

After these daunting exchanges it was none too easy to get back to straight question and answer,

153

to the small beer of where were you on the evening of Wednesday, September 26th. But he was forthcoming enough.

"I was down at my sister's place, in the village, until about eight o'clock that evening. Mrs. Jack Harness—you know her. Then I went to the Shock of Hay, and I was in the snug there a goodish time. I don't remember what time I left, except it was well before closing-time. Maybe about half-past nine, maybe not quite that. I dare say Io might have noticed, or Wedderburn, or some of the fellows who were there." He mentioned several names, indifferently, drawing heavily on the packed clay pipe. "I came home up the back way, over the fields. It's quicker. Didn't meet a soul, though; you won't get no confirmation of my movements once I slipped up the lane by the pub." He looked once around the clean, hard little room, monastically arid in the slanting light of the evening. "Nor you won't get no confiding woman here to tell you what time I got in that night. I could tell you, roughly— soon after ten. But I can't prove it. There's nobody here but me and the dogs, and they won't tell much."

Hearing himself mentioned, the collie thumped the floor with his tail for a moment, and lifted his head to look at his master. He was a one-man dog, nobody existed but Jim. He would gladly have deposed for him if he could.

"Then that's all you can tell me about this business?" said George.

"That's all I can tell you, and that's no better than nothing. I never touched him that night. If

154

I had, I'd tell you—but if I had, he wouldn't have been stuck in the brook to finish him off. My way'd be no better, maybe—but that ain't my way."

George looked at him with blankly thoughtful eyes, and asked: "Would you say it was more a woman's way?"

Jim straightened from his leaning attitude, not suddenly, not slowly, and came to his feet. The scrubbed deal table in between them, blanched and furry with cleanness, jarred out of line as his hip struck against it; and the startled collie rose, too, and growled from between his knees. He stood staring down at George, and his face had not taken fire, but only glowed darker and more savagely self-contained in shadow, averted from the window.

"What do you mean by that? What woman's way?"

"Any," said George. "Do you think they haven't got the same capabilities as you? But they might not have the same strength, or the same knowledge of how to do that kind of thing. And that's where the water would come in very handy. Wouldn't it?" He looked up at the gaunt, weathered face looming over him, and smiled, a little wearily. "Sit down, can't you! Do you think I found Helmut any more pleasing than you did?"

Said Jim, not moving: "You're on the wrong tack. She wouldn't hurt a fly." And it was somehow immediately apparent that he had in no sense been tricked into assuming a particular she. He knew which woman George had in mind, and he saw no point in dissembling his knowledge. All his cards went on the table. Or had he perhaps still one he wasn't showing, one he was never likely to show?

"Why should she?" said George. "No fly's been hurting her."

"I never knew her even feel like being violent to anyone or anything. She wouldn't know how. I tell you, Gerd Hollins is an angel."

"For all I know," said George, "I may be looking for an angel."

"Then why don't you stop looking?" asked the dark mouth very softly.

4

George went into the yard of the Shock of Hay by the private way, and tapped at the scullery door; and there was Io filling a kettle at the tap, and putting it on the gas-ring for the late cocoa on which they usually went to bed. It was getting round to closing-time, and warm, merry murmurs came in from the bar along the passage, the mellowest noise George had heard in Comerford all that day. It took a solid evening of drinking, leisurely but devoted drinking, to get rid of the hag on Comerford's back these days. There were no individual voices in this noise, it was as communal as the buzzing of a hive of bees, and as contented. He liked to hear it; it soothed his over-active mind, even while he was thinking out the first question for Io, who welcomed him with an unsuspecting smile. Pussy, of course, was

156

in bed already, though it was questionable whether she was sleeping. No one who wanted information would have dreamed of going to the Shock of Hay until after Pussy's bedtime.

"Come on in!" said Io resignedly. "We're nearly through, and you don't have to be official tonight—Dad's going to be only too glad to get 'em out on time, believe me. Go into the kitchen, will you, Sergeant, and I'll be with you in a minute. And keep your voice down, or the quiz-child will be out of bed and stretching her ears."

"Anybody'd think you were expecting me," said George, ducking his head under the low scullery doorway, where even Joe Hart, who was about five feet seven inches square, had to stoop.

"You'd have hard work to find one person among that gang out there," she said, nodding briskly in the direction of the murmurous bar, "who isn't expecting you—any minute. You're the most expected man in Comerford, bar none." But he could tell from the serenity of her voice and the undisturbed tiredness of her eyes that the true meaning of what she said had not yet penetrated into her own mind. She looked at him, and he was still human, he had not become a symbol. She smiled at him nicely, following him into the kitchen and patting the back of a chair at him invitingly. "Sit down until I can get Dad for you. I'll take him off in the bar until ten, it won't be long."

"No, stay!" said George. "I'd like to talk to you. In fact, I probably need to talk to you more than to your father—if you were looking after the snug last Wednesday, that is."

Io had already turned cheerfully away to relieve her father of his duties in the bar, but she swung round in the doorway and looked back at him with eyes suddenly widening and darkening, in a sharpened awareness. She came back slowly into the room, and closed the door behind her, one hand smoothing uncertainly at the skirt of her pink cotton frock.

"Me? The night before Pussy came in and—the night before they found him?"

"The night he was murdered," said George.

"Yes, I see! You know," she said slowly, "that's funny! I knew what you'd come about, of course. What else could it be? I guessed that much. And I knew everybody was somehow mixed up in it—I mean, from the impartial view. But the only person I didn't think of as being involved was me. Do you suppose that's the same with all those fellows out there? Everybody's talking about the murder, there isn't anything else worth talking about in Comerford just now. But how funny if every one of them sees all the rest as actors and himself as the audience!"

"Until I come along," said George wryly, seeing the first veil of removal drawn between his eyes and hers. He felt himself being geometricized into a totem as she looked at him. The law! An idol which does condescend to wield a certain benevolent guardianship over us; but beware of it, all the same, it exacts human sacrifice.

"Poor George!" said Io, breaking all the rules deliciously. "It isn't very nice, is it? But you can't help it. Go on, then, ask me anything you like. I don't quite see how I can be any good, I didn't know anything about it until you sent Pussy home, and even then she wouldn't let on what had happened, the monkey! She had an awful nightmare in the night, and then I found out. By next day it was a great adventure, and she was Sexton Blake and Tinker and Pedro all in one, but it didn't look quite such a picnic at one o'clock in the morning. I was in the snug as usual that evening—I mean the Wednesday evening. So go ahead, and ask me things. But I can't imagine I'll be much help." She sat down opposite to him, and folded her hands submissively in her lap, and looked at him gravely with her large brown eyes.

"Can you remember who was in, that night? All the regulars? Wedderburn and Charles Blunden? Jim Tugg?"

Io shut her eyes and recited a list of names, fishing them up out of her memory one by one, the first few readily, including the quarrelsome friends of whose presence she could never go unaware for long, then single names coming out of forgetfulness with distinct pops of achievement, like champagne corks. "And Tugg—yes, he was in some time that evening, I'm sure. I remember his dog having a bit of an argument with Baxter's terrier. You know what terriers are. Yes, he was here." She added disconcertingly, suddenly opening her eyes upon doubt and wonder, upon the crack in the wall of Comerford's peace: "Why did you ask me specially about him? You don't think that *he*—?"

"I just collect facts," said George. "If witnesses

159

can account for every minute of a man's time between nine and eleven on that evening, so much the better for him. Every one canceled out is one with a quiet mind—at least on his own account. So let's not look any further for my motives. What time did Jim come in?"

"Oh! Oh, dear, that's something quite different. I served him, of course, and I know he was there, because of the dogs—but what time he came in, that's another thing. The news was on when the terrier came in and started the row, I remember that. But honestly, I can't remember how long he'd been there then."

"Never mind! You could hardly be expected to keep the lot of 'em in mind." The news had been on, and Jim Tugg noticeably there at the Shock of Hay. The news had been on, and Chris Hollins talking cattle-transport with Blunden at the Harrow. "What time did he leave? Any clue?"

She shook her head helplessly. "I didn't notice him go. You know, he isn't a man who makes a noise about what he does. I think—I'm pretty sure he wasn't there at ten, when everybody was saying good-night. But he seldom stayed until ten, so perhaps I'm not really honestly remembering that, only taking it for granted. Doesn't he remember himself?"

"Not exactly. He thinks he left about half-past nine, maybe a little earlier."

"One of the others might remember properly," she said, with a sudden warming smile. "Baxter might, after having his dog nipped for its cheek. Only I'm not sure he wasn't away first himself. I never thought it would be so difficult to answer these questions, but it *is*. I didn't have any special reason to take note, you see."

"Of course not! Don't strain your memory, or you'll begin to imagine things and mix days up altogether. If anything flashes back of itself, well and good, but don't chivvy it. One of the others may have had things fixed in his mind by some little incident." He met her eyes squarely, and asked without warning: "What about Wedderburn and Blunden? Any clear recollection of their comings and goings?"

As if he needed to ask! Everyone knew that she had no peace from them, that she was forced to take notice of them because they took fierce notice of her, of every word she shed in their direction, and every glance, skirmishing over them like rival center-forwards in a hockey bully. Her pink-and-white face flamed, but she smiled, not too grudgingly, sensing first only his delicate little poke at her own self-esteem. Only then did the second stab reach her. Chad and Charles, they came into it, too. He saw her smile ebb, and her breath halt for an instant as it went home. Nobody is safe! Take care how you speak of one friend to another friend from now on. Take care particularly of every word you say to George Felse. After all, he is the police. And virtually, you've got everybody's life in your hands. Charles's life among the rest! Or was it Chad's she thought of first? Comerford would have said Charles's, but there was no way of being sure until she was sure herself.

George felt her withdraw herself, not stealthily, only delicately, in a shocked quietness, as deci-

161

sively as if she had walked backwards from him out of the room, to hold him in her eye every step of the way. Her look, which had been as limpid as crystal, grew opaque and shadowy as a thicket of bracken in its covert brownness. Her voice quietened by a distinct degree, answering discreetly: "Well, they were both here, but I didn't notice exactly when they came in, I was rather busy. Only when they began to fight, as usual, I couldn't very well help noticing, could I?"

"Literally fight?" asked George, with a smile he was far from feeling.

"No, of course not, it was only the same as it always is." Her brow darkened, clouding over at their idiocies. "But they were far too busy with each other to be wasting any time thinking of knocking anyone else on the head," she added firmly.

"They were there when the dogs began to scrap?" asked George again, doggedly ignoring his dismissal from individual personality.

"Yes, I'm sure of that. Charles was nearest, and he caught hold of the collie by the tail to make him break. They were both here before nine."

"And did they leave together?"

She said rather grudgingly: "No. They—behaved a little worse than most nights—at least, Chad did. Good Lord, wouldn't you think after all he's been through he'd have some sense of proportion? Wouldn't you, honestly? And yet, just because Charles asked me to go to the carnival dance at Comerbourne with him, and I said I would— Why shouldn't I go to a dance, if I'm asked?" she demanded of George, forgetting for the moment how much of a policeman he had become, and how little of a friend and neighbor. "Oh, not a word about the actual issue, of course, he just quarreled with Charles and with me and with the whole snug about everything else you can think of. Half of it was in Latin, or something; anyhow, I didn't even know what he was calling us. He got rather tight, and went off in the sulks, before ten o'clock. I can't be exact about the time, I didn't look at the clock, but it seems it must have been nearly half an hour before closing-time when he went."

"They don't give you much peace between them, do they?" said George, greatly daring.

Io looked at him for a struggling moment between indignation and laughter, and then collapsed without warning into an amused despair somewhere between the two. "Sometimes I'd like to knock their two silly heads together, and see if I could knock any sense into either of 'em. *I* don't want to be bothered with them, I've something better to do with my time; but I'd *like* them both, if only they'd let me. When they act like squabbling children, it isn't so easy."

Even in her confidences, now, there was a note of constraint, as if she watched him covertly to see how he took every word. Not only the wicked, apparently, flee when no man pursueth, for reach as he would, he could lay no hand on Io.

"Was he very drunk when he went off? That's most unusual for him, isn't it?"

"Well, it's hard to describe. He was more

drunk than I've ever seen him, and he'd been drinking in a more businesslike way than usual, but he was perfectly capable. Walked straight as an arrow. It seemed to make him more and more of a schoolmaster, if you know what I mean. By the time he went I couldn't understand a word he was saying, it was so high-flown."

"I take it he was heading straight for home?"

"Oh, you must ask him that, *I* don't know." She brightened at having reached something she honestly did not know, and stretched her small, shapely feet out before her with satisfaction. The murmurs from the bar, coming in only very softly, sounded like bees in lime flowers, drowsy and eased at the end of the day.

"I will. And what about Charles? He stayed till ten?" Why shouldn't he, reflected George, when he had got rid of his rival for once, and scored a minor triumph with the girl? He wouldn't go home until closing time that night, of all nights.

"Oh, he was the last out of the snug. He wanted to hang around and talk, even at that hour, but I was tired, and fed up with the pair of them." She made a wry face which somehow only accentuated the softness and sweetness of her mouth, the brown, harassed gentleness of her eyes. "I didn't behave so well myself. And he went home. But he was quite pleased with himself, was Charles. And Chad—well, I don't honestly think either of them had any time to think about anyone but himself that night."

"Probably not," agreed George, cocking an ear toward the bar, where the clock was just striking,

164

a few minutes ahead of its time. "Is Chad there tonight? I need to talk to him; perhaps I could catch him now."

Io let him go, watched him go with a grieved, withdrawn face. Chad was certainly there among the regulars stirring in the snug, they had both heard his voice lifted in good-nights just after the clock struck; and certainly he would go home to his rather rigidly retired cottage up the hill, where his mother kept house for him in a chilly, indifferent gentility, by the lane and the fields, on which quiet road one could talk to him very earnestly, and not be observed or interrupted. And of course she was sure that Chad could fill in the details of his better-forgotten evening minute by minute, like a school exercise. In any case, what was Chad to her but an ill-tempered nuisance? Still she watched George's purposeful exit to the yard and the lane with reluctance and regret, and would have liked to put a few miles between them until someone, someone who knew how to be more wary for Chad than he was likely to be for himself, had pointed out to him how times and people were changed in the village of Comerford.

A hand reached down through the banisters, and tweaked at the topmost of Io's brown curls. Green eyes shone upon her quietly from the stairs.

"What did I tell you?" said Pussy, dangling her plaits as deliberately as if they had been baited. "He thinks it's old Wedderburn! Now what are you going to do about it?"

5

When they fell into step on the way up the fields, neither of them was in the least surprised. This was the way home for only a handful of people, and Sergeant Felse was not among them, but Chad Wedderburn merely looked at him along his wide, knife-sharp shoulder, and smiled rather wearily, and left it at that. He said: "Hullo! On business?" Over the hill and beyond the ridge of trees was the small, genteelly kept house which had caused him such a panic of claustrophobia when he first came back to it, and the acidulated gentlewoman whom he had found it so hard to recognize as his mother. The likeness had come back into her unchanging face for him after a while, and they had fitted together the creaking parts of their joint life, and found it not so bad a machine, after all; but there were still times when he suddenly felt his heart fail in him, wondering what she had to do with him. She was so well-bred that she could not embarrass him by any parade of pride in him, nor shatter him by too unveiled a love, and altogether he was grateful to her and fond of her. But it could not be called an ecstatic relationship. She provided the background she thought most appropriate; he appreciated and conformed to it as his part of the adjustment. Only now and again did it pinch him badly, after a whole year of practice, and usually he could put up with these times and make no fuss. More than once in Croatia he had tasted surgery without anesthetics; it was a pity if he couldn't keep silence now when he got the anesthetic without the surgery.

The brown scar was like a pencil mark down his neck from the ear, a very small earnest of what he bore on his body. It drew his mouth and cheek a little awry, George noticed, a thing which was hardly observable by daylight; but now the twilight of a clouded three-quarter moon plucked his face into a deformed smile even when he was not smiling.

"On business, of course!" he said, answering himself equably. "Don't bother to be subtle about it, just say it. By now we all know that we're in it up to the neck—some of us rather above the neck, in fact. I know no reason why you shouldn't look in my direction rather pointedly. I know no reason why I should go out of my way to deny that I killed this particular man. I can hardly be indignant at the suggestion, can I, considering my history?"

His dark cheek, hollow and frail in the half-darkness, twitched suddenly. He looked as if a little sudden light would have shown dully clean through him; too brittle and thin to be able to beat in a man's head. And yet he spread his own hand in front of him, and looked at it, and flexed it, as if he stood off to regard its secret accomplishments, with awe that they should repose in such an unlikely instrument. The Fourth Form in their innocence had not wondered more at that than he had in his experience. He shivered in a quiet, inescapable disgust, remembering what was supposed to have been the achievement of his manhood. "It's almost a pity," he said, "that I can't make it easy for you, but I don't know the answer myself."

"I'm just beginning to find out," said George, rather ruefully, "what's meant by routine investigations. They don't follow any known routine for more than one yard before running off the rails. But if you want to ask the questions and answer them, too, go ahead, don't mind me."

"There was the Fleetwood affair," said Chad, mentally leaning back to get it in focus, "and I'm not going to try and make that any less than it was. Only an incident, maybe, but it was a symptom, too. And I seem to remember saying something rather rash about not wanting to start anything in case I killed him. Has been heard to threaten the life of the deceased man! And there was even the Jim Tugg affair, too; I was a witness to that if I needed any reminders."

"I didn't attach too literal a meaning," said George, "to what you said about killing him, if that's any comfort to you."

"Your mistake, I meant it literally. But you may also have observed that, because I was afraid of how it might end, I took good care, even under considerable provocation, not to let it begin."

"Granted!" said George. "Why go out of your way to make a case for and against, when nobody's accused you? I should sit back and wait events, if I were you, and not worry about it."

"I think you wouldn't. Haven't you noticed that that's the one thing none of us can do? Comerford's too small, and murder, even so piteous a specimen of the art, is too big. Besides, I find your presence conducive to talk, and I'm interested to see how good a case can be made—for and against." He was indeed talking to the night, which was no more impersonal than Sergeant Felse to him. "I find the motive angle a little under-supplied, don't you? The Fleetwood affair passed over safely, one doesn't kill this week for what one felt last week. A little roundabout, too. People do terrible things on behalf of other people, but things even more desperate for themselves. And what had Helmut ever done to me?"

This was more interesting than what George had foreseen, and he fell in with it adaptably enough, moving unhurried and unstampeded up the leisurely swell of the darkened field, with the vague black ghosts of the straggling hedge trees marching alongside on his right hand. Not too much attention need be paid, perhaps, to the matter, but the manner had peculiarities. Maybe Chad had drunk a little more than usual even tonight, in pursuit of some quiet place he couldn't find within his mind when sober. Or maybe he was instinctively putting up a barricade of eccentricity about his too questionable, too potential loneliness, to persuade the paths of all official feet to go round him reverently, as for a madman where madmen are holy. Or maybe he was just fed up, too fed up to be careful, and had set out to heave all the probabilities in the teeth of authority, and dare them to sort everything out and make sense of it.

"Jim Tugg suggested a very apposite motive, I thought," said George mildly. "It would apply

169

to you just as well. He said he had it against Helmut Schauffler that he was the living, walking, detestable proof of a war won at considerable personal cost by one set of men, and wantonly thrown away by others. If the Helmuts, he said, can sidle about the conquering country, only a few years later, hiding their most extreme nastiness behind the skirts of the law, what on earth did we tear our guts out for? I'm bound to say I find it a better motive than a great many which might seem more plausible on the surface."

"A motive for anger," said Chad, his voice slow and thoughtful in the dark, "but not for killing—not unless you could be sure that removing one man would make some difference. And of course it wouldn't."

"An angry man doesn't necessarily stop to work out the effects of what he does."

"Some do. I do. That's why I didn't do it. I had some training in calculating results, and doing it quickly, too. It comes almost naturally to me now."

"Moreover," went on George placidly, "the removal of Helmut might have been expected to have a very good effect indeed. He was like a penknife, chipping away industriously at the mortar between the stones of a perfectly good, serviceable wall—picking away at it and prising it apart bit by bit, for no positive purpose in the world, only for the love of destroying things. Nobody likes to feel the roof being brought down over his head, in my experience."

Chad turned his head suddenly, and looked along his thin shoulder with a small movement of such desperation and pain that even George was startled. "If you mean this damned inadequate society that's supposed to keep the rain off us, what makes you think I'd be sorry to see it go? What gives you the idea I've found it weatherproof, these last few years? Wouldn't I be more likely to forgive him the rest, if only he could bring this down on the top of us, and force us to put up something better in its place?" He drew a breath that hit George's consciousness like a blow, and caused him to flinch. No doubt of the hurt here, no doubt of the bitterness. He tried to close the door on it again, but his voice was labored. "Never in my life," he said deliberately, "did I strike a solitary blow for English society, and make no mistake, I'm never likely to start now."

"Perhaps not," said George, clairvoyant, "but for something bigger you might, or for something smaller. For the idea of human decency and dignity, for instance—"

"By reducing something human to an indecent and undignified mess in a ditch?"

"Something which had already offended so far that it had become a sort of renegade from its own kind. Perhaps! More is required to make up humanity than two arms, two legs, and all the rest of the physical catalogue. But far more likely, for the peace of mind of a very small unit of society—about as large as Comerford. "I'm not sure that the disintegration of this one little community would leave you so completely cold."

"I'm not so sure," said Chad, "that it would. But haven't you seen already, and don't you suppose I could have seen in advance, that Helmut dead is a more effective agent of disintegration than he was alive? My God, do you suppose you're still the same person you were ten days ago? Do you suppose I am? They talk, oh, yes, they shout over the garden fences just as usual, and talk their little heads off, and even enjoy it in a way. But they can all feel the ground quaking under them, just the same, and they can all see, now, that the bloke next door is just about as near to them as somebody from the moon. It's beginning to crumble apart, faster than one rather nasty young man could have prised it while he was alive. And the only way of stopping it is by catching and hanging some poor devil who probably meant well by all of us. Nobody could possibly deserve to die merely because he smashed Helmut's head in, but I'm not all sure that he doesn't deserve it for his damned stupidity, for what he's done to Comerford. While he was alive, Helmut was never quite real, but, by God, he's real enough now he's dead!"

"You have," allowed George ruefully, "very definitely got something there."

"I thought by the sound of you that you had it, too. Not a nice job, yours," he said more quietly, and even smiled in a wry, grudging way. But he had said too much already for his own peace of mind, and the less he added now, the better. He lifted his head with a gesture of putting something from his back, not without effort. "This is all a little in the air. Shall we touch down again? I loathed Helmut Schauffler, but I didn't kill him. I object to killing, for one thing, and for another, in this case it would have been the worst possible policy, and I think there never has been a moment in my dealings with him when I failed to remember that. But you don't, of course, have to believe me. Go ahead and ask me things, what you like!"

The voice in which he answered questions, George noticed, was not quite the same voice, but carefully flattened into a level of indifference, a witness-box voice. He had nerves which needed to be steadied by these little extra attentions; one does not drag one's life suddenly through half a dozen phases of chaos and emerge impervious, it seems one may even come out of it with sensitivities more acutely tuned than before to the vibrations of danger and exasperation.

"You were at the Shock of Hay last Wednesday evening about the usual time for a call. When the nine o'clock news was on you were there. Any idea what time you left?"

"Not exactly. I wasn't noticing time very much. Well before closing time, though, it was just getting really full—and a bit noisy. I'd say about twenty to ten, but somebody else might know more about it than I do. Charles might—I'd just called him something not very complimentary— and not particularly usual. In certain circumstances I tend to become polysyllabic—especially on brandy."

"So I've heard," said George. "What time did you get home?"

"You could, of course, get that from my mother. She always knows the time when everything happens, especially if the routine goes wrong."

"I'm trying," said George gently, "to get it from you."

"Clever of you," said Chad, "to be so sure I should know. She called my attention to it directly I came in. Oh, not in any very censorious manner, merely as you point out a slight error in the pence column to a junior clerk toward whom you are, on the whole, well-disposed. It's a habit, actually. I suspect she tells the cat when he's ten minutes late. One isn't, of course, expected or required to take very much notice of the small reproof. It was twenty-five minutes to twelve."

"And what happened to the two hours in between?"

"I spent them sobering up, and walking off a pretty evil temper. I bring enough moods home as it is—this one I preferred to leave somewhere in the Comer."

"You didn't go swimming?"

"I did. Half-tight—rather more than half—but I could still swim. It wasn't a cold night, and the pool's safe as houses if you know it well. I'm not saying I'd have done it if I hadn't been rather beyond myself, as a matter of fact—but something had to be done! I didn't go straight there, just walked; keeping off the roads. Over the mounts, through the larch plantation, down the woods the other side. Went a long way toward the bridge along the water-meadows, then changed my mind and came back to the pool, and bathed. After that I didn't linger, I was too damned cold, I came back into Comerford the same way, only dropped down from the mounts by the steep path through the quarry. Home— exactly twenty-five to twelve."

"Meet anybody anywhere along this route?"

"At that hour, along this route, I wouldn't expect to. And beyond that, I took good care not to meet anyone, that was the last thing I wanted. Nobody who isn't drunk or in love walks by the river at eleven o'clock at night, and the lovers choose the less exposed bits, even when there are no other people there. I did pass one boy pushing a bike when I crossed the lane on top there—we swapped good-nights, but I didn't know him, and don't suppose he knew me from Adam. After that it was fine, I never saw a soul."

"Might be finer for both of us now if you had," said George. "Why did you have to choose that night to be difficult? And come to think of it, when you crossed the mounts toward the larches you must have been fairly near to the basin by Webster's well. That would be about—let's see!—ten o'clock or soon after, wouldn't it?"

"About that, I suppose."

"You didn't see anyone hanging around there? There's a place where the ground dips from the high paths, and you can see down into the basin behind the well. Nothing out of the way to be seen there then?"

"Not that I remember. I can't say I do remember even glancing toward the well, really. But in the wooded part, just past the dip, there was somebody moving around. Nothing for you, though, I'm afraid. The preserve fence begins about there, and not being a gamekeeper I find it etiquette not to look in the direction of poachers when I hear 'em at work. I took it for granted that was what he was up to, but he was rather a noise of footsteps than anything I saw. Just somebody running lightly in the underbrush, away from me to get deeper in shadow. It was pretty dark; he didn't have to go far to be lost. But it was a man, all right. Just a blur with a face and hands, and then gone, but a man. It's happened before on occasions; and as I say, I was tactful, and went right ahead without another look."

"That's helpful!" said George glumly. "Nothing else to report at all?"

"No, I think not. Sorry about that, but I couldn't know it was going to be important. And as a matter of fact, I still think pheasants were all he was after. I know the kind of running, and the place and time were right for it. Still, it's your manhunt."

There was no more to be had from him, either directly or by observation. They parted at the junction of the field-paths, and in a few minutes a high hedge hid them from each other. George went very thoughtfully back into Comerford's deserted green, let himself into the station, and telephoned Inspector Logan at Comerbourne. There was something about Helmut's tunic that he wanted to confirm; and he thought, after all, he would go over and make certain now, and not risk leaving it until the morning.

V

Second Thoughts

1

"Well," said Selwyn Blunden, settling his considerable bulk well back in the big chair, "that was an experiment that didn't last long. Poor young devil!—but he was a devil! Pity, it seemed to be beginning rather well, so I heard from the manager fellow down on the site there." He nodded toward the window which lay nearest to the ravaged valleys of the coal-site, still out of sight and sound, still held at bay from the Blunden fences, but creeping steadily nearer. "Said he was an excellent worker, excellent! Well, nobody's going to get any more work out of him now—or have any trouble with him, either."

"Except us," said George. "My troubles with him seem to be only beginning."

"Yes, in that way I suppose you're right. Bad business altogether, bad for the village, unsettles everybody—bad for the boy himself, who after all might have made a decent fellow in the end—bad for your lad, and that young thing with the plaits, too, by God! How did your young man take it?"

"Oh, Dom's all right. Stood up to it like a professional, but it's had its effect, all the same, I wish it hadn't. He's taking far too proprietary an interest in the case for my liking."

The big old man looked up under his bushy eyebrows and smiled through the thin clouds of smoke from his cigar. "What, enjoying the sensation, is he? You never can tell with children. These things simply don't frighten them until some fool of a grown-up goes to the trouble to explain to them that they ought to be frightened."

"Oh, not that, exactly. Dom's rather past the stage of having to have these things explained to him. Consequently he's quite capable of frightening himself, without any help from anyone. No, I wouldn't say he's enjoying it. But it happened to him, and he doesn't want to let go of it until it's all cleared up. Feels committed to it. Neither soft words nor fleas in his ear discourage him."

"I see! Bound to admire his spirit, I must say, but damned inconvenient for you, I quite see that. One likes to have one's family kept rather separate from things like murder." He sighed deeply, and exhaled smoke like some wholesome old dragon in an unorthodox fairy tale. "Difficult times all round, Sergeant. I do appreciate your troubles. Got some of my own, but nothing to speak of by comparison. Result of that appeal should be through almost any day, and between you and me, win or lose, I'll be glad to see it. Can't carry this sort of war of attrition as well as I used to."

"How do you think it's going to turn out?" asked George with interest.

"Oh, it's anybody's guess—but I think the appeal will be allowed. Yes, I really expect it to go through. Site's almost an uneconomic proposition as it is, after the run of bad luck they've had down there. Well, bad luck!—more likely over-confidence and over-haste, I'd hazard, if the truth be told. Put any amount of machinery out of action in a very short time, crashed one grab clean over and damned nearly killed the lad driving it—too much of it to be simply bad luck. It's my opinion they were trying to rush this last stretch to make a good case for moving into my ground before the winter closed in, and were in such a hurry they took too many chances, and made a botch of it. But *I* don't know! Their business, not mine. I'll abide by the decision, this time, bad or good, but I admit I hope for success. Can't expect me to enjoy the prospect of having the place torn up by the roots, can you, after all?"

George allowed that it would be rather a lot to expect. He suppressed a grin which would have done no discredit to Dominic, and asked demurely: "How's the shooting this year? Client of mine tells me the pheasants have done rather well."

The white moustache bristled for a moment, the bold blue eyes flashed, but he relaxed into laughter before their blueness had quite grown spearlike. "Ah, well, haven't had too many taken yet, all things considered. And your job's a bit like the confessional, isn't it? So I won't ask you for his name. Yes, they've done quite well. With only half a keeper, so to speak, one couldn't ask more. Briggs is a complete anarchist, of course, won't be ruled by owner, expert or predecessor, but he does rear the birds, heaven knows how. I've stopped interfering."

"I heard the guns out for the first time yesterday evening. Sounded like autumn!"

"Oh, that would be Charles and a couple of

friends he had down. I haven't been out yet myself, haven't had time. Perhaps this weekend we may get out together for a few hours—can't let a whole week of October slip away without a single bird. But there won't be any big parties this year. I can't do with the social life, Sergeant Felse, it takes too much out of a man, and I'm not so young as I once was. And then, it needs a woman to take charge of the house, or there's no heart in it—"

For a fleeting moment his blue eyes glanced upward at the wide, creamy expanse of wall opposite, where the best light in the room gathered and seemed to cluster upon a large, framed photograph. A woman, young but not very young, pretty but not very pretty, somehow too undecided to be *very* anything; and yet she had a soft, vague charm about her, too. A lot of fluffy light-brown hair, a formless yet pleasing face which looked as if it might yet amount to something if every line in it could be tightened up, a soft, petulant mouth, a string of carved imitation stones round her plump neck. Why should so vigorous, hard and arrogant an old man have lost any sleep over the flight of such a wife?

The sight of the picture never failed to astonish George with the same query. But human affections are something over which even the most practical people cannot be logical. Nobody likes to be left naked to laughter, either, even if leaves have fallen and cold winds come, especially if he happens to be the local panjandrum. And since the quick glance was never more than a momentary slipping of his guard, George was no wiser after it than he had been before. Maybe it was love, maybe only outraged dignity, that dug knives into the old man. Or maybe both had worn off long ago.

But to think of a woman with a face like that having the brains and patience to go quietly about from dealer to dealer, selling her jewellery, getting rid of her securities, telling them all—and all in confidence, of course!—that he was sending her to safety in America. If two of them had ever compared notes they would have known that she was collecting together more money than she could possibly be allowed to take out of the country; but of course every deal was private and confidential, and they never did compare notes. In a way, thought George irreverently, the old man ought to have been rather proud of her, she made a thumping good job of it. And he appreciates tactics, as a rule! Maybe, at that, it was from him she learned all she knew.

But this was not what he had come for. He pulled his mind sharply back from this most fascinating sidetrack, and asked: "You're exhibiting at the Sutton Show, I suppose?"

"Yes, hoping to. Sending some stuff down by road, with Hollins. Pretty good prospects, I think." He began to talk stock, his eyes kindling, and George let him run for a while, though most of it went past him and left no mark.

"Hollins came to see you about the arrangements, I understand, last Wednesday night. He says he was here about nine. Do you remember it?"

"Yes, of course. Came just after I turned the

news on, I remember. Stayed maybe a quarter of an hour or twenty minutes. He was away before half-past nine, at any rate. Rather a dull stick, young Chris," said the old man, looking up suddenly under his thick eyebrows with a perfectly intelligent appreciation of the meaning of these questions, "though a good sheep-farmer. Not at all a likely suspect for murder, one would think."

"None of 'em are," agreed George. "All next-door-neighbors, everybody knowing everybody, murder's an impossibility, that's all about it. Only alternative to thinking nobody could have done it is thinking anybody could have done it—and that's a thing one hopes not to have to face."

"It's a thing nine out of ten of us couldn't possibly face. We know enough to shut our eyes tight when it comes along, and keep 'em shut until it's gone by. It's that or lose hold of every mortal thing. But still—I'd put Hollins well down the list of possibilities, myself."

"No one will be more pleased than I shall," agreed George, "if I can account for every minute of his evening, and put him clean out of it. You've accounted for twenty minutes or so, and that's something. What sort of frame of mind did he seem to be in? Just as usual? Not agitated at all? Not even more withdrawn than usual?"

"Didn't notice anything out of the way. He talked business in the fewest words that would cover it, as always. He never talked much. Came, and said what he had to say, and went, and that was that. No, there wasn't anything odd about him. Maybe a bit brisker than usual, if anything.

He was a fellow who liked to sit and light a pipe as a sort of formal preliminary to conference, and come to the point briefly, but at his leisure. This time he got off the mark without smoking. That's positively all there is to be said about the interview, as far as I remember."

"He didn't say anything about where he was going when he left you? Nothing about any calls intended on the way home?"

"No, nothing that I remember."

"Oh, well—thanks for your help, sir." George rose, and old Blunden's heavy bulk heaved itself out of the armchair to accompany him to the door. Again he noticed the ageing thrust of the big shoulders, the slight stoop, for all the glint of his eye which had still more devilry in it than Charles could compass in the whole range of his moods.

"I won't ask you anything," said Blunden, leading the way through the sudden dimness of a hall which faced away from the morning sun. "But I don't mind telling you, Sergeant Felse, that I feel very concerned for that poor woman Hollins married. Not much of the truth ever came out, but I gathered what sort of a life young Schauffler had been leading her, all the same. Wish you luck all the more when I think about her. I do indeed! The sooner this case is closed, once for all, the better I'll be pleased."

"So will I," said George with even more fervor; and went away very thoughtfully to find Jim Tugg, who was leaning on one of his hurdles at the lambing-fold down in the bowl of the fields beyond the farm, chewing a grass and contemplating a number of well-grown and skittish Kerry Hill lambs. He appeared to be doing nothing beyond this, but in fact he was calculating the season's chances, and putting them pretty high, if nothing went wrong with the weather. He was dead sure he'd got the best tup he'd seen for years, and was looking forward to an average higher than last year. He was not thinking of the police at all, and even when he looked up from the black knees and black noses of the fat young ewes to the incongruous navy-blue figure of George, the contemplative expression of his eyes changed only very slowly and reluctantly.

George was nonetheless familiar by now with this change. In most people it happened instantaneously, the brief flare of intensified awareness, and then the quick but stealthy closing of the door upon him, with an almost panicky quietness, so that he should not hear it shut to. In Jim the pace was slower, and only the eyes changed, the rest of the dark face never tightening by one muscular contraction; and in Jim the closing of the door had a deliberation which did not care so much about being observed. The collie stopped bossing the sheep about, and came and stood at his knee, as if he had called it.

"Well, Sergeant?" said Jim. "Thought of some more questions?"

"Just one," said George, and found himself a leaning-place on the hurdles before he launched it. He wanted more than an answer to it; he wanted to understand the expression that went with the answer, but in the end all he could make

186

of Jim's face was a mild surprise when he asked at length:

"That green door in the orchard-wall up at the house— Which day did you paint it?"

2

Gerd Hollins put down the large hen-saucepan she had been about to lift to the stove, put it down carefully with a slow relaxing of the muscles of her olive forearms, and straightened up wiping her palms on the hips of her apron, where they left long damp marks in a deeper blue. She stood for a long minute looking at George without saying a word or moving a finger, quite still and aware, with her big eyes, strangely afraid but more strangely not afraid of him, fixed steadily on his face.

"How did you know?" she said. "Was there someone who saw us? Who was it who told you?" And suddenly the tensions went out of her, ebbing very quietly, and she sat down limply in the nearest chair, and leaned her linked hands heavily into her thighs, as if the weight of them was too much to hold up any longer. But it was odd that she should first ask that. Why should she want to know if someone had told him? Because in that case the same person might have told someone else?

There was only one someone who could count for her in such an affair or at such a moment. Or perhaps two? The second of whom had just manifested nothing but rather scornful surprise at being asked about the newly painted door. But in any case her husband was in all probability the only creature about whom she really cared. Was it safe to conclude, then, that, as far as she knew, her husband was unaware of Helmut's last visit, and that the fear she felt was of the possibility that, after all, there might have been someone willing and able to enlighten him?

When she let herself sag like that she was middle-aged, even though her face continued dark, self-contained and handsome. She looked at him, and waited to be answered.

"On Helmut's tunic-sleeve," he said, "there were very faint traces of green paint, not much more than a coating on the hairy outside of the pile. The kind of just noticeable mark you get from a quick-drying paint when it's tacky. It tallies with the new paint on the door in your orchard-wall. Jim painted the door, he says, last Wednesday afternoon."

She passed her hand across her forehead, smoothing aside a strayed end of her black hair. "Yes," she said, "he did. He left it unlocked afterwards. Yes—I see! So no one actually told you?"

"No one. I've come so that you can do that."

She looked up suddenly, and said: "Jim—?"

"Jim is still wondering what the devil I meant by the question. He doesn't know it could have anything to do with Helmut. This is just between me and you."

She gave a long sigh, and said: "I'll tell you exactly what happened. It affects no one but me.

Chris didn't know. Jim didn't know—at least— no, I'm sure he didn't know about that night, at any rate. He was down in the village before Helmut came near me."

Yes, she could care about more than one man at a time, it seemed, even if not in quite the same way. A stubborn, deliberate loyalty to Jim Tugg crossed at right-angles the protective love she felt for her husband. Might there not even be some real conflict here in this house, where the two of them went about her constantly, either loving her in his fashion? George caught himself back aghast from this complication of human feeling. Good God! he thought, I'm beginning to see chasms all round me, complexes in the kitchen, rivalries in the rickyard. Why, I've known these people for years! But he was not quite reassured. How many of the people you have known for years do you really know?

"It was the fifth time he'd been up here," said Gerd, in a level voice, "since he left us. He didn't come too often, partly because it was a risk— and you know he always liked to have the odds on his side—but also, I think, because he wanted me never to get used to it, always to be able to think and hope I'd seen the last of him, so that he could come back every time quite fresh and unexpected. Twice he came over the fence and through the garden, when both Chris and Jim were off the place. He must have stayed some- where watching until they went. The third time he found the little door in the wall. That was perfect, because in the evening I have to go there to feed the fowl and shut the pens, and there it's quite private, right out of sight of the house or the yard. And narrow! I could never pass until he chose to let me. The fourth time was the same. There'd been eight days between, and I almost thought he'd tired of it. Then I had a lock put on the door, and kept it locked until the Wednesday. Jim forgot to lock it again after he finished. It never used to be locked, you see, it was no wonder it slipped his mind."

She paused, rather as if to assemble her thoughts than in expectation of any comment from George, but he asked her, because it had been mystifying him all along: "But what could he *do* here? What satisfaction did he get, to make the game so fascinating to him? I mean, you'd expect even a Helmut to tire of simply tormenting someone—especially, if I may say so, when the victim was quite beyond being frightened."

She weighed it and him in the deeps of her appallingly patient eyes, and explained quietly: "Fright is not everything. There may even be a new pleasure to be got out of someone who is not—frightened, exactly. I think Helmut must have got rather bored with people who were just frightened of him, during the war. They seem to have stopped being amusing to him. He liked better someone who was desperate, but couldn't do anything about it. I was desperate, but there was nothing I could do. Maybe it wouldn't be easy to make you understand what Helmut was like, those times when he came here after me. Since I'm telling everything, I'll try to tell you that, too. He very seldom touched me, usually just stood between me and where I was going.

Toward the end he began to finger me. Even then it was in his own way. My flesh was only attractive to him because it was in a way repellent, too. He just kept me with him while he talked. He talked about all those places in Germany where my kind of people were herded, and used, and killed. He told me how it must have been for my family. Especially how it must have ended. He told me that all in good time it would be like that for me, that I was not to believe I had finished with these things. He said England would learn, was learning fast, what to do with Jews, niggers, Asiatics, all the inferior breeds. Do not be obvious, and tell me that I am in England, and protected. He was real, was he not? He was there, and he was protected. Oh, I never believed literally in what he said. But I believed in *him*, because every word he said and every thought he had in his mind proved that he was still very much a reality. Things have been so badly mishandled that, after all we've done to get rid of him, he's still one of the greatest realities in the world. In some countries almost the only reality—except poverty. And not quite a rumor in other countries—even here!"

She had regained, as she spoke, the power and composure of her body, and looked at him with straight, challenging eyes, but palely unsmiling.

"I wasn't afraid of him," she said steadily, "but I was afraid of the effect he had on me. I'd forgotten it was possible to hate and loathe anyone in that way."

"I can understand it," said George somberly. "But did he really get so much satisfaction out of these visits that he went on taking such risks for it?"

"He got the only bits of his present life that made him feel like a Nazi and a demi-god again. What more do you suppose he wanted? And he took very little risk. Almost none at all. He was always careful, he had time to be careful."

"He could watch his step, yes, but at any moment you chose you could have told your husband the whole story. Why didn't you? I can understand your keeping quiet at first, but after Jim's flare-up with Helmut the story was out. Why didn't you keep it that way? Why go to such trouble to pretend the persecution had ended? If you didn't lie to your husband, you must have come pretty near it. You certainly lied to me. Why?"

She did not answer for a moment, and somehow in her silence he had a vivid recollection of Helmut's body lying in the brook, with ripples tugging and twisting at his blond hair. Perhaps, after all, it was a silly question to ask her. With that ending somewhere shadowy at the back of her mind, she had gone to some trouble to ensure that for the one person who mattered there should be no motive. And Hollins was a man for whom she could do such a service successfully, a limited man, a gullible man, a fond man, not so hard to blindfold. A woman like Gerd, experienced in every kind of evil fortune, might easily take it upon herself to shut up his mind from anger, his heart from grief, and his hands from violence. What was another load more or less to her, if he was back in the sun and serenity of his fields, innocent of any anxiety?

"Did you have any suspicion," said George suddenly, "that this would happen?"

"This?"

"Schauffler's murder." He used the word deliberately, but there was no spark.

"Like it did happen—no, I never thought of that. I thought of anger, and fights, and magistrates' courts, and newspapers, and all the stupidity of these things. I didn't often think of him dead, and when I did, it was openly, in a fight—some blow that was a little too hard. But that would have been enough, you see."

Yes, he saw. So perhaps the motive she was so resolute not to let slip into her husband's hands had only lain waiting and growing and hardening in her own.

"It seems, you understand," he said carefully, "that, but for whoever killed him, you must have been the last person to see Helmut alive. The last word we had on him was from the boy who saw him leave the lane for the field-path at Markyeat Cross, soon after seven. It was after that, obviously, that he came here, since he seems to have been heading straight for you then. Tell me about that visit. What time did he come in by the green door? How long did he stay?"

She told him as exactly as she could, dragging up details from her memory with a distasteful carefulness. It must have been nearly eight o'clock when she had gone out to the poultry-houses, therefore according to the time when he had passed Markyeat Cross he must have waited for her coming at least twenty minutes, but his savoring patience had not given out. He had left her, she thought, rather before a quarter-past eight. Where he had gone on closing the green door between them she did not know. By eleven o'clock, according to the doctors, he had been dead and in his brook, snugly tucked into the basin of clay under the edge of the Harrow woods and the waste lands. And between the last touch of his pleased and revolted fingers on her bare arm, and the blow that killed him, who had seen him?

"I wish to heaven," said George suddenly, "that you'd told me the truth long ago!"

"When you questioned me about these things there was already a body to be accounted for. In such a case one lies—rather too easily."

"I meant long before that, before it ever came to that. If you wanted your husband protected, as I'm sure you did, at least why didn't you come to *me*?"

She gave him a long look which made him feel small, young and nakedly useless, and said without any irony or unkindness: "Sergeant Felse, you over-estimate yourself and your office. To the police people simply do not go. Nor to the Church, either. It seems there are no short cuts left to God."

It was horribly true, he felt as if she had thrown acid in his face. All the good intentions, all the good agencies, seem to have grown crooked, grown in upon themselves like ingrowing toenails, and set up poisoned irritations from which people wince away. In real trouble, unless he is lucky enough to possess that rare creature, a genuine friend, every man retires into himself, the one fortress on which he can place at any rate some reliance. As Gerd had withdrawn into herself and taken all her problems with her, that no one else might stumble over them and come to grief.

The only people who still ask the police for protection, thought George bitterly, are the Fascists. What sort of use are we?

"It sounds impossible," he said, "that a woman can be persecuted in her own house, like that, and have no remedy she can feel justified in taking. Tell me honestly, had you yourself ever thought of a way out?"

She looked at him impenetrably, and said: "No. Except to go on bearing it, and take what precautions I could to avoid him."

"Did your husband ever say anything to make you think he had his suspicions? I mean, that Helmut was still haunting you?"

"No, never."

"Nor Jim, either?"

"No, nor Jim."

She heard, just as she said it, Christopher's feet at the scraper outside the scullery door, methodically scraping off his boots the traces of one of the few damp places left in the hollows of his fields, the shrunken marsh pool in the bottom meadows. George heard it, too, a slow, dogged noise like the man who made it. He saw the slight but sudden rearing of Gerd's head, the deep, perceptible brightening of her eyes, the quickening of all the tensions which held her secret.

But not a gleam of welcome for him now, no gladness. Not for the first time, Chris had done the wrong thing. She got up with a quite daunting gesture of dismissal, picked up the hen-saucepan, and put it on the large gas-ring, and resolutely lit the gas under it. But George did not move. Just as the porch door opened he said clearly:

"In that case I hope you realize, Mrs. Hollins, that you seem to be the only person in Comerford who had an excellent motive for wanting him dead, and who knew his movements that night well enough to have followed him and killed him."

3

Chris Hollins heaved himself into the doorway and stood there looking up under his lowered brows, like a bull meditating a charge. Gerd, turning with the matches in her hand, gave him a look so forbidding that at any other time he would have retired into a dazed silence, following her leads, saying what he believed she wanted of him; but now he stood and lowered his head at her, too, in his male indignation, and demanded menacingly:

"What's this you're saying to my wife, Sergeant?"

George repeated it. Not because he was proud of it; indeed, the second time it sounded even cheaper. But it had certainly made Hollins rise, and that was almost more than he had expected.

He said it again, almost word for word, with the calm of distaste, but to the other man's ears it sounded more like the calm of rocklike confidence.

"And what grounds have you got," he said thickly, "for saying any such thing to her? How do you know a dozen more people didn't know of his movements, and hadn't better reason to want him dead than ever she had?"

"There may have been a hundred," agreed George, "but there's curiously little sign of even one. You find me the evidence, and I'll be more than interested."

Gerd said: "In any case, it's no desperate matter, so don't let's get melodramatic about it. Sergeant Felse has his job to do. I haven't been accused of killing him, so far, and there's no need to act as if I have." Her eyes were large and urgent on her husband now, with no time for George; and for that reason he was able to make more sense of their questioning than ever he had made before. She wanted the subject dropped. She wanted either an end of the interview, or Chris miles away; for it was plain, for one dazzling moment, that she simply did not know what he might be about to say, and feared it as she had never feared Helmut Schauffler. "I've told all I know," she said. "I don't think he can have anything more to ask you."

"I might," said George, "ask him why it doesn't surprise him to hear that you knew all about Helmut's movements the night he was killed. After all, yesterday you both denied you'd seen hide or hair of him since he was in court.

He seems to take it all as a matter of course that we should have come to a different conclusion today."

The exchange of glances was fluid and turbulent, like the currents of a river. One minute he thought he had the hang of it, the next it seemed to mean something quite different. They were at cross-purposes, each in fear of what the other might give away, each probing after the other's secrets. Certainly it seemed that Helmut's last visit to the farm had been no secret from Hollins, however securely Gerd had tried to hide it. Now she was at a loss how to say least, how to keep him most silent, agonized with trying to understand at every stage before George could understand, and so steer the revelations into the most harmless channel. But Hollins was past giving her any cooperation in the endeavor. Concealment was alien to his nature, and he had had enough of it, if it could end in his wife's being singled out as a likely suspect of murder. He swung his heavy head from one to the other of them, darkly staring, and said bluntly:

"Well I knew he'd been here, and talked to her, and carried on his old games at her, like before! And well I knew she told you lies when she said the opposite yesterday. Do you wonder she kept as much as she could to herself? If it was a mistake, it was a mistake ninety-nine out of a hundred would have made."

She stood there staring at him with blank, shocked eyes. When she could speak she said: "Why didn't you tell me? I thought you at least knew nothing about it—I wanted you not to know! But when you found it out, yo... told me!"

"Trying to shut up trouble doesn't ... well," he said grimly. "But I thought it wa... job to think of something, and not to put ... weight of it any harder on you. Not that it cam... to anything—not even murder. I might as well say, why didn't you tell me, and not leave me to find out for myself what was going on. But I don't ask you any such thing."

"Well, having gone so far," said George, "you may as well tell me all you know. Look, I don't pretend to be the children's friend to any very wonderful extent, but wouldn't it have been better to trust me a little further in the first place?"

"Maybe it would, but try being in our shoes, and see what you'd do. Not that we'd anything guilty to hide," he said with quite unwonted violence, as if he were trying to convince himself, "but just the run of events can put you in a bad spot without any help on your part, and it comes natural to play down the awkward bits that don't mean anything, but have a nasty way of looking as if they do."

George, with his eyes on Gerd, agreed reasonably that this made perfect sense. "But now let's have all the facts you've got to give, even if they look nothing to you. They help to fill in an evening, and reduce the time about which we know very little. For instance, we know now that Helmut came here, accosted Mrs. Hollins in the orchard at about eight o'clock, made himself as objectionable as usual, and left at about a quarter-past the hour. From then until eleven o'clock,

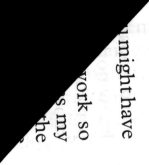

he must have been dead, we
ɔut him. It seems you knew the
till going on. How long had you
that night?"

his head from side to side,
1 both as if they might make
not concerted attack. After a
.d, quite quietly: "No."

"You found it out that night?"

"Yes. She was a long time. I had a devil nagging
me that there was still something wrong. I went
down the garden and looked through the trees
there, and saw them. He had her by the arm—"

Gerd cried out suddenly, in a voice too high-
pitched for her: "He's lying! I do not believe it.
He's making up a tale for you, to draw you off
from me. Don't listen to him! He knew nothing,
he saw nothing, I am absolutely sure he was not
there—"

"I did more than see. It was all I could do not
to come out at him and wring his neck on the
spot, but if you could keep me out of things for
my own good, so could I you. I went back to the
house," he said, breathing hard, "and got my old
revolver, and loaded it, and then I went round
to the edge of the spinney, where I knew he'd go
sneaking away after he left you. Oh, no, Sergeant
Felse, my wife wasn't the only one to know all
about his movements that evening. I knew them
better than she did. I saw him alive long after she
did. When he went off up the mounts and into
the wood, I went after him."

Knotting her hands at her waist into a tight

contortion of thin, hard fingers in which the knuckles showed white, she said: "You are a fool! You take the wrong way, the foolish way, to protect me."

George, looking from one to the other, prompted delicately: "You said, Mrs. Hollins, that he went out halfway through the evening."

"I was gone before she got back to the house."

"It's true, he was gone," she said, trembling now, "but I knew he was going to Blunden's, I took it for granted that he should simply leave when he was ready. And he did go to Blunden's— the old man will tell you so."

"He has told me so already. But it doesn't take three-quarters of an hour and more to go from here to the Harrow."

"On a fine evening, why should he hurry? There was nothing else to claim him. But this other story he has made up, to help me, to make you think that Helmut lived long after he left me, and there can be no suspicion on me—"

"Look!" said George, suddenly going to her and taking her firmly by the elbow. "Take it easy, both of you! You sit down, and don't rush things before you come to them." She looked surprised, even, he suspected, a little amused, as he put her into a chair, but she sat there obediently looking up at him, and her face was eased. "Look, I know I started this, and in a not particularly fair way, either. But I'm not trying to get more out of you or anybody than just the plain, stupid truth. Just because you're anxious to show me that he didn't kill Helmut, there's no need in the world to fall over backwards and tell me that *you did*. It's long

201

odds Helmut *was* seen alive long after he left here, maybe by several people, if only we knew how to find 'em. If your husband can fill in a bit of the missing time, so much the better for both of you in the long run. Only give up the idea that pushing the bits you don't much like under the rug is going to make things better for anybody. It's only going to make me mad, and that does nobody any good."

She began to smile, and then he felt better, even though the smile was faintly indulgent, as to a crazy juvenile. "All right, if it's understood that you don't either of you have to talk in a hurry, we can hear the rest." He looked up at Hollins, but the heavy remoteness of that face had not changed at all. "You followed him. Go on!"

Hollins shook back his shoulders, and went on: "I kept behind him all up the woods, out of sight and hearing of him, but close. The revolver was in my pocket. I don't know whether I meant to kill him or not. I know I meant at least to half-kill him, maybe I meant more."

"But it was after nine when he was killed," cried Gerd, "and at nine—"

"At nine, or a couple of minutes later, your husband was at the Harrow," said George. "Also, Helmut was not shot. And it does seem a little unlikely that a man with a loaded revolver in his pocket should go to the trouble to use a less certain method for the same job."

"I didn't use it for any job, in the end. It's still fully loaded, it hasn't even been used to bash somebody over the head. I suppose those fellows of yours who examine these things can tell that by looking at it?"

"They can try, at any rate," said George. "Go on, where did you leave Schauffler, and at what time?"

"I kept behind him until he came on to the ridge above the river, and sat down there for a while. He was very pleased with himself, humming and singing to himself in German, and grinning as if he'd pulled off something very clever. He sat there quite a time. I had time to think, and I thought better of it."

George asked, with genuine and personal curiosity: "Why?"

"Well, he wasn't such big stuff. I meant getting him, and I watched and waited for him to move on; but he got to looking smaller and smaller as it got dark. And I cooled off this much, that I began to think how much trouble I should be laying up for her, as well as myself, with how little use or satisfaction. I knew about him now, and I could put a stop to him as far as my wife was concerned, without starting something worse for her, like murder in the family. She'd gone to a lot of pains to avoid what it looked like I was bent to bring on her. So I went off and left him there. I went to the Harrow—we weren't two hundred yards from the wicket in the fence—and left him to go to hell for all I cared."

"Virtually," said George, "he did. What time did you quit?"

"I'd say about ten to nine. I went straight to Blunden's, and it wouldn't take above ten minutes to do it from there."

"And you didn't see anything of him on the return journey?"

"Not a sign. I told you the way I came home, and that was all truth, if the rest wasn't. I took my time over it, to get it all off my mind before I came back where anybody could see me. I needed to walk him out of my system, or *she*'d have known with one look at me. From my point of view, after I turned my back on him up there we were both done with Helmut Schauffler."

Unfortunately no one was yet done with Helmut Schauffler. That was the devil of it. Not George, not all the spasmodically talkative, suddenly quiet neighbors leaning over Comerford garden fences, not the cheated heroes looking for a world fit for humankind, certainly not these two unquiet lovers. It was plain when their eyes met, drawn together unwillingly, that wells of doubt were opened within them, never to be filled by any amount of protestations or promises. Only certainty was of any use; nothing else held any peace for anyone in this haunted village.

She looks at him, thought George with pity and horror, as if she believes he's lying. And he looks at her as if he *knows* she's told only part of the truth. And yet he could not be sure even of this. "My lad," said George to himself, "you'd better get a move on, for everybody's sake!"

4

"I never noticed before," he said to Bunty, in the late evening, when Dominic was safely in bed and his ears no longer innocently stretched after a solution of problems which were his as surely as anyone's, "I never realized how opaque people's looks can be. We read meanings into them every day, but suddenly when it's a matter of life and death it makes you look again, and start weighing possibilities and separating them from suppositions—and altogether in the end you're terrified to think anything means anything. For a moment I could have sworn that each of those two was seriously afraid the other had done it. And then I couldn't be sure if that was really the meaning of the looks they were giving each other, or if it was something shared, or what it was."

Bunty looked at him with her practical partisan sympathy, and agreed: "That's a pity. Because if each of them really believed the other had done it, that would mean neither of them had done it, and then at least somebody would be safely out of it."

"Not quite, because an expression in the eyes isn't evidence. But at least I could have felt sure of something in my own mind. Now I'm sure of nothing. It's as open as ever it was—in their direction rather wider open. Because there was an intent to murder, I'm sure of that, and while it's credible that it should evaporate as suddenly as that—because he's a sane man with both feet on the ground, and only too deeply aware how much trouble his wife's been dragged through already—still it's also a strong possibility that it *didn't* evaporate."

Bunty, aware of his hand's vague undirected searching for something in his pockets, got up and brought him the tired man's solace, his tobacco pouch and pipe, and the necessary matches. She put them into his lap, and watched his fingers operate them mechanically. Even over the first deep draws he made a face of disappointment. It was his own growing, and he always forgot to be prepared for the shock; but he was too stubborn to admit that it was unsmokeable. Maybe he hadn't got the knack of curing it properly; anyhow, it was pretty awful. Bunty had never before noticed his distaste quite so clearly, and she made a mental note to buy a tin of his old brand the very next morning, and leave it somewhere for him to find, quite by accident.

"And another eye-opener," said George fretfully, "is the ease with which well-known citizens can walk about this darned place for hours at a time, and meet nobody. You wouldn't think it possible."

"In the dark, in a scattered country district where everybody drops off home by his own particular beeline across the mounts, well, it isn't really so astonishing as it seems," said Bunty reasonably.

"Not when you come to weigh up everything, perhaps. But it's confoundedly inconvenient. Here we've got Wedderburn going off in the sulks

206

to walk off a slight load before he goes home to his mother. And Jim Tugg wandering home by devious ways, alone but for his dog—but I grant you, there's nothing new about that, Jim likes his dog's company far better than most men's. And Hollins stalking Helmut, by his own confession, with intent to knock hell out of him at the very least, and then taking his disordered fancy for a walk until the agitation set up by the thought of murder had passed—"

"And Mrs. Hollins," said Bunty very soberly, "at home by herself all this time, shut up with the thought of Helmut. Nobody to take her mind off it, nobody to see what she did, nobody even to tell us whether she was really there or not."

George looked through the detestable smoke of his unthrifty crop at her, and found her looking very solemn and rather pale under the ruffled red hair. Awfully like the shivering but acute waif, so pale, so important, so large and scared of eye, who had met him on the clay-flats by the shrunken brook, standing over the blond head of Helmut.

"You don't really think, do you, that she might have done it?"

"I think *I* might," said Bunty, "in her place. Especially if I had reason to think that *you* might be thinking of doing it for me. She had a background of desperation. I don't mean it came naturally to her, but her scope had been rather forcibly widened, you see. And she had, if we come to it in earnest, the finest motive you could wish to see."

"But the fact that her mind was used to dealing

with these awful things would also mean that it was trained and equipped to resist them. I mean, she could not only seriously consider murder, after all she'd experienced—she could effectively reject it, too. I'm not satisfied that it's the strongest motive we have to look for. People of insignificant balance kill for insignificant things— sometimes almost lightly. And we haven't quoted the tenth part of Helmut's enemies. There are dozens of them, more trivial ones but real ones, round this village unaccounted for. There's at least one good union man who began the ideological feud with him long before young Fleetwood ever opened his mouth. And plenty of others, too. And there's something about this whole affair that makes me feel it never was planned. It came out of nowhere, out of some man's mind through his hands so fast he never had time to stop it or even see what it was, until it was done. That's how it feels to me."

"It could still have been a woman," said Bunty, "even that way."

"It could. Women have murderous impulses, too. But wouldn't a woman have been—more disastrously subtle about it, afterwards? I don't know. This was so short and simple. No messy attempts to cover up, but a clean walk-out."

"And no weapon," said Bunty, biting her underlip. "I suppose the revolver didn't show any sign?"

"Not a mark. Nobody's head was beaten in with the butt of *that* gun recently, that's certain."

"If only," burst out Bunty, speaking for Comerford with authentic passion, "if only it weren't for all the people whose lives are being bent out of shape now, I'd pray like anything that nobody'd ever solve it. But it's the village that's being murdered, not Helmut. Oh, George, isn't there any way out of it?"

"Only one. Straight ahead and out the other side—one man short or one woman short," said George, "whichever it turns out to be. And the sooner the better, for everybody concerned!"

VI

Feathers in the Wind

1

It was odd how all the games which came into season with the autumn, the ranging games which can extend over a whole square half-mile of country, had gravitated this year toward Webster's well, which sat, as it were, in the midst of a charmed circle of play. The younger boys evacuated their gangs from the village into this particular wilderness out of all the circle of pit-mounds open to them, and files of Indians moved up the shadowed side of the high field hedge there, while the hollows of birch saplings scattered in the clay wastes began to heave with commandos. There had always been cycles of fashion in playgrounds, of course, and usually for the most unsuitable reasons. Once for a whole autumn the favorite place had been the ruined engine-house on the brambly, naked mounds near the station. An elderly man of none too sound mind had been found hanged there, and horrid fascination had drawn all the boys and many of the bolder girls to haunt it for months after, especially at the shadowy hour between evening and night, when it was most terrifying, and lingering there repaid terror well-concealed with the most enviable kudos.

Another year a farmer's horse, grazed in a field with a brook at the bottom, got itself bogged to the neck during the night, and had to be rescued by the inevitable and long-suffering fire-brigade, whose entire working life, in these parts, appeared to be spent in fetching kittens down from telegraph poles, or dogs out of pit-shafts. The rescue lasted all day, and a crowd large enough for a fair-ground had gathered to witness the end of it; after which the marshy corner had become haunted ground for at least a month, and all the mothers of Comerford had more than usually muddy children.

But this year it was Webster's well. Webster's well and the mounts round it had no rival. Even the older children, past the stage of pretend games, took their elaborate versions of hide-and-seek up there to play. Pussy had a splendid variation of her own, which involved dusk, and pocket torches, and therefore could only be played in the end of daylight, which meant at the extremest end of a thirteen-year-old's evening, until summertime ended, later in October. Usually they wound up the fine evenings with a bout of it, before they went home to bed. Pussy was trailing a gang at the time. She had her solitary periods and her periods of communal activity, and Dominic, largely independent of his company though willing to cooperate with any numbers, acquiesced in her moods but retained to himself, formidably and irrevocably, the right to secede. He didn't care how many people she collected about her, if the result continued to entertain him; but if they proved boring, and began to waste too much time in argument and wrangling, he was off. Life, even at thirteen, was too short for inaction.

It was growing dark on this particular early October evening, with the silvery darkness of autumnal, clear nights when frosts have not yet begun. The occasional reports of guns in the preserves had already become so snugly familiar that they fell into the silence almost as softly as drops of dew from the trees. They sounded warm when the warmth of the day ended, prolonging activity long into the inactive hours like an echo; and now with dusk they chimed once or twice more, and ceased upon a stillness. The earth sighed, stretched and relaxed, composing itself for sleep.

At this point even the games grew stealthier, brigandage molten into witchcraft. The fat child with the gym tunic, and the sandy-haired boy with glasses, who were hunters for the occasion, sat in the grass close beside Webster's well, counting up to two hundred in leisurely, methodical whispers, no longer shouting out the numbers belligerently as by daylight. The flock scattered into the waste woods voiceless and soft of foot. Pussy and Dominic scrambled across the ridges of clay and went up the terraced slope beyond on hands and knees, for it was steep, and it does not take long to count to two hundred. Through the hedge at the top, by enlarged dog-holes which no one bothered to repair, and headlong into a wilderness of furze and birch saplings, tunneling like rabbits among the spiny places, slithering like lizards through the silvery, slippery leaves.

"Where shall we go?" asked Pussy in Dominic's ear; and at this eerie hour even Pussy whispered.

It was the tail-end of the evening's play, and they had almost exhausted the charms of every ordinary hiding-place. At this hungry and thirsty and yearning hour, with the uneasiness of the dark and the inevitability of bedtime clutching at them, something more was needed than the spidery tunnels of the furze and broom, and the clay hollows of elders and watery pits of willow, full of lean shadows. Rustlings and whisperings and tremors quivered across the vanishing face of the waste land after the feet of their companions. The pit mounds inhaled with one great sigh, and the children were swallowed up. And Pussy and Dominic, straight as arrows, restless, wanting something more, set their course directly upward from the well across the ribbon of wilderness, and fetched up breathlessly under the pale fence of the Harrow preserve, looking into a sweet, warm, olive-green darkness within.

Dominic panted: "I never thought it was quite so near." He shook the pales, and looked along the fence, and saw nothing on his side but the same thickets in which he had already buried himself grubbily half a dozen times this same evening.

"Where shall we go?" repeated Pussy. "Quick, they'll be coming, if you don't make up your mind."

But he had made up his mind already. It might not have happened, if the pale had not been broken out of its place, rotted away with its top still dangling in the circle of wire. Only fifty yards along the fence there was a gate, and with no wire atop, either, and a path ran tidily away from it into the dark of the plantation, heading for the Harrow farm; but the gate would not have charmed him, because it was a right of way, whereas this was a way to which he had no right. And all the guns had ceased now, and the darkness had a hush upon it as if the wood held its breath to see if he would really come. He slid one leg through. The pale behind him gave unexpectedly, swinging aside to widen the gap as his negligible hip struck it. He didn't even have to wriggle.

"You'll catch it," said Pussy practically, "if anyone comes."

"Who's going to come, at this time of night? Come on—unless you're scared!"

But though she put the case against it, she was already sliding through the gap after him. Her head butted him in the side smartly. He tugged her through and away into the warm grassless deeps of the trees. "Come on! I can hear Sandy moving off. You take an *age*!—and the gap's big enough for a man."

Pussy said giggling: "Who d'you suppose made it? I never knew about it before, did you?"

"No, but I'll bet there are dozens like it. Poachers, of course! Who d'you think would make quick ways out, if it wasn't poachers?"

"Dope, I meant which poachers! Because I know several of the special ways that belong to special people, so there!"

"Oh, yes, they'd be sure to tell *you*!" said Dominic, unkindly and unwisely.

"I keep my ears open. You ought to try it some time! I could draw you maps—"

They crashed suddenly a little downhill, slithering in the thin, shiny coating of pine-needles, blind, wrapped in a scented, sudden, womblike darkness. They were not accustomed yet to the black of it, and Dominic, treading light and quick upon the light, quickening heels of his intuition, suddenly checked and felt ahead cautiously with one toe, putting out a hand to hold Pussy back as she made to pass him.

"Look out, there's a hole!"

"I can't see a thing," she said blithely, leaning forward hard against the pluck of his arm.

"Shine the light! You've got it."

"But they'll see it. We don't want to show it till we have to."

"They won't see it from here, if you keep it this way on the ground. Be quick!"

Clawing it indifferently out of the leg of her school knickers, she felt for the button of the pencil-slim torch, the button which always stuck, and had to be humored. "Besides, I'm not sure we're not cheating, coming in here. They'll take it for granted it's out of bounds beyond the fence. Nobody ever does come in here."

"Well, there's never been anything to stop 'em. We never *said* it was out of bounds. And anyhow, when we have to shine the torch they'll know."

"I don't believe the silly torch intends to be shone. I can't get it on." She shook it, and it made a ferocious rattling, but no light. "Maybe the bulb's gone. And if old Blunden comes along and hears us in here there's going to be trouble."

"Well, why did you come, if you're scared? *I* never made you! And I don't believe old Blunden would be so very fierce, either; he's always quite decent about things, if you ask me."

"Not people with torches in among his pheasants at night," said Pussy positively.

"Well, we haven't got what *I'd* call a torch—"

But they had. The button sprang coyly away under her finger at that precious moment, and a wavering wand of light sailed out ahead of them and plucked slender young tree-trunks vibrating out of the dark like harp-strings, with a suddenness which sang. They saw each other's eyes brilliant and large as the eyes of owls in the night, as the eyes of cows encountered unexpectedly nose to nose when short-cutting by gaps in the hedges. Their hearts knocked hard, for no good reason except the reminder of the combat of light and dark, before they even saw the chasm yawning under their toes. Then Pussy squeaked, and scuffled backwards and brought them both down in the pine-needles.

But it wasn't the abyss it had seemed at first glance. Dominic took the torch from her, and crawled forward on his knees to shine it into the hole, and the plunging hell of dark dwindled into a pocketful of dingy, cobwebby shadows. A filled-in pit-shaft, narrow among the trees, but still thrusting them a little aside to make room for it. Gray clay slopes breaking barrenly through poor grass and silt of needles, like a beggar's sides through his tattered shirt; a few bricks from the shaft beaten into the composite of clay and earth, showing fragmentarily red among the gray and green. The place had been leveled, long before the trees were planted, but the earth's hungry

219

empty places underneath had not been nearly satisfied, and now the inevitable shifting fall had made once again a pit, ten or a dozen feet deep, and steadily settling deeper. Grass clawed at the rims of it, trying to hold fast. The slopes of clay which descended into it were furrowed and dried and cracked into lozenges by the dry season, and down in the bottom a small abrupt subsidence within the large and slow one had exposed a curved surface of brickwork pitted with darker holes. Round it the young trees leaned, fearfully and inquisitively peering in, and Dominic with the torch in his hand was only one more strange young staring tree, curious and afraid.

"Just another old shaft!" said Pussy, recovering her aplomb.

"Yes. I didn't know about this one, did you? But there are dozens all over the place."

"'Tisn't a nice sort of place, is it?" said Pussy, wrinkling her nose with distaste. "Look at those holes down there! I bet you there are rats!"

"I bet there are! It's all right, though. I thought for a minute it was an open shaft, didn't you?"

They had forgotten Sandy and the fat girl, until a sudden howl and hubbub broke out on the other side of the fence, rustle of stealthy footsteps first, then giggles, then a shriek of triumph and discovery, and crashing of running bodies among the bushes. "It's Pat and Nancy—I heard you! Come on, Pat, you devil—show!" And a pencilly beam of light, wavering and striped among the branches as the detected pair switched on, and the thunder and protest of pursuit, sibilant slith-

220

ering of willows, hard obstreperous clawing of gorse, dangerously near.

"Duck!" hissed Dominic, clamping a hand over the torch until she could wrestle the button back. "Quick, they're coming this way!" She struggled, and the thread of sheathed light dwindled away into the warm dark of his palm. The hunters, returning in triumph, quested along the fence, traced by their steps back and forth, back and forth, whispering.

"Someone else up here! Sure of it! Who? Can't be! Can't hear a thing! But there *was* somebody. Who? Try Dickie! Oi, Dickie! Come on, show a light—Dick-ie!!" No light, no sound. "Hullo, here's a paling loose. Think anybody'd dare go inside?" "It's trespassing. And there might be traps!" "Rot, it's against the law."

The pale creaked. Danger prickled at Pussy's spine, at Dominic's. Only one way to go for cover. Softly, softly, over the rim of the slope, his hand on her wrist, down the smooth-rough, needle-glazed, heat-ridged sides of the funnel, down into the pit, down among the cobwebs, down where the rats go. They slid down inch by inch on their bellies, feeling the way gingerly with outstretched toes, and holding by the tufts of coarse grass which had such a different texture in the dark. Right down into the uncomfortable oubliette at the bottom, by the invisible shatterings of the arched brickwork and the black holes which Pussy preferred not to remember. The darkness here had a smell, dry, musty, faintly rotten. It made their nostrils curl with repulsion and yet quiver with curiosity—like the vaults of the Castle

of Otranto, perhaps, or the family tomb of the
Baskervilles. They huddled together in it and
froze into stillness, until the stealthy crunching
of feet in the pine-silt had withdrawn again, afraid
to venture so far beyond the pales.

"How if they fall in?" breathed Pussy in
Dominic's ear, tremulous with giggles.

"Can't fall far—and we'll be under. Shut up!"

But the night, settling lower in its pillows,
breathing long and gently toward sleep, brought
no more echoes of pursuit down to them; and in
a few minutes they relaxed, and sorted out their
tangled legs from among the dirty trailers of
bramble and spears of discouraged grass.

"They've gone!"

"I think! But don't shout too soon. Give them
a minute or two more."

"Be damned!" said Pussy elegantly. "I want
to get out of here." She fumbled at the torch
again, and swore because as usual it refused to
light until she had almost broken her nail on it.

"Why, what's the matter with it here? Been in a
lot worse places." Dominic stretched and heaved
himself upright by the edges of brickwork, and
fragments came away in his fingers and all but
tumbled him down again. He groped, and
encountered dankness, the caving softness of
earth hidden from the sun, cool, dirty, unpleasing
opening of one of the holes. Strange how cold!
Touch the clay above in the open mounds, and it
warmed you even after dusk, but this involuntary
contact added to the shock of its recession the
shock of its tomblike, dead chill, striking up his
wrist, making the skin of his arm creep like

running spiders. He was glad that Pussy was busy stamping on his little vaunt, as usual, so that she failed to hear his minute gasp of disgust.

"Oh, yes! Old Tubby's study this morning, for instance—I heard all about it!"

Half his mind gathered itself to retort, but only half, and that uneasily. How could she have heard all about it? Nobody knew all about it except the headmaster and Dominic himself, and he was jolly sure neither of these two had told her anything. And anyhow, the old boy had been in quite a good mood, and nothing had resulted except a lecture and a few footling lines, which he hadn't yet done. Oh, hell! Silly old-maid things, lines! The hole went back and back; he stretched his arm delicately, and couldn't feel any end to it. Filthy the cold earth felt in there. And there was something, his fingertips found it, something suddenly soft, with a horrid, doughy solidity inside it, soft, clinging to his fingers, like fur, perhaps, or feathers. He drew his hand back, and the soft bulk followed it a little, shifting uneasily among the loosened soil. Not alive, not a rat. It just rolled after the recoil of his hand because he had disturbed it, but it was small and dead. Rabbit? But not quite that feel. Spines in the softness, longer here. Feathers—a tapering tail.

"Something in here," he said, drawing his hand out; and his voice had the small awareness which could stop Pussy in mid-scramble, wherever they happened to be at the time, and make her turn the beam of the suddenly compliant torch upon his face. He was a little streaked and dusty, but not so bad, on the whole; it took a second and longer look to discover how far his mind had sprung from hide-and-seek. He sniffed at his own hand, and wrinkled his nose with shock. A clinging odor of rottenness prodded him in the pit of his vulnerable stomach, but his inquisitiveness rose above that. "Wait a minute! Shine the light this way again. There *is* something there. I believe it's a bird—"

He was groping again, more deliberately this time, with his eyes screwed up, as if that would prevent his nose from working since he had no free hand with which to hold it, and his teeth tight clenched, as if through their grip was produced the power which propelled him.

Pussy said, sitting firmly halfway up the slope, where she had turned to stare at him: "Don't be so daft! What would a bird be doing down a hole like that?"

"Daft yourself! He's just lying there, dead, because someone put him there, that's what. And why did somebody put him there? Why, because he didn't want to be caught carrying him— Wait a minute, I can't— There are two of 'em! What d'you know? A brace!"

"Pheasants!" said Pussy, leaping to catch up with him, and came slithering to his side again, a minor avalanche of clay dust and pine-rubbish accompanying her.

They were not, when he drew them out into the light of the torch, immediately recognizable as anything except a draggled and odorous mess, fouled with cobwebs and earth. He held them away from him, swiveling on his heels to get to windward, even where there was no apparent wind; and his stomach kicked again, more vigorously, but he would not pay attention to it. A nasty, mangled mess, with broken feathers, and soiled down. Rat-gnawed, too, but the wobbling light failed to show Pussy the traces. Dominic's spine crawled, but the charm was already working, his tightening wits had their noses to the ground. He reared his face, taking a blind line across country, clean over Pussy's stooped, inquisitive head. The fence only a few yards away, the hole in the fence, the tongue of waste land, the clay bowl under the outflow of Webster's well. He himself had said, only ten minutes ago: "I never thought it was quite so near." And how long did it take for birds to get—like these were? In a hole in the earth like this, with rats for company, would—he calculated with lips moving rapidly, tantalizing Pussy unreasonably—would ten, eleven days produce this stage of unpleasantness? He thought it might. He shifted the draggled corpses uneasily, shaking his fingers as if he could get the unclean feeling off them that way. Must tell Dad, as soon as possible. It might not be anything, but then it might, and how was he to be sure? And he hadn't even been looking for them, they were honestly accidental. Except that he would certainly be told, for Pete's sake keep away from that place!

"Well, some poacher got disturbed," said Pussy easily, "and thought it best not to be caught with the goods on him, so he dumped them in here. That's simple enough. If he used this ground he'd know all about the holes already. Maybe he's hidden things there before. Anyhow, what's the song and dance about? Ugh! Put them back, and let's get out of here. They're horrid!"

"Well, but," said Dominic, leaning into the thread of wind which circled the funnel of the pit, and surveying his finds out of the wary corners of large eyes, "well, but if a poacher just put them there because he thought he was going to meet somebody who could get him into trouble—maybe the owner, or the keeper—well, he put them away pretty carefully so they'd stay hidden until he could come and collect them, didn't he? He wouldn't want to waste his trouble."

This she allowed to be common sense, jutting her underlip thoughtfully. They had forgotten the very existence of Sandy and his partner by this time.

"Well, then, why didn't he collect them afterwards? Look, you can see for yourself, they've been there days and days. He must have meant to go back for them when the coast was clear. Why hasn't he been?"

"I don't know. There could be any amount of reasons. He may have been ill ever since, or something."

"Or dead!" said Dominic.

The minute the idea and the word were out of him the darkness seemed a shade darker about them, and the malodorous carrion dangling from his reluctant hand a degree more foul. Dead birds couldn't hurt anyone, but they could suggest other deaths, and bring the night leaning heavily over the pit-shaft in the wood, leaning down upon two suddenly shivering young creatures who observed with quite unusual unanimity the desirability of getting to some cleaner, brighter place with all haste.

"Outside," said Pussy uneasily, as if they had been shut in, "we could see them better. It won't be quite dark yet."

"We don't want the others to know," said Dominic, suddenly recalling the abandoned game. "We'll go the other way, down the little quarry. They'll soon give us up and go home. Or you could go and tell them I—tell them my mother wanted me, or something—while I go straight home with these."

Pussy turned at the rim of the pit to give him a hand, because he had only one free for use. She took him by the upper arm in a grip lean and hard as a boy's, and braced back, hoisted his weight over the edge. Waves of nauseating, faint rottenness came off the drooping bodies. She had no real wish to see them, by this or any light; she reached the open and still kept going, only drawing in a little to be just ahead of Dominic's other shoulder.

"Oh, they'll go home, they'll be all right. I'm coming with you." As they crawled through the swinging pale she asked: "Do you really think they were that German's pheasants? Dominic, really do you?"

"Yes, really I do. Well, look down there the way we came, it's only a few minutes to the path by the well, to the—to where he was. And unless it was someone who was dead, wouldn't he go back for his birds? Some time before a whole week there *must* be a chance. After he hid them so carefully, too, because they weren't just

227

dropped in the bushes, he wasn't in as big a hurry as all that. He just wanted them out of his pockets, because there was someone he heard in the woods, and he wanted to be able to pop through the fence and march off down by the well quite jauntily, nothing on him even if it was the keeper, and if he got awkward."

"But we don't know that Helmut had been poaching," she objected.

"Well, we know he was as near as that to the preserves. And don't you remember, the lining of his tunic was slit across here, to make an extra-large pocket inside. Why should he want a pocket like that, unless it was to put birds or rabbits in? And where we found him—well, it's so near."

They skirted the high hedge, and took the right-hand path down into the small overgrown quarry, instead of bearing left toward the all-significant well. What was left of the light seemed warm and kind and even bright upon them, greenish, bluish, with leaves, with sky, and the soft distant glimmering of stars almost invisible in the milky blue. Not even a hint of frost now, only the cool regretful afterbreath of summer, mild and quiet, ominous with foreshadowings, sweet with memories. Clamor of voices from the slackening game they had left came after them with infinite remoteness.

"He put them there until the coast was clear," said Pussy, hushed of voice, "and he went slipping back on to the lawful path, bold as brass. What harm am I doing? Because he heard someone coming in the wood, you think? It might

228

have been the keeper? Or it might have been anyone, almost—"

"Yes. But by the well, going along looking all innocent, as you said, he met someone. And that was the person who killed him. So he never had the chance to go back for them."

Once out of the closed, musty, smothering darkness, where panic lay so near and came so lightly, they could discuss the thing calmly enough, and even step back from it to regard its more inconvenient personal implications. As, for instance, the unfortunate location of the pit where the discovery had been made.

"Of course," said Pussy, "the very first thing he'll ask you will be where did you find them? And you'll have to admit we were trespassing."

"He won't have to ask me," said Dominic, on his dignity. "It'll be the very first thing I shall tell him."

"Well, I suppose that's the only thing to do—but I don't suppose it'll get you off."

"Can't help that," said Dominic firmly. "This is more important than trespassing. And anyhow, everybody trespasses sooner or later, you can do it even without knowing, sometimes." But to be honest, of course, he reflected within himself, that was not the way he had done it. However, he was not seriously troubled. What is minor crime, when every official mind is on a murder case?

They hurried down through the narrow, birch-silvered path which threaded the quarry, and into the edges of the village where the first street-lights were already shining. Horrid whiffs of decay tossed behind them on the small breezes of coolness which had sprung up with the night. They let themselves in unobtrusively by the scullery door of the police-station, and sidled into the office to see if George was there. But the office was empty. George had to be fetched away from his book and his pipe in front of the kitchen fire, and brought in by an incoherent Pussy, almost forcibly by the hand, to view the bodies, which by this time were reposing on an old newspaper upon his desk, under the merciless light of a hundred-watt bulb. The effect was displeasing in the extreme, and Dominic's self-willed inside began to kick again, even before he saw his father's face of blank consternation halted on the threshold.

"What in the name of creation," said George, "do you two imagine you've got there?"

2

Halfway through the explanation, which was a joint affair, and therefore took rather longer than it need have done, Bunty began to be suspicious that she was missing something, and as the parties involved were merely Dominic and Pussy, she had no scruples about coming in to demand her share in their revelations. Besides, there was a chance that someone would be needed to hold the balance between her husband and her son, who on this subject of all subjects still obstinately refused to see eye to eye. The note of appeasement, however, was being sounded with quite unusual discretion as she entered.

"It was an absolute accident," Dominic said, "honestly it was. We weren't even thinking about that business, and it was only one chance in a thousand we ever found them. If the pale hadn't been loose we shouldn't ever have gone in, and if Pussy's torch hadn't been phoney I shouldn't have grabbed off in the dark for a hold in the grass, and put my hand down the hole. It was just luck. But we couldn't do anything except bring them to you, once we'd got them, could we?"

"You'd no business there in the first place," said George, heavily paternal. "Serve you right if Briggs had caught you and warmed your jacket for you. Next time I hope he does."

Bunty remembered certain events of George's schooldays; but she did not smile, or only within her own mind. Dominic grinned suddenly, and said: "Oh, well—occupational risks! But old Briggs isn't so hot on running."

"I'm surprised at you, Pussy," pursued George, not strictly truthfully. "I thought you had more sense, even if he hasn't."

There was really no need to argue with him, for his mind was all the time on the dingy draggle of nastiness obtruding its presence from the desk. Thirteen days now! It could be. And the minute fluff they had harvested from Helmut's tunic-lining came easily back to mind. On his last evening he had been observed on the edge of the preserves, his body had been found not a hundred yards from the fence, and at about ten o'clock,

231

melting into the shadows with the typical coyness of his kind, Chad Wedderburn had caught a glimpse of what he could only suppose to be a poacher. And among the miscellaneous small belongings found in Helmut's pockets—

"He had a torch, didn't he?" said Dominic, his eyes fixed insatiably on his father's face. "A big, powerful one. I remember—"

Yes, he had had a torch on him, big and powerful, dragging one pocket of his tunic out of line. Trust Dom to remember that! Found practically on the spot, equipped for the job, and dead just about as long as these birds; and as the kids had pointed out, what poacher but a dead poacher would leave his bag cached until it rotted on him? He supposed he had better call at the Harrow, instead of making straight for the pit.

"Can we come back with you?" asked Dominic eagerly. "We could take you straight to it—and there are several holes down there, you might not know which it was."

"It's almost bedtime now," said Bunty, frowning upon the idea. "And Io will wonder where Pussy is."

"Oh, Mummy, there's nearly half an hour yet, we came away before any of the others. And we'd come straight back, really, it wouldn't take long."

"Nobody'll be worried about me," said Pussy, elaborately casual. "I'm not expected home till half-past nine."

"Better have a look on the spot," said George to Bunty. "I'll send them straight back as soon as they've told their tale."

The trouble was, of course, that he would and

did do precisely that. As soon as they had collected Charles Blunden from the farmhouse, with brief explanations, and led their little party to the pit in the pinewoods, and indicated the exact repellent hollow from which they had removed the pheasants, the adults, of course, had done with them. Pussy expected it, Dominic knew it. In the pitchy, resiny darkness, even with lights, expressions were too elusive to be read accurately, but dismissal was in the very stance of George, straightening up in the heel of the pit to say briskly:

"All right, you two, better cut home now. Unless," he added unkindly, putting ideas into Charles's easygoing head, "Mr. Blunden wants to ask any questions about fences before we let you out of it."

"Eh?" said Charles, with his arm rather gingerly down the dank hiding-hole, and only a corner of his mind on what had been said, just enough to prick up to the sound of his own name.

"Violating your boundaries, you realize— that's how the thing began. Knock their heads together if you feel like it, I'll look the other way."

"It was my fault," said Dominic, demurely sure of himself. "We only wanted somewhere new to hide, and we didn't mean to go far or do any harm. And anyhow, we did come straight back and own up to it as soon as we found the birds. You're not mad, are you, Mr. Blunden?" He daren't be, of course, even if he wanted to; Pussy wasn't Io's young sister for nothing. Io might call her all the little devils in creation on her own account, but it wouldn't pay Charles

Blunden to start the same tune; families are like that. So Dominic trailed his coat gracefully close to impudence, and felt quite safe. They were about to be thrown out of the conference, in any case, so he had nothing to lose.

"Oh, that's all right," said Charles, disappointingly not even very interested. "A fence like that asks to be violated. Not that I'm advising you to try it while Briggs is about, mind you, or even to let my father spot you at it. But there's no harm done this time. Just watch your step, and we'll say no more about it."

"And we did right to go straight back and report, didn't we?" pursued Dominic, angling for a reentry into council through Charles, since George certainly wouldn't buy it. "I say, do you think it was really like we worked it out? Do you think—"

George said: "Git! We want to talk, and it's high time you two went home to bed. You're observant, intelligent, helpful and reliable people, no doubt, in fact almost everything you think you are; but there isn't a thing more you can do for us here. Beat it!"

"I suppose it's something to be appreciated," said Pussy sarcastically, as they threaded their way out of the wood by the slender gleam of the torch, and went huffily but helplessly home.

3

"Nothing more there, I'm certain," said Charles, after twenty minutes of combing the pit and its spidery caverns inch by inch with torches. "Try it again by daylight, of course, but I think there'll be nothing to show for it. It looks as if the kids weren't far out."

"Oh, that was a deliberate cache, all right," agreed George, frowning round at the queer gaunt shadows and lights of the young tree trunks, erect and motionless, circling them like an audience. "Things don't fall into sidelong holes like that, even if they were dropped over the edge of the pit in a hurry. They were meant to be well out of sight, and I must say only the merest freak seems to have unearthed them again. There's only one thing worries me—"

"About the Helmut theory? I thought it was pretty sharp of your boy to have jumped to it like he did. Why, what's the snag? I can't see any holes in it."

"I wouldn't go so far as to say it is a hole. People do such queer things, and do the simplest things so queerly. But in my experience poachers *don't* go to such elaborate shifts to hide their birds, even when they have to ditch them for safety. This place is isolated enough to begin with, and here's the pit, ready to hand, what's wrong with just dropping the birds in one of the hollows under the hang of the grass? Ninety-nine fellows in a hundred would."

"Just wanted to make doubly sure, I suppose."

"He didn't expect to be leaving 'em a week or more, I take it. It's long odds the things would have been safe as houses like that for the time they'd have had to wait."

"Still, if he had to scramble down into the pit in any case to find a hiding-place, why not go the whole hog? And anyhow, isn't the very thoroughness of the thing an extra argument for thinking it was Helmut who planted them? He being a poacher rather out of our experience than in it, and given to habits of Prussian thoroughness? Where another bloke might favor rapid improvisation and a bit of risk, I should think he might easily have proceeded with this sort of methodical mak sikker. Makes sense, doesn't it?"

"Maybe, if you put it like that. But it still looks farfetched to me! Let's get out!" he said, digging a toe into the crumbling clay slope. "Nothing more we can do here."

They ploughed their way to the upper air, which was scarcely lighter by reason of the enclosing trees; and on the rim of the pit George turned to look down once again into the deep, dismal scar. "How far back does this date? It's not one of your father's wartime operations—trees are too well-grown for that by—what, ten years? Must be that at least."

"Oh, yes, this patch is one of the first, though mind you these beastly conifers do give a false impression, they're such mushrooms. Can't remember the exact year, but late in the 1920s it must have been. He had all this mound leveled and planted. But you can see it wasn't a very good job they did on the pit-shafts." His own voice, regretful and even a little bitter, sounded to him for a moment like an echo of Chad's. He wasn't succumbing to Chad's persuasions after all, was he? But the old man could have made a job of it, while he was about it. And if he was alert enough in the 1920s to level a mound for his own preserves, why couldn't he see that he owed the village a bit of leveling, too, for all the chaos the get-rich-quick mining grandfather had created? Still, it was easy to be both wise and enlightened twenty years after the event. They were of their kind and generation, no better but anyhow no worse. "With proper protection on replacing and leveling," he said, almost apologetically, "some of these ruined villages could still have been rich. Why don't we think in time?"

"Up to a point," said George dryly, turning on his heel from the unpleasing prospect, "they did."

"Up to the point of private preserves they did, but not an inch beyond."

"Strictly on that principle," said George, "the century proceeded."

"The old boy's late operations were all out on the heath patches the other side of the house," said Charles. "Near the boundary, actually. The opencast gang will be ripping them all up again, *if* they decide it's worth their while after all these disastrous expenses they've run their noses into recently, and *if* they win the dispute."

He didn't sound to George as if he cared very

much either way about that, or indeed knew very clearly what he did want. They walked singly through the close-set trees, Charles leaning the torch-beam to the ground for George's benefit. "We didn't even make a good job of the planting," he said sadly. "I'm all for mixed woods myself, these quick payoffs with conifers play hell with the soil." They came out from the warm, cloying stomach of the wood, where the soft darkness beyond seemed almost light by comparison, a striped light through the pales. "This time," said Charles, "I really think you should leave by the gap in the fence. See for yourself!" He groped along the pales until the loose one swung in his hand. "Here we are! I must get that seen to right away. No need to encourage 'em!"

George, looking through the film of trees beyond the fence, could trace at a little distance the cleared line of the path by which Chad Wedderburn had plotted his angry course that night of the death. Somewhere about here he had heard and glimpsed, if his tale was true, the figure of a man, presumed to be a poacher, withdrawing himself rapidly and modestly into the shadows. Could it have been Helmut Schauffler himself? Last heard of previously at about ten to nine, about five hundred yards from this same spot, very pleased with himself, singing to himself in German. Sitting, waiting for the spirit to move him to the next mischief. Or perhaps for the night to fall.

If the shy figure seen at somewhat after ten had really been his, the time during which his death might have taken place was narrowed to slightly under one hour; and Chris Hollins, marching home at last about half-past ten, was almost certainly absolved from any shadow of guilt. For though it did not, as George had said, take three-quarters of an hour to reach the Harrow from Hollins's farm, it did take at least twenty-five minutes to do the journey even in the reverse direction, which was mostly downhill. And the time of Hollins's arrival did not rest solely on his wife's evidence, for there was the carrier's cottage at the bottom of his own drive, and the carrier who had leaned over his gate and exchanged good-nights with him. At twenty-past ten, he said, and he was a precise man. If he was right, and if the shadow among the shadows was Helmut, then Chris Hollins could not have killed him.

"Not a very promising line, after all, I suppose," said Charles, sounding, as everyone did, quite cheerful at this reflection. In a way, no one wanted the wretched case solved; in another way no one would have any peace, and nothing would ever be normal again, until it was solved. "Still, you never know. Some witness may turn up yet who'll really have something to say. Anyhow, if there's anything I can do when you come up again, you know where to find me."

George went home to Bunty very thoughtfully It was all *if*, whichever way he turned. *If* Chad's elusive figure at ten had been Helmut, Chris Hollins was out of it. *If*, of course, Chad was telling the truth. And that was something about which no one could be sure. His whole attitude was so mad that it was quite conceivable he had not only seen him, but knocked him on the head and rolled him into the brook, too, and come back to tell half of the tale, when he need have mentioned none. It sounded crazy, but Chad was hurling provocations into the teeth of fate in precisely this bitter-crazy manner. Or, of course, he could be telling the whole truth, in which case it became increasingly desirable to identify his poacher. Most probably some canny regular who had nothing to do with the business, but still he might know something. See Chad again, in case he could add anything to his previous statement. See all the poachers he could think of; business is business, but murder is murder.

And did it necessarily follow from the (hypothetical) clearing of Chris Hollins, that Gerd was equally innocent? George looked at it from all directions, and could only conclude that it did not. Chris had been home shortly before half-past ten, just as he said, because Bill Hayley had seen and talked to him. But there was no proof that Gerd had been there to meet him, except her husband's word. And what was that worth where her safety was concerned? What would you expect it to be worth?

Exhausted with speculation, George's mind went back and forth between Hollins's household, Jim Tugg, Chad Wedderburn, with the uneasy wraiths of Jim Fleetwood and many like him periodically appearing and disappearing between. There was no end to it. And the mere new fact that Helmut had added poaching to his worse offenses did not greatly change the picture. All it did was slightly affect his actual movements on the night of his death, and perhaps give an imperfect lead on the time of his exit, since it argued that he had been alive and active after the darkness grew sufficiently positive for his purposes. In George's mind the death drew more surely into the single hour between ten and eleven; but stealthily, and he feared unjustifiably.

Bunty met him in the office, and indicated by a small gesture of her head and a rueful smile that Dominic was just having his supper in the kitchen. She closed the door gently in between, and said with a soft, wry gravity: "Your son, my dear George, is seriously displeased with you."

"I know," said George. "I don't blame him, poor little beast. He finds 'em, I appropriate 'em. But this time, as a matter of fact, he isn't missing a thing, there's nothing to miss. Only a lot of useless speculations that go round in circles and get nowhere."

"Then you can afford to talk to him, and at any rate pretend to confide in him a little. Now's the time, when you can do it with a straight face." She took his cap from him, laid it aside, and reached up suddenly to kiss him. "I wouldn't trust you to try it when you really had anything on your mind, because he'd see through you like glass. But if there's nothing to tell, even you can say so and remain opaque. Let's go and be nice to him, shall we? Or he'll only imagine all sorts of lurid discoveries."

"That's all I'm doing," said George bitterly. But he went, and he was nice. Somebody might as well get some satisfaction out of the incident, if it was any way possible; it was precious little George was getting.

4

It was Constable Cooke who said it, after they had been over and round and through every fact and every supposition they possessed between them. They had it now in positive terms that not only had Helmut's tunic-lining retained rubbings of down from the pheasants' feathers, but the pheasants' feathers had acquired and guarded, through their long repose in the clay of the pit, distinct traces of the fluff from Helmut's tunic-lining. Leaving no doubt whatever that these were the very birds, and very little that they had been planted in precisely the same way, and probably for the same reasons, as their discoverer had supposed. That was something at any rate, though it led them no nearer to a solution. They were left counting over their possibilities again, reducing them to the probabilities, which seemed to be four, and weighing these one against another to find the pennyweight of difference in their motives and opportunities. And Constable Cooke, who was light of heart because he was less surely involved, said what George had refrained from saying.

"Among four who had equal reasons for wanting him dead, and equal opportunities for killing him," he said brightly, "personally I'd plump for one of the two who're known to have had enough experience to be good at it. A sweater, after all, is most likely to have been knitted by someone who can knit."

George sat looking at him for a moment in heavy silence, jabbing holes in the blotting-pad of his desk with a poised and rapier-pointed pencil, until the over-perfected tip inevitably broke off short. He threw it down, and said glumly: "You may as well elaborate that, now you've said it."

Cooke sat on the corner of the desk, swinging a plump leg, and looking at his sergeant with the bland, blond cheerfulness which filled George sometimes with a childish desire to shock him; like a particularly smug round vase which no right-minded infant could resist smashing. He would have been quite a nice lad, if only God had given him a little more imagination.

"Well, it's obvious enough, isn't it? There's Mrs. Hollins, admittedly she was being pushed to extremes, and you can never be sure then what a person can and can't do. But I'm not professing to be sure, I'm only talking about probabilities. There's a woman who never hurt anybody or anything in her life, as far as we know, and never showed any desire to; and even if she got desperate enough to try, it would be a bit of a fluke if she made such a good job of it, the first time, wouldn't it? And then old Chris, how much more likely is it with him? I bet he never killed anything bigger than a weasel or a rabbit in his life. A more peaceful chap never existed. Not to mention that he had less time for the job than some of the others. But when you come to the other two, my word, that's a different tale!"

"The other two, however," said George, "had much less solid motives for murder. I'm not saying they had none, but there wasn't the urgency, or the personal need. And I'm inclined to think, with Wedderburn, that while people will certainly do desperate things for the sake of other people, when it comes to it they'll do far more desperate ones for their own sakes."

"Well, but according to that, even, they had as much motive as Hollins had. More, because they had more imagination to be aware of it. If Hollins might kill for his wife's sake, so might Tugg, if you ask me, he thinks the world of her. And Wedderburn had a grudge on Jim Fleetwood's account, as well as a general grudge that a German, and a near-Nazi at that, should be able to live here under protection while he stirred up trouble for everybody in the village."

"Very natural," said George, "and common to a great many other people who'd come into contact with Helmut round these parts. You could count me in on that grudge."

"Well, yes, most of us, I suppose. But in different degrees. And still you're left with this great difference, that Tugg and Wedderburn have both had, as you might say, wide experience in killing. They knew how to set about it, easy as knocking off a chicken. And even more, they'd got used to it. Most people, even if they could bring 'emselves to the actual act, would shrink from the idea. But those two lived with the idea so long that it wouldn't bother them."

George continued to stare at him glumly, and said nothing. The door of the office, ajar in the

244

draught from the window, creaked a little, naggingly, like a not-quite-aching tooth. It was evening, just after tea, and faintly from the scullery came the chink of crockery, and the vague, soft sounds of Bunty singing to herself.

"Well, it's reasonable, isn't it?" said Cooke.

"Reasonable, but not, therefore, necessarily true. You could argue on the same lines that people in London got used to the blitz, and so they did, but the reaction against it was cumulative, all the same. It was in the later stages they suffered most, not from the first few raids. Long acquaintance can sicken you, as well as getting you accustomed to a thing."

"Yes, but in a way this death was like a hangover from the war, almost a part of it. You can easily imagine a soldier feeling no more qualms about rubbing out Helmut than about firing a machine gun on a battlefield. For years it had been their job, a virtue, if you come to think of it, to kill people like Helmut. And it was a job they were both pretty good at, you know—especially Wedderburn, if all the tales are true."

George thought what he had been trying not to think for some time, that there was something in it. Not as much as Cooke thought, perhaps, but certainly something. In time of war countries fall over themselves to make commandos and guerrillas of their young men, self-reliant killers who can slit a throat and live off a hostile countryside as simply as they once caught the morning bus to their various blameless jobs. But to reconvert these formidable creations afterwards is quite another matter. Nobody ever gave much thought to that, nobody ever does until their recoil hits the very system which made and made use of them. Men who have learned to kill as a solution for otherwise insoluble problems in wartime may the more readily revert to it as a solution for other problems as desperate in other conditions. And logically, thought George, who has the least right of any man living to judge them for it? Surely the system which taught them the art and ethics of murder to save itself has no right at all. The obvious answer would be: "Come on in the dock with us!"

And yet he was there to do his best for a community, as well as a system, a community as surely victims as were the unlucky young men. And the best might have to be the destruction of one victim for the sake of the others. But he knew, he was beginning to feel very clearly, where the really guilty men were to be found, if Jim Tugg or Chad Wedderburn had committed murder.

"So your vote goes to the schoolmaster, does it?" he asked, stabbing the broken point of the pencil into the wood until powdered graphite flaked from its sides. The door went on creaking, more protestingly because the outer door had just opened, but he was too engrossed to remark it.

"Well, look at his record! It's about as wild a war story as you could find anywhere, littered with killings." Cooke, who had not suffered the reality, saw words rather than actualities, and threw the resultant phrases airily, like carnival balloons which could not be expected to do any harm. "He must be inured to it by now, however much he was forced into it by circumstances to begin with. After all, to a fellow like Wedderburn, who's seen half the continent torn into bloody pieces, what's one murder more or less to make a fuss about?"

Dominic's entering footsteps, brisk in the corridor outside the open door, had crashed into the latter part of this pronouncement too late to interrupt it short of its full meaning. Too late Cooke muttered: "Look out! The ghost walks!" There he was in the doorway, staring at them with his eyes big and his mouth open, first a little pale, and then deeply flushed. George, heaving himself round in his chair, said resignedly but testily: "Get out, Dom!" but it was an automatic reaction, not too firmly meant, and Dom did not get out. He came in, indeed, and pushed the door to behind him with a slam, and burst out:

"Don't listen to him, he's crazy, he's got it all wrong! Chad Wedderburn *isn't* like that!"

"Now, nobody's jumping to any conclusions," said George gently, aware of a vehemence which was not to be dismissed. "Don't panic because you hear a view you don't like, it's about the five hundredth we've discussed, and we're not guaranteeing any of 'em!"

"Well, but you were listening to him! And it's such a lot of damned rubbish—" he said furiously. His hazel eyes were light yellow with rage, and his tongue falling over the words in its fiery haste.

"Dominic!" said George warningly.

"Well, so it is damned rubbish! He knows nothing about old Wedderburn, why should he go around saying such idiotic things about him?

247

If that's how the police work, just saying a man was a soldier five years ago, so this year killing somebody comes easy to him—I think it's *awful*! I bet you hang all the wrong people, if you've got many Cookes! I bet—"

"Dominic!" George took him by the shoulders and shook him sharply. "Now, let's have no more of it!"

"You listened to him," said Dominic fiercely, "you ought to listen to me. At least I do know Mr. Wedderburn, better than either of you do!"

"Calm down, then, and stop your cheek, and you'll get a better hearing." He gave him another small, admonishing shake, but his hands were very placid, and his face not deeply disapproving. "And just leave out the damns," he said firmly, "they don't make your arguments any more convincing."

"Well, all right, but he made me mad."

"So we gathered," said Cooke, still complacently swinging his leg from the corner of the desk, and grinning at Dominic with impervious good humor. "I never knew you were so fond of your beaks, young Dom."

"I'm not! He's not *bad*! I don't like him all that much, but he's decent and fair, anyhow. But I don't see why you should just draw farfetched conclusions about him when you don't even know him beyond just enough to speak to in the street."

"And you do? Fair enough! Go on, tell us what you think about him."

"Well, he *isn't* like what you said. It went just the opposite way with him. In the war he got pushed into the position where he had to learn to live like you said, because there wasn't any other way. And he did jolly good at it, I know, but he *hated* it. All the time! He only got so good at it because he had to—to go right through with it to get out, if you know what I mean. But he just *hated* it! I don't believe anything could make him do anything like that again. Not for any reason you could think of, not to save his life. It's because he learned so much about it, because he knows it inside-out, that he wouldn't ever bring himself to touch it, I'm absolutely sure."

"He may talk that way," said Cooke easily, "but that doesn't necessarily prove anything."

"He doesn't talk that way. He acts that way. Well, look what happened when he came home! The British Legion wanted him to join, and he wouldn't. He said he was only a soldier because he was conscripted, and it was time we forgot who'd been in uniform and who hadn't, and stopped making differences between them, when they'd most of them had about as much choice as he had. And at school some of the fellows tried to get him to talk about all those things he'd done, and he wouldn't, he only used to tell us there was nothing admirable in being more violent than the other fellow, and nothing grand about armies or uniforms, and the best occupation for anyone who'd had to fight a war was making sure nobody would ever have to fight another. He said fighting *always* represents a failure by *both* sides. He said that to me, the day I started a fight with Rabbit. He was always down on hero-worship, or military things—any fellows

249

who tried to suck up to him because of his record, he was frightfully sarcastic with them at first, and then he got sort of grave and sad instead, because he isn't usually sarky. But he always squashes those fellows if they try it on."

"Some of those who value their own achievements most," said George, with serious courtesy, and looking him steadily in the eye, "also resent being fawned upon publicly."

"Yes, but I think not when it's that kind of achievements, really, because the kind of man who loves being a hero, and getting decorated, and all that—well, don't you think he has to be a bit *stupid*, too?—kind of blunt in the brain, so he doesn't see through all the bunk? Mostly they *love* being fussed over, so they must be a bit thick. And old Wedderburn isn't stupid, whatever he may be."

George looked at his son, and felt his own heart enlarged and aching in him, because they grow up, because their intelligences begin to bud and branch, to be separate, to thrust up sturdily to the light on their own, away from the anxious hand that reaches out to prop them. Even before their voices break, the spiritual note has broken, odd little rumblings of maturity quake like thunder under the known and guarded treble. Little vibrations of pride and sadness answer somewhere in the paternal body, under the heart, in the seat of shocks and terrors and delights. My son is growing up! Bud and branch, he is forward, and resolute, and clear. It will be a splendid tree. This is the time for all good parents to try their mettle, because the most difficult thing in life to learn is that you can only retain people by letting them go. George looked at Dominic, and smiled a little, and elicited an anxious but confiding smile in return.

"That's quite a point," he said. "No, he isn't stupid, and he doesn't like adulation, I'm sure of that. D'you want to tell us about that row you had over the fight? It might explain more than a lot of argument."

"I don't mind. It was funny, really," said Dominic with a sudden glimmering grin, "because it was about him, only he didn't know it. He turned out such a mild sort of beak, you see, old Rabbit started throwing his weight about and saying he didn't believe he'd done any of the things he was supposed to have done, and it was all a pack of lies about his adventures in the war, and all that. Well, I didn't care whether old Wedderburn wanted to get any credit for all those things or not, but I didn't see why Rabbit should be allowed to go about saying he was a liar. Because Wedderburn isn't sham, anyhow, that's the biggest thing about him. So we argued a bit about it, and then I hit Rabbit, and we didn't have time to get any farther because old Wedderburn opened the window and called us in. He never jaws very much, just says what he means. He said what I told you, that fighting never settles anything, it's only a way of admitting failure to cope with things, and the only thing it proves is who has the most brawn and the least brain. He said it was always wrong short of a life-and-death matter, and anyhow, he just wouldn't stand for it. And then he said we'd say no more about it, if we'd both give him our word not to start the fight again.''

"And what did you say?" asked George, respectfully grave.

"Well, Rabbit said O.K. like a shot, of course he *would*! And I was a bit peeved, really, because you want time to think when you get something like that shot at you. So he sent Rabbit away; I thought that was a pretty good show. And I thought pretty hard, and I said I thought he was right, really, about fighting being a bad thing, but still he *had* fought. But he wasn't mad, he just said yes, but not over nothing, like us. And he said I had to make up my mind, and promise not to start scrapping over it again, or else! He'd never licked anybody, not since he came, but he told me straight he would this time, so I had to think frightfully fast, and maybe it wasn't such a bright effort. Only I couldn't see why *I* shouldn't be allowed to judge what was nothing and what wasn't, and I still couldn't see why Rabbit should call him a liar and a cheat, and get away with it. At least," he said honestly, "I could see that I couldn't exactly be *allowed* to judge, but I didn't see why I shouldn't *do* it, all the same. So I explained to him that I'd rather not make any promises, because I thought that I ought to decide for myself what was worth fighting for, and what wasn't.''

"And what did he say to that? Was he angry?"

"No, he— You know," said Dominic doubtfully, "I think he was *pleased*! It sounds awfully daft, but honestly, he looked at me as if he was. Only I can't think why, I expected him to be mad as the dickens, because it sounded fearful cheek, only it really wasn't meant to be. But I honestly *didn't* see how it could be right just to let somebody else make the rules for you, without making up your own mind at all."

"Did he agree with you?"

"Well, he didn't exactly say. He just said that when you've got to that stage of maturity, you have to go the next bit, whether you want to or not, and realize that in any society you have to be prepared to pay for the privilege of making up your own mind. I can't remember all the right words, but you get what he meant. He didn't seem a bit angry, but I knew he wouldn't let me off, and he was giving me a chance to back out. But I wasn't going to. So I said yes, all right, I *would* pay."

"And then he licked you," said George.

"Well, he had to, really, didn't he?" said Dominic reasonably.

"Wasn't that a bit illogical," suggested Cooke, with his hearty, good-natured, insensitive laugh, "for a bloke who'd just been preaching nonviolence?"

Dominic replied, but punctiliously to his father's look, not to Cooke who was in his black books: "No, I don't think so, really, because he had to make up his mind, too. If you see what I mean!"

"Yes," said George, "I see what you mean."

"So you see, don't you, that what Cooke was saying about him is just bunk? He didn't get used to it, it *sickened* him, only there just wasn't anything else then for him to do. And honestly, he's the last man in the place who could have done a murder—even that murder. Dad, don't make an awful mistake like that, will you?"

"I'll try not to," said George, softened and gentle with astonishment at seeing his son's face all earnest anxiety on his account. "Don't worry, Dom, I'll remember all you've told us. It's perfectly good evidence, and I won't lose sight of it. Satisfied?"

"Mmmm, I suppose so. You know, it's so easy to say things like Cooke was saying, but it isn't true. All kinds of fellows had to fight, thousands and thousands of them, but they were still just as much all kinds in the end, weren't they? I think it may have got easier for some, and harder and harder for others. And anyhow, you can't just lump people all together, like that." He flushed a little, meeting George's smile. "Sorry I swore! I was upset."

"That's all right. Going out again now?"

"Yes, I came to tell Mummy I might be a bit late, but I shall only be at the Harts'. Mr. Hart is picking the late apples, and they want to finish tonight, so a few extra hands—" For whom, thought George, there would be ample wages in kind at the end of the picking, even if they came only half an hour before the daylight began to fail.

"All right, I'll tell her. You cut along." And he watched him spring gaily through the door without a glance at Cooke, with whom he was still seriously annoyed.

An odd, loyal, disturbing, reassuring kid, sharp and sensitive to currents of thought and qualities of character. If he didn't like Chad Wedderburn "all that much," very decidedly he liked him in some degree, and that in itself was an argument. But the weakness of the evidence of a man's own mouth is that it often has two edges. Fighting never settles anything, cannot be right short of a life-and-death matter. But a man must and should be his own judge of what is and what is not a matter of life and death, because that is ultimately an issue he cannot delegate to any other creature. And having reached that stage of maturity, he must realize that in any society— because societies, state or school or church, exist to curb all the nonconforming into conformity— he must pay for the privilege. So far, if he had perfectly understood him, Chad Wedderburn.

Even Cooke was thinking along the same lines. He looked after Dominic with an indulgent smile, and said appreciatively: "Well, I hope the folks who don't like *me* all that much will stick up for me as nobly. Poor kid, he doesn't know what it all adds up to. Call your own tune, pay your own piper! Well, and what if he did just that? He allowed Dom the right to, you can bet he'd insist on the same rights for himself. What did he decide about Helmut, do you suppose? That it would be worth it?"

George said nothing. It could follow, but it need not follow, that was the devil of it. Only something else echoed ominously in his mind, the hot, reiterated note of Chad's revulsion from bloodshed, genuine, yes, too terribly genuine, but was it perhaps pitched in an unnatural key? Did it not sometimes sound like the prayers of a man's

255

mind for deliverance from his own body? Might not a man thus passionately denounce what he feared most of all in himself? A man who was wise enough and deep enough to dread his own facility in destruction, an adept whose skill terrified him. And then the last remote, unexpected case, argued over and over in the mind, where this dreaded efficiency in killing, held so fiercely in restraint, began to look once more legitimate, began to argue its right to a gesture almost of virtue.

"Call your own tune, pay your own piper!" said Constable Cooke, brightly. "Some merely get hammered, some get hanged. It's a matter for the individual whether he finds it worthwhile!"

VII

Treasure in the Mud

1

Pussy and Dominic were in the loft over the stables at the Shock of Hay, in the warm, clean, high roof, smelling of straw and fruit; they were polishing and wrapping the biggest, soundest apples for keeping until the spring, and laying them out on wooden trays slatted to let the air through. The picking was already done, and the great unsorted baskets of fruit lay below them in the horseless stables, keeping company with the car, and the lawn-mower, and all the garden tools. From time to time Dominic slid himself and his basket down through the trapdoor by the shaky stairs, and selected the finest to haul back with him into the loft. They were working so hard that they forgot to eat, and neglected to light their lantern until the light was almost gone. It was middle evening, the sky outside suddenly clouded, the air heavy as a sad cake.

The end of the long drought came in a puff of air and a thudding of heavy drops down the roof. When the thunder had spent itself the sweet green night would smell heavenly of fresh foliage; but first the noise and the downpour, the ominous drumroll of the earliest scud, and then the clouds opening, and the crashing, splattering fall.

Somebody caught in the garden, where the benches circled the chestnut tree, gave a squeak of protest and ran headlong for the stable door.

The two above heard the door crash back to the wall before a precipitate entry, and a gasping laugh, and quick breathing. Sounds came up to them with a strange, dark clarity, cupped and shielded and redoubled in the arch of the roof-beams. They went on peaceably wrapping, intent on finishing their job and earning their wages. Kneeling in the straw by the low shelves, they themselves made no sound.

A second person running, a sudden foot at the brick threshold, and a perceptible check. The rain streamed coolly, wildly, over the tiles of the roof, giving the voice from below a brook's moving but monotonous sound.

"Oh, it's you! I'm sorry—I'll go!" And he actually turned to go, his heel harsh on the gravel. Dominic and Pussy heard, and knew Chad Wedderburn's voice, but it hovered only in the borders of their consciousness, so occupied were they with their apples.

And the other one was Io, and Io instant in exasperation, bursting out after him angrily: "Come *back*! Good Lord, haven't you got *any* sense? Come out of it, and don't be a fool! I shan't give you the plague."

The slightest of scuffles indicated that she had proceeded beyond words, and unceremoniously hauled him back into shelter. They stood gasping, and shaking and slapping the rain from their clothes, and he said in a harsh, constrained voice: "Aren't you afraid you might take it from me?" But he made no second attempt to leave her. She must have looked formidably angry.

"What's the matter with you? Can't you even

act naturally for ten minutes, till the rain stops? Am I diseased, or something, that you take one look at me and run for your life? Don't be afraid, I'm going back to the house as soon as I can get there without being drowned on the way. You won't be bothered with me a minute longer than I can help."

Shrinking away from her in the shadows within the door, he stood drawn into himself hard, and said nothing; and in the moment of silence Dominic and Pussy looked at each other guiltily, stirred back from a world of nothing but apples to a situation they had not foreseen. In the greenish, watery gloom under the skylight, with the refractions of rain flowing across their faces like the deeps of the sea, they stared stilly at each other, and wondered silently what they ought to do. It was now or never. In the first minute you can cough loudly, or drop a tray, or kick over the watering-can, or burst into song, but after that it's too horribly obvious. And if the first minute passes and is away before you can clutch at it, there is absolutely nothing to be done except hold your breath, and pretend you are not there. To be sure, in other circumstances they would have nudged each other, and giggled, and made the most of it, but somehow it was immediately apparent that this was not the occasion for such behavior. The voices, both of them, had overtones which raised the blood to their cheeks hotly.

"I'm sorry you had to be marooned with such an uncongenial company." Such a tight, dark voice, a disembodied pain. "It could just as easily have been someone more pleasing. Charles, for instance!"

"Oh, lord!" groaned Io. "I expected that! Must you carry on like a bad-tempered child?"

"I hope to God," he said, "there are no children in any way resembling me. It would be better to put them away quietly if there are."

"How can you talk like that! I suppose you're half-tight," said Io viciously.

"Not even half. What's the use, when it doesn't take?"

And now it was palpably too late to do anything about it. There they were, crouching mouse-still in the loft, holding their breath with shock, and not even looking at each other any more, because it was as disturbing as looking into a mirror. It would be awful if the two below should ever find out that they had been overheard. It was awful having to sit here and listen, but it was far too late to move.

The voice resumed, corrosive and unnatural in the void quiet, under the liquid lash of the rain.

"I can't make you out. *I* call it cowardice, to carry on as if you had nothing to live for, as if you were crippled, or something, just because things don't fall into your hand. For God's sake, what happened to you during the war? You got the reputation of being able to stand up to anything, but it must have been a mistake."

"It was a mistake," he said harshly, "the worst I ever made. The intelligent people lay down, for good."

"You make me mad!" she said furiously.

"Moping like a sick cow, for want of your own way! And you haven't even the wits to see that if you're not careful, and don't pull yourself together, you could die yet. Do you *want* people to believe you're a murderer? The police think so already."

"Why not? I am—a hundred times over."

"Don't go on talking like that! What happened in the war wasn't your fault, and it's over. And anyhow, most people found your part of it rather admirable," she said indignantly.

"Admirable!" he said, in a soft, indrawn howl. "My good God almighty!"

"Well, I didn't invent your reputation. I can't help it if you don't like being a hero!"

"I don't like it!" he shouted hoarsely. "I loathe it! Don't insult me with it! I never want to hear it from you, whatever the damned herd choose to think. Hero! Oh, yes, it's a fine thing to be a hero!—to have the identity ripped clean out of you—to be violated—in the middle of your being—"

It was awful, frightening; his voice broke in a terrible ugly sound, and then there was just an almost-silence, full of a sort of heaving and struggling for breath, like a drowning man fighting to regain his footing. Dominic turned his face right away from Pussy's sight, and leaned hard against the shelves, because he was trembling. His inside felt hollow and molten-hot. His heart hurt him. He wanted to think that Chad was really a little drunk, but he didn't believe it. He wasn't very experienced, but he knew a true grief from a drunken one even by its sound. And now somebody was crying. Io was crying, very quietly and laboriously and angrily, muffling it in her hands and the shadows and an inadequate handkerchief. And the painful quaking of the air which emanated from Chad had suddenly stilled into a listening silence.

"Why are you crying? As you said, it's over. And if it wasn't, you've no reason to shed any tears over it—you find it admirable."

"I find you detestable," cried Io furiously.

"I know! You've made that quite plain." And after an uneasy moment of the rain's song he said with sour, grudging gentleness: "Don't cry, Io! It isn't worth it."

"I'm not crying! Go away! Get to hell out of here, and leave me alone!"

He seemed to hesitate a moment, and then the heel of his shoe rang violently on the threshold, and he ran lurching through the downpour away from her.

Instant upon his going, she began to cry in earnest, candidly and stormily in a long, diminishing outburst, until her tears and the thunderstorm ebbed together. She went out slowly, plashing mournfully across the gravel path starred with sudden pools, and in a few minutes the two in the loft could move and breathe again. They stirred and looked at each other with quick, evasive, scared glances.

"Wasn't it awful? If they'd heard us!"

"Awful!"

They relaxed, and sat trembling, stiff with bracing themselves in one position, all large, wild eyes in the green gloom under the skylight.

"I've been worrying about her," said Pussy, "for a long time. You know, it's true what she said—your father thinks it was him who did the murder. Doesn't he?"

"I don't know. I tried to tell him it was crazy, but I'm afraid he does think it. I know he's making an awful mistake."

"He jolly well mustn't make it, then!" said Pussy with fierce energy. "I'm not going to have my sister made miserable like that all her life, no fear I'm not. If nobody else will do anything about it, we've got to, Dom, that's all."

Dominic, a little puzzled and still shaken by the sudden and searing contact of other people's misery, blinked at her for a moment without understanding. "Well, but I thought your sister—I didn't know that she—everybody always said it was the other one. And she—well, she wasn't being exactly nice to him, was she?"

"Oh, use your loaf!" said Pussy impatiently. "He wasn't being exactly nice to her, but everybody knows he's stuck on her so bad it's half-killing him. What d'you think she was crying about? Of course he's the one! I've thought so for a long time. They wouldn't bother to fight if they weren't gone on each other, because there'd be nothing to fight about. But, Dom, what on earth are we going to do?"

"If only we could solve it ourselves," said Dominic wistfully.

"Well, couldn't we at least try? It doesn't seem as if anyone else is doing much about it, and somebody's got to."

"My father—" began Dominic, his hackles rising at once.

"Your father's a dear, and I know he's trying all he can, and listen, I'm too upset to argue with you. I'm only asking you, couldn't we try? It's awful when you think about people being so miserable. If only it wasn't for this business hanging over them, maybe they could act a little more sensibly, maybe it would come out right. But as things are, what chance have they got? Dom, let's at least try!"

"I'd like to," said Dominic, "I want to. But I'm trying to think. What is there we can do? We haven't got a clue. We don't know where to look for one. There's only the basin by the well, where we found *him*. And the pit where the pheasants were, but there's nothing there, the police have been over it with microscopes, practically. And we don't even know what we're looking for," he admitted despondently.

"If only we could find the weapon—or even a trace of it—"

"Well, there's only one thing we can do, and that's go over and over the ground inch by inch, for *anything*, anything at all. Anyhow, there's no harm in trying. Are you game?"

"Yes, of course I am. When shall we go? Tomorrow?"

"The sooner the better. I'll meet you there as soon as I've done my homework. I'll bring a really good torch. Anyhow, if there is anything there, this time we won't miss it." He looked at Pussy crouching on the floor among the straw, and was touched to see the bright scornful eyes blinking back tears. He knew they were only going on a wild-goose chase, he knew they might just as well start going through the Harrow stacks for the proverbial needle, but he wouldn't admit it, if the pretense could comfort Pussy. He clapped her on the shoulders, a hard, comradely clout. "It'll be all right in the end, old girl, you see if it isn't. We'll try tomorrow, and we'll go on trying till we jolly well get somewhere. We've got to get ourselves and everyone else out of this mess, and we're going to do it, too."

Pussy said: "You know, Dom—I know I go on about Io, sometimes, but she's really not bad. I—I *like* her!"

2

It rained heavily most of the night, and the thirsty earth drank madly, but still there was water to spare next day, lying in all the dimples of the road, and making a white slime of all the open clay faces on the mounds. By the time Dominic came home from school the clouds were all past, and the sky from east to west hung pale and faint and exhausted into calm.

Just when he wanted to rush his tea and his homework, and be away on the job in hand—though when it came to expecting any results from it he might have been regarded as a despairing optimist—Cousin John was at the house visiting, and without his mother, so that it inevitably followed that Dominic was expected to help to look after and amuse him. Not that young John was such a bad kid, really, but who could be bothered with him on this particular day? Dominic made an ungracious business of it, so much so that Bunty was a little hurt and put out at his behavior. He was usually an accommodating child. Still, she admitted his right to his off-days, like the rest of us, and good-humoredly, if a little coolly, relieved him of his charge as soon as she had washed up. Dominic rushed through his French, made a hideous mess of his algebra, and scuttled out at the back door in a terrible hurry, with George's best torch in his pocket. It wasn't that he expected to find anything, really, but there was somehow a satisfaction in furious activity, and, after all, if one raked around persistently enough, something might turn up. At least he had keyed himself to the attempt, and he meant to leave no blade of grass undisturbed between Webster's well and the Harrow fences.

This was the day on which the news went round Comerford that the Harrow appeal had been allowed. In view of the objections raised by the owner, the Ministry had decided not to proceed with the extension of the open-cast site, but to cut their losses and end their operations in Comerford at the Harrow borders. Nobody was much surprised. The Blundens almost always got their own way, and it wasn't to be expected, in view of what Comerford had yet seen of nationalized industries, that the new setup was going to alter the rule very much. It took more than a change of name to upset the equilibrium of

Selwyn Blunden when it was a case of manipulating authorities.

Dominic had heard, distractedly from behind a French prose extract, the discussion round the tea-table. He wasn't surprised, either; everyone had been saying for weeks that it would go that way, but somehow long delay raises disconcerting doubts far back in the mind, behind the façade of certainty. Every speculation always ended with: "But after all, you never know!" Well, now they did know, and that was done with. Now there was only one topic of conversation left in Comerford.

At the last moment, just as he was sliding out at the gate, Bunty called him back, and asked him to see John safely on to the bus for Comerbourne Bridge; which meant that he had to go all the way round by the green, and stand chafing for five minutes until the wretched bus arrived, instead of taking all the most convenient short cuts to his objective. But as soon as John was bundled aboard, off went Dominic by the fields and the lane and the quarry, heading by the longer but now more direct route for Webster's well.

He came to the stile in the rough ground outside the Harrow preserves, where the silvery green of birches fluttered against the background black of the conifers; and there was Charles Blunden sitting on the stile, with a shotgun on his arm and a brown-and-white spaniel between his feet. He was looking straight before him with mild, contemplative eyes, and he looked vaguely pleased with the contents of his own mind, and rather a long way off. But he smiled at Dominic when he came up, and said: "Oh, hullo, Dom! Made any more interesting discoveries yet?"

Dominic had walked off the remnants of his impatience and ill-temper, and grinned back quite cheerfully at him. "No, nothing new! Did you get any birds tonight?" He peered through the stile, and saw a brace dropped in the grass by the side of the path. The spaniel, sad-eyed, poked a moist nose into his palm; its brow was covered with raffish brown curls, and its front legs were splayed out drunkenly, spreading enormous feathered paws in the wet grass. It had a pedigree rather longer than its master's, and shelves of prizes, and rumor had it that he had refused fabulous sums for its purchase; but it was not in the least stuck-up. Dominic doubled its ears and massaged them gently in his fingers, and the curly head heeled over into his thigh heavy and lopsided with bliss.

"I heard," said Dominic, looking up into Charles's face, "about the result of the appeal. I bet you're glad it's settled, aren't you?"

"Settled? Ah!" said Charles absently. He grew a little less remote, his wandering glance settling upon Dominic thoughtfully. "Tell me, Dom, as an intelligent and unprejudiced person, what do you think of that business? What were the rights and wrongs of it? Don't mind me, tell me your opinion if it kills me."

"I hadn't exactly thought," said Dominic, taken aback.

"Neither had I, until the thing was almost settled. D'you know how it is, Dom, when you want a thing against pressure, and want it like

270

the dickens—and then the pressure's withdrawn, and you find you don't really want it, after all?"

"Oh, yes," said Dominic readily, "of course! But I don't—"

"Well, after all, we seem to have made all this fuss about twenty acres of second-rate pasture. It got to looking like the fattest agricultural land in the county to me, while the fight was on. What do you think we ought to have done? I'll bet you had an opinion one way or the other. If you didn't, you're the only person over the age of five in Comerford who didn't."

"Well, I don't know much about it," said Dominic doubtfully. "It does look an awful mess when the land's being worked, but the old colliers say the shallow pits made a worse mess in the end. And it's all shallow coal, isn't it? So if it's ever going to be got at all, it's got to be one way or the other, hasn't it? It seems almost better to have the mess now, and get it over. It doesn't last so long as when the ground caves in, like under those cottages out on the Comerbourne road—all pegged together with iron bars. And even then the walls are cracking. I know a boy who lives in one. The bedroom floors are like this," said Dominic, tilting his hand at an extravagant angle.

Charles looked at him, and the odd, finished peacefulness of his face broke into a slow, broad smile. "Out of the mouths—" he said. "Well, so you think we raised a song and dance for next to nothing, and on the wrong side?"

"Oh, I don't know about that. I only said— And I told you, I don't really know much about it." Dominic was uncomfortable, and found it unfair that he should be pinned into a corner like this. He scrubbed at the bunched curls of the spaniel's forehead, and said placatingly: "But anyhow, in the end it seems the Coal Board didn't want it as much as they thought they did, either. Especially after they started to have such rotten luck. If it was luck! You remember that grab that went over the edge? I was talking to one of the men off the site once, and he told me *he* thought somebody'd been mucking about with the engine. He said he thought a lot of those repairs they had were really sabotage, only he couldn't say so openly because he couldn't find any proof. I don't suppose there's anything in it, really," owned Dominic regretfully, "because I've often talked to the same man, and he likes a good story, and anyhow if there wasn't the least bit of evidence there may not have been any sabotage, either. But still, it was funny that they had so much trouble so quickly, wasn't it?"

"I never heard that story," said Charles.

"Oh, he wouldn't dare tell it to anyone responsible, he's known for an awful old liar. Anyhow, the whole unit will soon be packing up now, I suppose, so there isn't any point in guessing."

Charles looked at him, and smiled, and said: "Maybe they won't, after all. It rests with them entirely."

"But—they've nearly finished the rest of the site, and now that they've allowed the appeal—"

"Oh, I took it to a further appeal, Dom. I told you, I stopped being indignant as soon as I got my own way. I've been walking round having another look at all my grandfather's wreckage this evening, since we heard the result. I'm going to withdraw my objections, and waive the result of the appeal. Tomorrow, while I know my own mind. They can carry right on, and be damned to grandfather and his methods."

Dominic, staring with open mouth, perceived that Charles meant what he was saying. This was no joke. The tired, satisfied, almost self-satisfied glow which Charles had about him this evening emanated from this decision, and he wanted someone to share it so that it would be irrevocable, underlined, signed and sealed, with no room anywhere for another change of heart. For which rôle of witness even Dominic had sufficed.

He asked, swallowing hard: "Does Mr. Blunden know?"

"Not yet!" Charles laughed, a large, ruddy, bright sound in the evening, breaking the sequence of gunshots, far and near, which were now the commonplace of the season, and almost inaudible unless one consciously thought about them. "Expecting me to get a thick ear? Don't you worry, if I know him he's lost all interest since he heard he's carried his point. That's what mattered with the old man, to have his own way. I suppose it's in the family. Besides, it'll please his cussed nature, making 'em sweat blood losing the ground to him, and then chucking it to 'em when he's won. Take his side of any argument, and he's sure to hop over to yours. No, this is really hot news, young Dom. You're positively the only one who knows it yet."

As a consequence of which accident, he was now unusually pleased with Dominic, and suddenly fishing out a half-crown from his pocket, flipped it over into his startled hand. "Here, celebrate the occasion, while I go and break the news." He swung his legs over the stile, hoisting the shotgun clear of the gate-posts, and gathered up his birds from the grass. Dominic was stammering delighted but rather dazed thanks, for he was not used to having half-crowns thrown at him without warning, or, indeed, at all. The cost of living, so his mother said, was turning her into a muttering miser, and causing her to cast longing eyes even on her son's weekly one and sixpence, and occasional bonuses.

"That's all right!" said Charles, laughing back from the shadow of the trees. "Buy your girl a choc-ice!" And he whistled the spaniel to heel, and marched away into his dark woodlands with his half of the momentous secret.

3

Pussy and Dominic hunted all the evening, inexhaustible, obstinate, refusing to be discouraged even by the fact that they were hunting what appeared to be a different country. After a night of thunder and heavy rain, the bowl behind the well, the frozen sea of clay, had thawed most alarmingly. It was now a glistening expanse of yellow ocherous slime, indescribably glutinous and slippery, with swollen, devious streams threading it muddily; and the overflow from the back of the well was a tight, bright thrust of water as thick as an arm, jetting out forcibly with a mule's kick. It was always strong of course, but this was storm pressure, and would soon diminish. In the meantime, they had chosen the worst possible conditions for their search, as they found after the first skid and fall on the treacherous greasy slopes going down into the bowl. Pussy got halfway down, and then her feet went from under her, and down she slid, to rise with the seat of her gym knickers one glazed gray patch of wet clay. Dominic, trying to enjoy the spectacle and pass her at speed at the same time, made a terrifying spin and left long ski-tracks behind him, but merely came down on one hand and arm to the elbow, much to the detriment of his jacket. He had also to work his way sidelong a dozen yards by the current sheep-track to find a tuft of grass big enough and dry enough to wipe his hands fairly clean.

As for their shoes, in a few minutes they were past praying for, clay to the ankles; but at the time they brushed these small catastrophes aside as of no importance. In any case, after the first fall there was not much point in being careful, and they began to stride recklessly about, skidding and recovering, slithering on to their behinds and climbing precariously up again, with their tenacious minds fixed on their objective, and fast shut to all regard of consequences to their clothing or skins. They'd come to look over the ground yet once more, and look it over they would, even if the rain had transformed it overnight and a fortnight of time made the quest practically hopeless in the first place.

The dusk came, and they did not even notice it until they were straining their eyes upon the ground. Then the torches came out, and the dark came, and as their eyes were bent assiduously upon the circles of light upon the trampled ground, it quite startled them to look up suddenly and see that the sky had stars already, and was deeply blue between the clusters of them, fully dark. The gradual brightening of the discs of gold, the gradual darkening of the walls of dark, had passed unnoticed.

"It must be getting late," said Pussy dubiously.

"Oh, rot, can't be!" He had not his watch on him, but he was quite confident, because it seemed to him that he had been there no time at all. "It gets dark very quickly, once it starts. But it can't be past nine o'clock yet."

"Seems as if it's hopeless, though," said Pussy, staring at the well. They were disheveled, tired and unbelievably dirty. Clay even in Dom's hair, where he had come down full-length once, and slid downhill on his back. Smears of ocher down his face. She had an uneasy feeling that she did not look very much better herself. Now that she came to look at him, the effect was awe-inspiring. She said: "Wait till your mother sees you! My word, isn't there going to be a row!"

"My mother will listen to me," said Dominic firmly, "she always lets people explain. If you're scared, go on home, or anyhow, go on up to the level and wait for me. I'm not afraid of my mother."

"Well, anyhow, we've looked everywhere, and it seems a dead end."

"I know," he said, dismally smearing a clay-stiffened cheek. He had not expected much, but he did not admit that, there was no point in making Pussy feel worse than she did already. "And yet if we quit now, there won't be any chance of finding anything after. We've trampled the whole place up, and after a few more rain-storms it'll be hopeless. But I suppose it was a thin chance—after so long. If we couldn't find a weapon or any sign of one that first time, we couldn't very well expect to find it now." He stared at the back of the well, where the fierce, quiet jet of the outfall poured into a little pebbly hollow, and ran away downhill through boulders and small stones to join the stream. "You know, I always thought—"

"Thought what?" asked Pussy, following his stare and the strong beam of the torch.

"Well, if *I'd* hit somebody over the head with a club, or whatever it was, close here by the well, I shouldn't throw it away and leave it to be found. And of course he didn't, either, or we should have found it. But if—if there was any blood, or anything, I shouldn't want to carry it away like that, either. They said it was something thin, like a walking-stick or a crop, so if it was you could easily walk away carrying it, even if you met a dozen people on your way home, if it was just clean and normal. But you have to be careful about getting even the smallest drop of blood on your clothes, because they can tell even months after what group it is, and everything."

277

"Plenty of water down there," said Pussy, shivering, "where he put the body. He could wash it."

"Yes, but that's the stream, and it's ocher water; I should think if there were any grooves, or if there was a plaited thong, like in some crops, or anywhere that dirt could lodge, that fearful yellow stuff might get left behind. Enough to be traced, they don't need much. But here," he said, jerking his solemn head at the muscular arm of the outflow, and gnawing at his knuckles forgetful of their coating of clay, "here's clean water, and with a kick on it that ought to wash anything off anything if you just stood it in it firmly for a few minutes. Very nearly wash the paint off, too. Only, of course, it wasn't quite so strong as this then. But it was pretty hefty, all the same. Remember, we were mucking about with it that next night, throwing jets around, and it was all you could do to keep your hand still in it."

Pussy drew a little nearer to him at the stirring of that memory, steadying herself by his arm. "Yes, that's right! I remember, just before you found him—"

"If I'd had to get a stick cleaned up after a job like that," said Dominic, "I should have wedged it in among the stones there so that it stood in the outflow. I should think if you left it there just while you dragged the body down and put it in the stream, and then came back for it and walked right on into the village, or wherever you were going, there wouldn't be even a hair or a speck left on it to show. Anyhow, that's what *I* should have done. Like anybody who had a drop of blood on his hands here would just run there and wash them. It stands to sense."

She agreed, with a shiver, that it seemed reasonable. Dominic climbed up the slope and pulled a stick out of the lush foot of the hedge, and scrambled with it up into the stony fringes of the outflow. "Like that!" He planted it upright, digging the point deep between the stones and into the soft underneath of the bed, and it stood held and balanced in the direct jet of the water, which gripped it solidly as in ice. "You see? It couldn't be simpler."

The spray from the tiny basin spattered him, and, shifting a precarious foothold, he stepped backward to one unluckily more precarious still. A rounded, reddish stone rocked under his foot, and slid from its place, bringing down in one wet vociferous fall Dominic and a large section of the stony bank together. He yelled, clawing at the boulders, and tumbled heavily on one hip and shoulder into the descending stream below the outfall. His hands felt for a firm hold among the stones under the water, to brace himself clear of it and get to his feet again; and sharp under his right palm, deep between the disturbed pebbles, something stung him with a sharp, metallic impact, denting but not breaking the skin.

Pussy, slithering along to help him out, sensed his instant excitement in his sudden quietness. She had reached for his arm, but he was grubbing instead in the bed of the brook, bringing up some small muddy thing which was certainly not the weapon with which anyone had been killed; and until he had it washed clean of encrustations of silt he was not even interested in getting out of the water. He scrambled backwards to his feet, and dipped the thing, and rubbed it on his handkerchief, which in any case was already soaking wet and smeared with clay.

"What have you got?" asked Pussy, craning to peer over his shoulder with the torch.

"I don't know. We'll have a look at it in a minute, when you can see it for muck—but it's something queer to find in a brook. Look, it's beginning to shine. I believe it's silver."

"Tin, more likely," said Pussy scornfully.

"No, tin would have rusted away in no time, but this was so covered in mud it must have been there some time, and you can see it's only sort of dulled. If one edge hadn't stuck in me I wouldn't have known there was anything there at all."

He climbed out of his stony bath, shivering a little in the chill night air, but too intent on his find to pay much attention to his own state. It was Pussy who observed the shiver.

"Dom, you're terribly wet. You'll catch cold if we don't get home double-quick."

"Yes, all right, we'll go in a minute. But look—now look!"

In the light of the torch they examined, large-eyed, a small irregular oval of silver, mottled and discolored now, but showing gleams of clean metal; a little shield for engraving, but never engraved, dinted a little, very thin, apparently from long use and sheer old age, for all the lines of its pattern were worn smooth and shallow. Round the outline of the shield curved decorative leaves, the flourish of the upper edge buckled and bent a little. It bore five tiny holes for fastening it to a surface, and by the strong round curve of its shape they could guess what kind of a surface.

"It's like on that walking-stick we gave to old Wilman when he left school two years ago," said Dominic in a hushed voice, "only a different pattern, you know. And a bit smaller, not so showy. But you can see it *is* off a stick. I can't think of anything else that would make it curve like that."

"Or an umbrella," said Pussy. "It could be."

"Yes, only people don't often give umbrellas for that sort of present, and put names on them, and all that. They're such stupid things it would look too silly. But lots of walking-sticks have these things on. And—we were looking for something that might belong to a walking-stick." He looked up at her across the tarnished glimmer of his treasure, and his eyes were enormous with gravity. She stared back, and asked in an almost inaudible whisper:

"But how did it get *there*?"

"I think it was like I said. He *did* shove the weapon in there to wash off the traces. And this plate had worn very thin, and the top edge was bent up, like you see, so the water had something to press against there, and it tore it right off and washed it down among the stones there, and it lodged tight. And when he grabbed up the stick again to make his getaway—because he wouldn't want to hang around, when for all very few people do come here, somebody easily *might*—he was in too much of a hurry to notice that the shield was gone. Or if he did notice it, he didn't think it safe to stay too long looking for it, and so there it stayed. Well, it's reasonable, isn't it? How else should a silver plate off a stick get in a place like that?"

How else indeed? Pussy said with awe: "Then we *have* found it! After all, we didn't come out for nothing. And now if we can find the stick this shield came off—" She shivered in her turn, remembering the strange pale island of Helmut's hair in the center of the brook's channel; and suddenly she didn't at all like this place by night, and wanted to be anywhere out of it. She clutched urgently at Dominic's arm with a thin, strong, dirty hand, and besought him in a low voice: "Let's go, Dom! We've found it, now let's get home. You ought to get it to your father, quickly—and anyhow, it's awfully late, I'm sure it is."

He could not tear himself away too easily, now that he had something to show for it, something to advance as sure proof that he had real ideas about the case which they wouldn't allow to be his, that he wasn't just being inquisitive in a totally aimless way. He was torn two ways, for he had an uneasy feeling that he had let time slip by more rapidly than he had realized, and it would be well for him to make all haste to placate his parents. But also he wanted to pursue success while he had hold of her skirt. What more he could expect was not certain. He knew only that he was on an advancing wave, and to turn back seemed an act of folly.

"And you're terribly wet," said Pussy. "You will catch cold if we don't run for it."

So they ran, taking hands over the rough places, he with the little shield clutched fiercely in his left palm in his damp trouser-pocket, she with the beam of the torch trained unsteadily on the path ahead of them. Halfway down the mounds, Dominic remembered the other item of information he had to pass on to his father, the odd decision of Charles Blunden to reverse his policy toward the Coal Board. Not, of course, that that had anything to do with the Helmut affair, or could compete in importance with the silver plate; but still it was, in its way, interesting.

4

Dominic arrived blown and incoherent at the back door just as the church clock chimed the half-hour, and wondered, as he let himself in with unavailing caution, whether it was half-past nine or half-past ten. It couldn't really be only half-past nine, though the thought of the later hour made his heart thump unhappily. What on earth had made him forget to put on his watch? But he had a talisman in his pocket, and a tongue in his head; and anyhow, they were always willing to listen to reason.

He had no time to steel himself, for the kitchen door opened to greet him, though he had made no noise at all; and there was George bolt upright in front of the fire looking distinctly a heavy father, with one arm still in the sleeve of a coat which he had just been in the act of putting on, and was now in the act of taking off again, with some relief; and there was Bunty at the door, with a set, savage face like angry ice, and eyes that made him wriggle in his wet clothes, saying as he halted reluctantly: "So you decided to come home, after all! Come in here, and be quick about it!"

Quite ordinary words, but a truly awful voice, such as he had never heard from Bunty in the whole of his life before. Dominic's heart sank. Suddenly he was fully aware of every smear of grime on his face, of his encrustations of clay, of his appalling lateness, of the fact that George had been about to come out and look for him, and, into the bargain, of every undiscovered crime he had committed within the year. The scrap of silver clutched in his hand no longer seemed very much to bring home in justification of all these enormities.

He stole in unwillingly, and stood avoiding Bunty's fixed and formidable eye. In a small, wan voice he said: "I say, I'm frightfully sorry I'm late!"

"Where," said Bunty, levelly and coldly, "where have you been till this hour? Do you see that clock?"

Now that she pointed him to it so relentlessly, he certainly did, and he gaped at it in consternation. But it couldn't be true! Half-past ten he could have believed, though even that seemed impossible, but half-past eleven! He said desperately: "Oh, but it can't be right! It was only seven when I went out, it just *can't* have been as long as all that—"

"And what *have* you been doing? Just *look* at you! Come here, and show yourself!" And when he hesitated discreetly among the shadows in the doorway, his heart now somewhere in his filthy shoes, she took two angry steps forward and hauled him into the light by the collar of his jacket, and like any other mother gasped and moaned at the horrid sight. "George!" she said faintly. "Did you *ever*—!"

George said blankly: "My God, what an object! How in the world did you get into that state?"

"I'm most awfully sorry," said Dominic miserably, "I'm afraid I *am* a bit dirty—"

"A bit!" Bunty turned him about in her hands, and stared incredulously, despairingly, from his ruined gray flannels to her own soiled fingers. "Your *clothes*! They'll never clean again, never! Why, it's all over you. It's even in your hair! How on earth did you get like this? And where? Nearly midnight, and you come strolling in as if tomorrow would do. And filthy! I never saw anything like you in my life. And you're wet!" She felt at him with sudden exasperated palms, and her ice was melting, but into a rage which would need some manipulating. "You're wet through, child! Heavens!" she moaned, "you're supposed to be thirteen, not three!"

She usually listened, and tonight she wouldn't listen. She was always just, yet tonight she didn't care whether he thought her just or not. She didn't give him a chance to explain, she just flamed at him as soon as he opened his mouth.

285

It was a shock to his understanding, and he simply could not accept or believe in it.

"But, Mummy, I—yes, I know, I fell in the brook, but it was because—"

"I don't want to hear a word about it. Upstairs!" said Bunty, and pointed a daunting finger.

"Yes, I'll go, really, only please, I want to explain about—"

"It's too late for explanations. Do as you're told, this minute."

George, an almost placating echo in the background, said dryly: "Better go to bed, quick, my lad, before something worse happens to you."

"But, Dad, this is important! I've got to talk to you about—"

"You've got to get out of those wet things, and go to bed," said George inflexibly, "and if I were you I'd do it without any arguing."

"No, honestly, I'm not trying to make any excuses, it's—"

Bunty said, in the awfully quiet voice which indicated that the end of her patience was in sight: "Upstairs, and into that bathroom, without one more word, do you hear?"

It wasn't fair, and it wasn't like her, and Dominic simply couldn't believe it. A flash of anger lit for a moment in the middle of his confusion and bewilderment. He burst out, almost with a stamp of his clay-heavy foot: "Mummy, you've *got* to listen to me! Don't be so *unreasonable*!"

Bunty moved with a suddenness which was not natural to her, but an efficiency which was characteristic, boxed both his ears briskly, took him by the scruff of his neck, and ran him stumbling and shrilling out of the room up the stairs, and into the bathroom, quite breathless with indignation. She sat him down upon the cork-topped stool, and swooped down upon the taps of the bath as if she would box their ears, too, but only turned them on with a crisp savagery which made him draw his toes respectfully out of her way as she swept past him.

"Get out of those clothes, and be quick about it."

She stooped to feel the temperature of the water, and alter the flow, and when she turned on him again he had got no farther than dropping his jacket sulkily on the floor, and very slowly unfastening his collar and tie. She made a vexed noise of exasperation, slapped his hands aside quite sharply, and began to unbutton his shirt with a hard-fingered, severe speed which stung him to offended resistance. He jerked himself back a little from her hands, and pushed her away, childishly hugging his damp clothes to him.

"*Mummy*! Don't treat me like a baby! I can do it myself."

"I shall treat you like a baby just as long as you insist on behaving like one. Do it yourself, then, and look sharp about it, or I shall do it for you."

She went away, and he heard her moving about for a moment in his bedroom, and then she came back with his pyjamas, and his hairbrush, and gave an ominous look in his direction because he was still not in the bath. The look made him move a little faster, though he did it with an expression of positive mutiny. She was in a mood he didn't know at all, and therefore anything could happen, especially anything bad; and the bath seemed to him the safest place, as well as the place where she desired him to go. He wanted to assert himself, of course, he wanted to vindicate his male dignity, his poor, tender male dignity which had had its ears soundly boxed, exactly as if it had still been a mere sprig of self-conceit; but she looked at him with a pointed female look, and reversed the hairbrush suggestively in her hand, and Dominic took refuge in the bath very quickly, with only a half-swallowed sob of rage.

The silver shield, which he had fished carefully out of the pocket of his flannels and secreted in his tooth-mug while she was out of the room, must on no account be risked. If it came within her sight she might very likely, in her present mood, sweep it into the waste-bin. But he was in agony about it all the time that she was bathing him. For she wouldn't trust him to get rid of the clay unaided, even though he protested furiously that he was perfectly competent, and flushed and flamed at her miserably: "Mummy, you're *indecent*!" She merely extinguished the end of his protest with a well-loaded sponge, and unfairly, when he was blind and dumb, and could not argue, told him roundly that she intended to get him clean, and to see to it herself, and further added with genuine despondency that she didn't see how it was ever to be done.

The battle was a painful one. Having no other means of expressing his resentment of such treatment, Dominic developed more, and more obstructive, knees and elbows than any boy ever had before. Bunty, retaliating, adjusted his suddenly unpliable body to the positions she required by a series of wet and stinging slaps. The tangled head which would not bend to the pressure of her fingers was tugged over by a lock of its own wet hair, instead. Dominic fought his losing fight in silence, except when her vigorous onslaught on the folds of his ears dragged a squeal of protest from him:

"Mummy, you're *hurting*!"

"Serve you right!" she said smartly. "How do you suppose I'm ever going to get you clean without hurting? You need scrubbing all over." But for all that, she went more gently, even though the glimpses he got of her face in the pauses of the battle, between soapings and towelings and the rasp of the loofah, did not indicate any softening in her anger and disapproval. Still, in spite of her prompt: "Serve you right!" so determinedly repeated, she wiped his eyes for him quite nicely when he complained that the soap was in them; and suddenly, when her fingers were so soft and slow with the warm towel on his sore, sulky face, he wanted to give in, and say he was sorry, and it was all his fault, even the bathroom war. But when he got one eye open and glimpsed her face, it still looked dauntingly severe, and the words retreated hurriedly, and left an unsatisfied coldness in his mouth. And then he was angrier than ever, so angry that he determined to make one more attempt to assert himself. The thought of his hard-working evening, the feel of the little shield stealthily retrieved and secretly cradled in his hand as he pulled on his pyjamas, stung him back to outer realities.

He waited until he was padding after her into his bedroom, his hair smugly brushed, his tired mind stumbling with sleep but goaded with hurt self-importance. Bunty laid the brush on his tall-boy, turned down the bed, and motioned him in. He felt the sharp edges of his discovery denting his palm, but she didn't look any more approachable than before, and there was still no safe ground for him to cross to reach her.

"I'll bring you up some hot milk," she said, "when you're in bed. Though you don't deserve it."

But for that fatal afterthought he would have got across to her safely, but as it was he turned back in a passion of spleen, and said ungraciously: "I don't want any, thank you!" He wasn't going to want anything she said he didn't deserve.

He hesitated at the foot of the bed, gazing at her with direct, resentful eyes, his newly washed chestnut hair standing up in wild, fluffy curls all over his head. "Mummy, there's something I want to talk to Dad about, seriously. I've got to tell him—"

It was no use, she rode over him. "You're not going to talk to anyone about anything tonight. We've both had enough of you. Get into bed!"

"But it's awfully important—"

"Get into bed!"

"But, *Mummy*—"

Bunty reached for the hairbrush. Dominic gave it up. He made a small noise of despair, not unlike a sob, and leaped into the bed and swept the clothes high over him in one wild movement, leaving to view only the funny fuzz of his hair, soft and delicate as a baby's. Under the clothes he smelled his own unimaginable cleanness, revoltingly scented. "The wrong soap," he muttered crossly and inaudibly. "Beastly sandalwood! You did it on purpose!"

Bunty stooped over him, and noticed the same error in the same moment. He hated a girl's soap. She wished she had noticed in time. She kissed the very small lunette of scented forehead which was visible under the hair, and it and all the rest of Dominic's person promptly recoiled in childish dudgeon six inches lower into the bed, and vanished utterly from view in one violent gesture of repudiation. Unmoved, or at any rate contriving to appear unmoved, Bunty put out the light.

"Don't let me hear one word more from you tonight, or I'll send your father in to you," she warned.

"I wish you would!" muttered Dominic, safely under the clothes. "At least he'd listen to reason."

When she was gone, he lay clutching his treasure for a few minutes, and then, mindful of the danger of bending its thinness if he fell asleep and lay on it, and so losing perhaps the most vital aspect of his clue, he sat up and slipped it into the near corner of the little drawer in his bedside table. Then he subsided again. He was still very angry. He lay tingling all over with hot water, and scrubbing, and slaps, his mind tingling, too, with offended pride and slighted masculinity. He was too upset to sleep. He wouldn't sleep all night, he would lie fretting, unable to forgive her, unable to settle his mind and rest. He would get up pale and quiet and ill-used, and she would be sorry—

Dominic fell off the rim of a great sea of sleep, and drowned deliciously in its most serene and dreamless deeps.

5

When he awoke it was to the pleasant sensation of someone rocking him gently by the toes, and the gleam of full daylight, with a watery sun just breaking into the room. He opened one eye into the rays, and closed it again dazzled and drowsy, but not before he had glimpsed George sitting on the foot of his bed. He lay thinking about it for a moment, trying to orientate himself. Around his snug and blissful sense of immediate well-being there was certainly a hovering awareness of last night's upsets, but it took him an interval of thought to remember properly. He opened his eyes, narrowly against the glare, and yawned, and stared at George.

"Come on, get out of it," said George, smiling at him without reserve, but he thought without very much gaiety, either. "I've given you a shake three times already. You'll be late for school."

"I didn't hear you," murmured Dominic, with eyelids gently closing again, and nose half-buried in the pillow.

"You wouldn't have heard the crack of doom if it had gone off this morning. That's what you get for staying out till half-past eleven. Remember?"

He did remember, and became instantly a shade more awake; because a lot of uncomfortable trailing ends from yesterday suddenly tripped his comfortably wandering mind, and brought him up sharp on his nose. He sat up, fixing George with a sudden reproachful grin.

"You're a nice one! Why didn't you help me out last night?"

"More than my own life was worth," said George. "I'd have been the next to get my ears clouted if I'd interfered. You be thankful you got off so lightly." He gave his waking son a nice smile, full of teasing and reassurance in equal measure, the intimate exchange between equals which had always been an all-clear after Dominic's storms. "Now, come on, get up and get washed."

"Don't need washing," said Dominic, reminded of his many injuries, and looking for a moment quite seriously annoyed again; but the morning was too fine, and his natural optimism too irrepressible to leave him under the cloud any longer. He slid out of bed, and stuck his toes into his slippers. A slightly awed, pink grin beamed sideways at George. He giggled: "If you'd seen what she did to me last night, you'd think I could skip washing for a month. Anyhow, I haven't got a skin to wash, she jolly well scrubbed it all off."

"She had to relieve her feelings somehow. If she hadn't skinned you with washing, I dare say she'd have had to do it some other way. You be thankful she only used a loofah!"

"She didn't," said Dominic feelingly, "she used a hairbrush, too. *My* hairbrush, of all the cheek! At least, she threatened me with it. She wouldn't listen to a word. And I really did have something important to say, because I didn't go off and stay out all that time and get into all that mess for nothing. *Do* I do things as stupid as that, now, honestly?"

George, thus appealed to, allowed that he did not, that there was, somewhere in that disconcerting head, the germ of a sense of responsibility. Dominic, vindicated, completed the interrupted shedding of his pyjamas, and turned to reach for his clothes in the usual place. A clean shirt, his other flannels, the old blazer; Bunty had laid them there with a severe precision which indicated that some last light barrier of estrangement still existed between them, and it would behove him to set about the process of sweetening her with discretion rather than with audacity. There is a time for cheek and a time for amendment; Dominic judged from the alignment of his clothes upon their chair that this was the time for amendment. He sighed, a little damped. "Is she still mad at me?"

"No madder than you were at her last night," George assured him comfortably. "Just watch your step for a few days, and be a bit extra nice to her, and it'll all blow over. Now hurry up! Go and wash the sleep out of your eyes, at least, and brush your teeth. Your breakfast's waiting."

"But I want to talk to you. I still haven't told you about it."

"You can talk through the door, I'll stay here."

Dominic talked, and rapidly, between the sketch of a wash and the motions of cleaning his teeth, and padded back into the bedroom still talking. "It was only a thin chance, but that was the only place we could think of to start. And I know you told me to keep out of it, over and over, but honestly I couldn't." He paused in the middle of slithering into his flannels. "*You*'re not mad at me now, are you?"

"What's the use?" said George. "That wouldn't stop you. So that's why you went to such a daft place on a night when it was sure to be sodden with rain!"

"Yes, and honestly, I hadn't the remotest notion how late it was, it didn't seem to have been any time at all. I suppose we were just busy, and didn't notice, but really, I had a shock when I saw the clock. Well, then we were in a bit of a mess already, and I thought of the outflow, and climbed up on the stones. And one of the silly things rolled away and let me down in the water, and that's when I put my hand on this thing I told you about, right down between the pebbles in the bed of the stream. And that's what I wanted to tell you about last night, only I couldn't get a word in for Mummy. Look, it's here!" He loped across to the drawer, and fished out the shield, and laid it triumphantly in George's palm. His light, bright hazel eyes searched the judging face anxiously. "You do see what it is, don't you? It's off a walking-stick—or anyhow, off something thin and round like a walking-stick. And tapered, too, because look, the curve at the bottom of the shield is a little bit closer than at the top. I was awfully careful not to bend it out of shape at all. And you see, it fitted in with what I'd been thinking so exactly. So I brought it for you. Because how else would a silver plate from a stick get in there under the outflow, except the way I said?"

"How, indeed?" said George absently, staring at the small thing he turned about in his fingers. "Can you show me exactly where this was? The very spot? Oh, I'll guarantee you absolution this time, even if you fall in the brook again."

"Yes, of course I can!" He began to glow, because George was taking him seriously, because George wasn't warning him off. "I made a note—there's a special dark-colored stone with veins in it. I could put this right back where it was wedged. You *do* think it's important, don't you?"

"I think it is, I'm sure it may be. But we shall see if they can find anything interesting in these grooves of the pattern. Can't expect much of a reaction after a fortnight in the brook, I'm afraid, but with a crumpled edge like this top one you never know."

"And it was partly silted over," said Dominic eagerly. "That would protect it, wouldn't it? And if we could find the stick it came from, there ought to be marks, oughtn't there? Even if he tried to hide them. The shape of the shield might show, and anyhow, the tiny holes where it was fastened. Dad, before you take it away, d'you mind if I make a tracing of it? In case, I mean, I might see a stick that might be the one."

George gave him a distracted smile, and said: "Yes, you can do that. But make haste and brush your hair—straighten it, anyhow. Detective or no detective, you've got to go to school, and you'd better be in good time. Don't worry, I won't shut you out of your own evidence. You shall know if it helps us. Fair's fair! Now get on!"

"But my copy," said Dominic agitatedly, through the sound of the brush tugging at the ridiculous fluff of his hair. "I shan't have time to make it now, and you'll take it away before I come home."

"I'll do it for you. Mind you, Dom, I should like it much better if you'd do as I asked, and stay out of it. It's not the sort of business for you, and I wish you'd never been brought into it in the first place." Dominic was very silent indeed, for fear of being thought to have made some response to this invitation. George sighed. "Well, it wasn't your fault, I suppose. Anyhow, you shall have your copy."

"If only Mummy had let me speak, I could have told you all about it last night." The point was still sore, because it was so unlike Bunty to close her ears; and Dominic kept returning to rub incredulously at the smart. "It wasn't a bit like her, you know. I mean, she's always so *fair*. That's what I couldn't understand. What got into her, to make her like that? I know it was awful to be so late, and all that, but still she always listens to what I've got to say, but last night she wouldn't let me say a word."

"It's quite understandable, in the circumstances," said George. "If I could have been at home with her it wouldn't have been so bad. But I came home only about ten minutes before you did, and found her frantic, still waiting for you. She'd been along finally to the Shock of Hay, and found that Pussy was missing, too, but nobody'd got a clue where either of you had gone. She'd just finished telling me all about it, and I was putting my coat on again to come out and look for you, when you sneaked in. No wonder you caught it hot, my lad!"

"Well, no, but still— Mummy isn't like all the others, who fly off the handle for nothing. I mean, she doesn't *panic* about lateness, and jump to the conclusion that people have been run over, or murdered, or something, just because they don't come in when they ought to. Not usually, she doesn't."

"Not unless there's a reason," said George, "but last night was a bit different. She was scared stiff about you, and that's why you got rather a rough time of it when you did turn up. I may as well tell you," he said soberly. "You'd hear all about it at school, anyhow, and I'd rather you heard it from me." Dominic had stopped brushing, with the length of his disorderly hair smoothed down over his forehead, partly obscuring one eye, and in this odd condition was staring open-mouthed at his father. Something made him move close to him, the brush still forgotten in his hand. George took him by the arms and held him gently, for pleasure and need of touching him.

"You see, Dom, last night there was another death. Briggs, the gamekeeper up at the Harrow, rang up soon after eight o'clock from the top call-box, and told me he'd just found Charles Blunden in the woods there, with his own shotgun lying by him, and both barrels in him. He hadn't dared tell the old man, I had to do that when I got up there. It may have been suicide. It could just, only just, have been an accident. Only people here don't believe in accidents any more. It went round the village like wildfire. That's why," he said, soothing Dominic's blank white stare with a rather laborious smile, "a late son last night was a son who—might come home, or might not. Like the old man's son! So don't hold it against Bunty if she took it out of you for all the hours she'd been waiting. If I'd known you weren't home I'd have been pretty edgy myself."

Dominic's sudden small hand clutched hard at his arm. "Did you say Charles Blunden?" His voice was a queer small croak in moments of stress, already beginning to hint at breaking. "But—when did he find him? And where?"

"He rang up soon after eight. The doctor said Charles hadn't been dead any time, probably not more than half an hour. It's by sheer luck he was found so soon, because nobody would have paid the least attention to the shots. There were several guns out all round the village, one report more or less just vanished among the rest. He was up in the top wood, apparently heading toward the house."

Dominic, with fixed eyes and working lips, made frantic calculations. "I went out a bit before seven, didn't I? The bus from the green is at five minutes to. Yes, I must have gone out more like a quarter to, because John dawdles so, it would take nearly ten minutes down to the green. And where was it they found him? In the top wood?"

"Yes, lying by the path about two hundred yards in from the stile on to the mounds. You'll be late, Dom. Go and eat, and we'll talk about it this evening. After all, the poor devil's dead, we can't do anything for him." George put a rallying arm round his son's shoulders, and gave him a shake to stir him out of what appeared to be a trance; but Dominic seized him by the lapels, and hung on to him with frantic weight.

"No, no, *please!* This is frightfully urgent, don't make me go until I've told you. You see, I *saw* him! Last night, at the stile! He gave me a half-crown—it's in my pocket, Mummy must have found it." Odd, excited tears, such as he had not experienced by Helmut's body, came glittering uncertainly into his eyes now, and his voice wouldn't keep steady. Disgusted and distressed, he clung to George, who was solid and large, and held him firmly. "It's awful, isn't it? It didn't seem to matter so much when it was somebody I didn't know much, and nobody liked. But Mr. Blunden—I was talking to him last night. I think I must have been the last person who talked to him, except—you know—if somebody killed him, the somebody. He gave me half a crown," said Dominic, with trembling lips. "He was *pleased* with himself, and everything. I'm sure he didn't do it himself, not on purpose. Oh, I don't want his half-crown now, I wish he hadn't given it to me—"

George drew him round to sit on the bed beside him, and shut him in with a large, possessive arm, and didn't try to hurry him, or even to keep him to the point. School could wait. Indeed, if this meant what it appeared to mean, Dominic would be occupied with other matters than school for most of the morning, and if he seemed in a fit state to benefit by a return to normality he could easily go in the afternoon. Meantime, he leaned thankfully into George's side, and shook a little at intervals, but with diminishing violence.

"Why shouldn't he give it to you?" said George reasonably. "And why shouldn't you spend it? He wanted you to have it, didn't he? He'd be a bit hurt, wouldn't he, if he knew you'd let it be spoiled for you. What did he say when he gave it to you?"

"He said: 'Go and celebrate for me.' And when I thanked him, he said: 'That's all right. Buy your girl a choc-ice.'"

"Then that's what you do, and don't disappoint him. You don't have to tell Puss where the money came from, that's just between you and him, and none of her business."

"I suppose not." His voice sounded a little soothed. "I'd better tell you about it, hadn't I? I wish I'd had my watch, because I can't be quite sure about all the times. Only I know I started from the green as soon as the bus had gone, and it was on time, and that's five minutes to seven."

"Well, that's a good start. You went up the

lane to the quarry, did you? That's the nearest way."

"Yes. And when I got up to the stile, Charles was sitting on it. How long do you think that would be after I started? I should think it would take me about twenty minutes from the green, because I went as quickly as I could, to have some of the daylight left. But I could walk it again and time it, if you liked. I think it must have been about a quarter-past seven when I got there. He'd been shooting. Did they find any pheasants with him?"

"Yes, Briggs found a brace. Charles spoke to you first, did he? And then you stayed there for a few minutes, talking to him?"

"Yes, I told him I'd heard about the appeal being granted, and then he asked me what I thought about it. I didn't know what to say, really, because I'd never thought much about it, but I said maybe surface mining was better than shallow mining, anyhow. And then he said that although the appeal had been upheld, it was up to the Coal Board whether the contractors went on working the site, because he was going to tell them tomorrow—that's today—that they could have the land, after all."

"What?" George held him off incredulously to stare at him, but the intelligent, slightly stunned hazel eyes stared back firmly, and with an admirably recovered calm. "But they'd been fighting like tigers to keep it, why should he change his mind now? Are you sure you didn't misunderstand him? That couldn't have been what he said."

"Oh, yes, really it was. He said he'd been walking round having another look at the mess his grandfather left behind, the old way. He said you want something like the devil when someone tries to get it from you, but if they give up trying you can see it's only twenty acres of not very good pasture that'll have to come up sooner or later, one way or the other, if there's really that much coal there. So he'd made up his mind to tell them he'd give up his objections, and they could go ahead. I think he wanted to tell somebody quickly, so he wouldn't get uncertain again, and it was just that nobody happened to come along except me."

"You mean he hadn't told anyone else at all?"

"No, he hadn't. Because I thought there might be a row about it, and like a crumb I said, did his father know? And he laughed, and said no, he didn't yet, but it was all right, he wouldn't care, what mattered to him was getting his own way, and after all, he *had* got that."

This had a credible sound to George's ears. And wasn't it possible that the long arguments with Chad Wedderburn, which had made life wearisome for so long in the snug of the Shock of Hay, had had some odd, cumulative effect in the end? When, as Dominic had said, the pressure was removed, and Charles could afford to think, instead of merely feeling, in the contra-suggestible way of all his family? The whole thing began to make a circumstantial tale, and the stimulation of telling it had pulled Dominic together valiantly after the shattering shock of learning its ending. He had drawn a little away, leaning easily into the circle of George's arm, facing him with color in his cheeks again, and animated eyes.

"And then he said this was really hot news, and I was the first to hear it. And he threw me the half-crown, and told me to go and celebrate, and said he was going home to break the news. Then he got over the stile, and picked up his birds and went off along the path toward the Harrow, and I went on to the well to meet Pussy. I don't think I can have been there at the stile with him more than ten minutes, but that would make it about twenty-five past seven, wouldn't it? And he only got such a little way along the path. You know," said Dominic, his eyes getting bigger and bigger, "you go over a ridge there to the well, although it's not far, and I don't think the sound would carry so sharply. Especially when there were quite a number of guns going at the time, you know, all round the valley. But I think it must have happened awfully soon after I left him, don't you?"

"It looks like it. You didn't see anyone else up there? While you were talking, or after you left him?"

"No, not a soul. I didn't see anyone else until Pussy came up from the village."

"There's nothing else strikes you about it?"

"No," said Dominic, after a minute or two of furrowing his brow over this. "Should it?"

"Oh, I'm not being clever and seeing anything you didn't see. Just collecting any ideas you may have. Usually they seem to me worth examining," said George, and smiled at him.

Unexpectedly Dominic blushed deeply at this,

and as suddenly paled under the weight of being appreciated and praised thus in intoxicating intimacy. Something inside him was growing so fast, these days, that he could feel it expanding, and sometimes it made him dizzy, and sometimes it frightened him. It was deeply involved, whatever it was, with George, and George's affairs, and when George trusted him and paid him a compliment it quickened exultingly, and opened recklessly like a deep, sweet flower feeling the sun. He said hesitantly: "There is one thing. Only it isn't evidence, really; it's only what I think myself."

"I should still like to hear it."

"Well—it's only that I'm sure he didn't do it himself. At least, not on purpose. When I talked to him, he was in an awfully good mood. Something special, I mean. He wasn't thinking at all about ending things, more of starting them. He'd sort of gone off the deep end by telling me, and he was *glad*. It's like this!" pursued Dominic, frowning down at a slim finger which was plotting the obscure courses of his mind on George's coat-sleeve. "He's been in the Army, and all his life apart from that he's worked the farm for his father, and—well," he said, suddenly raising bright, resolved eyes to George's face, "he seemed to me as if it was the first real decision he'd ever made for himself in his life, and—and that's what he wanted me to celebrate."

VIII

The Pursuit of Walking-Sticks

1

At the opening of the inquest on Charles Blunden, only evidence of identification was taken.

The church room was packed on the occasion, and the air within heavy with an uneasiness which took effect like heat, though from ill-fitting windows an elaborate network of draughts searched out every corner. It was the first really cold day. Outside, the air pinched. Inside, the entire population of Comerford, or all those who could squeeze in, stared and sweated and whispered. Comerford was full of whispers, sibilant over fences, floating down lanes, confided over counters, drawn out across pints of bitter in the bar of the Shock of Hay, where Io Hart seldom showed herself now, and always with pale face and heavy eyes. From grief for Charles, people said to one another wisely. But Io withdrew herself, and said nothing at all. She did not come to the inquest, though the cord of tension which was tugging the whole village into one congestion of feeling had drawn to the hall even the most unexpected and retiring of people. It was not quite curiosity. In this case the community was a party involved, deeply, perhaps fatally, and it behoved them to sit watchfully over their interests so long as there was anxiety, so long as there was hope.

The old man came. Everyone had been sure that he would not appear, but he did, suddenly lumbering through the narrow gangway with a heavier lurch than usual, and a more ungainly stoop, as if his big, gallant body had slipped one or two of its connections, and was shaking unco-ordinated parts along with it in a losing struggle to reassemble them. His wholesome ruddiness had become a stricken mottle of purple and white, with sagging cheeks and puzzled old puffy eyelids, though the bright blueness of his eyes continued sudden as speedwell, alive and alert in the demor-alization of his face. Charles had been his only child. There was not much point in the Harrow for him now, and none in his old amusement of making money, of which he had more than enough already for a dwindling middle age without an heir. People pitied him. If he knew it, he gave no sign, though it must have galled him. He had been so long kowtowed to and envied. People held their breath, pitying him. He lumbered to his place, and sat as if he believed himself to be sitting alone. And when the time came, he identified his son in a harsh, shocked, but defiant voice, daring fate to down him, even with weapons like these. But George observed that the tell-tale back view, which had always betrayed him, was now that of an old man indeed, sunken together, top-heavy, disintegrating. The old, however, sometimes have astonishing recu-perative powers, because with one's own death at least fully in sight, few things are any longer worth making a lengthy fuss about, even the deaths of the young.

Three days' adjournment, at the request of the police, who were not yet ready to present their expert evidence; and therefore the tension remained and tightened, wound up with whispers, frayed with fears. Few people hesitated to use the word murder this time, though there was no verdict yet to support it. Few people waited for the evidence, to conclude that though the connection was not immediately apparent, this murder was fellow to the first. Murder begets murder, and the first step is the hardest. There even began to be a name in the middle of the whispers, blackening under them as under a swarm of bees settling. Who else had any motive for killing Charles Blunden, except his inseparable quarreling partner, his rival in love, his opponent in ideas, Chad Wedderburn? Who was already held to be the most probable suspect in the first crime, and showed now as almost the only one in this, unless Chad? The first death an impulse of understandable indignation, they said, from a man of his record and reputation; and the second one the fruit of the first success, adapted now, too easily, to his own inclinations and desires. Out at large, somewhere without witnesses, on the first occasion, and this time, by his own account, peacefully at home marking test papers in Latin, but alone, for his mother had been away for some days in Bristol, visiting a sister of hers who had arthritis. Again no witnesses to his movements all the evening. And when all was said, who else was in it?

Of course there was no evidence—yet—that he had gone out to meet Charles in the woods, and turned his own gun against him, and emptied both barrels into his chest. But there was no positive evidence that he had not, and by this time that was almost enough for Comerford.

Bunty came home shocked and distressed from her morning's shopping, having been offered this solution confidently with the fish. She had stamped on the theory very firmly, but she knew that she had not scotched it. As well join Canute in trying to turn back the tide. The strain on Comerford had to find outlet somewhere, it was only to be expected. And after all, who could say with certainty that they were wrong? The most one could say was that they were premature.

She argued with herself that the two young men had always been friends, in spite of their endless wranglings, for what else could have held them together? But some insecurity within her mind answered dubiously that human creatures cling together for other reasons besides love, that there are the irresistible attractions of enmity as well. And further, that friendship has often reversed its hand when some unlucky girl got in the way. She had no peace; no one had any peace, and no one would have now until the thing was finished. Meantime, there was Charles's funeral to focus public feeling, and she had ordered flowers, as much for Dominic's sake as anyone's. To lay the ghost of the flung half-crown, and the easy, gay voice which had bidden him buy his girl an ice to celebrate a gesture of self-assertion, the first and the last, made only just in time.

Pussy and Dominic compared notes in the loft, over the last of the apple-wrapping, and the note of desperation had somehow stolen into their councils unawares.

"She won't go out, or do anything, or take any interest in anything," said Pussy. "She just does her work, as usual, and says nothing all the day long. And he doesn't come in any more. He did come in once, and then it was so awful he went away very soon. I think that's when he realized how it was. And that's why he won't come near her now."

"She doesn't think he did it, though, does she?"

"No, of course not. But all the others do, and he won't even bring that feeling near her. If he's going to bring bad luck he's determined he won't bring it here. You know, everybody's saying it now, everybody."

"Well, everybody's wrong," said Dominic, cussed to the last.

"Well, I think so, too, but how to prove it? Was he at school today?"

"Yes, we had him first period this morning."

"It must be pretty awful for him," she said.

"He looked kind of sick, but he acted just the same as ever. But—" Dominic scowled down at the apple he was wrapping, and said no more.

"What are we going to do?" asked Pussy grimly.

"The same we've been doing, only twice as hard. Just go on watching out for walking-sticks—anywhere, doesn't matter where, doesn't matter how you do it, only get a close look at all you can, until we find the right one."

"I *have* been doing. And it isn't so easy,

313

because I'm not allowed in the bar and the snug, but I've done it. I bet I haven't missed many this week, and I'll bet almost every stick in the place has been in by now, but I haven't seen anything like we're looking for. And it's all very well for you, but I've nearly been caught two or three times creeping about with my little bit of paper, and you can't always think of something credible to say."

"All very well for me? I like that! You've got it easy, you just sit around and wait for people to bring the sticks to you, but I have to go out and look for them. I'm fagged out running errands, just to get into people's halls and see if there are any sticks. All this week I've run about for Mummy like a blinking spaniel," said Dominic indignantly, but miserably, too.

"I bet she thinks you're sickening for something," said Pussy cynically.

"Oh, well, she thinks I'm trying to get round her by being extra good because of the row we had when we came home late that night." He looked a little guilty at this, however convenient he had found it to be; for he had inherited something of Bunty's sense of justice, and was uncomfortable in even the shabbiest of haloes when he had not earned it. "But that's not all. Even from school I've collected notes to deliver, and all sorts of beastly errands, just to get into more places, and I can tell you it isn't such fun getting yourself a reputation like I'm getting with the other fellows. But I wouldn't care, if only we could *get* something from it."

"Is it any use going on?" asked Pussy despondently.

"What else can we do? And I'm absolutely sure that if we can only find that stick, Pussy, we've done it, we're through."

"Well, of course, it would be a big thing," she owned dubiously, "but I don't know that everything would be settled. This other business—it seems to make the stick a bit of a back-number now."

"It doesn't, I'm sure it doesn't. I've got a hunch. The two things are connected somehow, I'm certain. And the only clue we've got in either case is this." He fished the little paper shield out of his pocket, and smoothed it ruefully on his thigh, fingering the faint convolutions of the leaves. "So you can please yourself, but I'm jolly well going on plugging and plugging at this until I *do* find the stick it came from. Or until I can think of something better to do."

"O.K.!" said Pussy, sighing, "I'm with you. Only I can't say I'm expecting very much."

Dominic could not honestly have said that he was expecting very much himself, but he would not be discouraged. He had a hunch, and not being in a position of exact responsibility, as his father was, he could afford to play his hunches. That seemed to him the chief difference between them; he was a piece of George, bound by no rules and regulations except the normal ones of human decency, and he could do, and he would do, the things from which George was barred, like following will-o'-the-wisps of intuition, and butting his head obstinately against the weight of the evidence—such as it was—and taking subtle, implied risks which he himself could not define. And what he found he would give to George, and where he failed no one was involved but himself. But he must not fail. There was only one channel to follow, and therefore he could give every thought of his mind, every particle of his energy, to the pursuit of the walking-stick.

Sitting back on his heels among the straw, he argued the possibilities over again, and could get nothing new out of them. It is possible to burn a stick, or drop it down a pit; but would the murderer think it necessary, just because a tiny plate without a name had been lost from it? Because there was always a risk of things thrown away turning up again in inconvenient circumstances, and even things committed to the fire had been known to leave identifiable traces behind. Much simpler to keep the thing, and see if the plate came into the evidence at the inquest. And of course it had not, and even now no one knew anything about its discovery except Pussy, Dominic and the police; ergo, in all probability the owner would congratulate himself on the way things had worked out, and behave as normally as usual, destroying nothing where there was no need, not even hiding the stick, because no one was looking for it. He might use it less than usual for a time, but he wouldn't discard it, unless he'd been in the habit of ringing the changes on several, because its disappearance might be noticed and commented on by someone who knew him. Every man, even a murderer, must have some intimates.

Conclusion number one, therefore, and almost the only one: it was worth looking in the normal places, hallstands, and the lobbies of offices, and the umbrella-stands in cafés, or in the church porch on Sundays, where one could examine everything at leisure. And the obsession had so got hold of him that he had even crept into the private staff hall at school, and hurriedly examined the single ebony cane and two umbrellas discarded there. And almost got caught by old Broome as he was sneaking out again, only luckily Broome jumped easily to the conclusion that his business had been with the headmaster, and of a nature all too usual with Dominic Felse; and he couldn't resist making a rather feeble joke about it, whereupon Dominic took the hint, and got by with a drooping crest and a muttered reply, and took to his heels thankfully as soon as he was round the corner.

Sometimes even he became despondent. There were so many walking-sticks. Among the young they were not so frequent, perhaps, but lots of the older men never went anywhere without them, and the old grandees like Blunden, and Starkie from the Grange, and Britten the ex-coal-owner practically collected the things. Dominic had never realized before how many were still in constant use. Ordinarily they constituted one of the many things about the equipment of his elders to which his selective eyes were quite blind, they came into sight only when they threatened him; and the days of his more irresponsible scrapes, in which he had occasionally been involved with indignant old men thus armed, were some years behind him now, so that he had forgotten much of what he had learned.

Fortunately he had a strain of persistence which had sometimes been a nuisance, and could now for once be an asset. A single objective suited him very well; he fixed his eyes on it, and followed stubbornly.

George played fair with him. The silver plate was Dominic's piece of evidence, honestly come by, and he was entitled to know what they could discover of its significance. George would much have preferred to edge him out of the affair, even now, but if he insisted on his rights he should have them. Therefore the results of the tests on the shield were faithfully, if briefly, reported as soon as completed. Dominic expected it; almost the first thing he did when he came from school each day was to put his head in at the office door to see if George was there, and if he was, to fix his brightly enquiring eyes on him and wait for confidences without asking, with a touching faith.

On the evening after the inquest opened, George was late, and Dominic met him as he came in. Inky from his homework, the brat couldn't wait.

So George told him; it was like cutting out one of his own nerves to hold out any part of the complications of living and dying to Dominic, thus prematurely as he felt it to be; but he owed it to him. Yes, there were positive reactions. The crumpled upper edge of the shield had retained, soon covered by sand and silt as it had been, the faintest possible traces, in its threads of tarnish and dirt, of something else which was undoubtedly skin tissue and blood.

Dominic's eyes grew immense, remembering how the whole accumulation of matter in those furrows had been no thicker than a rather coarse hair, and marveling how any tests could extract from them exact information about particles he could not even see.

"Could it be his? Can they tell that, too?"

"They can tell that it could be, but not that it is. Yes, it may be Helmut's."

"Well—" said Dominic on a long, deep breath, "being found right there, and if it *could* be—there isn't much doubt, is there?"

George owned soberly that the odds in favor were certainly heavy.

"Then we've only got to find the stick!"

George merely smiled at him rather wryly, clapped an arm round his shoulders, and drew him in to supper. It sounded so very simple, the way Dominic said it.

2

The wreath for the funeral was delivered late in the evening. Dominic went into the scullery, where it reposed upon the table, and stood looking at it for a minute as if he hoped it had something to tell him, with his face solemn and thoughtful, and his lip caught doubtfully between his teeth. Then he said to Bunty, somewhat gruffly: "I'll take it up to the farm tomorrow as I go to school."

"It would mean getting up awfully early," said Bunty comfortably. "Don't you bother about it, I'll take it up later, or George will." Penitence was nice, but she didn't want him too good.

"No, I can easily get up in plenty of time. I'll take it."

For a moment she was at a loss what to say, and looked at him narrowly, hoping he wasn't genuinely moping about Charles and the unhappy meeting with him at the tail-end of his life, and hoping still more sternly that he wasn't doing a little artificial moping, dramatizing the encounter into something it had certainly not been in reality and his past interest in Charles into a warm relationship which in fact had never existed. She felt vaguely ashamed of supposing it possible, in this most healthy and normal of children, but round about thirteen queer things begin to happen even to the extroverts, and it pays to knock the first little emotional self-indulgence on the head, before it begins to be a necessity of life. But Dominic chewed his lip, and said joltingly: "You know, it wouldn't seem so bad if I'd even *liked* him. But I didn't much, and it's awful humbug trying to pretend you did because a fellow's dead, isn't it?" He misinterpreted Bunty's relieved silence, and looked at her a little deprecatingly. "It sounds a bit beastly, maybe I shouldn't have said that. I do think he was quite a good sort of chap—only sort of secondhand. You know—there wasn't anything about him you couldn't have found first somewhere else. And—and there ought to have been," said Dominic firmly, "he had plenty of chance."

"You didn't know him so very well," said Bunty. "I dare say there was more to him than you found out."

"Well, maybe. Only I don't want to go putting on any act. It doesn't seem decent sucking up to a fellow just because he's dead, and you were somehow sort of dragged into it at the end. It's awfully difficult, isn't it," said Dominic, turning on her a perplexed and appealing face, "knowing how you ought to behave to people, not to be dishonest, and not to be just beastly, either? I get all mixed up when I start thinking about it."

"Then don't think about it too hard," advised Bunty. "It only gets you a bit hypnotized, like staring at one thing till you begin seeing spots before your eyes. Mostly the spots aren't really there."

"Well, but does it go *on* being as complicated as this?" he asked rather pathetically.

"Much the same, Dom, but you get used to picking your way. Don't you worry about it, I'll back your instincts to be pretty near the right balance most of the time."

Dominic frowned thoughtfully at the brilliant bronze and gold chrysanthemums of the wreath, and said definitely: "Well, I've got an instinct I owe him something."

The half-crown? thought Bunty for a moment; for even that was a legitimate point, to a punctilious young thing who had lost the chance of returning satisfaction for a gift. But no, it wasn't that. What stuck in his conscience and made him feel bound to Charles was the confidence which had suddenly passed between them. It had hardly mattered to Charles, at the time, who first received his news in trust; but it mattered to Dominic.

So she made no demur, even in the way of kindness; and Dominic, rising half an hour earlier than usual, and without being called more than twice, at that, set off through the fields and the plantation for the Harrow farm.

It was a meek sort of morning, gray, amorphous, not even cold, the tufts of grass showery about his ankles, the heather festooned with wet cobwebs in a shadowy, silvery net, and the subdued, moist conversations of birds uneasy in the trees. Dominic hoisted the heavy wreath from one hand to the other for ease, and found it awkward however he carried it. His mind behind the musing face was furiously busy, but he was not sure that it was getting anywhere. Point by point he went over all he had told George, and wondered if he had left anything out. It isn't always easy remembering every detail of an encounter which you had no reason to believe, at the time, would turn out to be evidence in a murder case. They hadn't yet said it was murder, of course, officially, but all the village was saying it, and Dominic couldn't help imbibing some of that premature certainty. Charles, who had taken him into his confidence, and had thereupon astonishingly died, nagged at him now to make use of what he knew. He owed him that much, at any rate.

And seriously, who could have wanted Charles

dead? It wasn't as if he had been positive enough and individual enough to have any real enemies. You don't kill people you can't dislike, people who haven't got it in them to rouse you at all. As for old Wedderburn, that was bunk. Maybe Charles Blunden had been in his way where Io Hart was concerned, but then Io had never shown any obvious inclination to single out either of them. Maybe, thought Dominic doubtfully, fellows who've got it bad for girls imagine these things; but it seemed to him Chad regarded his chances with Io as marred at least as surely by his own past as by the existence of Charles. As though he'd lost a leg, or something, so that he could never think of marrying, and yet couldn't stop thinking of it, either. Was it really possible to feel yourself maimed for life, merely because you had been pushed into killing other people in a war in order to stay alive yourself? In a war, when most people thought themselves absolved for everything? But the fellow who goes the opposite way from everyone else isn't necessarily wrong.

So apart from his instinctive certainty that Chad was not the murderer, Dominic was not even impressed with the arguments of those who thought he was. People don't remove their rivals unless it's going to make enough difference to justify the effort, let alone the risk. And it didn't look as if Chad thought the removal of half her male acquaintance could ensure him a peaceful passage with Io.

And if Chad didn't seem a likely murderer, no more did anyone else of whom Dominic could think at the moment. What earthly reason could they have? Maybe, after all, it had been the result of an accident. Powder-marks on his jacket, but no particular scufflings underfoot or round about to indicate that there had been any struggle for the shotgun. Accident, they said, was a bare possibility. Suicide, thought Dominic definitely, wasn't even that.

He came through the broad rickyard, past the long barns and the byres, and into the kitchen-yard. He hadn't liked to go to the front door, where he might encounter the old man; and at this hour the cook-housekeeper and the maid, both of whom slept at home in the village and went in daily, would be in and out at the kitchen door, and see him coming in, so he would be giving the least possible trouble. Also, though he did not admit that this weighed with him, if he ran errands to the Harrow at this time of year, and took care to discharge them into Mrs. Pritchard's hands, there were usually late pears to be harvested, and yellow, mellow, large pears are very welcome at break.

In the yard, backed against the wall of the house, was a kennel, and lying before it, chin on outstretched paws, a brown-and-white field spaniel, staring indifferently at the day through half-closed lids. When he opened his eyes fully at Dominic's approach, their blank sadness seemed preternatural even for a spaniel. He did not move until Dominic stooped to scrub civilly at the curls of his forehead, then his tail waved vaguely, and he leaned his head heavily to the caressing hand, but made no warmer response. He was chained to his kennel. Dominic never remembered having seen Charles's dog chained up before.

Of course, that was one thing he'd forgotten to mention to George: the dog. Not that it made much difference. Only, now that he came to think of it, George hadn't mentioned him, either, when he told how Briggs had rung up to break the news. Dogs were taken for granted in Briggs's life, of course, maybe he wouldn't think to say there was a dog there. Only someone must have taken him home, for it didn't seem to Dominic that he would leave his master's body of his own will.

The dog was moping; that was natural. He liked being saluted by his friends, but even this pleasure he accepted now abstractedly, and soon let his broad head sink to his paws again, staring slit-eyed at the day. And Dominic went to meet Mrs. Pritchard in the kitchen doorway.

She took the wreath, and being touched by his somewhat misunderstood solemnity, desired to cheer him with pears. He went back to the dog while he waited for her, for the dog worried him. Such a fine creature, in such resplendent condition, and lying here so listlessly at the end of a chain. He set himself to woo him, and did not so badly, for the tail began to wave again, and with more warmth; and presently the great, sad head lifted, and the soft jowl explored his lowered face, blowing experimentally with strong, gusty breaths. So far they had progressed when a footstep sounded at the door, and the dog stiffened, peered, and then withdrew into the dark inside of the kennel, belly to ground, and lay there.

The feathery front paws disappeared under the spotted chin. Only a bight of chain coiling out from the kennel and in again, and the round luminous whites of two staring eyes, betrayed that there was any dog within. He made a small whining sound, and then was quiet, and would not come out again in spite of Dominic's wheedling fingers and winning voice.

Dominic gave up the attempt. He got up from his knees, dusting them busily, and looked up full into old Blunden's face. He had expected Mrs. Pritchard returning, and was speechless with surprise and shyness for a moment; but the old man smiled at him, and seemed quite himself, in spite of his ravaged face and forward-blundering shoulders. The loss was not by him, but the shock was, and his toughness had not let him down. The bold blue eyes had still a rather blank, dazed look, but the old spark of intelligence burned deep underneath the surface as bright as ever, lustrously intent upon Dominic.

"I shouldn't bother with him," he said quietly. "Poor brute's been temperamental since Charles went, you know. Pining here, I'm afraid. His dog, you see—with him when it happened—whatever did happen." He seemed to be talking as much to himself as to Dominic, and yet a sense of sudden isolation, of terrifying intimacy, made Dominic hold his breath. "You're Felse's boy, aren't you?" said the old man, smiling at him quite nicely but rather rigidly, so that his senses went numb, and his mouth dry. Very seldom in his life had Dominic been as tongue-tied as this.

"Yes, sir!" he whispered, like any second-former new at school.

"Wanting me? Or is Mrs. Pritchard seeing after something for you?"

"Yes, sir, thank you, she—she said she'd get me some pears."

"Ah, good! Plenty of 'em, goodness knows, plenty! No boys to make inroads in 'em here. May as well fill your pockets, take 'em where they'll be welcome, eh?" His eyes went back regretfully to the round, unwavering, white stare in the shadows at the back of the kennel. "Yes, poor brute, pining here! Might do well yet at some other place. Fresh start good for dogs, as well as for humans, eh, my boy? With him when it happened, you know. Came home alone!"

Dominic stood looking at him with awed eyes and wary face, wishing himself away, and yet painfully alive to every accent, every turn of voice or tension of body. And presently, as if soothed with staring, he did not wish himself away any more. He had an idea; at least, it felt like an idea, though it seemed to come out of his bowels rather than his brain, making him ask things before he knew he was going to ask them.

"Do you have to tie him up? He isn't used to it, is he?"

"Roams off, poor beast, if you loose him. Back to where it happened, mostly. Get over it in time, no doubt, but once off the chain now, and he's away."

"Isn't it odd," said Dominic, automatic as a sleepwalker, "that he should come home that night, and now he goes back there as often as he can."

"Don't know, my boy! I didn't think much about it at the time. Enough on all our minds, no time for the dog. But they're queer cattle, too, you know—individual as humans, every one, and almost as capricious. Suffer from shock, too, like humans. Poor brute came home and crept into the stables, and hid in a corner. Heard him whining when I came through the yard. Had to hunt for him, wouldn't come out. Found him only just before Briggs turned up with your father. Had to chain him, no doing anything with him since then. But he'll get over it, if he goes to a new home, with decent people—fresh surroundings, and all that—no reminders." He looked through Dominic with a fixed face, the smile dead on it, and repeated absently: "No reminders!"

Dominic ventured: "We're all most awfully sorry, sir."

"Yes, son, I know, I know! Your father's been very good—very good!" He patted Dominic's slight shoulder, and sighed. "Here comes Mrs. Pritchard with your pears now."

Dominic accepted a bag almost as heavy as his school satchel, and distributed thanks between them, as both appeared to be involved in the gift. To tell the truth, he had little energy or attention left over from coping with the idea, which was occupying his body with the intensity of a stomachache, making him feel light and sick with excitement. When Mrs. Pritchard had gone away again into the house, and left them moving slowly toward the rickyard together, he struggled to

328

grasp the moment and turn it to use, and for a minute or two was literally without words. Unexpectedly the old man helped him.

"You've been taking a real interest, so your father tells me, in this bad business that's got hold of Comerford." He sounded, in his preoccupied way, as indulgent about it as all the rest, as if it were something quite unreal and childish, a kind of morbid game. But he was old, and one had to make all kinds of allowances.

"Well, I don't know!" Dominic said uncomfortably. "It was just an accident that it happened to be Pussy and me who found him. And you can't just forget about a thing like that. But there hasn't been anything we could do."

"Very few leads of any kind, more's the pity," agreed the old man. "For you, or your father, eh?—see, now, what's your name? Dominic, is it?"

Never particularly pleased with this admission, the owner of the name sighed that indeed it was.

"Still, you're an intelligent boy. I hear you've been trying, anyhow—doing your best. That night you saw the last of my lad—" The hand on Dominic's shoulder tightened, just perceptibly, but the pressure sent a quaking shock through him; needlessly, for the old man's voice was level, spiritless and resigned, and Charles relinquished already, because there was no help for it. Only the old or the cold can resist trying to help what cannot be helped. "That was the occasion of some amateur sleuthing, wasn't it? Eh, Dominic? And got you into some trouble on the rebound, too, didn't it? No more late nights for a while, eh?"

To be teased with laughter so mournfully soft was dreadful. Dominic felt himself crimsoning to his hair, and vowed to reproach his mother bitterly for talking to outsiders about what should have remained a private matter between them. It wasn't like her, either; but that had been a night of near-panic among the households of Comerford, and no doubt all the women had compared notes in the greengrocer's and the butcher's afterwards. Maybe she hadn't really told very much, only that he was out late poking his nose into his father's business—she wouldn't have to tell them how angry she had been, that would be clearly visible without any words. Still, he would make his protest. It would be foolish to let one's parents get out of hand.

"It wasn't a great success," he said rather glumly.

"No, there's been no luck for the police from the beginning. No luck for the village, one could say." They had reached the gate of the rickyard, and here the hand left his shoulder, and the heavy feet pacing beside him halted. "So you didn't find anything of interest. Pity, after such a gallant try!" The old, indulgent, sad smile dwelt thoughtfully upon Dominic's face. He felt the fluttering excitement inside him mounting to speech, possessing his lips. And just for a moment of panic he had not the least idea exactly what he was going to say. Frightened of his instincts, trying with a too belated effort to control them into thoughts, and shape what was already shaped, he heard himself saying in a tight, small voice:

"I *have* got something now, though. I didn't give it to my father, because—well, it may be nothing at all to do with it, and they've had so many false starts, and—well, he doesn't like me butting in. So I thought, if I could find out first whether it really means anything, then he'd be pleased—and if it's no good, well, I shan't have caused him any trouble, or—or—"

"Or got into any yourself," said Blunden, the smile deepening almost affectionately in his blue, bright eyes. "Well, maybe you're wise. They've certainly got more than enough irrelevant nonsense to sort out, without our adding to it. You do that, Dom, my boy! You make sure of your evidence first!"

Dominic closed the gate between them, and hoisted the bag of pears into the hollow of his left arm. "Yes, sir, I think I will. Only I shall need *somebody's* help. You see, it's something I can't understand myself, it's—" He hesitated, flushed and smiled, resettling his satchel on his shoulders. "I say, sir, I'm awfully sorry! I didn't mean to start worrying you with my affairs—and I expect it's all tripe, really. I'd better get on now. Thanks awfully for the pears!"

"That's all right, my boy! If there's anything *I* can do—"

"Oh, I didn't mean—I say, I *am* ashamed, bothering you, when—" He made to say more, then resolutely turned himself to the drive. "Thanks, sir, all the same! Good-bye!"

"Oh, well, it's your pidgin! Good-bye, Dominic!"

Dominic went ten yards down the drive,

331

gnawing his knuckles in extreme indecision, and then turned, and called after him: "I say, sir!"

The old man was only a few yards from the gate, moving heavily, and at the call he turned at once and came back. The boy was coming back, too, dragging his feet a little, still uncertain. Big hazel eyes, dark with solemnity, stared over the bitten fingers. "I say, sir, do you really think I might— If you honestly don't mind—"

"Come on, now, better share it!" said Blunden kindly. "What is it that's on your mind?"

"I haven't got it here, but I could bring it to you. You see—can you read German, sir?"

They stared at each other over the gate with wide, conspiratorial eyes, half-hypnotizing each other. Then the old man said, not without some degree of natural bewilderment: "As a matter of fact, laddie, I can. But what's that got to do with it?"

Dominic drew a deep breath, and came back through the gate.

3

It was not a nice day for a boy with his mind anywhere but on his work. To begin with, he was late, which made a bad start; and a part of himself, the part with the brains, had been left behind somewhere on the way, to haggle out a worse problem than ever cropped up in algebra. It was a pity that the headmaster now took Fourth-Form maths. He wasn't a bad sort, and he wasn't even in a bad temper that day, but he was a man who liked a little application even where there was no natural aptitude, and above all he couldn't forgive lack of application where the natural aptitude did exist. Dominic suffered from the reputation of having a fairly liberal share of brains; it was usually what went on out of the classroom, rather than what happened in it, that got him into hot water. But today he couldn't do anything right. He was inattentive, absentminded, dreaming in a distant and rather harassed world where a and b, x and y indicated people, not abstract quantities. In the middle of theorems, Dominic floated. Challenged, he gave frantic answers at random, dragging himself back in a panic from some mysterious place to which he had retired to think. The Head was not convinced that what occupied him there was thought. Chewed to fragments, Dominic did not really seem to mind as much as he should have done, but only to wriggle and circle uneasily, like a dog anxious to get back to a bone from which it has been chivvied wantonly by spiteful children. If the tongue-lash left him unstung for two minutes, he was off again, blank-eyed, into the depths of himself.

It went on like that all day, and by last period in the afternoon, which was Latin, he had even begun to look a little ill with the indigestible weight of his thoughts. Virgil could hold him no better than x and y, though he had normally a taste for the full, rolling hexameters, which were round in the mouth as a sun-warmed apple in the palm, tactile satisfaction somehow molten into the ear's delight. He made a stumbling mess of passages which would ordinarily have made his eyes lighten into gold; and Chad, after a succession of rather surprised promptings and patient elucidations, gave him a more searching look, and on the strength of it let him out gently a few lines before he had intended to do so. Dominic retired ungratefully, with bewildering promptness and a single-mindedness Chad could not help admiring, and sank his teeth once again into the throat of his own peculiar problem. Which by then he had almost settled, in so far as it could be settled short of the assay.

Chad set some written work, and perceiving, as he expected, that one pen was loitering after only a few tentative words, called Dominic to him. "The rest of you," he said almost automatically, as the few inevitably inquisitive heads were raised to follow Dominic's resigned progress, "get on with your work. We're no better worth prolonged examination than we were five minutes ago." The "we," Dominic thought, was rather decent of him.

The Fourth Form, as always, looked mortally offended at being told to mind their own business, and elevated their eyebrows and looked down their noses in their best style to indicate their total lack of interest in anything so insignificant as Dominic Felse and Chad Wedderburn. And if here and there an ear was flapping a little in their direction, it flapped in vain. Chad had a quiet voice, and leaned forward over his desk to reduce the distance between them so that it might be even quieter and still adequate. He looked, now that Dominic examined him closely, distinctly worn and haggard, and his scar stood out more lividly than usual, though his manner was exactly as they had known it ever since his return, unhurried, calm, past surprise but wryly alert to impressions, and sensitive in response to them. If sleep had largely left him, if he knew as well as they did that the whole village was settling his guilt and seething with speculations as to his future, he gave no outward sign of it, made no concessions. And he could still see sufficiently clearly to observe that one of his boys had something on his mind. The only mistake he had made was in thinking that it might be something which could be got rid of by sharing it.

"Come on, now," he said quietly, "what's the matter?"

"Nothing, sir," said Dominic, but in a discouraged tone which did not expect to convince.

"Don't tell me that! Your mind hasn't been on what we're doing here for one minute this afternoon. I know your work well enough to know that. What's wrong? Are you feeling off-color?"

"Oh, no, sir, really I'm all right."

"Then there's something worrying you sick. Isn't there? Don't you dare hand me: 'Oh, no, sir!' again," he said smartly, warding off another disclaimer, "or I'll take you at your word, and make you pay through the nose for what you just did to the shield of Æneas. How would you like it if I kept you here for an hour after school, and let you make me a decent translation of the whole passage?"

Dominic's face woke into sudden alarm and reproach, because his inner world was touched.

He breathed: "Oh, but, sir, *please*— You don't really mean it, do you? Please not today! I've got such a lot to do this evening, honestly."

"I'm sure you have," said Chad, watching every change of the vulnerable face, and at a loss as yet to account for the success of his pinprick. "Suppose you tell me the truth, then, and talk yourself out of it. Or, of course, you could regard it as merely getting a load off your chest, in strict confidence. Wouldn't you like to unload?"

Dominic would, as a matter of fact, have liked to very much; but if he couldn't entirely trust George with it, how could he give it to anyone else? No, as soon as it was shared it was rendered ineffective. He had to carry it through alone, or some ham-handed well-intentioned adult would throw sand in the works. He had it ready now, exactly planned out in his own mind, and no one knew anything about it except himself, and no one was to know except Pussy, who had only a minor part and could in any event be trusted to the death. So nobody could ruin it. And that was the best, the only way.

"It's only something I have to do," he said carefully, "and I would like to tell you, but I mustn't—not yet."

"Something as anxious as you've been looking? Couldn't you use some help, then? It might not look so bad if you compared notes with somebody else over it."

"Oh, it isn't *bad*," said Dominic, opening his eyes wide. "It's a bit difficult, but really, it'll be all right. Only it's important that I should have

336

this evening free; truly it is. I'm sorry I mucked up the construe, I didn't have my mind on it."

Chad looked at him silently and thoughtfully for what seemed a long time; and by the pricking of his thumbs he was warned that the child was most certainly up to something. No light employment, no mischief, no slender personal affair to be squared up in half an hour of getting round someone; but a serious undertaking. Nothing less could account for the odd, withdrawn look of the hazel eyes, which regarded him from beyond an impassable barrier of responsibility. A look at once calm and desperate, resolved and appealing. "I'd like awfully to tell you," said the eyes, "but I can't, so don't ask me. I've got to do this myself." And deep within all the other expressions they held was a bright, still excitement which made him very uneasy.

"You'd rather I didn't pursue the subject. Well, I can't press you to tell me, if you don't want to. But at least remember, Dom," he said, suddenly flicking a petal of color into Dominic's cheeks with the unexpected use of his name, "that there's no need for you to look far for help, if you do want it. If it's something you don't want to take home—well, even beaks are capable of listening to something more important than Virgil, on occasion. I hope you'd feel you could come to me, if you ever did need a second judgment."

Dominic, pink to the temples, but remarkably composed, said: "Thanks awfully, sir! Only I can't—not yet."

"All right, leave it at that. You can go back to your desk."

Somehow the probing of that level, illusionless voice, and its unexpected kindness, had shaken Dominic's peace of mind, making him turn and look more closely at what he was doing; and he was a little frightened at what he saw, but it was fright without the possibility of retreat. He had started the thing already, and it would have to run.

When he was released from school he ran nearly all the way back into the village, and caught Pussy just biking into the yard of the Shock of Hay, wobbling across the dipping threshold with her eyes alert along the road for him. They retired into the loft, which was their usual conference hall when the cooler weather came; and before he was well out of the trapdoor and into the straw beside her, Dominic had her by the arm in a hard, sudden grip which made her stare at him in astonishment. Pussy saw the excitement, too, and glimpsed, but did not recognize, the desperation. She asked promptly: "What on earth's the matter? What's going on?"

"Listen! I've got to go, awfully quickly, so listen seriously, and don't make any mistakes. There's something you've got to do for me, do you understand? *Got* to! If you muff it, goodness knows what will happen."

"I'm no more likely to muff things than you are," she said, the hackles of her pride rising instantly. "Have I ever let you down? Have I?"

"No, you never have. You've always been fine. And listen, this is the most vital thing you ever did for me, and there's nobody in it but just us two. So you can see how I'm trusting you."

"Well, and you know you can. Is it something about the case, Dom? Have you found out something?"

"I don't know—I think so, but I don't know. It may turn out wrong, that's what we have to test. I'm taking a chance on something, and you've got to work this end of it, and you've got to work it right, or I shall be in a spot. And not only me, because everything may come unstuck, and then we'll be back where we started, or even worse off. So make absolutely sure for me, Pussy, *please!*"

"You don't have to go on about it," she said with spirit. "Just tell me what I've got to do, I won't make a mess of it."

Bright and feverish, his eyes gleamed yellowly in the shadows, burning on her with a frightening light. His hand kept its slightly convulsive hold of her arm. She had never seen him like this before, not even when they found Helmut in the brook.

"You know where the top lane from the station comes up to the gate into the Harrow grounds? The one among the plantations? You've got to get hold of my father, tonight, and make him go there with you. Cooke or Weaver, too, if you can get them, but there must be my father, and some other witness, too. You've got to get them into hiding in the wood there, near the gate, where they can hear and follow if anyone comes along the path, and you must have them there before nine o'clock. That's vital. I shall come along there just after nine. I want my father to hear and see

339

everything that goes on, and keep pretty close to me. Is that quite clear?"

"Clear enough! But is that all? What happens then?"

"Nobody knows that yet, idiot!" Dominic's nerves were a little ragged, and his manners frayed with them; but for once Pussy did not combat the issue. "That's what we've got to find out. That's what my father's got to be absolutely sure to see. You've got to keep him quiet until something does happen, and you've absolutely got to keep him within earshot of us, or I'm wasting my time."

"But how am I going to do it? What am I to say to him, to make him take me seriously? He may be busy. He may not listen to me."

"Tell him I'm on to something important. Tell him I'm in a jam— I probably shall be by then," said Dominic. "If he doesn't believe I've got anything for him, maybe he'll believe I've got myself into a mess, anyhow, trying. But it's your job. I don't care what you tell him, provided you get him there. Now I've got to go," he said, wriggling through the straw with a dry rustling, "but Pussy, please, for Pete's sake don't let me down. I'm relying on you." He slid his long legs through the trap, and his foot ground on the rungs of the ladder.

Pussy clawed at his sleeve. "No, wait, Dom! It's something dangerous you're doing—isn't it?"

"I don't know—I keep telling you, I just don't know what will happen. It may be!"

"Why not tell him about it, instead of just dragging him about by guesswork in the dark?

340

Wouldn't it be better? Tell him, and let him help properly, instead of being blindfolded. Think how much better and safer it would be!"

"Oh, don't be a fool!" said Dominic ill-temperedly. "If I told him, there wouldn't *be* any experiment. He'd never let me try it. All I'd get would be a flea in my ear, and we'd be no farther forward. And this is something I've started already—if he made me give it up we'd be wasting everything we've done. That's why I've got to go off tonight and give the thing a push without Dad knowing anything about it. And that's why you've got to look after his end of it, after I'm gone. Do talk sense! This is something the police couldn't do, it wouldn't be right for them. But *I* can! And then they've *got* to help me finish it, because it's the only way of getting me out of the mess." He ended a little breathlessly, and the sick shining of his eyes scared her.

"But can't you tell *me*? I could be more use if I knew what you were doing. If anything goes wrong, I shan't know what to do, because I don't know what you want. I shan't even know, perhaps, if something does go wrong. And suppose your father wants you at home tonight? How can you make a good enough reason for not doing what he wants? It's all so sloppy!" said Pussy helplessly. "A lot of dangling strings!"

"No, it isn't. I'm going to gobble my tea and be out before my father comes home. I'm not staying to ask any questions, or to answer any. Before nine o'clock I've got things to do. And if I'm right," he said, shivering a little in excitement, so that the ladder creaked as he stepped lower, "you'll all know what to do. And if I'm wrong, it won't matter, I'll have made such a mess of everything, nothing can make it any worse."

Watching him sink slowly through the floor, like a demon in a pantomime, resolutely drawing away from her and leaving her with all the weight of his project in her hands and none of the fun, she began to protest further, and then stopped, because there was nothing more to say. She would do as he asked, no matter how it enraged her to be treated in this fashion, because heaven knew what mess he would get himself into if she did not. And there would be time afterwards to take it out of him for hogging his secret.

"I can't stay any longer," he said, vanishing, "or I'd tell you everything, honestly. You'll know by tonight. Don't be late!"

"We'll be there," said Pussy, flatly and finally, and slithered after him down the ladder.

Dominic hurried home, by the same road which Charles Blunden's funeral had taken that morning, on its way to the church. It had been a long funeral, the biggest Comerford had seen for years. The coffin had been hidden under the mass of the old man's white and gold and purple flowers.

IX

Babes in the Wood

1

Chad Wedderburn hesitated until nearly eight o'clock, but he went in the end.

The remembrance of Dominic's overburdened eyes had haunted him all through the marking of two batches of homework, and made a small counter-circling pool of uneasiness on the borders of his own taut and isolated disquiet. He knew he was letting things go, lying down and letting events run over him, because he was sick of himself and his unsloughable memories; and because where one hope—but had it ever reached the stage of being a real hope?—had blotted out all lesser and more accessible consolations, and remained itself forever out of reach, there was no longer any inducement to stand upright, or any point in fighting back. He resented his own bitter acquiescence, but it was logical, and he could not stir himself out of it. He had suffered, whether by his own fault or the mismanagement of others, injuries to his nature which unfitted him for loving or being loved by an innocent like Io; and only the artificial stimulus of rivalry with Charles had ever made him quicken to the possibility of so happy and normal a relationship, exult in what seemed to be hopes, and sulk over what seemed to be reverses. Only seemed to be. With the stimulus withdrawn, the thing was seen to be still a simple and irrevocable impossibility. But surely poor

Charles didn't have to get killed to show him that.

He knew, none better, that they were already saying he had killed Charles. With all the acquired stoicism of six years of warfare, he found himself still capable of unpracticed emotions not so easy to contain as pain, exhaustion and fear had proved; and he supposed there was little Comerford did not know about his feelings for Io Hart. Busily misinterpreting what they knew, they had made him a murderer, because he was a dog with a renowned name, which the spiral courses of history were about to use to hang him. He had, had he not, been a great killer in his day?

So he let fall out of his hands every intention of defending himself. For what? There remained a certain interest in watching the events which moved in on him, but no point whatever in caring about the issue.

Yet other people went on existing, side by side with him in the world, with a certain intermittent warmth and poignancy which still troubled him. Especially when they looked at him with harried, adventurous young eyes like Dominic's, and reluctantly declined to confide in him. Another human being taking large and probably disastrous decisions, too early and too anxiously, perhaps mutilating himself before he was even whole. And because one had resigned all responsibility for one's own fate, did it follow that one could not care for his?

He hesitated a long time, but he went in the end. Down to the village, among the covert, regretful, fascinated eyes, and knocked at the door of the police-station, and asked for George. He wondered if the three youths passing with their girls believed that he was in the act of giving himself up. More than likely they did.

Bunty was surprised to see him. She stood the door wide, and asked him into the office, to close the door on the chill of the evening. He thought how very like her son was to her, even to the tilt of the head and the disconcertingly straight eyes.

"I'm sorry, but George is out at the moment. He's been gone ever since mid-afternoon, and told me he might be late getting home." She smiled at him, rather wryly. "I don't even know where he is. I haven't seen much of him myself, lately. Is it something urgent?"

"Well, I hardly know. It isn't business exactly, I only wanted to talk to him about Dominic. But since he's already out of reach, I dare say tomorrow will do as well."

Bunty, looking intensely serious in a moment, asked: "Dom isn't in any trouble, is he? He hasn't been getting himself into any bad scrape?"

"Not any scrape at all that I know of. Don't worry, it's nothing like that. Just that I think it might be useful if your husband and I compared notes about him. He's a nice kid, and got more gumption than most of his age. But perhaps he's reached a difficult stage of development rather early."

It sounded portentous, but Bunty seemed to understand better than the turn of phrase had deserved. Her eyes lit much as Dominic's did when his partisan interest was kindled. "Yes, hasn't he?" she said, and bit her lips upon a

347

slightly guilty smile, remembering how little respect she had paid to his budding manhood when her dander was up, and with how little subtlety she had approached his new complexities. Good old Dom, the first really adult quality he had acquired had been an ability to humor his elders and make allowances for them. "Have you been having trouble with him? He likes you, you know, and that's the first essential for being able to manage him."

A slow, dark flush mounted Chad's lean cheeks as he looked at her. She found it astonishing and touching that the mention of a child's liking for him could make him color so painfully. He must be awfully short of compensations to make so much of so small a one.

"I'm glad! I like him, too, and by and large, the sort of trouble he gives me is the most encouraging kind. No, I'm only concerned, probably quite unnecessarily, with Dom's own state of mind. Isn't there something weighing a bit heavily on him, just lately?"

Bunty hesitated, for they were approaching a subject which had thorns wherever one touched it. "Well, of course, he's been thinking far too much about this Schauffler case, but that was hardly avoidable, since he found the body. But naturally we've been keeping an eye on him, and I can't say I've thought there was much wrong with his reactions. One can't just forget a thing like that, but there's nothing morbid about Dom."

"Good God, no! I never meant to suggest it. No, he hasn't an ounce of humbug in him, I'm sure of that. I was thinking of something much more positive and active. Are you sure he's not up to something on his own? By the way, where is he now?"

"He went out, immediately after tea." Her eyes widened in suspicion and apprehension. "He was very quick and very quiet, but so he often is. He didn't stop to do his homework first, as he usually does, but that happens, too, when he has something on. And I've never asked questions, it's never been necessary, and I'm not going to start now. You don't think he's up to anything really hare-brained?"

"Never quite that," said Chad, and smiled, and was glad to see her smile in response.

"That's awfully nice of you. He *is* a capable boy, I know that. But we might not think exactly alike about what's crazy and what isn't. You see, trusting him and leaving him his privacy has been easy while he stayed transparent and calculable— maybe not so much of a gesture, after all, because we often didn't need to ask, we could see for ourselves. But now he isn't quite transparent, even though I think he's as honest as ever he was. And he isn't, he certainly isn't, quite calculable. That's when the pinch comes."

"I may be thinking more of it than it really is," said Chad, "and troubling you with what amounts to nothing. It's only today he's been in this peculiar state; so one can hardly blame Schauffler for it. It may even be some odd score he's got to settle with some other boy, only he seemed to be taking it very seriously. All today he's been miles from school, working out something which did seem rather to be giving him trouble. I wondered if between us we couldn't find out a little more about it, without treading too heavily on his toes."

"There was the bad business of Charles Blunden," said Bunty carefully. "That was rather on his mind, because—" She remembered in time that the adjourned inquest had so far produced only evidence of identification, that Dominic's last meeting with Charles, and the queer confidence it had produced, were known to no one except herself, the police, and the boy. Maybe Dom had stretched his promise of secrecy so far as to admit Pussy, who was half himself, but she was sure he had extended it to no one else; and it was not for her to publish it to Chad Wedderburn, whatever she believed of him. "But I'd swear he was all right," she said, "when he went off this morning. I wish I'd paid more attention to him at tea, but there was nothing particularly odd about him being silent and a little abstracted."

"Of course not! I had different opportunities. In the middle of the Æneid, Book Eight," he said with a fleeting smile, "one is apt to notice complete absence of mind. Especially in the intelligent. The middle of tea is rather another matter."

Bunty, looking uneasily at the clock, said: "With all his homework still to do, he ought to be thinking of coming back by now. Usually he does it first."

"You don't know where he's gone?"

"No, I rather took it for granted it was down

350

to the Shock of Hay to pick up Pussy for some project or other. I thought maybe they needed what was left of the daylight, hence the hurry. Now I don't know what to think."

"Go on thinking the same," said Chad, "and I'll go and see if he's down there. But I think I ought to apologize in advance for scaring you for nothing. We're all a shade jumpy, maybe it's affected my judgment."

She was nevertheless deeply aware that it had taken some very strong uneasiness to send him down here tonight on this or any other errand. It might prove baseless, but it had been profoundly felt, and since it was on Dominic's account she warmed to him for it. "Hadn't I better come down with you, and make sure?"

"Had you better? If he's harmlessly fooling around there with Pussy and their gang, it might be a little galling—"

Bunty thought deeply, and smiled, and said: "You're very right. He'll hardly suspect you of coming along simply to reassure yourself he isn't in mischief, but I couldn't get by so easily. All right, I'll wait. No doubt he'll come blithely in when it suits him, or when he's hungry. No, I couldn't make a fool of him in front of Pussy, of course."

"I'll come back this way, and let you know. But I'm sure it will be all right."

That, he thought and she thought, as the door closed between them, is precisely what one says when one is by no means sure of any such matter. The street-lamp just outside the police-station shone on him briefly through the near-darkness, which in unlit places would still be scarcely more than dusk. A small, slender figure, coming at a run, butted head-down into his middle, and being steadied from the impact, gave a gasp of relief, and called him Sergeant Felse. He held her off, and recognized Pussy. She had a certain fixed and resolute look about her which fingered the same sore place Dominic's eyes had left in his consciousness. He said: "Hullo, where are you off to in such a hurry? What's the matter?"

"Oh, it's you, Mr. Wedderburn," said Pussy, damped but well-disposed. "I thought you were Dom's father. I've got to see him."

"Bad luck! I came on the same errand. He's out, and he won't be back till late."

Pussy, with her hand already reaching out for the latch of the gate, stopped dead, and stared up at him with large green eyes of horror. "He's out?" she echoed in a shrill whisper. "Where? Where could I find him?"

"I doubt very much if you can. Mrs. Felse doesn't know where he is, only that he's been gone since this afternoon, and told her not to expect him back until late tonight. Why, what's the matter?"

"But what am I going to do?" she demanded in dismay. "I've got to find him." She pushed headlong at the gate, for a moment intent on bursting in to pour out the story to Bunty, since George was missing, and somebody had to take action. Then she closed it again, and stood chewing her underlip and thinking more deeply. No, it wouldn't do. She couldn't frighten his mother until she knew there was reason. The last time had been bad enough. "Is Weaver in there? Or even Cooke, but Weaver would be better."

"No, there's no one but Mrs. Felse."

"Oh, hell!" said Pussy roundly. "And they might be just anywhere!"

"No doubt they could be found, if it's as bad as that. And why won't Mrs. Felse do?"

"She—well, she's a woman," said Pussy in sufficient explanation. "I can't go scaring her, and anyhow there's nothing she could do. I need *men*. And I haven't got time to look for them." Her voice grew deeper and gruffer in desperation, instead of shrilling. "I need them now, at once. I was relying on Sergeant Felse. I left it as late as I dared, so he wouldn't have too much time to think. I was dead sure of finding him at home. He ought to have been home long before now. What on earth am I going to do?"

For answer, Chad took her by the arm, and turned her firmly about, and began to march her toward the distant lights of the Shock of Hay. "Come on, if it's as bad as that, you can walk and talk at the same time. You're going home, and on the way you're going to tell me what this is all about."

Not unwillingly trotting alongside, she uttered breathlessly: "But I can't—it isn't my secret, I can't just tell anyone."

"Don't be finicky! You want men, and I'm the nearest. In the bar no doubt we can find more, if you can convince me by then that you seriously need them. So go ahead, and tell me the whole story. Where's Dominic?"

She began to tell him, half-walking and half-running at his side in the dark, gratefully anchored by his large, firm hand. She had disliked the whole business from the beginning, as she disliked and distrusted any plan of which she possessed only half the essential outline; and now that it came to the point, she was glad to pour it out to him, glad of his unexclaiming quietness and terse questions, glad of the speed he was making with her, though it left her gasping; and more glad than ever of his procedure on arrival. For he released her arm at the main door, shepherded her by one shoulder straight through the bar, where she was not allowed to go, walked up to Io without hesitation, and said:

"Come through into the kitchen, please, Io. There's something bad afoot, we need five minutes' thinking."

Io pushed a draught Bass across the bar, scooped in a half-crown, and automatically dispensed change, without any alteration of her expression. She raised her eyes to his face suddenly, their rich brown a little stunned and misty with bewilderment, but large and calm, and ready to light up with pleasure. He had just shouldered his way clean through something which had hung between them for so long that she had almost forgotten how he looked when he was not obscured by it. She did not feel the eyes of every soul in the bar converging upon them, with a weight of speculation which would have hurt her only ten minutes ago. She was not aware of the sudden silence, and the equally sudden discretion of voices veiling it, rather too quickly, rather too obviously. She did not stop to argue, but did exactly as he asked her; she had been ready to do exactly as he asked her for quite a long time, and the real trouble had been that he had never asked her. She turned, and flashed through the rear door, holding it open for him to follow; and the surprising creature, turning to run a critical eye over the whole company assembled in the bar, singled out Jim Tugg as the most potentially useful and the most proof against astonishment, and jerked an abrupt head at him to join the conference in the kitchen.

"Lend us a hand on a job, Jim?"

Jim left off leaning on the corner of the bar, and hitched his muscular length deliberately after them, the collie padding at his heel soundlessly. The men of Comerford, glasses suspended in forgetful hands, watched his dark, shut face pass by them, going where Chad Wedderburn called him, uncommitted, apparently incurious, certainly unsurprised. They fell silent again, their eyes following him until the door closed between. Joe, rolling back from the snug with an empty tray, looked them all over and asked blankly: "Who's been through? The Pied Piper?"

When they told him, he shrugged his wide shoulders, and went on drawing beer. He was at sea already with Io; better to keep his fingers crossed and leave her alone.

In the kitchen Io turned on Chad and Pussy wide-eyed. "What is it? What's the matter? Where did you find her, Chad, and what's wrong with her?"

Chad looked at the clock; it was twenty-five minutes to nine. He looked down at Pussy, whose green eyes were blazing again hopefully, almost gleefully. "Now, then! Get your breath back, and tell all that tale again in less than five minutes. No interruptions, there isn't time. If you or he are pulling our legs, look out afterwards, that's all. But now, we're listening!"

Pussy recounted in rather less than three minutes the instructions she had received from Dominic, and the way he had looked and acted at that interview. Io and Jim kept their eyes on her throughout the recital, but Chad's were on Io, and when Pussy's breath and facts gave out together Io seemed to feel the compulsion of his glance, for she looked directly up at him, and both of them smiled. A rather anxious, grave, and yet very peaceful smile, confirming, where there was no time for more, that while what was about to happen was extremely uncertain, what had just happened was the most certain thing in the world, and neither accident nor mistake.

"Well, what's the verdict?" asked Chad.

"We must go, of course," said Io. "I don't say he's really on to anything important, but almost certainly he's going to be in some sort of trouble if we don't fish him out of it. Either way, he needs rescuing."

Jim said: "What is there to lose? If the kid's father isn't here to lug him out of mischief, somebody else better take over. All the more if there's more to it than mischief."

"There is," said Pussy earnestly. "I tell you, he's dead serious. I think he was a bit scared, really, but he's got some clue, I'm sure he has. Let's go, quickly! There's only just time."

They slid out from the scullery door to the yard, Io clawing a coat from the hooks in the passage as she went. It was the mackintosh she wore when feeding the hens, but she didn't care. And suddenly in the half-lit scullery Chad turned and caught her hand restrainingly as she struggled into it.

"No need for you to come, Io. Stay here! We shall come back."

"What do you take me for?" she demanded indignantly, and remained at his shoulder as they scurried across the yard. "This may be something real—have you thought of that? You know Dom. He isn't a fool. He doesn't go off at half-cock."

"Yes, I've thought of it. So go back and help your old man, and take Pussy with you. Who's going to look after the bar if you quit?"

"Damn the bar!" said Io. "If Pussy and I stay behind, who's going to look after you?"

2

Dominic went up the last fifty yards of dark birch-coppice with his heart bumping so heavily that it seemed to him its impact against his ribs must be clearly audible a long way ahead, like a clock with an enormous tick. If it went on like this, it would be difficult to talk. He tried to restrain its leaping, breathing deeply and slowly, clenching his hands and bracing his muscles to struggle with the pulse that shook him. It was ten minutes to nine. He had just seen the smoke of the train, a pallid streak along the line with a minute rosy glow at its forward end, proceeding steadily in the direction of Fressington. It would take the old man the full ten minutes to walk up the lanes from the station and reach his forest gate. So Dominic had time to think, and time to breathe slowly.

He came to the gate and waited there. Behind him the absolute dark of the first belt of conifers, beyond which the older mixed woods began; but in both, darkness enough, only the wide drive making a perceptible band of pallor until it lost itself among the trees. Very close to the pathway the bushes and trees leaned. He thought of them, and felt comforted. Before him, across the green track, the clumsy, crumpled mounds, half-clothed in furze and broom and heather, blundering away into a muddle of birch trees once more. On his left, the winding lane dipping down into meadows and coiling to the station; and on this side it seemed almost light by comparison with the blackness of the firs within the Harrow fence. On his right, grass-tracks meandering to the bowl of the well, autumnally filled now with coppery ocher-slime and stained, iridescent water.

Dominic's feet were caked to the ankle, and felt too heavy to lift. He groped along the dark ground for a broken end of stick, and began to clean the worst accumulations from under the waists of his shoes. The little notebook he was clutching, still damp to the touch, and soil-colored almost to invisibility in the last remains of the light, could hardly suffer by such smears as found their way to its covers. It was already a disintegrating mess. But he had better keep his face and hands fairly presentable. The former he scrubbed energetically with his handkerchief, the latter he rubbed even more vigorously on the seat of his flannels. The moist October night settled deeper about him, an almost tangible silence draping his mind like cobweb, when his wits had to be so piercingly clear. He pulled the little torch out of his pocket, and tried the beam of it. Not too big a light, not so bright that it made vision easy even when held to the page. The faint, faded ink-marks in the book, widened and paled by soaking in water, sunk into the swollen texture of the pulpy leaves, winked and seemed to change and shift under the light, sometimes to vanish altogether with his intent staring. But here and there a word could be read, and here and there a column of figures, conveying its general significance but not its details.

Down the lane from the station there began the sound of footsteps, heavy but fairly swift, though the old man was climbing a decided slope. Presently there was a bulky, increscent shape vaguely discernible against the sky, gradually lengthening to a man's full height; and Selwyn Blunden, puffing grampus-like, and leaning heavily on his stick, came laboring to the gate.

"Hullo, young man! So there you are! Afraid I'm late. Confounded train behind time, as usual. I hope you haven't been waiting long?"

"Oh, no, only a few minutes. I saw the train pulling out."

"Well, shall we go on up to the house? We can't

do anything here in the dark. You've brought this little book that's been worrying you so much, have you?" He put a hand to the latch of the gate, and his walking-stick knocked woodenly against the bars as he led the way through. Dominic followed, but rather slowly, with some appearance of reluctance, and closed the gate after him with a flat clapper-note of the latch which echoed through the bushes. Straining his ears, he thought how deathly silent it was after the sound, and his heart made a sick fluttering in him. "What's the matter?" said Blunden, wheeling to look at him with close, stooping head, in the darkness where the small shape was only another movement of shadow. "You have brought it, haven't you?"

"Oh, yes, look, here it is. But—couldn't you look at it here? I was only a bit worried—I don't want to be too late getting home, and if we go right up to the house won't it take us rather a long time? My mother—"

A large hand behind his shoulders propelled him gently but firmly forward. "That's all right, we won't give your mother any reason to complain this time. I'll take you home in the car afterwards. Mustn't get you into trouble for trying to be helpful, must we? But I'm not a cat, laddie, and I can't see in the dark. Come on up to the house like a good lad, and let's have a real good look at your find."

Dominic went where he was led, but walked no faster than he had to. He kept silence for a minute as they walked, and the black coniferous darkness closed behind them like another gate.

He listened, stretching his senses until he could imagine all manner of sounds without hearing one; and then he thought there was the lightest and softest of rustling steps, somewhere alongside them in the bushes, and then an owl called, somewhere apparently in the distance, with a wonderfully detached, undisturbing note. But he was aware by a sudden quivering of the nerves that it was not distant, and not an owl. He held his breath, in apprehension that what was perceptible to him should also be obvious to the old man; but the heavy tread never halted.

Dominic drew a deep breath and felt better. Someone, at any rate, had kept the tryst. He ought to have known; he ought to have trusted Pussy, she never had let him down, never once. He clutched the little book, braced his shoulders, and said firmly: "I'd better tell you about it, sir." His voice sounded clearly in the arching of the trees, a light thread through the darkness. "Look, you can see from the look of it why it took me a long time to make anything of it." The beam of the torch, shaken by his walking, wobbled tantalizingly upon the sodden grayish covers with their stains of ocher. "It was the day before yesterday, when we were coming up from the Comer and crossing by Webster's well there, and you know it's in an awful mess now, after the rain. We were fooling around, ever so many of us, and I found this right in one of the holes in the clay by the brook there. It must have been there some time, and I should have thrown it away again, only, you know, for the murder. But we all used to hope we'd find something that would be a clue."

"Every boy his own Dick Barton," said Blunden, with a laugh that boomed among the trees; and he patted Dominic with a pleased hand. "Very natural, especially in the police-sergeant's son, eh? Well, so you showed it around, I suppose, among you?"

"No, I kept it just to myself," said Dominic. "I don't know exactly why. I just did."

"Why didn't you give it to your father, right away?"

Dominic wriggled and admitted reluctantly: "Well, I should have, only—the last time I tried to help, there was an awful row. My father was awfully mad at me, and told me not to interfere again. He didn't like me being in it at all. And I didn't want to get into any more trouble, so I tried to make it out by myself, this time, at least until I could be sure I'd really got something. And I just couldn't, though I'd cleaned it up all I could. But honestly, I didn't like to risk showing him until I was sure. Most of the time I didn't think it was anything, really," he confessed, "only it just *could* be, you see. So then when you were so decent this morning, I thought perhaps if you could read German—and you could!"

"Could and can, old man, so we'll soon settle it one way or the other. How much did you find out on your own? This is very interesting—and damned enterprising, I may say!"

"Well," said Dominic, slowly and clearly, "it's got a lot of dates in it, and some columns of figures, though you can't make out just what they are, at least not often. It looks like somebody's accounts, and a sort of diary, and it *is* German,

362

honestly it is. Look, you can see here!" He stopped, the better to steady the light upon the warped and faded page, and the old man bent his head into the glow beside his, to peer closely, and shut one hand on the nearer side of the book; but somehow Dominic's hand was interposed, and kept its closer hold.

"Look, that's a German word, you can read that—it's the German word for machine. That's funny, isn't it? And look here, again—" He pulled himself up suddenly from a skid into enthusiasm, moving on again slowly from under the massive bulk of the old man.

Softly in the dark Blunden said, behind him, over him: "But, my dear boy, you're perfectly right, it *is* German. No doubt about it. Now what do you make of that?"

"Well, you see, it's just that it was found *there*—where we found him. And *he* was German. I know it seems farfetched, but I do sort of wonder if it can have fallen out of his pocket somehow. And at the inquest it came out how very careful he was, and kept records of everything he did, almost, even his washing and mending. Only there was quite a lot of money without any records. And in here, look, there's what seems to be something about money. Columns of figures, and everything. Could it be, do you think, that he was just as careful about that extra money he had, only it was a bit shady where he got it, and so he kept it in a separate book? You do see, don't you, how it would sort of make sense?"

"Oh, yes, I quite see that!" said the old voice softly, humoring him. A sudden hand reached out again for the book. "Let me see it closer! Of course, I don't want you to be disappointed, after so much ingenuity, but much better settle it quickly."

Dominic held on to it, bending the torch upon its pages industriously, and frowning over the unfamiliar syllables. When the hand would have touched, he stopped abruptly, the better to study the inside cover. "Just a minute, sir! It's funny— a trick of the light, I suppose—there's something here I've tried and tried to make out, even in a good light, and now, all of a sudden—"

"Let me see! Perhaps I can tell you." He came nearer. Dominic hesitated, and backed a step, looking up at him oddly. "Well, come on, child! You brought it for me to see, didn't you?"

The torch went out, and left them a moment in the dark, the velvet-black night between the trees extinguishing faces and voices. The wind sighed a little in the bushes, and somewhere on the left a twig cracked, but softly, moistly in the damp undergrowth. When the tiny beam erupted again, glowwormlike, they were three yards apart, and the small, upturned face, lit from under the chin and very faintly, was an awestruck mask with hollow, staring eyes.

"I think, sir," he said in a pinched voice, "I ought to go straight home now. If you don't awfully mind."

"Go home? After coming all up here for a special purpose, go home with nothing done? Nonsense, child! There's no hurry, you'll be home just as quickly in the car." And the big body, powerful and silent, leaned nearer, seemed to Dominic's fascinated eyes simply to be nearer, without a sound or a movement. He backed away by inches, trying to keep the distance between them intact. The hands of the bushes, sudden and frightening, clawed at his back; he did not know quite how he had been deflected into them, but they were there, nudging him. He felt sick, but he was used to that, it happened in every crisis, and he was growing out of it gradually and learning to control it.

"Yes, sir, but— It's very good of you, but I ought to go straight back to my father. I ought not to wait. And there isn't any need for me to bother you now, I've just found what we needed. It's quite all right now, thank you. So if you really don't mind—"

The darkness round his little glowworm of light confused him. He was trying to stay steadily between Blunden and the gate, now perhaps a hundred yards behind them; but somehow in his anxiety to keep his face to the old man he had allowed himself to be edged round into the rim of the drive, into the undergrowth; and now he had no sense of direction at all, he was just marooned on a floating island of inadequate light in a sea of dark. He knew he would see better if he switched the torch off, but he knew he must not do it. Other people, mere whispers in the bushes—and how if they were only owls and badgers, after all?—they had to see, too; they had to see everything.

"And what," said the old man softly, "what have you found? What is this magic word that settles everything? Show me!" And the ambling, massy darkness of him below the shoulders shifted suddenly, and he was nearer, was within touch. Something else moved, too, from left hand to right; the walking-stick on which he had leaned so heavily, so ageingly, since Charles was killed. He was not leaning on it now, his back was not sagging, the stoop of his head was a panther's stoop from muscular, resilient shoulders. Dominic felt behind him, and was lacerated with holly spines.

"It's his name," he said in a little, quaking voice which longed rather to shriek for George than to pursue this any farther. "I tried and tried, and couldn't read it before, but it *is* his name, Helmut Schauffler— So it's all right, isn't it? I must go quickly, and give it to my father. It was very kind of you to help me, but I've got to go and find him at once—"

"Pretty superhuman of you," said the old man's voice heartily, "not to have shown it to someone long before this. Didn't you? Not even to some of the other boys?"

"No, honestly I didn't."

"Not to anyone at all?" The hand that held the stick tightened its fingers; he saw the long line of descending darkness in the darkness lift and quiver, and that was all the warning he had.

"No, nobody but you!"

Then he gathered himself, as if the words had been the release of a spring, and leaped a yard to his right, stooping his head low, the light of the torch plunging madly as he jumped. He saw only a confusion of looming, heavy face, immense bristling moustache, exaggerated cheeks, set teeth and braced muscles steadying the blow, and two bright, firm, matter-of-fact blue eyes that terrified him more than all the rest, because they were not angry, but only practically intent on seeing him efficiently silenced. He saw a dark, hissing flash which must have been the stick descending, and felt it fall heavily but harmlessly on his left arm below the shoulder, at an angle which slid it down his sleeve almost unchecked, to crash through the holly-branches and thud into the ground. Then his nerve gave way, and he clawed his way round into the line of the drive, and ran, and ran, dangling his numbed left arm, with the heavy feet pounding fast behind him. He threw the little book away, and the torch after it, and plunging aside into the bushes, tore a way through them into somebody's arms.

He didn't know what was happening, and was too stunned to attempt to follow the sounds he heard, though he knew that someone had screamed, and was dimly and rather pleasurably aware that it had not been with his voice. Confused impressions of a great many people erupting darkly from both sides of the drive cleared slowly into a sharper awareness. Voices regained their individuality. Pussy had screamed, and he thought he had heard his father's tones in a sudden sharp shout, and then after the crashing of branches and thudding of feet and gasping and grunting of struggle, a heavy fall. He didn't care much. He was satisfied to be alive, and held with a sort of relentless gentleness hard against a big, hard body, into whose shoulder he ground his face, sobbing dryly, and past caring who heard him.

"All right, all right, son!" Jim Tugg was saying in his ear. "We was by you all the time. If you'd held still I had me hands on you, all ready to lug you backwards out of harm's way. Never mind, fine you did it your own way. All over now bar the shouting!"

There wasn't much shouting. It had gone very quiet. Dominic drew calming breaths that seemed to be dragged right down to his toes. "Did they get him? Is it all right?" he managed between gulps.

"We've got him all right. Don't you worry!"

So presently he took his face out of Jim's shoulder, and looked. Several torches had appeared in a random ring of light about the torn holly-bushes and the scuffled patch of gravel in the drive. Chad Wedderburn and Constable Weaver were holding Selwyn Blunden by the arms, but though all his muscles heaved a little in bewilderment against the restraint, he was not struggling. His big head had settled like a sleeping owl's, deep into the hunched shoulders, and his face had sagged into a dead, doughy stillness; but the blue, icy eyes which stared hard at Dominic out of this flabby mask were very much alive. They had not hated him before, because he had been only a slight bump in the roadway, but they hated him now because he was the barrier into which a whole life had crashed and shattered. He stared back, and suddenly, though he couldn't be ashamed, he couldn't be proud, either. He blinked at the rest of them, at Io just starting toward him a step or two in impulsive tenderness, with Pussy in her arm; at his father just picking up the fallen walking-stick in his handkerchief, hurriedly and without due reverence because his mind was on something else, and thrusting that, too, into Io's hands. It wasn't all over bar the shouting, at all; it had only just begun, and it was he who had begun it. He'd had to, hadn't he? There wasn't anything else to be done. But he turned his face into Jim Tugg's patient sleeve, and said:

"I want my father! I want to go home!"

George was by him already, lifting him out of Jim's arms as by right, hugging him, feeling him all over for breaks and bruises, and finding nothing gravely wrong. George was an inspired comforter. Jim Tugg heard him, and grinned. Dominic heard him, and came to earth with a fine corrective bump that braced his nerves and stiffened his pride indignantly, and did him more good just then than all the sympathy in the world. Having satisfied himself that his son was not a whit the worse, and still holding him tightly:

"You bat-brained little hellion!" said George feelingly. "Just wait till I get you home!"

3

When they really did get him home, of course, they wanted to put him to bed and keep him quiet, and not let him do any talking until next day. Pussy and Io went straight into the kitchen with him, while the others shut themselves into the office, and presently telephones rang, and cars came and went. Dominic was preoccupied with more immediate things, little ordinary things the charm of which he had not noticed so clearly for a long time, like the coolness of Bunty's bare arms when she hugged him, and the rough place on her finger where she always pricked it when she sewed, and the skin on top of very creamy cocoa, and the worn place on his favorite velvet cushion. He had been so abstracted at tea that he had eaten scarcely anything, and now he was hungry. Bunty fed him, and didn't ask him any questions. She didn't know the half yet, but it was scarcely even late, and he was home, and safe, and apparently in some obscure fashion both a hero and a criminal. Since he was there within sight and touch of her, and eating his head off, Bunty forbore from either scolding or praising him, and waited without impatience for explanations. And when George and Chad and Jim came in, she got them at last in very fair order.

"He's away to Comerbourne," said George, answering all the interrogatory eyes which turned upon him as soon as he entered the room. "And the stick's gone with him. Plenty of work and fuss yet, but virtually, that's over." He rubbed a hand over his forehead, and marveled that he felt nothing of satisfaction, little of surprise, only a flatness and a weariness, such as come almost inevitably at the end of tensions. When the cord slackens, and there ought to be a joyous relief, there seems instead to be only a slightly sick indifference. But later things right themselves. You can get used to anything in time, even to the idea that Selwyn Blunden, J.P., the nearest thing to God around Comerford, is a murderer. He looked down at Dominic, half-immersed in cocoa, and said darkly: "I ought to take the hide off you!"

But the tone was reassuring to Dominic's ears; he knew enough about parents to know that when they begin to talk about it as something they ought to do, the resolution necessary to the act has already left them. "The stick!" he said, emerging from the mug with a creamy-brown moustache, "I forgot about it! It was the one, wasn't it?" His face was beginning to melt from the slightly stunned immobility of shock to a rather painful excitement, with a patch of hectic rose on either cheek, and snapping yellow lights in his eyes. Bunty, having made room for everyone and given them all coffee, came and sat on the sofa beside him, and put a restraining hand on his arm. He liked the touch, and turned on her a brief, vague smile, but went back instantly to his question. "It *was* the right one, wasn't it?"

"Not much doubt about it," said George, eyeing him thoughtfully. "The shield fits, even to the crumpled edge. The place has been stained over to match the rest, and very well done, too, but the holes are there to be seen, and the outline of the shape, too, in a good light. It's a ridged horn handle, well polished with use, but it has some very deep furrows. Even if it was washed in the outflow, there ought to be some traces to be found in those furrows."

"And all this time," said Io, staring fascinated,

371

"he just hid it by carrying it everywhere with him."

"Can you think of a better way? And he didn't know actually that anyone was looking for it. The shield was never mentioned; it came too late for the inquest, and nothing was ever published about it even when it did turn up."

"No, and in any case people had another new sensation then," said Dominic, paling at the memory of Charles. "But there are lots of things I still want to know—"

"Lots of things I want to know, too," agreed George, "but frankly, I think you've shot your bolt for tonight. It's time you and Pussy went to bed and slept it off. The urgent part's over, and well over. We can talk it out properly tomorrow."

It was not their double grievous outcry that defeated him, but the resigned intercession of Bunty and Io, neither of whom saw any prospect of sleep for her charge if despatched to bed in this state. The crisis was too recently over. The echo of Pussy's enraged scream as she darted out of the bushes had scarcely ceased to vibrate in their ears, and Dominic was still shaking gently with excitement and erected nerves in Bunty's steadying arm. If he went to bed too soon he would probably wake up sweating with shock and leaping about in his bed to evade the fall of the terrible old man's loaded stick. If he talked himself into exhaustion and left nothing unsaid to breed, he would sleep without any dreams.

"Let him talk now," said Bunty, smiling at George across the room. "He'll be better."

"I'm quite all right," said Dominic indignantly. "I was only scared at the time, and anyhow, who wouldn't be? But there's nothing the matter with me now. Only look, it isn't even my proper bedtime, quite—well, only just a little past it, anyhow."

"All right," said George, giving in, "get it off your chest. I want to hear it quite as much as you want to tell it, but it wouldn't hurt for waiting a day. Still, go ahead! Tell me how you came to that performance tonight, and then I'll tell you what brought me to the same place. How soon did you start thinking in Blunden's direction, and what set you off on that tack?"

"Well, it was the dog," said Dominic, frowning back into the past. "I only started to get the hang of it today, really. I never thought of Mr. Blunden until this morning. I don't know why, but you know, he was sort of there like the rest of us, and yet not there. When we said everybody was in it, there were still people who weren't included in the everybody, and he was one of them. Until I saw the dog this morning, and I started to think, and I thought why shouldn't he be?"

He leaned back warmly into Bunty's shoulder; it was still rather nice, when he began remembering, to be sure that she was there. "It was Charles dying when he did! It was almost the very minute he made up his mind to let the land be torn up, that's what made me think. One minute he'd won the appeal, you see, and he was going out shooting in the evening, all on good terms with himself and everybody; and the very next, almost, he was shot dead with his own gun in his own woods. And the only thing that

373

happened in between was that he changed his mind about the land. He saw me, and told me, but that was just luck—nobody was supposed to know yet, he was just on his way home to tell his father. And then inside an hour he was dead. Well, I didn't think of it quite like that until today, because old Blunden still sort of wasn't there in the everybody who could have done it. But I did get to thinking awfully hard about the land, and it did seem, didn't it, that everything that happened round here was something to do with keeping that land from the coal people."

"Everything? Previous events as well?" asked Chad, from the background.

"Yes, I think so. Only I know there were lots of other things about Helmut, he was just Helmut, almost anyone would have been glad to kill him. But even he fitted in, in a way, because, you see, it was Mr. Blunden who got him the job with the open-cast unit, and then all those things began to happen there, all the machines going wrong, and the excavator falling over the edge, and everything. And Helmut had lots of money that nobody knew anything about, odd-numbered notes that couldn't easily be traced. And though he wrote down everything, he hadn't kept any records to account for this extra money. Don't you remember, we all wondered what his racket could have been, because he wasn't known to have got into any of the usual ones? So there was he with lots of money, and the unit with lots of trouble, so much that they were thinking of dropping the claim on the Harrow land, and closing the site. And so when I just began to put everything together, today, all this fitted in, too, with the bit about the land. It looked to me as if Blunden had put Helmut into the job just to make it not worth their while to go on. I did tell you, I told Charles Blunden, Wilf Rogers on the site told me those accidents weren't accidents at all, but somebody pretty clever monkeying with the machines, only they couldn't get any real proof. You didn't listen much, I didn't much believe it myself, really, just because Wilf's an awful old liar. He *is* an awful old liar, only sometimes he tells the truth."

Chad, staring down constrainedly at the note-book in his hand, asked: "You don't think—Charles was in on that deal, too?"

"No, I'm sure he couldn't have been. He might have backed up his old man in all the usual sorts of monkey business, you know, the legal ones. But I don't think his father would ever have let him in on anything like that, because he was—sort of honest. Even if he'd wanted to help, I don't believe he could have put it over."

Chad's face warmed into a singularly sweet smile. He looked up at Dominic, and then beyond his shoulder to where Io sat on a hassock by the fire, with Pussy on the rug at her feet, coiled up and purring, the domestic pussy for once. "Thanks, Dom! No, I don't believe he could."

"But according to this business of the stick," said Jim Tugg abruptly, "you're going to prove that Blunden killed Schauffler. How does that fit in, if he'd put Schauffler in a position where he wanted him for his own purposes? He was doing the job all right, wasn't he? Then why kill him?"

"Yes, I know it does seem all wrong, until you think a bit further. You think what sort of a person Helmut was. And then, the pheasants, you see, they gave the show away. You know," said Dominic earnestly, turning his brilliant eyes on Jim, "how it was with Helmut when he came to your place. First he was always as meek as milk, but as soon as he found his feet, and someone treated him well, he began to take advantage. Everybody who was decent to him he thought could easily be afraid of him, because he thought people were only decent because they were too feeble to be beastly."

"That's hellish true!" said Jim. "It was him to the life."

"Well, of course, it was a bit different with old Blunden, because he knew from the start what Blunden wanted with him, and he wasn't being decent, particularly, he was just getting value for money. But if he hadn't got that hold over him, he thought he'd got a better. Just think how a man like Helmut would love it if he thought he'd got a local bigwig like Blunden just where he wanted him! It wasn't only the birds he could poach, or the money he could get out of him, but the pleasure of being able to swagger about Blunden's land as he liked, and if the old man tackled him about it, well, he'd only got to sneer in his face, and say, one word out of you, and I'll give the whole show away. Because Blunden had a lot more to lose than Helmut had, if it came out."

"That's all good sense," agreed George. "But now you come to the real snag. Helmut wasn't trespassing on Blunden land when he was killed, and he hadn't got the pheasants on him, he'd been careful to dispose of them."

"Yes, I know that's what we thought. But when I began to sort everything out today, and got to thinking all this I've told you about, of course that didn't make sense anymore. Because if Helmut was just getting to the stage of being ready to spit in Blunden's eye, then of course he wouldn't bother to hide the birds. He wouldn't need to, and he wouldn't want to. He'd want to wave them up and down in front of his boss's nose, and say, want to make something of it? So then for a minute I thought, it's just coincidence, they can't have been Helmut's pheasants, but we know they were, they'd been in the lining of his tunic. So then I thought, of course, we've got it the wrong way round, the one who didn't want them connected with Helmut wasn't Helmut himself, it was the murderer. And why should the murderer care about giving Blunden a bit of a motive, unless he *was* Blunden? And I worked it all out that way. I think they met down beyond the well that evening, some time after Hollins had left the Harrow, and before Charles came home—between half-past nine and about half-past ten it would be, wouldn't it? I think Helmut *had* got the pheasants on him, and either Blunden knew he had, or Helmut boasted about it to him. Whoever started it, I think Helmut bragged how he could do as he liked, because he had the whip hand, and there was nothing the old man could do to stop him. Only, you see, they'd both picked the wrong man, but Helmut was even wronger about Blunden than Blunden had been about him. People couldn't threaten Blunden and get away with it. There *was* one thing he could do to stop it, and he saw he'd have to, sooner or later, and so he did it on the spot. When Helmut turned away from him he bashed him on the head with that walking-stick, just like he tried to bash me, and put him in the brook, and the stick in the outflow of the well, and the pheasants in the pit—so that no one should think his poaching had anything to do with his death."

He paused, rather for breath than for words, and looked round the circle of attentive faces. "And, of course, it hadn't, really. It wasn't for them he was killed, they were only a sign of the way things were going. You can't have two bosses in a partnership like that. They'd both mistaken their man, but Blunden was the first to see his mistake, and see he had to go all the way to get out of it. And you have to admit he could make up his mind fast, and act on it, too."

"Oh, yes," allowed George somberly, "he could do all that."

"Well, and then things went on, and nobody connected him with the murder; and everything went his way, even the appeal, so he had everything beautifully arranged as he wanted it. Only Charles had to go and tip it all up again. He started to look at the whole question again as soon as he'd got his own way—though it was really his father's way. And he went out with his dog and his gun, and thought it all out again by himself in the wood, and decided to hand the land over, after all. And going back toward the house he met his father, and told him so. The old man couldn't know, could he, that Charles had already told me? I mean, why should he? So he'd naturally think no one knew but himself, and it couldn't appear as a motive. He had to think very quickly that time, too, because Charles said he was going to tell them his decision first thing in the morning. He wasn't expecting any trouble with the old man, and when you come to think of it, the old man couldn't make any, because if he did it might all have to come out, the murder, too, and he couldn't trust Charles to feel the way he did about it. He could try to persuade him to change his mind again, but supposing he wouldn't? They were both pig-headed, and supposing he finally absolutely wouldn't? And after the next morning it would be done, too late to do anything about it at all. So he had to choose at once, and he did, and he took the gun from Charles on some excuse or other, to carry it, or to try a shot with it, or something, and he shot him dead."

Everybody exclaimed at this, except George, who sat frowning into the bowl of his pipe, and Jim Tugg, who looked on darkly and said no word.

"But, his own son!" whispered Io. "Oh, Dom, you must be mistaken there, surely. How *could* he?"

"Well, I don't know how he could, but I'm absolutely sure he did. Maybe it was done all in a minute, because he was in a rage—only he had to take the gun from him to do it, so I honestly don't think so. Anyhow, he *did* do it," maintained Dominic definitely.

"But, just over a few acres of land and a little defeat?" Chad shook his head helplessly, though Chad had known people kill for less. "It doesn't seem enough motive for wiping out his own family. It can't be true." But he was shaken by the revelation of Charles's change of heart, and had to remind himself over and over that Charles and his father were two different human creatures. He remembered, too, Selwyn Blunden's fixed, competent, unmistakably sane face in the glow of Dominic's torch, in the instant when the stick was raised for a third murder. There wasn't much, after all, which could not be true.

"It wouldn't be enough motive for most people," said Dominic hesitantly, "but he was a bit special, wasn't he? I think—it wasn't the number of acres, or the littleness of the defeat. There wasn't any proportion about it, there wasn't any little or big. It was *his* land, and it had to be *his* victory. And when Charles changed his mind he—sort of changed sides, too. He *did*, you know. And so he was a sort of traitor from the old man's point of view." He lifted his wide eyes doubtfully to George's face. "I can't help it if it sounds thin. It happened, anyhow, didn't it?"

"Go on, Dom!"

"Well, when I was telling you about meeting Charles that night, I clean forgot about the dog. He had that spaniel of his with him, you know, the brown-and-white one that won all the prizes. But when Briggs rang you up to report about the death of Charles, and how he found him, and

380

everything, he never said anything about the dog. And I wondered. You can't be *sure* what they'll do, but he was trained to a gun, he wouldn't be frightened by that; and I thought most likely he'd stay by the body until somebody came. There were plenty of people out shooting that evening, all round the village, one shot more or less made no difference. And then, it was done with Charles's own gun, and there didn't seem to have been any struggle for it, or anything like that, so if he didn't do it himself—and I was sure about that—then it must have been somebody who knew him well enough to walk with him, maybe to take the gun and carry it for him, or try it out as they went along. Anyhow, somebody who could get it from him without it seeming at all funny. That could still have been—" his eyes avoided Chad "—several people. But it *could* have been his father, easily. But it was the dog that really bothered me."

"He bothered me, too," said George.

"But I didn't tell you about him."

"No, but if he was out with a gun it was long odds the dog would be there. And, as you say, Briggs found no dog. He was gone from the spot pretty quickly."

"Yes, that was what got me. And then, when it really started with me, when I went up to the Harrow this morning, I saw the dog there chained up, and the old man told me he'd come home by himself after the shooting, and hidden himself in the stables and wouldn't come out—like they do sometimes for thunder, or shock, or fits. He said he'd been funny ever since, and they had to keep him chained up because he roamed off if he was loosed. Well, it all sounded on the level. But when he came near, the dog went into the kennel, and lay down right in the back and stared at him—you know, keeping its face to him wherever he went. It'd been all right with me—well, mopish, but fairly all right, it liked being petted. But he never touched it. And it was then I really started to think. I didn't believe him. I believe the dog came home after the shooting because he brought it home, for fear it should bring anyone there too soon, and give him away. But he only just had time, because by sheer luck Briggs found Charles very quickly. And if the old man dragged the dog home with him, and then told lies about it, of course it could only be because he'd killed Charles himself. There couldn't be any other reason for him keeping the dog out of circulation now, except because it acted so queer toward him that he was afraid to be seen with it. So then I was certain," said Dominic simply. "It came on me like a flash. And I thought, and thought, and couldn't see how we were ever to prove it, or get at him at all, unless he gave us an opening. Because what a dog would or wouldn't do isn't exactly evidence."

"So you set to work to make an opening yourself. And a nice risk you took in the process," said George severely.

"No, not really, because I knew you'd stand by me." But he said nothing about the panicky moment when he had strained his ears after them with no such perfect trust. He flushed deeper; he was getting tired, but he wasn't talked out yet.

"I had to think in an awful hurry, it was a bit slapdash, perhaps. I told him I'd found a little notebook, down in the clay holes close by where Helmut was killed. I said I was scared to show it to Dad, because I'd got into a row already for interfering; so I wanted to find out first if it really was something to do with the case, before I risked another row. I asked him if he could read German, and he cottoned on at once, though he pretended he was just humoring me. He said he could. I don't know if it was true, but you see, don't you, that if I'd really found it where I said I had, and it really was in German, he couldn't afford *not* to jump at the chance of having first look at it—whether he could read it without a dictionary or whether he couldn't. If it had really been something of Helmut's, why, it might have had *anything* in it, all about their contract, and the money that passed, and the jobs that were done for it, and everything. You know what Helmut was like about all his other business, and Blunden knew it, too. So then I said I hadn't got the thing on me, but I'd bring it up to him if he really wouldn't mind looking at it for me. I was careful to tell him I hadn't shown it to anybody yet, so he figured if he could persuade me it was just rubbish, I'd take his word for it, and throw it away. Anyhow, he just *had* to find out. I bet he thought it probably would be rubbish, but there was always the little risk that it might not be. He'd got to be *certain*. But he was in a spot, because he had to go somewhere by train after the funeral, and he wasn't coming back until the nine o'clock train in the evening. That must have been something important, too, or he'd have given it a miss. But instead, he said would I meet him up at the forest gate when he came from the train, and go up to the house with him, and we'd have a look at it together. And he told me very specially not to mention it to anyone—the book, or where I was going, or anything—because he didn't want to make any fresh troubles for you harassed policemen, and also to keep myself out of trouble. So you see, he figured that if—well, it was always possible that he might have to— well, if I didn't come back, you wouldn't have a clue to where I'd gone."

The same reflection had not escaped either George or Bunty.

"But if I produced some ordinary rubbish," went on Dominic, stumbling a little in haste to get past a thought which he himself, on reflection, did not like very much, "or even if it was really something, and I obviously didn't know it, and would take his word for it that it was rubbish— then he was O.K., he could just burn it and forget it, and I could forget it, too. Most likely that's really what he expected. Only he had to be *sure* I didn't know too much about it already, he couldn't take any chances on me. And I had to be sure, too. It wasn't any good half-doing it. So I went the whole hog. After school I got on to Pussy. I suppose she told you all that part—"

"I didn't know what you meant to do," protested Pussy. "I knew it was something desperate, by the way you looked, but I didn't know how bad. Or I'd have told your mother, right away, and put a stop to it."

"You would not! And if you had, you'd have spoiled the whole thing. But you wouldn't! Well, then I went up to the well, and took my German vocabulary notebook from school—" His eyes strayed rather dubiously toward Chad, who smiled, and laid the wreckage on the table. "I'm afraid it's rather past it now. Do you suppose we can square it? I had to have something fairly convincing, and with a bit of faking the figures, and then doctoring it in the mud, and drying it again, it made a pretty good show. Anything that came through, you see, was at least German."

"I dare say we can square it about the note-book," said Chad gravely, "all things considered."

"Well, you know everything else, you were there. It wasn't as bad as it sounded, truly it wasn't. And I couldn't think of any other way. I had to make him think I knew too much to be let go, or he wouldn't have given himself away. I *was* scared, but it was the best I could do. Mummy, you're not awfully mad at me, are you?" The reaction was setting in. He was very tired, his eyelids drooping; but he wanted to get rid of all of it, and sleep emptied of even the last dregs of his seething excitement.

"Not tonight," said Bunty comfortably. "I'm saving that up for tomorrow."

"But, Dad, if Pussy didn't bring you there, like I expected, how did you get there? I'm jolly glad you did, but *how* did you?"

"I followed Blunden," said George simply. "I'd gone part of the way you went, about Helmut's murder, about the way the land kept cropping up. But I won't say I seriously thought of Blunden, until the dog came into the picture, or rather didn't come into it when he should have done. I smelt the same rat. The spaniel more or less vanished. Nobody exercised him, he was never seen out with the old man. I got the same ideas you had. So I started a close watch on Blunden; and when he suddenly groomed the dog and took it down to the station after the funeral this afternoon, Weaver and I went after him. He went to get rid of it, of course, before anyone else could start noticing things."

"He didn't kill the dog, too?" asked Pussy anxiously.

"No, he sold him—to a man who'd made several attempts to buy him from Charles before, for a very good price. Quite a known name in the spaniel world, lives in Warwickshire, right in the country miles from anywhere. We found out all about him quite easily. No, dogs were something it hardly occurred to Blunden to kill. He used them to help him kill other things. It didn't seem necessary to kill the dog, and it could have been dangerous. But it was quite natural to get rid of him, after what had happened—a gesture to get rid of a bereavement, and give the dog a fresh start, too. Besides, when he had a thing of value, he couldn't resist getting a price for it. Well, he sold the dog, and he came home, and we were on his heels—just in time to come in on your little scene, and a nice fright you gave us."

"Do you mean you were close behind us all the time?" asked Dominic, opening his eyes wide.

"As close as was safe."

"I wish I'd known! I'd have felt a lot better," He yawned hugely. "And do you mean, then, that you'd have got on to him just the same, without all that performance? I scared myself nearly to death for nothing?"

"I wouldn't say that," said George, smiling. "I was certain he'd killed Charles. I might have got hold of the stick sooner or later, and got him on that charge. But to date we hadn't a shred of real evidence. You provided that—at least enough to let us get our hands on him, and the rest followed."

"I'm glad if I was useful," said Dominic, "anyway." He yawned again. Io took the gentle hint which poised on Bunty's near eyelid, and rose from her hassock.

"It's time we went home. Dad might be wondering, and we'll have a lot of explaining to do for him. Come on, Pussy, you can see Dom again tomorrow, he's had about enough for tonight, and so have you, I should think." And she turned with equal simplicity to Chad, and gave him the full candid look of her brown eyes, and her hand, too. "Come back with us, Chad! Just for half an hour!"

Jim Tugg's dog was stretched out on the office rug. He rose at the first sound of his master's step on the threshold of the room, and fell into his place in the little procession, close at the shepherd's heel. Subdued good-nights drifted back to Bunty in the doorway, soft, relaxed murmurs of sound, tired, content. She watched them go, and her gratitude went after them down the moist October street, where the lamps were just winking out for half-past eleven. Chad with his hand protectively at Io's elbow, as if he had had the right for years, Io with her arm round Pussy's shoulders. A lot of knots had somehow come untied, and when the nine-days' wonder had passed over, Comerford could sleep easy in its bed. Bless them all, Jim and the collie, too, everyone who had stood by Dominic and brought him back alive.

She went back to the kitchen. Dominic had come down to the fire, and was kneeling on the rug to warm himself, shivering a little from the cold which follows nervous strain. But he was still talking, rather drunkenly but with great determination.

"There was something in it, you see, about the people who get to take killing for granted. Only Cooke had hold of the wrong ones, *I* think. It isn't the people like old Wedderburn, who had to do it because there wasn't any other choice at all. You know, Dad, sometimes things get into such a jam that there isn't a right thing to do, but only a least wrong one. And that's how it was with the people like him, in the war. And then, even if you do the best you can, you feel dirty. And you hate it. You don't know how he's hated it! But it wasn't like that with Blunden at all. The only use he had for a lot of things was to kill them. He bred things to kill. He was brought up to it. The little things in the woods, that he could have left alone without missing much, the badgers, and foxes, and crows—anything that took a crumb of his without paying for it double, he killed. And the war didn't hit him, you see, because he was here, all he had to do was feel the excitement of it, a long way off, and talk about knocking hell out of the beggars. He didn't have to *do* it. He didn't have to feel dirty. Of *course* it came easy to him. Why shouldn't it? In a way it wasn't even real. Nothing was, that didn't happen to him."

"And do you really think," asked George, gravely and respectfully, "that even Blunden—about whom I wouldn't like to say you're wrong—killed two people and was quite ready to kill a third, simply to preserve twenty acres of land?"

"I suppose so, yes. It was *his*, you see. Whether he even wanted it or not, it was his, and so it was sacred. It might as well have been his blood. It made no difference if it was only twenty acres, or if it was only one. That didn't have anything to do with it." He rubbed a tired hand over his eyes. Bunty came and put her hands on his shoulders, and he got up obediently to the touch, and gave her a dazed smile. "Yes, Mummy, I'll go to bed. I *am* tired."

George drew his son to him for a moment in his arm. "Good-night, Dom! Look—don't waste any regrets on Blunden. You did what you decided you had to do, what seemed to be the right thing, for everybody. Didn't you?"

"Yes. Well—I thought I did. I thought I was sure about it. Only they'll kill him, won't they?"

"He killed, didn't he? And hurt more people even than he killed. Couldn't we agree, at least," he said very gently, "that what you did was the least wrong thing? In the circumstances?"

"I suppose so," said Dominic with a pale smile, and went away quietly to bed. But when Bunty went up to him, ten minutes later, he was lying with the light still on, and his eyes wide open, staring into the corner of the ceiling as if he would never sleep. She went to his bedside and leaned down to him without a word; and suddenly he put his arms out of bed and reached up for her, and clung to her desperately. She felt his heart pounding. He said in a fierce, vehement stammer: "Mummy, I'm never going to be a policeman, never, never!" And then he began to cry. "Mummy, don't tell him! Only I couldn't—I couldn't!"

She could have argued George's side of it, she could justly have told him that in an imperfect world *somebody* has to do the dirty work; but there was an answer to that, too, and she had a feeling that Dominic would put his finger on it. And in any case there would be a lot more days after tomorrow, time enough to get over this and be ready for the next inescapable tangle when it came. So she just hugged and soothed him, and said placidly: "No, darling, no, you shan't! Of course you shan't!" and held him gently rocking in her arms until he stopped crying and went to sleep.

X

Treasure Trove

1

He got over it, of course, very quickly, almost as quickly as Comerford did. Only half the story was ever allowed to leak out, but it was enough to cause people to turn and look twice at Dominic in the street, and attract a comet's-tail of envious boys to trail after him on the way to and from school. Pussy shared his notoriety, but Pussy was a born iconoclast, and delighted in pushing even her own false image off its pedestal. But Dominic could enjoy being idolized, even while he saw through it; and the jealous scorn of Rabbit and his coterie was even sweeter to him than the adoration of the rest. Pretty soon it became necessary to take him down a peg. George had not saved his ammunition for nothing.

Not that there was anything peculiarly displeasing about Dominic on the gloat. He enjoyed it so, and laughed so wickedly at himself and his gallery at the same time, that it needed a serious-minded father to find the heart to burst the bubble. And then it was not an unqualified success.

"You are undoubtedly," said George, laying down his office pen, "no end of a clever devil, my lad. But let me tell you this, that *coup* of yours was the most barefaced fluke that ever came off to the shame of the really clever. And now I'll say what I've been storing up for you, young man, for a long time. If ever you put your private oar into my affairs again, and put me or anyone else to the trouble of lugging you out of a spot like that, look out for yourself afterwards, that's all! You'll be due for the nearest thing to a real hiding you ever had in your life, just as soon as I get you home undamaged. I ought to have done it this time, but next time I won't make any mistake."

Dominic, when he could speak, gasped: "Well, I like that! I save you no end of a long, dreary job, and maybe one that would be a failure, anyhow, and solve your beastly case for you, and that's all the gratitude I get!" But he was laughing even then, at George as well as himself, until hard paternal knuckles rapped at the back of his head, and jolted the grin from his face.

"Better take notice," said George. "I mean it."

And he did. One sober look at him, and there was no more question about it. Dominic digested the steadying implications, and went away to think it over; but his spirits were too much for him, and he could not, in his present irrepressible state of gaiety, be put down in this way. Five minutes later he was back. He put his head in at the office door, and said sweetly: "I told Mummy what you said. She says if you try it, you'll have to deal with her."

"Tell her from me," said George grimly, looking up from his work, "that I'll be delighted to deal with her—after I've dealt with you! And if you come barging in here just once more today," he added, warming, "I'll start now."

Dominic laughed, but he went, and he did not come back with any more impudence that day, which in itself was enough to suggest that he had decided to pay a little attention. And presently the exhilaration which had followed on the heels of his first revulsion went the same steady, sensible way into oblivion, so that before Christmas his days had settled again into a beautiful reassuring normality. People didn't forget. It was rather that events slipped away into perspective, and left the foreground for what was newly urgent, end-of-term examinations, cake-mixing, present-buying, and all the rest of the seasonal trappings. Not even the very young can iron out flat all the unevennesses of the past, but the mountains of today are the molehills of tomorrow.

So Comerford got over the shocks to its nervous system, and the place where Selwyn Blunden and his son had fitted began to heal over even before the winter had set in. He had already ceased to be the main topic of conversation in the village by the time he died in prison in November, before he could be brought to trial. Medically his death was curious. He was old, of course, and parts of his economy were wearing out with over-use; but there seemed no special reason why he should dwindle away and stop living as he did. Bunty said he had died of frustration and cumulative shock at finding that, after all, he was not above the law. He was a bad loser, because he had always used his position and privileges to avoid any exercise in the art of losing gracefully. It seemed seriously possible that spleen should kill him.

So there was never a verdict in either of the

Comerford cases, except the verdict which had already been collectively pronounced by the village; but that was all that was required to set the village free to go back to its everyday occupations. The rift in the wall of society closed gently with the closing year. And there were other things to be discussed, other surprises to be assimilated, like Io Hart's quiet marriage to Chad Wedderburn, at Comerbourne registry office at the end of November. A quick decision, that was, said Comerford, considering the other one wasn't long dead; but this wasn't the first knot that had been cut by events when it couldn't be unraveled by humankind, and maybe it was all for the best.

Pussy confided to Dominic: "You don't know how much trouble she had with him, even after that night. The time he spent trying to tell her he ought not to let her do it! It would have taken more than him to stop her, once she knew he was only trying to be noble. You men are a silly lot of dopes, if you ask me. But she nagged him so much, he had to marry her in the end to shut her up."

The more usual interpretation of the affair was that Chad had managed to get Io at last, after infinite trouble, because Charles Blunden was no longer there to be his rival. But Pussy, though prone to sisterly derogations, was nearer the mark. The only thing for which her version did not quite account was the look of extreme and astonished joy on the bridegroom's face when the little registrar shut the book, smiled at them, and said: "Well, that's all! You've done it now—you're married!"

Then the rumor started, and proved by Christmas to be no mere rumor, that Gerd Hollins was expecting a baby at last, after nine years of hoping and one of quietly giving up hope. They'd even thought of adopting one, when it began to seem certain that they would have none of their own; but now there was a fair chance of a son coming to the farm in his own right, and good luck to him, said Comerford, and to his mother, too; she'd had more than her share of the bad. A bit late, perhaps, to start a family, but she was a strong woman, and older and less sturdy wives had produced healthy first babies before now.

So what with births and marriages, Comerford could balance a death or two.

A distant cousin came to the Harrow after the old man's death. He seemed a nice enough young man, and he had a different name, which made things easier; and he came in time to have the last mild word upon the open-cast site. As far as he was concerned, they were welcome to go ahead, and so they did, as soon as the year turned and the mild, lengthening days began. Later surveys stated that the amount of coal to be harvested would be even larger than had at first been supposed, and the project would certainly pay for itself handsomely.

In the first days of the spring, therefore, the red-and-yellow monsters crept over the border of Harrow land, from which so many pains had been taken to exclude them, and began to rip off the tangle of furze and heather and rank grass, to pile up the gathered topsoil, to burrow deep into the entrails of pennystone and clay, and lay bare the old shallow shafts one by one, the unfilled and the shoddily filled together, the ugly debris of last century's not much comelier civilization.

2

A worker from the coal site came to the police-station and asked for George. "You'd better come up, Sergeant," he said. "We've found something we'd just as soon not have found. It's in your line of business more than ours."

George went up with Weaver, and stood beside the giant excavator, on a broad shelf from which the topsoil had already been stripped, in the heath beyond the Harrow farmhouse, where were dotted the old shafts filled during the war years. Debris of one of them, plucked out wholesale, had spattered down the side of the new mountain where the pennystone and clay was being shot. Old brickwork, half disintegrated, old rotten timber, all the rubbish of a prosperous yesterday. The past had come up the shaft and lay in the sun, slanting above the gouged valleys where the water had drained off to a deep, cliff-circled pool. The hole of the shaft, a ring of brickwork, gnawed by time, filled with rubble, lay open to the noon light. They stood at the rim, and stared into it, and were struck suddenly silent.

"Well, that's it," said the manager, kicking at the crumbling bricks and hunching a helpless shoulder. "Your folks'd better come and get it, I suppose. Unless you'd rather we just ploughed it under and forgot it. I'd just as soon forget it, myself."

Weaver, very large of eye and solemn of face, looked into the pit, looked at George. He said, breathing gustily: "How long do you suppose it— she—" he looked again, and made up his mind "—she's been down there?"

There was still perceptible cloth, shoes, a handbag; and incomprehensibly there were two large suitcases, burst and gnawed and showing soiled colors of clothes. But the rest was bone. George said: "A few years. Not above ten, I'd say." For the skirt had a traceable length, the shoes a dateable fashion.

"But this is a skeleton," said Weaver. He was chalky-white, too shocked to reason very closely. George didn't like to remind him that the workings were alive with rats. "It must be longer than ten years. I don't know of anyone going missing, as far back as I can remember. She must have fallen down."

"Fallen down and taken her luggage with her?" said the manager.

"Then she must have committed suicide— wanted to vanish, I suppose. People do funny things."

"They have funny things done to them, too," said George. "Do you see what I see round her neck? Quite a determined suicide, if she strangled herself with a twist of wire, and then carried her cases to a pit-shaft, and jumped down it."

"My God!" said the sunshine miner blankly.

"That's right! You mean we been and found a new murder?"

"You dug up an old one," said George. By now he even knew the date of it. Noon sun on covered places brings out a lot of facts in a very little time, and queer things happen when men begin making the rough places plain. There she lay, a short, tumbled skeleton, falling apart here and there in the dirty folds of cloth which had now only slight variations from the universal dirt-color of buried things, among the soil and gravel and brick, jostled by the moldering cases. A few fragments of skin still adhering to the skull, and masses of matted hair. Front teeth touched with distinctive goldwork standing forward in the jaw; and two things round her neck, a necklet of carved imitation stones and a twisted wire. Loose enough now, but once it must have been tight round a plump, soft throat.

"Plenty of identifiable stuff there to hang half a dozen men," said the sunshine miner, in displeased but deeply interested contemplation.

"Yes," said George, "but it never will."

For he'd got the hang of it at last. The cases had jolted him, but it was the necklet of stones that made everything click into place. He'd seen it before, not so long ago, round a soft, plump throat in a photograph. It was all very, very simple once one had the missing bit. A house without servants after six o'clock in the evening, a son away in North Africa, nobody home but a wife with a fair amount of money in jewels and securities, and a husband with his affairs in bad shape, and a position and reputation which rated well above other people's lives with him. A situation in which she could easily be persuaded to turn everything into cash, and a plethora of pit-shafts round the house, into which she could vanish some night when she had done it, with enough of her personal belongings to give color to the story of her exit in quite another direction. A letter of farewell which didn't even have to exist, a lover who never had existed except in one proficient imagination. One man's word for everything, and an ingenious arrangement of circumstances which made it indelicate to probe too deeply. And then a broken, ageing, but reestablished demigod, who touched nothing he did not turn to profit.

Fill in the shafts, in a burst of local benevolence, and what have you left to fear? The war distracts attention from village events which might otherwise arouse too much interest; and Charles, the dumb, worthy Charles, comes home to swallow the story whole, and feel sorry for his father. What can you possibly have to fear?

Except, perhaps, red-and-yellow excavators ripping the bowels out of the secret places of the earth, laying bare the treasures of the mine, turning the soil traitor. For the land turned out to be neutral, after all. That was the one thing you hadn't bargained for. You were aware of ownership; but the land was not aware of being owned. And you had to fight some unexpected rearguard actions; and there were casualties—a tool that turned in your hand, and a son who innocently went over to the enemy. But you'd gone too far then to turn back or to hesitate. And as for small, inquisitive boys, they should be kept out of the battle area; total war is not selective.

"I always had a feeling," said George, "that the motive as we knew it was a little thin to account for Charles. Well, now we know! I'm afraid we'll have to stop your operations here for a few hours. Go down and phone the inspector, Weaver, will you? Tell him we've found what's left of Selwyn Blunden's wife."

IF YOU HAVE ENJOYED READING THIS LARGE PRINT BOOK AND YOU WOULD LIKE MORE INFORMATION ON HOW TO ORDER A WHEELER LARGE PRINT BOOK, PLEASE WRITE TO:

WHEELER PUBLISHING, INC.
P.O. BOX 531-ACCORD STATION
HINGHAM, MA 02018-0531